Reviewers' Cho...
function cook by trade, and lives in Melbourne,
Australia.

Visit Keri Arthur online:
www.keriarthur.com
www.facebook.com/AuthorKeriArthur
www.twitter.com/@kezarthur

Praise for Keri Arthur:

'Keri Arthur's imagination and energy infuse
everything she writes with zest'
Charlaine Harris, bestselling author
of *Dead Until Dark*

'Keri Arthur is one of the best supernatural
romance writers in the world'
Harriet Klausner

'This series is phenomenal! It keeps
you spellbound and mesmerized on

By Keri Arthur

Dark Angel Series:
Darkness Unbound
Darkness Rising
Darkness Devours
Darkness Hunts
Darkness Unmasked
Darkness Splintered

Riley Jenson
Guardian Series:
Full Moon Rising
Kissing Sin
Tempting Evil
Dangerous Games
Embraced by Darkness
The Darkest Kiss
Deadly Desire
Bound to Shadows
Moon Sworn

Damask Circle Series:
Circle of Fire
Circle of Death
Circle of Desire

Spook Squad Series:
Memory Zero
Generation 18
Penumbra
Nikki & Michael
Vampire Series:
Dancing with the Devil
Hearts in Darkness
Chasing the Shadows
Kiss the Night
Goodbye

Ripple Creek
Werewolf Series:
Beneath a Rising Moon
Beneath a Darkening
Moon

Myth and Magic Series:
Destiny Kills
Mercy Burns

DARKNESS
SPLINTERED

A Dark Angels Novel

KERI ARTHUR

piatkus

PIATKUS

First published in the US in 2013 by Signet Select
an imprint of New American Library
a division of Penguin Group (USA) Inc.
First published in Great Britain in 2013 by Piatkus

A CIP catalogue record for this book
is available from the British Library.

ISBN 978-0-349-40165-2

Printed and bound by CPI Group (UK) Ltd, Croydon, CR0 4YY

Papers used by Piatkus are from well-managed forests
and other responsible sources.

MIX
Paper from
responsible sources
FSC® C104740

Piatkus
An imprint of
Little, Brown Book Group
100 Victoria Embankment
London EC4Y 0DY

An Hachette UK Company
www.hachette.co.uk

www.piatkus.co.uk

DARKNESS SPLINTERED

I'd like to thank all the usual suspects:

My editor, Danielle Perez; copy editor Karen Haywood; and the man responsible for the fabulous cover, Tony Mauro.

Special thanks to:

My agent, Miriam; my good buddies Mel, Rob, Chris, Carolyn, and Freya; and last—but not least—my lovely daughter, Kasey.

Chapter 1

I woke up naked and in a strange bed.

For several minutes I did nothing more than breathe in the gently feminine—but totally unfamiliar—scents in the room, trying to figure out how, exactly, I'd gotten here.

And where the hell "here" was.

My brain was decidedly fuzzy on any sort of detail, however, and that could only mean my mission to consume enough alcohol to erase all thought and blot out emotion had actually succeeded. And *that* surprised the hell out of me.

Thanks to our fast metabolic rate, werewolves generally find it difficult to go on a bender. I might be only half were, but I usually hold my alcohol fairly well and really *hadn't* expected to get anywhere near drunk. I certainly hadn't expected to be able to forget—if for only a few hours—the anger and the pain.

Pain that came from both the worst kind of betrayal, and my own subsequent actions.

My eyes stung, but this time no tears fell. Maybe

because I had very little in the way of tears left. Or maybe it was simply the fact that, somewhere in the alcohol-induced haze of the past few days, I'd finally come to accept what had happened to me.

Although it wasn't like I had any other choice.

If I *had*, then I would have died. *Should* have died. But Azriel, the reaper who'd been my follower, my guard, and my lover, had forced me to live and, in doing so, had taken away the very essence of what I was.

Because in forcing me to live, he'd not only ensured that my soul could never be reborn, but he'd made me what he was.

A dark angel.

The next time I died, I would not move on and be reborn into another life here on Earth. I would join him on the gray fields—the unseen lands that divided this world from the next—and become a guard on the gates to heaven and hell.

And that meant I would never see my late mother again. Not in any future lifetime that might have been mine, because he'd stolen all that away from me.

What made it worse was the knowledge that he'd saved me not because he loved me, but because he needed me to find the lost keys to the gates.

And because I was carrying his child.

The stinging in my eyes was *nothing* compared to the pain in my heart. I curled up in the bed and hugged my knees tightly to my chest, but it did little to stop the tidal wave of grief washing over me.

If he'd said, just once, that I mattered more than any quest or key—or even the child we'd created—then perhaps the bitterness and anger would not have been so deep, and I wouldn't have banished him from my side. But he hadn't, and I had.

And now all I could do was try to figure out what had actually happened in the days that had followed his departure, and move on.

Because despite his actions, my task in *this* world had not changed. I still had keys to find, and I very much doubted whether the patience of either my father or the Raziq—the rebel Aedh priests who'd jointly created the damn keys with my father before he'd stolen said keys from their grasp only to lose them himself—would hold for much longer.

Hell, it was surprising that one or both of them hadn't already appeared to slap me around in an effort to uncover what the hell had gone wrong *this* time.

But maybe they had no idea that I'd actually found the second key. After all, this time it had been stolen not only from under my nose, but *before* I'd managed to pinpoint its exact location. Which meant the thief—the same dark sorcerer who'd stolen the first key, and who'd permanently opened the first gateway to hell—wouldn't know which of the many military weapons he'd stolen was the second gate key in disguise. Thanks to the fact that my father's blood had been used in the creation of the three keys, only one of his blood could find them.

And I *would* find them. Without my reaper. Without my protector.

A sob rose up my throat, but I forced it back down. *Enough with the self-pity*, I told myself fiercely. *Enough with the wallowing. Get over it and move on.*

But that was easier said than done when my entire world had been turned upside down.

I scrubbed a hand across gritty eyes, then flipped the sheets off my face, and finally looked around the room. It definitely wasn't a place I knew, and I very much doubted it was a hotel room. There were too many florals—the wallpaper, the bedding, and the cushions that had been thrown haphazardly on the floor all bore variations of a rose theme—and the furniture, though obviously expensive, had a well-used look about it. There was a window to my left, and the sunshine that peeked around the edges of the heavy pink curtains suggested it was close to midday.

Curious to see where I was, I got out of bed and walked over to the window. My movements were a little unsteady, but I suspected the cause was more a lack of food than any residual effect of my drinking binge. Alcohol cleared out of a werewolf's system extremely fast, which is why it was so damn hard for us to get drunk. And *that* was definitely a good thing, because it meant my desperate attempt to forget wouldn't have done any harm to my child.

I drew one curtain aside and looked out. In the yard below, a dozen or so chickens scratched around a pretty cottage garden. To the left of the garden were several outbuildings—one obviously an old stable, another a large machinery shed—but to the right, there was nothing but rolling hills that led up to a thick forest of gum trees.

It definitely *wasn't* somewhere familiar.

Frowning, I let the curtain fall back into place and turned, my gaze sweeping the small room again. My clothes were stacked in a neat pile on the Georgian-style armchair, and flung over the back of it was a fluffy white dressing gown. Sitting on the nearby mahogany dressing table was a white towel, as well as bathroom necessities. Whoever owned this place at least didn't intend to keep me naked or unwashed. Whether they intended me other sorts of harm was another matter entirely.

Not.

The familiar, somewhat harsh tone ran through my mind and relief slithered through me. I might be without my reaper, but I still had my sword, so I wasn't entirely without protection. Amaya—the name of the demon trapped within the sword—

was as alert and as ready for action as ever. The sword itself was shadow wreathed and invisible, so the only time anyone was truly aware of her presence was when I slid her dark blade into their flesh. Although she *did* have a tendency to be vocal about her need to kill, so she certainly could be heard on occasion—generally when she was about to kill someone.

What do you mean, "not"? I walked over to the Georgian chair and started dressing. Like the room itself, my clothes had a very slight floral scent, although this time it was lavender rather than rose, which was definitely easier on my nose.

Harm not, she replied. *Foe not.*

Which didn't mean whoever owned this place was a friend, but my sword had saved my butt more than once recently and I was beginning to trust her judgment.

Should, she muttered. *Stupid not.*

I grinned, not entirely sure whether she meant *she* wasn't stupid, or that *I'd* be stupid not to trust her. I sat down on the chair to pull on my socks and boots, then headed for the door. It wasn't locked—another indicator that whoever had me didn't mean any harm—but I nevertheless peered out cautiously.

The hall beyond thankfully was free of the rose scent that had pervaded my room, and it was long, with at least a dozen doors leading off it. To the left, at the far end, was a wide window that poured sunshine into the space, lending the pale green walls a warmth and richness. To the right lay a staircase. There were voices coming from the floor below, feminine voices, though I didn't immediately recognize them.

I hesitated, then mentally slapped myself for doing so and headed toward the stairs. My footsteps echoed on the wooden boards, and the rhythmic rise and fall of voices briefly stopped.

I'd barely reached the landing when quick steps approached the staircase from below. I paused on the top step and watched through the balusters. After a moment, a familiar figure strode into view and relief shot through me.

"Ilianna," I said. "Where the hell am I?"

She paused and looked up, a smile touching the corners of her green eyes. Ilianna was a shifter, and her human form echoed the palomino coloring of her horse form, meaning she had a thick mane of pale hair and dark golden skin. She was also a powerful witch, and one of the few people outside my adopted family I trusted implicitly. Tao, our flatmate; Mirri, Ilianna's partner; and Stane, Tao's cousin, were the others.

"We're at Sable's winter retreat," she said. "And it's about time you woke up. I was beginning to think you intended to sleep the rest of your life away."

Sable was Mirri's mom. I'd met her only once, but I'd seen her often enough on TV. The woman was a cooking phenomenon, with two TV shows behind her—the repeats of which still pulled good ratings—and a slew of books on not just cooking, but herbs and natural healing. Mirri's dad, Kade, had worked with my aunt Riley at the Directorate years ago, but had unfortunately been killed when Mirri was little more than a baby. It had been Sable who had looked after his herd and kept them all together when he'd died.

"After the events of the last week or so, sleeping the rest of my life away certainly has its appeal." I couldn't help the grim edge in my voice. "Why the hell are we at Mirri's mom's rather than home?"

"Because we figured a change of scenery might get you out of your funk. You coming down for lunch?"

"Funk" was definitely the *polite* description of what I'd been through the past few days. "Lunch would be good," I said, even as my stomach rumbled rather loudly.

Ilianna's eyebrows rose at the noise. I grinned and walked down the rest of the stairs, only to be enveloped in a hug so fierce I swear she was trying to squeeze the last drop of air from my lungs.

"God," she whispered. "It's good to have you back."

I blinked back the sting of tears and returned her hug. "I'm sorry, Ilianna. I didn't mean to worry you. I just—"

"Needed to cut loose a little," she finished for me. "I understand. More than anyone else ever could."

It was gently said, but nevertheless a reminder that I wasn't the only one who'd been played and abused. Guilt swirled through me and I pulled back, my gaze searching hers.

"Are you—"

"Yes," she said, interrupting before I could finish. "As I said in the hospital, my pregnancy was meant to be, even if the method of conception was both unforeseen *and* unwelcome. But we are *not* discussing me and my pregnancy right now."

I half smiled. No, we were discussing me and mine. "I've a feeling I'm about to be told off."

"Not told off. Just . . . warned."

Tension rolled through me. "About what?"

She hesitated. "While I understand your need to cut loose after everything that has happened recently, others do not, and they are looking for you. Specifically, one person. And she's not someone any of us should piss off."

"Hunter." I practically spat the word.

Madeline Hunter was the head of the Directorate, a top-ranking member of the high vampire council, and a monster clothed in vampire skin. She was also, unfortunately, my boss, thanks to an agreement I'd made the day I'd scattered my mother's ashes.

Of course, that agreement technically no longer

stood, because I'd been the one to find and kill the man who had murdered my mother, not Hunter. That man had been my Aedh lover, Lucian, who had managed to fool me in more ways than I was willing to think about. Not only had he been responsible for my mother's murder, but he'd also been involved in the theft of the keys.

And, as a parting gift, he'd kidnapped and impregnated Ilianna, and had tried to do the same to me. Thankfully, I'd already been carrying Azriel's child by that time.

Ilianna grimaced. "Yeah. Tao's fobbed her off a couple of times now, but she's getting pretty scary."

Scary was a normal state for Hunter, but I certainly didn't want to piss her off any more than necessary. Not after what I'd seen her do to the dark spirit who'd murdered her lover.

Still, it was decidedly odd that she didn't know where I was. "Why would she be hassling Tao, or anyone else, for that matter? She knows *exactly* what I'm doing every single minute of the day, thanks to the fucking Cazadors."

Cazadors were the high vampire council's kill squad, and they'd been following me astrally for weeks, reporting my every move back to Hunter.

"In this case, she doesn't, because they *can't* follow you here." Ilianna tucked her arm through mine and escorted me down the hall.

I raised an eyebrow. "You've *spelled* the place?"

She nodded. "Mom found a spell that automatically redirects astral travelers every time they approach the spell's defined area."

Just astral travelers, not Aedh, I guessed. Which was logical, given that the only spell we had to keep the Aedh out was the one we were using around our home, and *that* had originated from my father. Which meant my father and the Raziq could get to me here. I shivered and tried to ignore the premonition that I'd be confronting both far sooner than I'd want.

Still, some protection was better than nothing, and at least we could plan our next move without the Cazadors passing every little detail on to Hunter. "There wouldn't happen to be a mobile version of that spell, would there?"

"Unfortunately, no."

Of course not. Why on earth would fate throw me a lifeline like that? "Then I guess I'd better give the bitch a call ASAP."

And pray like hell she didn't have another job for me. I really didn't need to be chasing after escapees from hell right now—especially, I thought bleakly, when chasing hell-kind was all I had to look forward to in the long centuries after my death.

Besides, I needed to find the sorcerer and snatch the second key back. While he might not know which one of the items he'd stolen it was, there was nothing stopping him from taking them all to hell's gate and testing them out one by one.

And while my father and the Raziq had been

relatively patient so far when it came to my lack of progress on the key front, I doubted that would last. They'd already threatened to destroy those I loved if I didn't find the keys. I wouldn't put it past any of them to actually kill someone close to me, just to prove how serious they were.

As if tearing *me* apart to place the tracker in my heart hadn't already proved that.

"Calling her should definitely be a high priority," Ilianna agreed. "But come and eat first. You look like death warmed up."

No surprise there, given I nearly had been. "So what's stopping Hunter or the Cazadors from *physically* finding us?"

"She probably could, given enough time. While the spell is designed to confuse astral senses, they'd still have a general idea of location."

"But all she has to do is hack into my phone—"

"Which was left at home," Ilianna interrupted. "Along with anything else that could be used to track you. We're not that dumb."

No, they weren't. And Hunter was undoubtedly hassling Tao simply because she couldn't get to anyone else. Even *she* had more sense than to contact Aunt Riley. I might not be related by blood to Riley, but she and her pack were the only family I had left. They would not have reacted nicely to the news that Hunter was after me. "Knowing Hunter as well as I now do, I'm surprised she hasn't done more than merely threaten him."

Hell, she probably considered a spot of bloody torture a good way to start the day. Although, given that Tao was rapidly losing the battle with the fire elemental he'd consumed, maybe I should be hoping the bitch *did* attempt to torture him. Crispy fried Hunter was a sight I wouldn't mind seeing.

"She's given him until tonight to find you, so there's time. You need to regain some strength before you run off to confront that psycho bitch."

"Ain't that the truth," I muttered. "Especially now that I have to do it alone."

Ilianna hesitated, then said quietly, "Look, I don't know what actually went on between you and Azriel, but—"

Something twisted deep inside me. Pain rose, a knife-sharp wave that threatened to engulf me. *No*, I reminded myself fiercely, *you can't go there.* Not just yet. Not so soon after waking. I needed at least *some* time to mull over the implications of my actions by myself.

"Ilianna," I said, when I could, "leave it alone."

"But he wouldn't have left you—"

"He did, because he had no choice. I banished him." *How* I'd actually managed that I had no idea. I mean, he was a reaper, a Mijai, and me telling him to leave me alone had never worked before now. So why the change?

"Why the hell would you do that? Damn it, Ris, you need—"

"Ilianna," I warned, the edge deeper in my voice this time.

She drew in a breath, then released it slowly. "When you want to talk about it, I'll be here. But just remember one thing—he's not human. He's energy, not flesh, and he doesn't operate on the same emotional or intellectual levels as we do. But whatever he did, he did for a reason. A *good* reason. And no matter how absolute or final his actions may seem to you, it may not be a truth in his world."

"The truth," I replied, bitterness in my voice, "is that the keys were always first and foremost to him."

And I wanted more than that. Wanted him to feel about me the way I felt about him. But was love an emotion reapers were even capable of?

I blinked at the thought. I *loved* him. Not just cared for him, but *loved* him.

When the hell had *that* happened?

I'd spent far more time with Lucian than I ever had with Azriel . . . I paused at the thought. No, that wasn't true. Not really. I may have spent more time *sexually* with Lucian, but for every other part of the day—and night—Azriel had been by my side. Somewhere, somehow, he'd snuck past my guard and stolen my heart. How that was even possible when we were still little more than strangers, I have no idea. It wasn't like love and I were on familiar terms. Quite the opposite really,

given the only other man I'd loved had been Jak—
the werewolf reporter who was one of the people
we'd pulled in to help with our key search—and
that had turned out to be a complete and utter di-
saster.

Obviously, my heart had no damn common
sense when it came to picking men. Or it just liked
to be broken.

Ilianna said, "I would not be so sure of that—"

"Ilianna," I warned yet again.

She sighed, then pushed open the door and ushered me through. The twin scents of curry and
baking bread hit, making my mouth water and my
stomach rumble even louder than before.

The room itself was a kitchen bigger than our
entire apartment. The country-style cabinets
wrapped around three of the four walls, providing massive amounts of storage and preparation
space, and there were six ovens and four stove-
tops. A huge wooden table that would have seated
at least thirty people dominated the middle of the
room, and it was at this that Sable, Mirri, and two
other women sat.

They glanced around as we entered. Sable
smiled and rose. In either human or horse form
she was stunningly beautiful, with black skin and
brown eyes that missed very little. Mirri, a mahogany bay when in horse form, had taken after
her dad.

"Risa, so glad you're recovered." Sable kissed

both my cheeks, then stood back and examined me somewhat critically. "Although you do need some condition on you. You, my girl, are entirely too thin."

I smiled. "Werewolves do tend to be on the lean side."

"Not this lean, I'll wager. The ladies and I are just about to go out, but there's a curry in the oven and the bread should be done in about five minutes."

"Thank you—"

She cut me off with a wave of her hand. "Ilianna is family now, and her family is my family. So please, don't be thanking me for something we'd do for anyone in the herd."

I smiled. At least Mirri's mom had accepted her relationship with Ilianna. The same couldn't be said of Ilianna's parents—although I personally thought they *would* come round if they actually knew about it. But Ilianna refused to even tell them she was gay.

Sable collected her coat and bag from the back of one of the chairs; then she and the two women retreated out the glass sliding door.

I raised an eyebrow and glanced at Mirri. "That felt like a deliberate retreat."

Mirri grabbed a couple of tea towels and rose. "I told them you and Ilianna need some alone time for a war council when you woke up."

"War council? Sorry, but whatever I do next—"

"You're *not* doing alone." Ilianna began setting

the table for the three of us. "Azriel may be gone, but Tao and I are still here. And we're a part of this now, Risa, whether you like it or not."

I didn't like. Not at all. She and Tao had been through enough because of me and this damn quest. I wasn't about to put them through anything else. But I also knew *that* tone of voice. It was no use arguing—not that *that* ever stopped me from trying.

"The first thing I have to do is find the damn sorcerer who stole the key, and that's not something I want you involved with. It's too dangerous, Ilianna."

"Maybe." Ilianna gave me a somewhat severe look. "But the Brindle is more than capable of taking care of a dark sorcerer. There aren't that many in Melbourne, you know, and they'd be aware of all of them."

The Brindle was the home of all witch knowledge, both ancient and new. Ilianna's mom was one of the custodians there, and Ilianna was powerful enough to have become one—and in fact had started the training when she was younger. She'd walked away for reasons she refused to discuss, but if the predictions of the head witch, Kiandra, were to be believed, Ilianna would one day not only finish that training, but her daughter would save the Brindle itself.

"Yeah," I said, "but given Lucian was probably working with him, he'll know about my connection to both you and the Brindle." I grimaced, then added, "I'd bet my ass he's taken steps to ensure you—and they—can't find him."

"But it would take *major* magic to achieve something like that, and it would create a 'hot spot' that could be traced."

Maybe that sort of ruling would apply to Earth-based magic, but would it apply to magic that was Aedh sourced? And even if it did, that still meant dragging more people into the search, and I really didn't want to do that unless absolutely necessary. It was just too damn dangerous.

"It's an option." I sat down. "But it wouldn't be my first."

Ilianna placed the hot bread on the table. "Why not? There's no easier way to find a sorcerer than to trace his magic."

"A normal sorcerer, perhaps. But this one has been working with an Aedh, remember, and has probably acquired much of his knowledge." Which was another reason to be glad Lucian was dead. At least the bastard couldn't pass anything else on to our ever-elusive sorcerer. "Besides, our best option right now is to go through Lucian's things and see if he left any clues behind."

Mirri snorted as she began dishing out the huge chunks of curried vegetables—which wasn't normally a favorite of mine, but it smelled incredible. "Forgive me for stating the obvious, but you've been on a bender for three days. That would have given our sorcerer plenty of time to go through Lucian's things and ditch whatever evidence there might have been."

"Lucian was clever enough *not* to leave such information in easy reach. If there *is* incriminating evidence to be found, then it would be somewhere ultimately safe from everyone but him."

And that, I realized suddenly, could mean the gray fields. They might be the unseen division between worlds, but they were as filled with life as anyplace in *this* world. And given Lucian had once been an Aedh priest under my father's tutelage, then maybe the first place I should look was in temples near the gates of heaven and hell. I had no idea whether they still stood now that the priests had all but disappeared—or if someone like me would even be able to see them—but what better place would there be to secure information? It was doubtful whether the reapers or the Raziq would bother to look through ruins in an effort to find information on a dark sorcerer.

Of course, that was presuming Lucian *could* get onto the fields. The ability to attain full Aedh form had apparently been ripped from him by the Raziq, but that hadn't stopped him from shoving his fist into my mother's chest and blowing her apart.

Which is exactly how I'd killed him.

I'd had my revenge, but its taste wasn't as sweet as I'd expected.

I swallowed heavily and added, "The bastard was more cunning that a basketful of foxes."

Ilianna's smile was grim. "But not cunning enough in the end."

"No." I tore off a chunk of bread as Mirri slid a plate of curry my way. "I'll search his place first, then I'll do the same to his lover's place."

"And if you find nothing either there or on the fields?"

Then we were in trouble, because I honestly didn't think the Brindle would be able to help us. Not in this. Not when Aedh magic was involved. And there *had* to be: The ancient cuneiform that gave the magic to the transport pillars we'd found—pillars both the dark sorcerers and Lucian had been using to move around undetected—could have come only from Lucian.

"If I find nothing," I muttered, as I dipped a chunk of bread into the curry, "we're up shit creek without a paddle."

"Then," she said, "talking to Kiandra can't hurt. At least she'll be able to tell us if there is some sort of hot spot near the intersection. Until we know that, we can't make any other plans."

"We?" My gaze shot to hers. "There's no damn we—"

"Oh yes there *is*," she cut in, voice fierce. "You can't do this on your own anymore, Ris."

I snorted. "I was never doing it on my own, and look where it's gotten—"

I cut the words off as awareness ran through me. Something approached the house.

Something that wasn't human, or in human form. An invader that was as silent as a ghost, and yet accompanied by such a wash of heat and power that the hairs on my arms stood on end.

It was a sensation with which I was more than a little familiar.

An Aedh approached the house, and he was in energy form rather than physical.

Only it wasn't any old Aedh.

It was my father. And he was *not* happy.

Having to face a parent as prone to violence as mine certainly wasn't what I needed right now—especially when I didn't have Azriel at my back.

I closed my eyes, trying to remain calm, trying to contain the fear that galloped away at the thought of another confrontation. The desire to reach out to Azriel, to tell him that I needed him, that I wanted him back in my life, was fierce. But that was just a reaction born of fear. After all, the last time my father and I had met face-to-face, he'd just about killed me—and that was *with* Azriel present.

But if it *was* my father approaching, why hadn't the Raziq device woven into my heart reacted? It had been designed to summon them the minute my father appeared in my presence, and when it activated, it felt as if someone had shoved their hand into my chest and was intent on squeezing every ounce of life out of my heart. Painful didn't even come *close* to describing the experience.

This time, however, there was nothing. And while it was curious, I wasn't about to complain. I might not want to confront my father, but I sure as hell had no desire to be caught in the middle of a battle between him and the Raziq.

He hurt not, Amaya commented. *We stronger. Fight.*

I snorted. Fighting was my sword's answer to every problem.

Not every, she said. *But kill better.*

I ignored her and said, "Ilianna, Mirri, get upstairs. *Now.*"

Ilianna opened her mouth to protest, then took one look at my face, grabbed Mirri, and got the hell out of the kitchen.

And not a moment too soon.

An instant later I was hit by a blow of energy so fierce it smashed the chair and flung me backward. I was thrust along the floor with such force that I crashed into one of the cupboards, sending jagged pieces of wood and china flying. Then a band of iron settled around my neck and hauled me upright.

"Where is the second key?" The voice was a deeper, angrier version of mine, and so thunderous it rattled the remaining crockery in the cupboard.

I opened my mouth to answer, but no words came

out. No air was getting in, either, but it was anger rather than panic that bloomed through my body.

Damn it, I was getting rather tired of being thrown about by all and sundry. My father, the Raziq, Hunter—they *all* needed my help, and it was about time they started remembering it.

Even as the thought crossed my mind, energy surged through my body and Amaya was suddenly in my hand. I gripped her hilt tight and swung at the invisible band of steel wrapped around my neck. She screamed in pleasure and anticipation, eager to kill.

No, I warned. *Not yet.*

Fun not, she bit back.

Then shadowed steel met Aedh force. Lilac fire flared down her length, leaping from the tip of her steel to race along the cord that was my father's energy. He roared, the sound one of fury and pain combined, and released me so suddenly I hit the ground knees first. Pain shot up my legs, but I ignored it and held Amaya in front of me. Her fire flared out from the sides of her blade, forming a curved circle that completely encased my body. And just in time.

Energy hit the barrier, and once again pushed me back into the cupboard. Amaya screamed her fury, her shield burning bright where my father's energy flayed her. But she held firm.

"Try to remember you need my fucking help," I said, my voice surprisingly devoid of the fury and fear that tumbled through me.

"I am your *father*," he roared. "I may have given you life, but I can also give you death."

Amaya's hissing got stronger in my head. Whether that meant she was finding it harder to maintain the shield or she was simply getting more pissed off, I couldn't say. But the sooner this attack ended, the better for us both.

"My death will hardly help regain control of the two remaining keys," I countered, still managing to keep my voice even. "Besides, I've already been dead. It holds no fear for me."

The words were barely out of my mouth when the attack stopped with a suddenness that had me blinking. There was a moment of silence before he said, "You died?"

A hint of amusement had replaced the anger, and I frowned. What in the hell was funny about me dying?

"You didn't feel it?" Amaya was beginning to quiver in my hands, which generally meant she was running low in resources and would soon start leeching mine. And while that was something I couldn't afford, given that I wasn't exactly at the top of my game after the last few days, there was no way in hell I was about to ask her to drop the shield. Not until I knew the reason behind my father's sudden mood switch. "I thought the blood bond meant you could feel my presence no matter where I was?"

"When you wear flesh, yes," he replied. "But

place yourself in death's hands, and it is a different matter entirely."

"Why? I mean, wouldn't me dying break any sort of connection? That in itself should tell you something happened."

"It is not that simple."

"It never is."

His amusement got stronger, but it didn't make me feel any safer. Quite the opposite, in fact.

"If you had remained on death's plane, then, yes, I would have sensed it. But you chose to come back."

"Which clarifies nothing, given the gray fields themselves are the realm of death." And the Raziq certainly had no trouble finding me whenever I stepped onto the fields.

"Stepping onto them as an Aedh is very different from stepping on them as a soul ready to move on."

Which I would never be able to do again, thanks to Azriel's actions. Bitterness stabbed through me—bitterness and anger and a splintered sense of loss. I swallowed heavily and somehow said, "So is the fact I basically died the reason why the device in my heart hasn't summoned the Raziq?"

"Yes. As I told you previously, only death could stop it."

Which only meant I was free from the pain of the device, not from the Raziq themselves.

Unfortunately.

"And is *that* the reason you seem to find my death so amusing?"

"It was not so much your death, but the mere fact that you succeeded in short-circuiting Malin's plans."

Malin was the head of the Raziq, and my father's former lover. She was also a woman scorned, as my father had apparently refused to give her the child she'd wanted, deciding instead to seek out and impregnate my mother. It was a combination that made her less than benevolent when it came to me and, in part, the reason behind my latest kidnapping. What she'd actually done to me during that time I couldn't say, because she'd erased all memory of it.

Although given that she'd told me my father would more than likely kill me if he ever found out about it, I'm guessing it was something pretty bad. Something that perhaps tied me to *her* just as much as my father.

"I hadn't exactly planned to die, you know."

"Humanity rarely does. It is one of their greatest failings."

Strength fade, Amaya said, annoyance heavy in her mental tones. She didn't like having to admit to any sort of failing. *Must draw—*

No, I cut in. *Drop the shield*.

And I mentally crossed my fingers that my father hadn't been waiting for that very event.

The faint lilac haze around me flickered, then

died, and Amaya's blade became shadowed once more. I tensed but, despite my fears, my father didn't immediately attack.

Not that I relaxed any. "It's a failing also shared by the Aedh. I hardly think Lucian had planned to die so soon."

"Perhaps not, but he was aware of its approach, as you well know."

He paused, and that vague sense of amusement vanished. My grip on Amaya tightened so abruptly it was a wonder my knuckles weren't glowing.

"Lucian's plans are no excuse for you having lost the second key, however."

"No, because you own some of *that* blame." My voice was curt, which was perhaps unwise given the state of both my strength and Amaya's. "You not only knew he was fucking the sorceress Lauren, but also that he was working with the sorcerer who stole the first key. You didn't tell me the first fact until *after* I'd questioned you about her, and you didn't even bother mentioning the second."

"Because it should not have been relevant. No human should have been able to access the fields, let alone the gates."

"But he had Lucian's help, and he's a very powerful dark sorcerer."

"Lucian could not attain full energy form, and therefore should not have been able to step onto the fields."

"So how the hell did the sorcerer get to the gates with the first key if he didn't have Lucian's help?"

His anger swirled around me, fierce and frightening, but this time, its force was not aimed at me. And it had a rather frustrated edge to it.

"*That* I do not know."

And it killed him to admit it—a situation that cheered me up no end. "We think the sorcerer accessed the fields via stone portals formed by both black and Aedh magic—"

"While *that* is more than possible," my father interrupted, "he should not have been able to see the light and dark paths, let alone access them."

"Unless he had Lucian's help."

"Even Lucian would not have been so foolish as to direct a human to their location. Not when he had his own plans for them."

"Lucian's plans had *nothing* to do with the gates. He not only wanted revenge on the Raziq, who'd made him less than he was, but to turn back time and once again become full Aedh."

An aim that seemed right up there with pigs flying, and yet Lucian had totally believed it was possible.

"Only the strongest magic raised on the strongest ley-line intersection could feasibly allow a human to achieve something like that."

I frowned at his slight emphasis on the word "human." "Meaning Aedh are capable of transcending time?"

"Of course." Amusement filtered through his words again. "How do you think Lucian came to spend so much time here on Earth? He was not only stripped of his ability to become full Aedh, but he was relegated to suffering eons of human development."

"And all it did was not only give him plenty of time to plan his revenge, but plenty of time to find a ley line strong enough for him—and his sorcerer buddy—to place their portal."

And it was so well protected we'd yet to find the damn thing. According to Ilianna, the sorcerer had to be using a containment spell to keep us from sensing it, but surely the amount of power he'd need to suck from the intersection just to change form—let alone access the fields—would not be so easily restrained . . .

I added, "I'm gathering Lucian would have been able to access the fields that way?"

"Certainly. But both he and this sorcerer would have to alter the composition of their bodies to that of energy, if only temporarily. Souls are the only other entity outside Aedh and reapers who can walk the fields, and only then with the help of a guide."

"What about the temples?"

"What about them?"

I bit back my impatience. I wasn't about to rock the boat too much when my father was being helpful. Or as helpful as he was ever likely to get.

Although it *did* seem somewhat surreal to be having such a calm and collected conversation with him after his initial entrance. "Would either Lucian or the sorcerer have been able to access the temples in their altered forms?"

"Lucian could have, as he was my chrání. The sorcerer has no need to enter the temples. The gates are within the grounds that surround the temples, not in the temples themselves."

A chrání, in Aedh speak, basically meant student or protégé. "That doesn't actually answer my question."

Yet again his amusement touched the air. While it was nice that he was in such a jovial mood, I suspected it wouldn't take much to bring back his wrath.

He said, "Only those of Aedh blood can enter sacred temples."

Meaning the gates weren't considered sacred? Why not? "So I could enter them, if I needed to?"

His energy swirled around me, contemplative in its feel. I wasn't entirely sure why, given he could access my thoughts and would have to know where this was heading.

And yet, his next question suggested the exact opposite. "Why might you wish to access the temples?"

"Lucian was a devious bastard who trusted no one." And rightly so, given it was my father who'd betrayed him to the Raziq in the first place. "Not only would he have kept information about the sorcerer's identity, but he would have kept it somewhere not even the sorcerer could access."

"Being Aedh does not automatically give you access to the temples—indeed, only those initiated into the order can move freely within the inner realm of the temples."

"Which is a roundabout way of saying I'll need your help?" And it would come at a price, of that I had no doubt. Still, it was worth reminding him exactly what was at risk. Hell, he might even surprise me and offer help without threats or strings.

And tomorrow, those damn pigs will fly.

"You will need help to access the temples, yes, but I will not be able to provide it. The Raziq have traps waiting around them." Contempt darkened his tone as he added, "They hope to ensnare me should I be foolish enough to go near."

"So how in the hell am I supposed to get into the place if you can't help me? I'm thinking you don't want me asking the Raziq for help."

Anger surged, strong enough to snatch my breath and send lilac sparks skittering down Amaya's sides. "That *would* be unwise."

"Then how about offering a fucking solution, instead of just threats?" I snapped. "Because if you want the sorcerer shut down before he can use the key, I need some help."

"There's your reaper. While they are not initiated into the order, they have always had access to the temples."

My reaper ... pain and regret stormed barely shored-up defenses, and once again tears were stinging my eyes. Damn it, *no*. I was stronger than this. I'd survived Jak's betrayal, and I'd get over this, too. I had to, because this time, there was more than just my heart and my mother's reputation at stake. This time, there were lives on the line. Many lives.

A world of them, in fact.

I fiercely thrust the pain aside. "Didn't you just say the gates are within grounds? Why, then, would the reapers be able to access the temples?" After all reapers, as soul guides, needed access to the former not the latter.

"At one time, they did not. But the priests have long gone, and the reapers have been forced to do what the priests once did."

And that was keeping the gates in working order, as well as stopping anything—and everything—that tried to escape hell. With the first hell gate now open, more and more demons were escaping into the fields and subsequently onto Earth, and the Mijai—who were the reaper soldiers—found themselves spread very thin indeed.

God, I hope Azriel is keeping himself safe . . .

I shoved the unbidden thought back into its box. "My reaper is no longer part of this mission, so it's not like I can get his help."

"It is not like one of the Mijai to abandon a mission before it is finished."

"He didn't abandon it. I banished him."

"But you could not do that unless he—" He stopped, and once again I felt his amusement. "That *is* an interesting development."

"And what, exactly, is so interesting about me banishing him?"

"The mere fact that you could."

Which in no way explained his amusement. Goddammit, could no one ever give me a straight answer? "Care to go into a bit more detail?"

"No." Again that glimmer of amusement trailed around me. "You are not unprotected, however. The Mijai still need you, just as the Raziq and I still need you."

"Meaning someone else is now guarding me?" Someone who was keeping their distance, and refusing to interact with me in any way? Because I certainly hadn't sensed their presence.

"Yes. What their plans are beyond that, I have no idea. Nor do I have any interest, other than reminding you your allegiance must lie with me. Otherwise—"

"My friends will die," I cut in, annoyance back in my voice. "I've heard that song before. So tell me, how the hell am I going to access the temples if I can't get reaper support?"

"You are not the only half Aedh in this city, and the other is also trained as a priest. He could get you in." He paused. "However, you will not gain access into the quarters the chrání and I shared without *my* help."

He was talking about Uncle Quinn. And while I really *didn't* want to involve either him or Aunt Riley in this fucking quest any more than I already had, it was looking more and more like there was no other choice. "And the price of your help is no doubt the key."

"No," he said, voice so ominous it sent chills racing down my spine. "The price of the key is the life of your friend."

And just like that, the facade of civility snapped.

Power surged, an energy so fierce it momentarily felt like he was trying to pull me apart. Amaya screamed in response, and flames leapt from the point of her blade. But they swirled around aimlessly, as if she couldn't find anything to attack.

And she couldn't, because my father had disappeared. Completely disappeared.

A heartbeat later, Ilianna screamed.

Chapter 2

Oh fuck, *no!*

I spun and raced out of the kitchen. Ilianna's screams stopped as abruptly as they'd started, and the only noise in the house now was the thunder of my footsteps as I raced up the stairs. If he'd hurt Ilianna in any way—

I swallowed heavily—as much against fear as fury—and followed the tendrils of power that was my father's presence.

"Enter," he said, as I approached a door near the end of the hall. "And witness what awaits should you fail."

I flexed my fingers, my palm suddenly sweaty against Amaya's hilt, then opened the door and stepped inside. The room was a mirror image of the one I'd woken in, although lilac rather than roses seemed to be the dominant theme here. Ilianna and Mirri stood in the middle of the room and, despite my fears, both were not only alive, but apparently unhurt.

But this was my father we were talking about.

He was perfectly capable of tearing one or both of them apart in an instant.

I hoped to god that *wasn't* what he was planning now.

My gaze met Ilianna's, and in the green depths I saw fear and fury combined. She didn't say anything—maybe she couldn't—but her gaze flicked toward her mate. I stepped closer, and saw the luminous blue threads that had been wrapped around Mirri's neck.

Only it wasn't any type of thread found here on Earth. It was energy.

I stopped and stared. "What the hell have you done?"

"It is what you would call an insurance policy." His voice was heavy with menace. "I have threatened the life of both the witch and the wolf, but it hasn't appeared to make much difference to your actions—"

"*My* actions?" I all but exploded. "What about *your* fucking actions? If you'd been up front about what Lucian was and who he was working with, the damn sorcerer would not have grabbed the first key, nor would he have gained access to the second. That blame lays on your shoulders, *not* mine."

"Indeed," he continued darkly, as if I hadn't spoken, "one could almost think you do not take my threat seriously."

"That is *not* true—"

"And yet, you appear to fear the Raziq more than you do me. That cannot be allowed."

I clenched my fingers against Amaya's hilt, but resisted the urge to throw her into the haze of energy that was my father. I had no idea what that thread around Mirri's neck was and, until I did, I had to practice restraint.

Thread bad, Amaya muttered.

I knew *that* without asking. *Can you destroy it without hurting Mirri?*

Know not, she replied. *Taste first.*

And if you taste it?

Kill might.

Mirri, or the thread?

Amaya hesitated. *Both.*

Then there'd be *no* tasting. "What the fuck have you done, Father?"

"If you wish this shifter to live, then you must not only retrieve the second key, but find the last one."

"As I've repeatedly said, I can't find the second key without your fucking help," I spat back. "And I can hardly find the third key when you haven't even *told* me where the fucking thing is."

"I will send directions for the third key, and a means of getting into our temple rooms," he said. "But the latter will require several hours to construct. You are not an initiate, so I will also have to create a means of circumventing that particular restriction. I suggest you use that time to search this plane for the sorcerer and the second key."

"And if I don't succeed in finding it, Mirri will die." It was a statement, not a question. I don't think I've hated anyone as much as I hated my father at that moment.

Except, perhaps, for Hunter.

"Yes. And there *is* one other restriction."

My stomach was churning so badly it felt like I was going to throw up. It was enough that she could die—what the hell else could he do? But even as the thought crossed my mind, the answer came. He was Aedh, and Aedh, like reapers, could command souls. He could rip hers free and make her one of the lost ones—a ghost confined to the astral field, never to move on, never to be reborn. I licked dry lips and croaked, "Meaning?"

"The lariat will begin tightening at forty hours. At that time, she will have eight hours left."

And with that, he was gone.

"Bastard!" Ilianna exploded, and swung around to face her mate. She touched a hand to Mirri's cheek. "Are you okay?"

Mirri nodded, her face pale and fear in her eyes. "Yes. For now."

I stopped beside Ilianna. "I'm sorry, Mirri, really sorry—" My voice faded. I seemed to be saying that an awful lot of late and, as ever, it was useless.

Mirri gave me a taut smile. "You can't be held accountable for your father's actions, Risa."

No, but I could be held accountable for my own

and if Mirri died . . . god, it would kill Ilianna. My gaze dropped to the thin cords of power around her neck and I raised a hand. Mirri hissed before I could actually touch it.

"Don't," she said quickly. "It tightens."

I swore vehemently and glanced at Ilianna. "I don't suppose hoping for some sort of magical intervention is worthwhile?"

Her gaze came to mine, green eyes filled with fury. Though it wasn't aimed at me, I felt the force of it nevertheless. It *would* be unleashed my way if anything happened to Mirri.

"No. It's a type of energy I've never felt before."

No surprise there given its source was one of the most powerful Aedhs around. "Would the Brindle be able to do anything?"

It was, after all, the home of all witch knowledge, so surely they *had* to have something, somewhere, about the Aedh and their abilities. And some way of counteracting something like this.

"I'll take her there immediately." The doubt in her expression suggested she held little hope of them being able to do anything. She gently squeezed my arm. "Find the keys, Risa. *Fast*."

Easier said than done, and she knew it. But I pressed my hand over hers in reassurance, then spun and walked back into the room I'd woken in. I gathered my keys and wallet, shoving them into pockets as I looked around to see if there was anything else I'd left behind.

There wasn't. I'd obviously travelled light when I'd gone on my drinking binge. I took a deep breath and released it slowly, vaguely hoping it might help calm the turmoil inside. I may as well have tried to stop the moon from rising.

I swore softly, wrapped my fingers around my keys, and called to the Aedh within. She came with a rush that literally blew me away. Energy tore through every muscle, every cell, numbing pain and dulling sensation as it broke them all down, until my flesh no longer existed and I became one with the air. Until I held no substance, no form, and could not be seen or heard or felt by anyone or anything who wasn't reaper or Aedh.

In that form, I swept out of the house and into the sunshine, speeding away from peace and quiet of the rolling hills, heading toward Melbourne and the Collins Street building that housed Lucian's apartment.

I didn't re-form as I neared the building—there were too many people walking along this end of Collins Street to risk that. I didn't immediately go into the building, either, but scanned it carefully, looking for anything that seemed odd or out of place.

It was one of those grand old Victorians the top end of Collins Street was famous for and, like many of them up here, only five stories high. Lucian's apartment was on the top floor, at treetop level, and would have been beautiful once it had been finished. Not that being unfinished had ever stopped us from using the place—and we'd certainly shared many good times within the half-constructed interior walls. But it had all been a lie.

Well, not so much the joy he'd gotten out of sex—in *that* area, at least, he'd been real and honest. And yet the sex had been nothing more than a means to an end for Lucian. What he'd wanted—what he'd always wanted—was the keys.

The keys were *everything*. To Lucian, to my father, to the Raziq, and Hunter. Hell, even Azriel . . .

I cut the thought off abruptly. Don't think about him, I reminded myself fiercely. Just *don't*.

But it was hard *not* to when I was carrying his child.

I cursed and moved warily into the building. There didn't seem to be any traps, but that didn't mean they weren't here. After all, Lucian's other lover—and his partner in key-stealing crime—was a dark sorceress. And while we had no actual proof Lauren had been working with both Lucian *and* the key thief, my father certainly hadn't denied the possibility, and that was good enough for me. And given *that*, she'd want to protect his identity just as much as Lucian had. After all, the game was far from over—for them, as much as for us.

I slipped under the locked gate and into the building's foyer. New marble had replaced much of the old, but the floor was covered in dust and

the breeze rustled the plastic sheeting still covering some of the walls. There were no workmen
here, despite the fact it was only early afternoon.
With Lucian dead, I guess they'd have no choice
but to shut the site down—at least until his estate
was sorted out, anyway.

That's presuming he'd made a will. Lucian had
never suffered from a lack of confidence, and he
certainly wouldn't have expected to die as he
had—especially by my hand. But it might be
worth doing a search through the probate office
records. If he *did* have heirs, maybe he'd left information with them.

There would be something, somewhere, of that
I was sure. Lucian had been betrayed once, and it
had cost him his Aedh powers. He wasn't likely to
let anything like that happen again. He *would* have
had some form of insurance.

I moved forward again, but tiredness washed
through my particles and I stopped. I might shift
to Aedh with far greater accuracy and power these
days, but it still took a lot of energy to hold this
form, and I wasn't at my best. Not to mention the
fact I was now pregnant. I had no idea how far
along I was, but even if it was little more than a
week or so, it would no doubt drain my strength
faster. After all, there were now two beings for the
energy to alter. I just had to hope that being in this
form wouldn't affect my child. But Azriel was energy rather than flesh, and I was half werewolf *and*

half Aedh, so our child belonged to all three. Surely something that was part of my child's heritage would not harm him or her.

Still, given the building site was closed, there was little reason to remain in Aedh form. I called to the transforming magic once again, and it stormed through me, rearranging cells until I was once again wearing flesh.

Dizziness immediately swept me, and I had to grab at the nearby wall to remain upright. But the pain that raced through my being was next to nothing when compared to my usual state after a shift.

My clothes, however, came through the change as disastrously as ever. They always disintegrated just fine, but re-forming them was trickier, as the magic didn't always delineate bits of me from the other particles. Which meant I often ended up with a dustlike sheen covering my skin rather than fully formed pieces of clothing. My jeans generally came through relatively intact, although the breeze teasing my left butt cheek suggested a rather largish hole around that area. My underwear, as usual, hadn't fared all that well, given both my knickers and bra were little more than fluff that clung to my skin and itched like hell. My sweater had also survived—a good thing, considering the state of my bra. Being nearly naked on a building site probably wasn't a great idea, even if the building site was currently empty.

But I'd barely pushed away from the wall when a familiar scent teased my nostrils. I swore softly and turned around, my gaze scanning the plastic sheeting. As I did, Jak Talbott stepped out from behind it and said, "Well, that was certainly one *hell* of an entrance. Care to explain how you did that, exactly?"

"No," I bit back. "Care to explain why the *hell* you're here?"

Because he was certainly the *last* person I wanted—or had expected—to see here. Not only was he my first love—though one, thankfully, I'd finally gotten over—but also a reporter with a nose for a story. I did *not* want said nose sticking in this particular story, even if I'd been using him—and his resources—to help find the ley-line gate.

His answering smile was slow and sexy. At five ten, he was pretty much the average height for a male werewolf, and while he wasn't what I'd term drop-dead gorgeous, his rough-hewn features could certainly be classified as handsome. His hair, like his skin, was black, but there was a whole lot of gray in it these days. More, perhaps, since he'd become part of my quest. As for the smile— well, it had certainly enabled him to slay more than his fair share of maidens. Me included.

"Where else was I supposed to be?" he said, his dark eyes showing little of the amusement evident in his expression and his voice. "You wouldn't answer the phone, Tao threatened to cut my nuts off if I went near you, and Ilianna—well, heaven only knows what *she* would have threatened had I contacted her."

Amusement bubbled briefly. Given Ilianna's opinion of Jak's reappearance in my life, her threat would probably have been a whole lot nastier than Tao's. "None of which explains your presence here."

"Where else might I be given the Directorate's reticence about answering questions concerning Lucian?" He eyed me for a second, the amusement fading. "I figured that, given your involvement with the man, sooner or later you'd come here."

A statement that made me wonder just how much he knew about Lucian's death. "You could have been waiting a long time—"

"I doubt it. Now, it's your turn."

I grimaced. "Look, the way I reappeared . . . it's not something—"

"Don't try that," he cut in. "We passed the whole 'it's not something I need to know' thing around the time we were attacked by hellhounds. I deserve some honesty, Ris, if nothing else."

I sighed. He was right. He did. After all, I could hardly bitch about people lying to *me* when I was doing the exact same thing to him.

"You know how Azriel comes and goes—"

"You're *not* a reaper." His gaze swept me, though I wasn't entirely sure why. When Azriel wore flesh, it wasn't obvious he was anything else.

"No, I'm not." Not yet, anyway. "But I *am* partially an energy form. My father is an Aedh, just as Lucian was."

Something sparked in his eyes. The reporter within had the scent of a story. "So you *do* know he died?"

I hesitated, though there was little point in denying it. "Yeah."

"And do you happen to know *how*?"

"Why? What have you heard?"

"Interesting way of not answering the question, Ris." He studied me for a moment, then added, "I talked to several people who were near the warehouse at the time of his murder. By their accounts, it appeared that Lucian had been blown up— something later refuted by the Directorate. They said the cause was accidental."

If the Directorate were saying *that*, it could only mean Uncle Rhoan was cleaning up my mess and protecting my ass. They knew, as much as I did, that it had been no accident.

But if Jak had been talking to people who'd been near the warehouse at the time of Lucian's death, it was more than possible he knew my part in it. Still, I returned his gaze steadily. "And you don't believe the Directorate's statement?"

He snorted. "I saw the photographer, remember? From what the witnesses said, the manner in which Lucian died was almost identical."

The photographer had been one of the many

leads Lucian had erased before we'd had the chance to talk to him. I'd forgotten Jak had been there when I'd discovered the body. "Whoever killed Lucian didn't kill the photographer."

"Never suggested they did." He quirked an eyebrow. "And that wasn't actually a question I asked."

Perhaps not out loud, but it was nevertheless implied. And I didn't have to be psychic—although, technically, given my somewhat unreliable clairvoyant abilities, I was—to predict his next question.

"It does, however, force me to ask—did you kill him?"

I didn't pull my gaze away, didn't react, even if my insides were churning so badly it felt like I was about to throw up. "What do you think?"

"I think it's possible, and I'd like to know why."

I considered my options, weighing honesty—and what that might mean—against the knowledge that I still needed his help. Probably more so now than ever before thanks to the fact that I'd pushed Azriel away.

And yet, it was no more right to draw Jak deeper into this whole mess than it was to involve Ilianna or Tao.

"It's possible," I said eventually, "that Lucian died the way he did simply because that's the exact same way he killed my mother."

Jak blinked. "Lucian killed your mother? Why the hell were you fucking him, then?"

"Why do you think, asshole?" I spun around and stalked toward the elevator.

He took several quick steps and grabbed my arm, stopping me. "Look, I'm sorry, but you've got to admit, it's an obvious question."

I drew in a deep breath, though it did little to calm the rush of anger—anger that was aimed just as much at myself as at him.

"Do you think I haven't agonized over the fact I was having sex with my mom's murderer? It makes me want to puke every time I think about it." I pulled my arm from his and continued on to the elevator. "And the worst of it is, that *wasn't* the end of his crimes. It was just the beginning."

Jak fell in step beside me. "What else did he do?"

"Just about everything." I punched the Call button. "He was working with the sorcerer who stole the keys, and he was reading my thoughts during sex to keep up-to-date with everything we were doing to find them."

"Wow," Jak murmured. "Even *I* wasn't that much of a prick. At least when *we* were making love, I concentrated on the business at hand."

A reluctant smile touched my lips. "Oh, I don't know about that. There were definitely occasions when it seemed your thoughts were elsewhere."

"If my thoughts were elsewhere, you can bet it was because I was trying *not* to come. You, my dear, can sometimes make a man a little too quick on the trigger."

My smile grew. "I did notice you had a tendency to fire off a little too soon—"

"It didn't happen *that* often," he said, nudging me with his shoulder.

"If you say so," I murmured, amused. The elevator door opened and I stepped inside.

He followed close behind. "What floor are we heading to, and why?"

"Top floor, to what would have been Lucian's apartment. I'm looking for clues."

He punched the appropriate button. "Clues for what?"

I grimaced. "I wasn't Lucian's sole bed partner. Not only was he bedding a dark sorceress, but we're pretty sure the two of them were partners in crime with the sorcerer who stole the keys."

"Well, speaking from experience, the man had to have superman's stamina if he could cope with more than *you* in his bed."

I raised an eyebrow. "You and I are over, so you really can stop with all the compliments."

"Hey, throwing a compliment doesn't mean I want back in your bed. I mean, yeah, I'd love it, but I've come to accept it's not going to happen." He paused, then added more seriously, "So we're looking for something to pin down the sorceress?"

"No, because we know who she is. However, *we're* not looking for anything. *I'm* looking. I don't believe you were invited to this particular party."

"Unfortunately, you're stuck with me. I mean,

considering the options and all, what choice do you have?"

"*That* sounded like a threat, and really? That's not a place you want to go."

"It wasn't so much a threat," he murmured. "Not considering you could probably get your uncle to throw my ass into jail or erase my memory."

"Then what the hell was it?"

"More a . . . reminder. I know what I know, simply because I have the contacts. Contacts you still need."

I should have been annoyed, but the reality was, he was right. I'd gone to Jak in the first place because of those contacts, and I still very much needed them.

But given the fact that everything that could go wrong *had* gone wrong, I at least owed him the chance to back away. Not that I thought he would—not when the scent of a story was in his nostrils.

"Jak, the people who want the keys are threatening the life of everyone I care about." I met his gaze again, hoping he'd see that I was totally serious. "The more you attach yourself to this quest, the more likely the chance of you becoming one of its victims."

"And tomorrow I could die crossing the road," he said, with a shrug.

"Jak, I'm not kidding—"

"I know." He squeezed my arm lightly, his fingers warm against my skin. "I don't mean to downplay the danger, but it's a danger I've faced before. I'm a paranormal and occult news investigator, remember?"

"You've never faced this sort of danger before," I muttered, glancing up at the floor indicator as the elevator came to a bouncing halt.

The doors swished open. "Perhaps not," he agreed. "But it doesn't alter the fact that I always do whatever is necessary to get my story."

And one of those necessary things was hooking up with me to get a story on my mother. While I knew not everything about our relationship had been faked, it had certainly been more real to me than it ever had been to him.

The elevator opened directly into what Lucian had planned to be the living room of his penthouse apartment. It was still filled with building debris, although many of the plastic sheets that had defined the different areas the last time I was there were gone. But the new walls hadn't yet received a coat of paint and cables hung everywhere, looking like a network of intertwined snakes.

Snakes were better than spiders, I thought with a shiver. And then wondered whether that was clairvoyance or merely paranoia speaking.

"Wow," Jak said, looking around. "This place is huge."

"And this is just the living area."

"Obviously, Lucian wasn't lacking in cash."

"No." I picked my way through the building rubbish, heading for the newly constructed doorway into the kitchen area. "But considering he'd had centuries to accumulate it, that's no real surprise."

"Centuries?" Jak said, surprise in his voice.

"At least."

I paused just inside the doorway, quickly scanning the vast kitchen-dining area. It still held the remnants of the old kitchen—an oven, a fridge, and the bare bones of two small counters—but the framework for the new kitchen was in place.

The folding chairs we'd briefly used the time I'd met Lauren here were propped up against an outer wall. I'd asked her—against Azriel's warnings and my own misgivings—to create a spell that would nullify the device the Raziq had placed in my heart. She'd subsequently presented me with a cube designed to prevent magic escaping its boundaries. The idea, supposedly, was that once the cube had been "tuned" to my aura, it would prevent the device in my heart activating. But the cube hadn't been created from the magic of this world. It hadn't even been created from blood magic. That, perhaps, I might have risked, even if only as a last resort.

The source of the cube's power had come from hell itself. While I might have made some very stupid mistakes lately, and had often placed too much trust in entirely the *wrong* people, even *I* knew better than to use a device created by a woman who not only considered it natural to play in hell's fields, but perfectly normal to draw on its energy to create her magic.

It was certainly one of the few decisions I didn't regret. Unlike all the time I'd wasted with Lucian . . .

I shoved the thought aside and continued looking around the room. But aside from the fact there were now doors dividing this room from the bedroom area, little else had changed.

And yet, something *felt* different.

An odd sense of wrongness crawled across my skin, and that was usually a precursor to me walking into a shitload of trouble.

"I don't suppose you have any weapons, do you?" I studied the doorway leading into the bedroom. If any clues were going to be here, they would be found in the place where he'd made so many conquests. Like most Aedh, he'd been able to charm the pants off any woman he desired with just a kiss, simply because an Aedh's kiss was designed to sweep aside objections and fuel lust.

And Lucian had certainly been more than willing to employ the power of it. Maybe it had been his way of passing time—when he *wasn't* plotting his revenge, that was.

Jak glanced at me, expression sharp with concern. "Why would I? And why would you be asking something like that?"

"Because I have a very bad feeling we could be walking into trouble."

And along with it came a very bad desire to reach for Azriel. Not so much for his protection, but simply because I felt stronger—more capable of coping with the weird shit that kept getting thrown at me—with him by my side.

I don't want to do this alone. And that, right there, was a truth I might not have any wish to face, but one I inevitably would. Because no matter how angry I was, no matter how determined to prove that I could do this alone, the truth of the matter was, I really didn't *want* to.

I'd banished him in anger and confusion and grief, and it wasn't *just* that he'd made me Mijai and ended any possibility of me being reborn and seeing my mother again. It was that he'd destroyed our one sure way to end this key madness and keep everyone I cared about safe.

The simple fact was, no one but me could find the keys. No me, no key, no threat.

I had every right to be angry. And I was. Very much so. But Ilianna was right. I owed him the chance to explain his reasons. He had tried—in his own stoic, say-as-little-as-possible way—but I'd been too locked in misery to listen. I'd wallowed in that particular pool long enough, though, and I was ready to listen now. Besides, I'd faced up to

Jak's betrayal, and had given him a second chance, even if it extended only as far as friendship. Did Azriel deserve anything less?

"What sort of trouble?" Jak asked.

"The kind that comes from a seriously annoyed dark sorceress."

"Oh, delightful."

He gave the bedroom doors a somewhat dubious look. He wouldn't have seen anything more than I did—an innocuous, unpainted double entrance into another room. But the more I looked at those doors, the more the sensation of danger crawled through me.

"You know," he added, "common wisdom would suggest walking away from trouble rather than into it."

I half snorted and glanced up at him. "Seriously? You're actually suggesting we turn around and walk away?"

"You know me better than that." His grin flashed. "I was merely pointing out what the wise would do."

"I don't suppose suggesting you at least wait here would do any good?"

"No. Besides, you're armed and I daresay your reaper is near."

"I daresay *a* reaper is near," I commented, voice a little harsher than necessary. "Whether they'll come to our assistance should we land in trouble is anyone's guess."

I forced my feet forward. Jak fell in step beside me. "I take it from *that* there's been a lover's quarrel?"

"It means exactly what it says. A reaper is near, just not Azriel. More than that you need not know."

"Which, of course, just fuels the fire," he murmured. "This case gets more interesting by the day."

"And more dangerous." I slowed as I neared the double doors, scanning them quickly and still seeing nothing. Yet that niggling sense of wrongness was growing.

Amaya? Can you feel anything? I twitched my fingers but resisted the urge to reach for her. Not every problem could be solved by her presence, however much *she* might believe otherwise.

Not, she replied, and sounded a little miffed. I wasn't entirely sure whether it was over my thought that she couldn't solve every problem, or the fact that there didn't seem to be a problem.

"So what lies beyond the doors you're giving the evil eye to?" Jak asked.

"A bedroom."

He frowned—something I sensed rather than saw. "I thought you were looking for clues?"

"I am, but I'm not likely to find them where the builders could inadvertently stumble upon them."

"And the builders couldn't stumble into the bedroom?" Jak asked, a slight edge in his voice.

Whether it was sarcasm or concern, I wasn't really sure.

"Well, yes. But it would suit Lucian's twisted sense of humor to hide stuff in a half-finished bedroom."

"So are we going to enter, or are we just going to stand here and stare at the door?"

"I prefer the latter option myself," I muttered. "But I guess we should do the first."

I gripped the handles and slid the doors back into their respective recesses. The large room beyond was more finished than it had been the last time I'd been here. The king-sized bed still dominated the middle of the room, but the three bathroom walls had been plastered and the fourth side was now a half-height glass-and-brick wall that would have provided some modesty to those sitting on the toilet but little else.

My gaze swept the rest of the room, but I couldn't see anything out of place. Couldn't see anything that suggested there was, in any way, something dangerous lurking in wait for us.

And yet that's exactly what I sensed.

It would be sensible to retreat. Totally. But retreating wouldn't get the damn keys found. Wouldn't save Mirri's life.

I swallowed heavily and forced myself forward. Felt a featherlight press against one shin, then a snap. Quickly looked down and saw the glimmer of pale thread.

I froze, waiting for the hammer to fall.

"What?" Jak's voice was little more than a whisper.

"Someone placed a cotton line across the door. I just broke it." I scanned the room again. Still nothing, and yet the sense of danger was growing.

Energy whisked across my skin. It was the barest caress, little more than a hint of darkness, but it nevertheless made my skin crawl. Amaya's hiss began to flow through the back of my thoughts.

"Why would someone do that?" Jak asked. "I mean, anyone could spring it."

I didn't get the chance to reply, because at that precise moment all hell broke loose.

Chapter 3

The air exploded, filling the room with a tidal wave that was both heat *and* magic. As it stormed toward us, I swore and spun, wrapping my arms around Jak and calling to the Aedh.

"What the *fuck*—"

The rest of his words were abruptly cut off as my magic ripped through us both, shredding skin and blood and bone with quick efficiency, until there was nothing left but two streams of tremulous smoke, separate but entwined.

Then the wave of energy and magic hit, and the doors, walls, and ceiling all around us disintegrated. I very much suspected the wave would have done the same to us had we been in flesh form.

The wave rolled into the kitchen–dining area, its progress trackable through the pulverization of everything it touched. Not just walls and ceilings, but the half-built kitchen as well as the old remnant. But the force behind the wave obviously began to fade as it neared the far wall, because while some of the plaster fell, most remained intact.

I turned, peering through the dusty gloom, wondering if that explosion was all there was to the trap. Wondering if it had been aimed at me, specifically, or just anyone who entered this room. That brief caress of darkness before the explosion certainly seemed to suggest the former rather than the latter, but if that was the case, why not create an explosion that would do damage to an Aedh? Whoever had set this trap—be it the dark sorcerer or Lauren—had to know what I was.

But then, why would they want me dead? The final key still had to be found, and I was the only one who could do that.

Maybe this trap had been set more out of spite and emotion than levelheaded thinking, and *that* suggested Lauren more than the dark sorcerer. If the argument I'd interrupted between Lucian and her had been any indication, Lauren hadn't been happy about my presence in his life. And she certainly *had* to suspect my part in his death.

Maybe destroying any possible evidence had been the main intent of the blast. Damage to *me*, if I hadn't been quick enough, might have just been a bonus.

Which made me wonder if the reaper who'd replaced Azriel would have stepped in to save me had my life truly been in danger.

Or wouldn't it have mattered to him? Or to any of them?

I mean, I was now destined to become Mijai the

next time I died, and Mijai could become flesh. Maybe it would be better for them if I *did* die.

But with Azriel gone, there was no way to get any answers to questions like that . . .

Except, he doesn't have to remain gone . . .

The thought rose like a ghost, seductive and enticing. I pushed it away. If I was going to invite him back into my life, then I'd do it the fair way— when I was safe rather than in trouble.

I studied the mess now that the white dust had started to settle. What it revealed was the broken remnants of the bed and bathroom. Wiring hung like limp snakes from the remains of the ceiling, and the lines of silver ducts that crossed the room had been torn open in several places.

I couldn't see anything that suggested there was another trap waiting, but that didn't mean there wasn't. There was only one way I could ever be sure, however.

I carefully imagined Jak and me as two separate beings, and reached for the Aedh. The magic stitched us back together, until flesh was fully formed and we became ourselves once again.

There was nothing at all elegant about my reappearance this time. I landed with a splat on the dust-covered concrete, shivering and coughing and generally feeling like shit. Back to the old days, I thought bleakly. But I twisted around, ignoring the red-hot pokers that jabbed into my brain as I looked for Jak.

He was lying within arm's reach, his clothes shredded but his flesh whole. And he was breathing.

Relief spun through me, but I didn't entirely relax. I reached out and poked him with a stiffened finger. "Jak? You okay?"

"No, I'm fucking *not*." His voice was raw and somewhat shaky. "You just tore my whole body down to atoms and then re-formed it. To say I feel like shit is something of an understatement."

"Welcome to my usual state of being," I muttered, my gaze sweeping the room again. Given the mess and destruction, it was likely that if there *had* been clues here, they would have been destroyed. But I still had to look.

At least I would when I no longer felt like throwing up.

"Why the hell would you put yourself through something like that?" Jak raised a hand and scrubbed his forehead rather gingerly. "I mean, it *hurts*."

"Better that than being dead." I carefully pushed up into a sitting position, but no amount of care could stop my stomach from leaping into my throat. I swallowed heavily and added, "And that was our only other option. Just look at the walls."

He cracked open an eye, and swore fluently. "To repeat an earlier question, why the hell would someone do that? It could have been anyone walking through that door."

"Which is why the magic checked us out first."

He glanced at me. "It did?"

"Yeah." My stomach was beginning to settle again, although the madmen in my head didn't seem too inclined to follow suit. I nevertheless stood upright, and held out a hand. "Need some help getting up?"

"Yes." His fingers gripped mine. I couldn't help noticing the slight tremor in them. "Although I have to say, the view from this angle isn't half bad."

I glanced down as I hauled him upright. My sweater had not come through the second shift at all well. Not only had I lost a sleeve, but there was a gaping hole down my left side that exposed one breast. And my jeans weren't in much better shape, hanging on my body in shredded bits.

"It's nothing you haven't seen before," I commented. "And your clothes haven't fared much better."

"No," he muttered, glancing down. "Although it does explain the sudden feeling of freedom."

I half laughed—which I regretted the moment the madmen in my head sprang into action with their pokers—and released Jak's hand. "I think you'd better stay here while I check—"

"No way on god's green earth," he cut in. "If I'd hung back last time, I'd be dust like those walls. Consider me your shadow until we get out of this place."

I couldn't exactly argue given it was totally

true. I took a careful step. The air stirred, and the hairs at the back of my neck rose.

Something else *was* here.

I stopped and scanned the room again. The dangling electrical wires swayed lightly, even though the place was hushed and the air up here still.

The images of snakes rose again. I swore under my breath and drew Amaya. She began to hum with excitement and flames flickered down the edges of her steel.

"Drawing your sword is *not* a good sign," Jak said. "What can you see that I can't?"

"Moving electrical wires."

"Electrical wires? *Seriously?*"

"I'm afraid so."

I took another step. The swaying got stronger. It was almost as if they were attempting to grab us. My skin crawled and I quickly swiped at the nearest one. It plopped to the ground and didn't move.

Not that it should. I mean, it was electrical *wire*.

"You don't think you're overreacting, do you?" Jak's breath was warm against the back of my neck. He might not believe the wiring presented a threat, but he still wasn't taking any chances.

"Can you feel a breeze?" I swung Amaya around as another piece of wiring snapped toward us. It retreated.

Definitely *not* the behavior of inert wiring.

"No, but—"

"Then tell me why the hell those wires are moving like they are."

"I'm sure there's a reasonable answer, but fucked if I can think of it right now." He paused. "Maybe we should leave?"

"What makes you think whatever magic inhabits these wires doesn't also inhabit the ones that control the elevator?"

"There are stairs—" He yelped and jumped, cannoning into me and sending me sprawling forward.

I caught my balance and swung around, Amaya ablaze in my hand. Jak was jumping around like a madman, frantically pulling at the piece of wire slithering up his leg. It was the piece I'd sliced moments earlier.

Amaya, destroy that thing—but don't hurt Jak!

Won't, she said, as flames leapt from her blade to Jak's leg. He yelped again, and raised a hand to batter her away, but I grabbed it.

"She won't burn you," I said. "Just stay still."

"There are flames near my *nuts,*" he shouted, his expression one of horror. "You stay still—"

"Jak," I cut in harshly. "Trust me."

His gaze flashed to mine; then he gulped and stopped moving. Sweat beaded his forehead as Amaya's flames wrapped almost lovingly around the two-foot snake of wiring stretching from just below his knee up to his groin. When the last of the snake was covered, her flames flared briefly, then disappeared. The snake was gone, and there was little evidence of its presence on Jak other than a few scorch marks on his jeans.

Magic bitter, Amaya commented. *Hate made.*

Lauren for sure, then. I still had to wonder why, though. It made little sense for anyone to want me dead, even if Lauren *did* want revenge for Lucian's death. Unless, of course, both she and the other sorcerer—if indeed there *was* another sorcerer; we still weren't entirely sure about that, despite the fact it had definitely been a male who'd snatched the first key from me—had decided they were happy enough having two of the three hell gates open. I guess, if nothing else, it would make accessing hell's minions a whole lot easier for them.

Although the effort-to-reward ratio seemed way out of whack to me. But then, we were talking about a pair of dark sorcerers. Maybe they planned to hold the world for ransom or something equally insane.

I released Jak's hand. "You okay?"

He took a deep breath, then nodded. "What the hell are we going to do about the wiring? Severing it doesn't stop it, and there's too much hanging down for us to do a proper search of the room without risk."

"True." I turned around. *Amaya, are you able to burn a path between here and the bed?*

She didn't answer, but flames leapt from her

blade, shooting forward, creating a six-foot-wide avenue between us and the bed. The remaining wiring shivered and snapped, as if in anger or frustration.

Another chill ran down my spine. There was no way in hell I was going to use the elevator to get out of this place.

With our path clear, we moved forward. The bed had borne the brunt of the explosion, and was little more than a blackened, twisted mass of frame, springs, and fabric remnants. If there *had* been something hidden within it, it was unlikely to have survived.

I checked the remnants anyway, and found precisely what I'd expected—nothing.

I bit back a frustrated curse and looked around the rest of the room. Where would Lucian have hidden something if not in the bed?

"If I'd wanted to secure something," Jak commented, "I would have chosen the loo."

I shot him a glance. "Why?"

He shrugged. "It's the last place anyone thinks to look."

It was certainly a place that would have appealed to Lucian's warped sense of humor. I cleared more wiring snakes, then walked across to the remnants of the bathroom. Surprisingly, the glass wall had held up well, as had the toilet, which had been positioned behind it.

"Try the tank first," Jak said. "It's been plumbed

in, so anywhere else would have caused an ob-
struction."

I unscrewed the flush button, then lifted the lid
off the tank. And there, attached to the plunger,
was a small plastic-wrapped envelope.

"Bingo," I said softly, and pulled it free. I
handed Jak the lid, then unwrapped the envelope,
slicing it open with a fingertip, then carefully un-
folding the piece of paper inside.

It read "-37.76759373693766, 144.88306045532227."

"Coordinates," Jak said, looking over my shoulder. "Latitude and longitude, I'd guess."

"If you're right, then *for what?* is the next big
question." I flipped the bit of paper over, but there
was nothing else written on it.

"Why don't I Google it and find out?" He reached
into his pocket and frowned. "What the hell . . . ?"

He drew out his hand and held it out, palm up.
A collection of broken bits of metal and plastic sat
within it. The remains of his phone, I knew without asking. I closed my eyes and cursed again. In
the rush to get out of the way of the blast, I'd totally forgotten *anything* metal not touching flesh
would be shredded. Which meant not only *his*
phone, but mine too *and* my keys.

"Sorry, that's my fault."

His gaze jumped to mine, and after a moment,
he said, "That change thing?"

"Yeah. Metal not touching flesh doesn't get re-
formed."

"Meaning we'll have to go somewhere else to decipher the clue." He paused, and a sudden, somewhat cheeky smile touched his lips. "My place is nice and close. And I probably still have some of your clothes hanging around."

I blinked. "Why the hell would you still have those?"

He shrugged. "Couldn't be bothered throwing them out. And it wasn't like they were taking up a whole lot of space."

"I bet that must have pleased the hell out of the girlfriends that followed me."

"It wasn't a problem because there weren't any. Only bed partners."

I snorted. "You seriously expect me to believe—"

"Yes, because it's true." His gaze held mine. "My work may be the most important thing in my life, then *and* now, but you were, believe it or not, the next best thing."

"Being the next best isn't exactly a compliment," I noted dryly. "And it doesn't exactly explain why you've had no girlfriends since."

"Ours wasn't the first relationship I wrecked over a story, but it *was* the last. I decided it was better for everyone if I just didn't go there."

I stared at him for a minute. "Good god, was that a touch of remorse in your voice?"

"More an acknowledgment that forming attachments to get a story probably isn't the best way to go about things."

Which was probably as close to a sorry as I was ever likely to get. I folded the piece of paper and slipped it into my pocket. "You could have decided that before you printed the story about my mom and destroyed what we had."

"No, I couldn't have."

Because it had taken that destruction for him to see the light—although I had no doubt the threats from Uncle Rhoan, Aunt Riley, and Ilianna had also played a part. They'd certainly prevented him from printing the remaining part of the story. "I can see you becoming a very lonely old man."

"Not lonely, because there has never been a lack of partners. Just alone."

Meaning he'd faired better in the after-relationship sex stakes than *I* had. At least until Lucian and Azriel had come along to liven things up.

"Your place, then." I paused. "Are you parked somewhere very close? And do you still keep your spare key taped under the rear wheel arch?"

"Yeah, but why . . . ?" He stopped, and tucked a hand into his other pocket. What came out was a handful of metal shards. "Well, shit."

I glanced down, amusement touching my lips. "There's also the free willy problem."

"I don't see it as much of a problem, but I agree that others might." He grinned. "So, do we make a mad dash and hope no one notices?"

"Wiring snakes aside, my clothes won't stand

up to a mad dash. I'll get us out of here, but you'll
have to bring the car around to the building's entrance."

"Sounds like a plan." He turned sideways and
waved me forward grandly. "After you, my dear."

We carefully retreated. Amaya's steel was quivering by the time we made the stairs, so it was
with some relief that I realized not only had the
wiring in the stair shaft remained unaffected by
the blast, but also by the magic.

When we reached the foyer, Jak pulled off the
remains of his sweater and wrapped it around his
waist, effectively hiding the ventilation spots
around his balls.

I waited until he'd left, then said, "Reaper, show
yourself."

For several seconds there was no response; then
heat washed across my skin and the reaper appeared. He wasn't what I'd expected—although
I'm not entirely sure what I *had* been expecting.

I mean, he, like Azriel, was of medium height,
with warm brown skin and mismatched blue eyes,
but his hair was a rich honey color rather than
black, and there was a multitude of scars criss-
crossing his chest and well-muscled arms. Another scar stretched from just below his right
temple to his chin. He also bore two swords rather
than one.

What surprised me, though, was his expression. It was positively hostile.

"What do you wish?" His voice was cold. Unforgiving.

I eyed him warily. "Do you intend to intervene if I get into trouble?"

"I am here to keep you safe until the keys are found," he said. "Nothing more, nothing less."

Meaning, I suspected, that he would keep his distance and be totally unsociable. Azriel might have done the latter when he'd first appeared, but never the former. "What of Azriel?"

He crossed his arms. "We all bear the name of Azriel to those of flesh."

Animosity practically oozed from his pores. Why? What in the hell was going on? "You know who I mean."

"Perhaps I do. And perhaps it is none of your business."

"But it *is* my business. I don't—" . . . *want my child growing up like I did—not knowing anything about his father*. But I swallowed the words, not wanting to admit something that personal to a stranger—especially such a hostile one.

Besides, it was something I should have thought about *before* I'd banished Azriel—and it was yet another reason to call him back. I added, "I just want to know he's okay."

"He lives. Anything more you have no need nor right to know."

The urge to smack *this* particular reaper was strong enough that I actually clenched my fists.

But I very much suspected that would *not* be a good move. He was angry enough to stab me with his swords and claim provocation to higher powers. "Why the attitude, reaper? What the hell have I done to you?"

"What have you done?" He shook his head, as if in disbelief. "Duty is all to those of us who guard, and duty unfinished is a crime against all."

Meaning *my* Azriel was in trouble. Serious trouble. My gut twisted at the thought, but even so, anger flared. "What of the way he failed *me*? He forced me—"

I cut the rest of the sentence off. I was talking to air anyway. The reaper had disappeared.

"You could at least have the decency to hear me out, you bastard."

The reaper no doubt heard, but he was unlikely to care one way or another. And to be honest, no amount of lashing out—whether verbally or physically—was going to make me feel any better.

Only getting Azriel back in my life was ever going to do that.

I swore again and stalked out of the building. Jak's red Honda pulled up a heartbeat later, and I quickly climbed in.

He glanced at me as he pulled away from the curb. "You look like a woman with a problem."

"Yeah, and it's a universal one called men."

He grinned. "May I point out that we males think much the same about you females?"

"When you're not trying to get into our pants, you mean?"

His grin grew. "Even *when* we're trying to get into them. So who's trying to get into yours?"

I crossed my arms. "No one."

"That is a problem, I agree."

I snorted and whacked his arm. "That's not what I'm annoyed about."

"Then what's upset you? You were fine when I left to get the car. What happened in the five minutes it took me to get back here? Did the wiring attack again?" He hesitated, his brief glance shrewd. "It's to do with your reaper, isn't it?"

"Yeah. I banished him—justifiably, I might add—but I wish I hadn't."

"Then unbanish him."

"It's not that simple."

"Why not?"

Why not indeed. I hesitated. "What he did—it was bad, and it's something that can't be undone."

"Was it worse than me starting a relationship with you to get a story? Worse than Lucian killing your mother, then bedding you for information?"

I opened my mouth to say yes, then stopped. Put like that, the answer was actually no. Even if Azriel had a tendency to keep secrets, he'd *never* been anything less than honest about his intentions or his priorities—and his priority had always been, first and foremost, his duty to secure the keys for the reapers. All else was secondary.

I might be furious with him, might feel betrayed by his actions, but he'd *always* warned me he would do whatever he deemed necessary to get those keys. Or die trying.

Why would he think my life—or rather, all my future lives—were any less expendable?

He wouldn't. As the hostile reaper had pointed out, duty was all to a reaper. It rose above everything, even family and love. He might care for me, but that would not have stopped him from doing what needed to be done in order to finish his mission.

The only thing that *had* stopped him was me. I'd sent him away, thereby forcing another to take his place. I'd made him fail, and he was now paying the price.

I scrubbed a hand across suddenly stinging eyes and swore yet again.

"So," Jak murmured. "Not as bad."

"No." I hesitated. It felt a little weird discussing this with Jak, of all people. And yet, he was also the one person who would understand betrayal, even if from the other side. "But I don't know if I can move past—"

"Relationships are hard work," he interrupted. "They're all about give and take. If Azriel did the latter rather than the former, the question you have to ask yourself is, are you willing to walk away? Or is whatever lay between you special enough to work on a fix?"

Yes, it is. I stared at Jak for several heartbeats. "When the hell did you start doling out such astute relationship advice?"

He smiled. "I've had more than my fair share of broken relationships, remember. And you didn't answer my question."

"That's because I haven't actually got one." A lie, but I wasn't about to admit my feelings to Jak before I admitted them to Azriel.

"Then I suggest you do so—and before the gulf between you gets too wide to traverse. Besides, running away from a problem is never a good idea."

Which was an echo of what Aunt Riley had said to me when I'd first woken in hospital after being dragged back from death.

I hadn't wanted to listen to her back then. Hadn't really wanted to listen to anyone—not even when my own intuition had suggested that banishing Azriel was the worst possible move I could ever make. I'd been far too angry.

But somewhere between waking this morning and now, my brain cells had finally started functioning again. The truth of the matter was, despite the pain and the hurt, despite the sense of betrayal, I needed Azriel in my life. I just had to hope that it wasn't already too late to get him back.

I grabbed a quick shower at Jak's in the vague hope that it'd wash away all the bits of fluff and debris that were both on and *in* my skin—the

Aedh magic didn't always re-form clothing as precisely as it deformed it, and it wasn't unusual for me to have annoying bits of fiber sticking out of my flesh for days after becoming Aedh—then went in search of clothes. I found a pretty, knee-length dress at the back of the wardrobe in the spare bedroom, but had no such luck when it came to underwear—for which I was kind of glad. It would have been a little too weird if he'd kept any of that after all these years.

But just as I was about to pull on the dress, I caught a glimpse of my reflection in the mirror behind me, and froze. Because my reflection now bore a series of tattoos that ran up the back of my neck and disappeared into my hairline. They were a mix of patterns that sometimes resembled the known—one looked vaguely like a rose, another like an eye with a comet's tail—and at other times looked nothing more than random swirls. But these weren't any old tats. They were a tribal signature—Azriel's tribal signature.

Obviously, when he'd leashed our energy beings and bound us together forever, I'd become part of his tribe. His family. The one he was apparently refusing to see because of his shame at being a dark angel.

And for the first time since I'd woken up in the hospital, I had to wonder—at what cost to himself had he made me one?

He'd once said that if we'd assimilated—if we'd

become so attuned to each other that our life forces merged—his reaper powers would become muted, and he would never again be able to function as a soul bearer. So in saving me, had he sacrificed his own desire to once again escort souls?

As much as I hated that he'd taken away my right to die as I was destined, it seemed very wrong that he'd also suffer the loss of his own dreams. Becoming a Mijai had been a punishment for him, and it wasn't something he'd wanted to spend eternity doing.

So when he'd put the mission first and dragged me back to life, had the cost been as great to him as it had been for me?

God, I hope not. I closed my eyes for a moment and took a deep, shuddery breath. It was time, I thought, I not only started *acting* like a rational adult, but thinking like one.

And that meant putting on my big girl knickers to not only confront the man I'd banished, but sit down to discuss where the hell we now went relationship-wise.

Or even if we *had* a relationship.

But I couldn't do that here. It would have to wait until later, after I'd gotten home and contacted Hunter.

I tugged on the dress, finger-combed my hair, then went in search of Jak. I found him in the study.

"Did you find out where those coordinates were?" I asked.

His gaze skimmed my body as he swiveled around in his chair. "Always did like you in that dress. The lilac matches your eyes. And yeah, it's smack bang in the middle of an old Department of Defense site in Maribyrnong. They sold it off thirty years ago for development."

I frowned. "That's nowhere near the other warehouse."

"No, but it *is* on a ley line."

My eyebrows rose. "Since when did you become an expert on ley-line location?"

"Since you dragged me into this goddamn quest. I thought it might benefit the story if I actually knew what I was writing about." His expression was somewhat wry. "That's presuming I'm actually allowed to write about it once it's all over."

"Uncle Rhoan said you could."

"Yeah, but I'm betting they'll vet it before it goes to print."

Undoubtedly. "Being on a ley line could suggest it's hiding another transport gate."

The first one certainly had—we'd witnessed a Razan using it, right before hellhounds had attacked us. What it *wasn't* was the gate they were using to get onto the gray fields. But that *had* to be somewhere near the first warehouse, because that was where the intersection was. I guess it wasn't all that surprising we were having trouble finding it, though—it wasn't like they'd want anyone accidentally stumbling onto it.

"Well," Jak said, rising. "There's only one way we're going to find out what's out there."

"As long as it doesn't take all day. I have to be back home by five." It was just after two, so that gave me a couple of free hours before I had to contact Hunter. "And you might want to grab that knife Ilianna gave you, just in case."

"It's stashed in the car." He hesitated. "I haven't heard any whispers about weird things happening out that way. No reports of dogs with red eyes, like the first one."

He touched my back, guiding me out of the house and into his car.

"That doesn't mean they're not there," I said, once he'd climbed into the driver's seat.

"I know. It would be nice, however, if just once we could enter a building without getting attacked."

"Amen to that," I muttered. Hell, it would be nice if just once we caught a decent break. Maybe even a decent clue or two.

Mirri's life might just depend on it.

It took us just over half an hour to scoot across to Maribyrnong. The old defense site was easy enough to find, although much of it was now warehouses in various states of ill repair. Jak wound his way through the estate until we'd reached the coordinates, and parked up the road from a line of boxlike concrete buildings. There were no cars other than Jak's in this immediate area, and all the warehouses seemed empty of movement or life.

"It's the unmarked one in the middle." Jak crossed his arms on the steering wheel and studied the building through the windshield. "It looks harmless."

"So did the first one."

"True that."

I opened the door and climbed out of the car. The air swirled around me, rich with the scent of humanity. There was no one close, though. These warehouses were definitely as empty as they looked.

Jak came around the back of the car and halted beside me, the sheathed knife gripped firmly in his right hand. "The lady with the psychic skills may lead the way."

I smiled and walked down to the warehouse. It was a two-story structure, with small, evenly spaced windows lining both levels. The bottom ones were protected by metal bars, but not the top. I couldn't see anything unusual or out of place, yet tension crawled through me. Maybe it was just the expectation of trouble rather than the sense that anything lay in wait.

The double gates were padlocked but there didn't seem to be any other security measures in place. No cameras or sensors, anyway. Amaya could have dealt with the padlock easily enough, but that would tell whoever owned the building someone had been here.

"Looks like we're climbing over," I said. "And no looking up the dress."

His grin was decidedly cheeky. "Would I do something like that?"

"In a heartbeat."

"I'm mortified you think me so uncouth."

I rolled my eyes. "Will you just get over the fucking gate?"

He grinned and leapt up, grabbing the top of the gate and hauling himself over. I was right on his tail, landing beside him in a half crouch as I scanned the building again. Still no sense of anything untoward.

I rose and padded forward. There were pigeons strutting about on the roof, but little else moved.

The main entrance was on the side of the building, near the large loading bay. The door was locked, as were the bay doors.

"Now what?" Jak said.

I studied the side of the building, then said, "Maybe we should check the windows around the back."

He frowned. "The windows are barred, and not even you're skinny enough to squeeze through them."

"The top ones aren't. Maybe we'll get lucky and find one open."

He snorted. "Since when has luck been on our side?"

There was that. We checked anyway and, as it turned out, lady luck had obviously decided to throw us a small morsel. One of the rear top windows was open an inch or so.

Jak eyed it dubiously. "I'm gathering you're going to use your magic trick to get up there?"

"Yeah." I hauled off my dress and handed it to him. I'd already destroyed one set of clothes today—I wasn't about to destroy another. "I'll get you in if I can."

His gaze skimmed me; then he sighed. "As lovely as ever. I really am an idiot, aren't I?"

I grinned, but didn't answer. I simply called to the Aedh, then whisked upward, slipping in through the small gap and cautiously looking around. The room appeared to be some sort of storeroom—metal shelving lined the walls, but there was little else here other than dust. I scooted under the small gap between the door and the concrete floor, then checked out the various rooms—all of which were empty—before making my way downstairs. Other than the offices that lined the road side of the building, it was a vast, empty space. Once I'd checked there were no hidden security cams, I shifted back to human form.

The madmen in my head went a little crazy with their knives, making my eyes water and my stomach twist alarmingly. But that was to be expected. Not only had I changed shape a fair bit so far today, but I'd yet to eat anything other than a few mouthfuls of bread. I waited until the ache eased and my stomach seemed less inclined to jump up my throat, then slowly rose. The chill air caressed my body, hardening my nipples and sending goose bumps skittering across my skin. But there was no sense of magic in its touch, nothing that suggested anything or anyone had been in here for some time.

"Jak? You there?"

"Right outside the loading bay door. You see anything?"

"No." I spun around, my gaze sweeping the area. There was nothing here that prickled my psychic senses, either. "The place is empty."

"The warehouse near Stane's that we searched a few days ago looked empty," he pointed out. "Until we fell through the damn floor and almost ended up a hellhound's dinner."

"Yeah, but we knew something *had* to be there because of the hellhound reports."

"Lucian wouldn't have hidden the coordinates of this place for no reason," Jak said. "There *has* to be something—you just can't see it."

"Well, I certainly don't want to find it by falling into it."

But the truth was that might be the only way we would uncover what secrets this place might hold. I walked over and opened the window, but the bars were welded securely in place. As werewolves, we could have ripped them off easily enough, but again, that would only announce our presence to whoever owned this place. "How high can you jump?"

He raised an eyebrow. "Fairly high, especially with a run up."

"Then go around the back. I'll open that top window wider for you."

He nodded, and disappeared. I ran back upstairs, and five seconds later he was scrambling in—sans my dress. I peered out the window. It was neatly folded next to the wall. "Why the hell did you leave it there?"

He grinned. "I may not be able to touch these days, but no wolf in his right mind is going to pass on the chance to look. Besides, we have to leave this place as we found it, and that means you closing the window and slipping back out in that other form of yours."

"It's bloody cold in this building, you know."

He sighed dramatically, and proceeded to take off his cotton sweater. "You do spoil all my fun."

"Sorry. But thanks." I pulled it on. It was long enough to cover my butt, and was filled with the warm spicy scent of him. As I rolled up the sleeves, I added, "We do this the old-fashioned way—search every room carefully and see if we spring any traps."

Which is precisely what we did. After more than an hour of walking up and down both levels of the building, we found precisely nothing.

"Damn it!" He thrust a hand through his dark hair. "There *has* to be a reason he hid the coordinates of this place."

"Obviously." I plonked down on the window-sill and rubbed my arms. "But maybe you need to be a sorcerer to find it."

"Fat lot of good that does us when neither of us are."

No, but Ilianna, while not a sorcerer, might be able to see what we could not. I hated the thought of dragging her here, but I really couldn't see what other choice we had.

"Maybe we need to tackle this from another angle." Jak crossed his arms and leaned back against the wall. "I could search public records, see who owns the place, and track them down. And in the meantime, we could keep a watch on the place."

"A physical watch would be too noticeable. The area isn't exactly a hive of activity."

"What about Stane? He owns an electronics shop, doesn't he? Couldn't he get you a camera or something?"

Stane could get me a whole lot more than just a camera, thanks to the fact the shop was a cover for his black marketeering business.

"Good idea." I glanced at my watch. We'd wasted a whole two hours and gained absolutely nothing—nothing except moving Mirri two hours closer to death. Frustration and anger surged anew, but there was little I could do but ignore it and keep on searching. I pushed myself off the sill and headed for the stairs. "Right now, I need to go home. I have to get to that damn meeting."

He followed me. "You want me to drop you off, or are you going to get there under your own steam?"

"You can drive me, if you wouldn't mind. Becoming Aedh drains the hell out of me."

"Which probably explains why you're so damn thin these days." He held out a hand. "Sweater. Don't want it wrecked."

I hauled it off and handed it over. He studied me for several seconds, his gaze lingering on my breasts, then he sighed again. "Do you know how hard it is *not* to touch right now?"

I resisted the urge to glance down and see for myself just how hard it was. "Will you just get out the window."

He grinned and jumped down to the ground. I slid the window back into its original position, then changed form and followed him out. Once the knives and my stomach had again settled, I redressed and we headed to the car.

He dropped me off on the corner of Punt Road and Tanner Street, then zoomed off to begin his hunt for the warehouse owners. I walked down toward Lennox Street, half wishing I'd borrowed his sweater again. The bite in the air was getting stronger, and a dress, however pretty, wasn't enough to keep me warm.

I swung left into Lennox, then stopped dead. There were cops, firemen, and others everywhere.

And the old building that was our home was a half-burned-out shell.

Chapter 4

For several heartbeats, I couldn't move, couldn't think, couldn't even breathe.

My home was *destroyed*. While there were no flames, smoke drifted lazily from several sections of the building and the air was thick with its acrid scent. Firemen were rolling up long lengths of white hoses, and there were both firemen and cops picking their way through the remains of the kitchen end of the building. The other end of the building, which housed both the garage and the bedrooms, showed some evidence of scorching on the bricks and on the half-open roller door, but otherwise, it seemed to have escaped any major damage—at least from the fire. Whether it had escaped water damage was another matter entirely.

Oh, god. *Tao.* He'd been home. He could be hurt, injured . . .

I pushed through the gathered crowd, then ducked under the police tape that fenced off a wide area around our warehouse building. A cop caught me before I got three steps.

"Miss, you can't go in there—"

"I fucking live there!" I yelled back, and brought my heel down on his foot as hard as I could. He cursed freely, but he didn't release me. "Damn it, let me go! I need to find—"

Hands gripped me, shook me. "Ris, it's okay. I'm okay."

I blinked, staring up almost owlishly at the figure that held my arms so tightly. Then it registered that it was Tao, that he was here and whole, even if a little singed. I threw my arms around him and hugged him fiercely. "Oh, thank god," I whispered. "For a moment I thought—"

"For a moment there, I almost was." His voice was grim. He glanced at the man behind me, and added, "She's my flatmate."

"She's damn lucky I don't press assault charges," the officer replied grimly. "Both of you, get back behind the tape and stay there until otherwise advised."

Tao slipped his hand under my elbow and guided me across the road, finding us both a perch on the old brick fence five houses down from our place. He didn't say anything, just sat beside me, a brooding figure that smelled of smoke and fire and fear. It was that last scent that had unease stirring through me.

I'm not sure how long we sat there, watching and not talking. Long enough that night came in, long enough for me to get colder than I'd ever thought possible, despite having a man of fire sitting beside me. Or maybe even because of it. Long enough for the fire marshals to finally declare the old building safe and the police to unwrap the tape and allow everyone back into their houses.

Even us.

Without comment, Tao rose and offered me his hand. I placed my fingers in his, and he tugged me upright. His flesh was hot, and it wasn't the natural heat of a werewolf. It was the heat of a man who was barely controlling the fire elemental he'd consumed to save Ilianna's life—an elemental he was now battling for control over his own body.

Of course, both he and Ilianna had been present at the sacred site where the elementals had been created only because I'd needed their help to uncover information from a book my father had left me. Which meant that the battle Tao faced now was very much *my* fault. I should have stopped them from coming . . . should have done a lot of things. But I couldn't change the past. I could only change the future.

And hope like hell that Tao won his battle.

My gaze raked the black, broken end of our warehouse home. Was that what had happened here? Had the elemental tried to wrest control from him again?

I very much suspected it might be.

As we ducked under the scorched roller doors, I noted what looked suspiciously like a handprint melted into the side of his Ferrari. My motorbike was safely tucked away in the secure parking lot near RYT's, our open-all-hours café, but my old SUV was here. Luckily, it appeared undamaged.

The security door at the top of the stairs was open but undamaged, and water trickled out, a steady stream that tumbled down the metal steps like a mini waterfall. I followed Tao through the door, then stopped. The main living room was a goddamn mess. The walls, floors, and furniture had all sustained both smoke and water damage. Even the industrial fans situated high in the vaulted ceiling were damaged, the big blades bent and twisted by the heat of the blaze. The ceiling itself, though scorched, appeared relatively intact overall. It was in the kitchen where the fire had obviously started, because even from where I stood, it was easy to see that there was very little left except a twisted and blackened mess of wood and metal.

Thankfully, the fire hadn't gotten anywhere near the bedrooms, although I had no doubt that even with all the thick doors closed, everything inside would reek of smoke.

"What the hell happened, Tao?" I said softly.

He wearily scrubbed his eyes with a soot-grimed hand. "What do you think happened? I lost fucking control again."

"How?"

I rubbed my arms in a vague attempt to warm

up. The wind blustered through the broken windows, stirring the ash and making paper remnants pirouette across the floor. The room was cold, wet, and stunk to high heaven, but there was nothing more miserable in the room than the wolf who stood before me.

"I don't really know." He moved across to the kitchen; a long, angular figure that was far too skinny these days, even for a wolf. Even his warm brown hair looked lank and unhealthy. It was as if his body was using everything it could to fight the monster that resided within. "One minute I was getting a roast ready for our dinner, the next I was standing in the middle of an inferno."

I picked my way through the puddles and stopped beside him. "You had no warning of any kind?"

"Not this time." His gaze came to mine. The fear and desperation in his warm brown eyes had my stomach flip-flopping. He wasn't only losing the battle, but very near giving up. "It's stronger than before. Stronger than—"

"Don't say it," I said fiercely. "Because it's *not* true. You're the strongest man I know, and the mere fact that you're still here, still fighting this thing, proves it."

He snorted. "You've known a lot of people who've consumed a fire spirit, have you?"

"No, and that's the fucking point." I glared at him. "If it *has* happened before, then those people obviously haven't survived the merger, because there's no record of it anywhere. But you've not only survived, you've retained control. Most of the time, anyway."

"Yeah, but it's the times I *don't* that worry me. They're starting to happen more and more, Ris." He waved a hand at the ruined kitchen. "I don't want to do this to either you or Ilianna, or anyone else for that matter."

"But even when the elemental has taken over, you've never hurt anyone—"

"I hurt you," he cut in. "And if not for Azriel, you'd have lost use of your damn hand."

"That happened because I grabbed you. My fault, not yours." I squeezed his arm gently. "And the minute I did touch you, you regained control." And I'd do it again in a heartbeat, even if Azriel wasn't around to heal me. What was a ruined hand when it came to saving a friend's life?

"Next time it may not make a difference." He took a deep breath, then blew it out. It was a heavy, frustrated sound. "I guess I'd better ring Ilianna and tell her what happened."

"Good idea." I glanced around the sodden living area. "There doesn't seem to be much in here worth salvaging."

"No. But hopefully the bedrooms will be relatively untouched."

Hopefully. The doors still being closed was a good sign, at least. "You planning to stay the night?"

"Yeah. The fire burned out the security system, so I'll keep watch until we can get it fixed." He studied me for a moment. "What about you?"

"I've got a key to hunt down, and a deadline to beat."

He frowned. "What deadline?"

I briefly explained what my father had done, and he swore softly. "Shit, we can't seem to catch a break, can we? Not from fucking anything."

"It would certainly appear that way."

He hesitated, then said, "You can't do this on your own, Ris. You need help—of the reaper kind."

"I know." I'd known it since I'd woken up earlier this morning. It had just taken me a whole lot of angst and arguing with myself to come to the conclusion everyone else had already reached. "I'm just not sure what to say, given the way we parted."

"It's simple. You need to explain why you were so angry, and he needs to explain why he did what he did. And then you both need to apologize and move on." He half smiled. "There's a world of people who are relying on you both, even if they don't know it."

I sighed. "I know. Trust me, I know."

He placed his hand over mine and squeezed lightly. "You feel hungry? The lamb I was preparing is more than a little overcooked as a result of the fire, but I can wander down the street after I ring Ilianna, and pick up some burgers and coffee."

"That would be lovely. In the meantime, I might just bite the bullet and contact Azriel."

"Then I shall take my time getting back. Just in case there's fireworks."

"I'm not intending to argue—"

"I wasn't talking about arguing," he replied, a cheeky smile touching his lips. He bent and kissed my cheek. "Good luck."

"Thanks." I was no doubt going to need it.

Tao left, closing the door behind him. I turned and retreated to my bedroom. I really didn't want to confront Azriel in the ruins of our living room, just in case, one way or another, things did get heated.

My bedroom had a definite smoky smell, and plenty of water had crept under the door, soaking a good portion of the carpet near the door, but otherwise, everything was as I'd left it. Which meant it was messy—tidy I am not. I grabbed a bunch of towels from my en suite and dropped them over the soaked carpet in the vague hope they would sop up some of the water. Then I walked to the center of the room, my stomach twisting into knots—as much from fear that he *wouldn't* respond as from anything else.

I took a deep breath—though it didn't do a whole lot to calm my nerves—then said mentally, *Rephael, we need to talk.*

Rephael was Azriel's real name, a name known and used only by those very close to him. Which meant I couldn't say it out loud simply because, in the reaper world, names were a thing of power, and knowing someone's true name gave you a measure of control over them. That he'd told me meant he not only trusted me, but he cared more than he'd let on. Only I'd been too damn lost in my own misery and anger to even realize it.

For several minutes, nothing happened. Sweat began to trickle down my back and my heart thumped so fast it felt as if it was about to tear out of my chest. God, what if he didn't come back? What if he *couldn't*? He might have said I only had to say his name and he'd hear me, no matter what he was doing or where he was, but he'd also warned that the powers that be might not *allow* him to come back once I'd sent him away.

If I had to spend the rest of eternity as a goddamn Mijai, I sure as hell didn't want to spend it alone. Or with any other reaper, for that matter.

"There would never be another reaper in your life," he replied quietly. "In that, also, the choice has gone."

I spun around, a turbulent mix of relief, happiness, and fear surging through me. He appeared near the end of my bed, the electricity of his presence playing gently through my being, a sensation as intimate as the caress of fingers against skin. Longing shivered through me, but the fear sharpened. There was nothing, absolutely nothing, in his expression, and not even the slightest whisper of warmth in the mental line between us. There was no sign whatsoever that he was, in any way, happy to see me.

I swallowed heavily, but it did little to ease the sudden dryness in my throat. "Thank you for coming."

"It is not as though I had any other choice, given you used my name." He crossed his arms, an action that not only emphasized the muscles in his arms and shoulders, but brought into stark relief the jagged pink scar that now marred his left arm.

My fault, I thought, feeling sick. I'd sent him away, not only disgracing him but ensuring punishment in the form of being ordered into the battle being waged against escaping demons at hell's second gate. I swept my gaze over the rest of him, searching for other signs of injury. His face—which was chiseled, almost classical in its beauty, but now possessing an even harder edge than before—was untouched. But his well-defined torso bore a new scar, one that ran from the left edge of his belly button and up under his arm, slashing through the middle of the stylized black wing tattoo that swept around from his spine, the tips brushing across the front side of his neck.

Only it wasn't a tat. It was a Dušan—a darker, more stylized brother to the lilac one that resided on my left arm—and had been designed to protect us when we walked the gray fields. That the scar swept through the middle of the Dušan suggested that perhaps it, too, was battle scarred.

My gaze rose to his again. His blue eyes—one as vivid and bright as a sapphire, the other as dark as a storm-driven sea—gave as little away as his expression.

"Azriel, we need to talk—"

"So you said," he interrupted coolly. "About what? I was under the impression you had no desire to see me again, let alone talk to me."

Anger slipped through me, brief and sharp. It wasn't like he was the only injured party here . . . I took a deep breath, and thrust the thought away. Calm, cool, rational. That's what I had to remain. It was acting in anger that had gotten me into this mess in the first place.

Well, that and his actions.

"Look, I understand why you pulled me back from death. Your mission—"

"Was only part of the reason," he cut in. There was a flicker of either fury or frustration in his eyes, but it was gone as quickly as it had appeared. But a muscle along the side of his jaw pulsed, a sure sign of annoyance.

I took a deep breath and plowed on regardless. "The mission to reclaim the keys has always been first and foremost in your thoughts, and your actions have always reflected this. I should not have reacted as I did, in anger and sorrow."

He didn't say anything, just continued to regard me steadily.

I took another deep, steadying breath. It still wasn't helping. "So, I apologize for reacting as I did, and for sending you away."

"But?" It was practically growled.

"But," I added, "I think you owe me both an apology and an explanation. Not only did your actions rob me of all my future lives, but given I am the *only* one who can find the keys here on Earth, my death would have meant they'd remain unfound. Both our worlds would have been safe, Azriel, and isn't that what we're both trying to achieve?"

"The problem," he said, voice flinty, "is that your death would *not* have meant the keys were safe. If I hadn't reacted as I did, the Raziq—and in particular, Malin—would have called you back from the path of light and, in doing so, would have had control over both you and your actions."

I frowned. "But if my body was dead and my soul had reached heaven—"

"It would not have mattered," he cut in. "The Aedh could have not only forced you back into this world, but into the flesh of another. It is your being, your soul, that is vital to finding the keys. The outer layer does not matter."

"Then why couldn't my father have just claimed another body and found the keys himself?"

"Because souls cannot be transferred at will. It can only occur at death."

"Then why didn't the Raziq just kill me? Wouldn't that have been easier for them?"

"They would not have done it unless there was little other choice. And they also know I would have killed you had they chosen such a path. Once dead a second time, your soul would have become one of the lost ones—inaccessible to both them and us."

A ghost, I thought with a shiver. At least I'd been saved from that. "So why is what you've done so very different?"

"Because I merged our beings rather than just pulling you back. It made you more. Made you what I am."

"But in the process, made *you* less." Because he could never again become a soul guide. He would remain a Mijai for the rest of eternity.

"I am well aware of the price," he replied coldly. "But I had no choice—and no desire—to do otherwise."

It was a statement that could have meant anything, but even so, something inside me leapt in hope. "So this is what you meant when you said that death was not the answer?"

"Yes."

"Then why the *fuck*," I practically exploded, "didn't you explain that to me at the time? Why keep something like that secret? If I'd known—"

"Would telling you have made you any less angry at my actions?"

"No, but I wouldn't have *banished* you." My gaze dropped briefly to his scars, and my stomach twisted again. "And you wouldn't have been hurt."

He made a short, sharp movement with his hand. "It is the price I paid for foolishness."

I frowned. "What is that supposed to mean?"

"It means, I was foolish enough to believe you trusted me," he bit back, and there was no holding back his anger this time. It was evident in his voice, and it blistered through the link, strong enough that I took a step back in surprise. "Foolish enough to believe you would understand *why* I would never harm you."

"But I *do* trust you—"

"No, you do not," he cut in again. "Always, in everything I do, you search for a motive."

"Because there always *has* been one!" My voice rose again, but I couldn't help it. "You, the Raziq, my father, Hunter—hell, even Jak—every one of you came into my life wanting something from me. It was not about me. It was never *just* about me."

"You know that was *not* the case with the two of us. Not in the end."

"And *how* would I know that, Azriel? You fought our relationship until the bitter end and, even then, only gave in because you needed to recharge so you could heal me."

"Because I could not bear to see you hurt like that again. It would kill me."

His words sung through me. He might never

come out and say he loved me—hell, for all I knew there was no reaper equivalent of love—but he'd finally acknowledged that he cared, deeply, and that was really all that mattered right now.

But it didn't erase any of the problems that stood between us. The barrier of being from different worlds might now have disintegrated because of his actions, but that didn't lessen any of the other problems. Quite the opposite, in fact.

"And you not being completely honest is killing *me*," I said softly. "There's been too many secrets and half-truths between us, Azriel. If we're to have any hope of a long-lasting relationship, then *that* has to stop."

He studied me for a moment, his expression as still as ever save for that muscle along his jawline. And it spoke volumes. "And this is what you wish? A long-lasting relationship?"

"I don't know if it's possible, Azriel. There's more to our differences than just physiology." I hesitated, and gave him a twisted half smile. "But yeah, I'd like to at least see if this thing between us could become permanent."

"Why?" His voice was still harsh. Unforgiving. And yet, just for an instant, a turbulent mix of joy and fear surged down the link, briefly threatening to fry my mind. "Do you wish it because we are now tied through eternity and you have little other choice? Or is it merely for the sake of our son that you desire it?"

Shock coursed through me and for a moment I could do nothing more than stare at him. Then I licked my lips and said, a little hoarsely, "Our *son*? We're going to have a son?"

He smiled. It was like sunshine breaking through storm clouds, and it bathed me in a heat that echoed through every part of me. "Yes. I felt his resonance when I pulled your soul back from the brink of death."

I stared at him for a moment longer, then threw myself across the distance that divided us. His arms came around me, his hug fierce, as if he never intended to let me go again.

"You have no idea how ridiculously happy that makes me." I pulled back a little, my gaze searching his. "But to answer your question, I don't want a relationship because I'm stuck with you or because I carry our child. I want a relationship because I woke up this morning and realized I might just damn well love you, despite your being one of the most pigheaded, stubborn, and downright frustrating beings I've ever known."

He took a deep, shuddering breath, and slowly released it. He skimmed my cheek, then my lips, leaving them tingling with warmth as he tucked his fingers under my chin and gently tilted it upward. "Those words are a music I never thought I'd hear."

Then he kissed me. Softly, sweetly, tenderly. And there was so much warmth and caring swirling through the link it felt like I was drowning. But oh, what a way to go.

The kiss, however, ended far too swiftly for my liking. I growled softly, and he half smiled. "I know, and I'm sorry, but we still have a problem."

"And what might that be?"

"I am no longer the Mijai assigned to this case. My task now lies with defending the gates, rather than you."

I frowned. "Even though I carry your child?"

"It is my duty, not my desire. Believe that."

"Well, duty can fuck off. And so can the powers that be. I want you guarding me, and no one else."

"It is not that easy—"

"It *is* that easy," I bit back. "Or they can forget any fucking hope of me giving them the keys."

He was silent, his gaze suddenly distant, distracted. After a moment, he said quietly, "The powers that be suggest withholding the keys from them would not be wise."

My heart just about stopped. "They're listening in to our conversation?"

"Of course. You are now Mijai to-be, so discussions of importance, such as this, will always be monitored."

Celestial eavesdropping. Just what we needed. I shrugged, a casual movement that belied the tension riding me. "What's the worst they can do? Kill me again?"

"It would bring you under their control more

fully," he said. "You will, after all, become Mijai after your next death."

"Which means squat. It's not like they can go all autocratic on my ass and force me to do their bidding, is it?" I hesitated, frowning suddenly. "Is it?"

"No, that is not their way. They can, however, make life rather unpleasant."

My gaze dropped briefly to his scars. If they were a result of "unpleasantness," then it definitely wasn't something I wanted to face. But I wasn't about to try to find the other keys without Azriel by my side, either.

"We started this together, we finish it together. End of story, Azriel." I took a deep breath, then added resolutely, "And if they don't like it, then hey, they can do their worst. As I told my dad this morning, I've been dead, and I've had all my future lives ripped away from me. There's nothing much more *they* can do, except take you away from me. And *that* will only achieve the exact opposite of what they want."

His expression went all distracted again. I waited—though I wouldn't say patiently—and eventually he said, "They will accede to your wishes. However, they are less than happy."

I snorted. "Like I really care."

"You might when you become Mijai. They have long memories."

"And we have a whole lot of shit to face and

survive before we ever get to that point." I hesitated. "If I die, I become Mijai. What happens if
you die?"

"Reapers, like Aedh, are extremely long-lived,
but we are not immortal. If I die, then I will become just another celestial star awaiting rebirth."

"So reapers don't move through heaven and
hell gates like the rest of us?"

"No. We are energy, and we return to the cos-
mos that gave birth to us."

Huh. "Then I guess you'd better make sure you
don't get dead, then."

"That would be my plan also," he said, voice
solemn, but with a smile touching his lips. He
gently tucked a stray hair behind my ears. "Tao
returns, and you need to eat."

Eating wasn't what I wanted to be doing right
now. Not when Azriel and the bed were in such
close proximity. But the hours of life Mirri had left
were steadily counting down, and it would be
selfish to waste even ten minutes of it.

"Ten minutes," Azriel commented, placing his
hand against the base of my spine and ushering
me toward the door, "is hardly enough time to
warm up, let alone do justice to our lovemaking."

"You obviously have never experienced the
benefits of a quickie," I said, amused.

"No, but if we survive this, then perhaps I
might."

"If we survive this, I'll make sure that you do."

Tao was standing in the middle of the living room, a brown paper McDonald's bag in each hand. "Not sure where to put these. The sofas are sodden and the dining chairs are a write-off."

"We can sit on the table." Which had, surprisingly, survived pretty much unscathed, despite its close proximity to the kitchen. But then, it was made from aluminosilicate glass, and therefore had a higher melt point.

He nodded almost absently and, as I drew closer, the heat radiating off him caused pinpricks of sweat to roll across my skin. *Shit.* The elemental was threatening his control again.

I stopped beside him and gently touched his arm. He jumped; then his gaze swung to mine. Just for a moment, his brown eyes were consumed by fire; then he swallowed heavily and the danger retreated.

"I'm okay," he said softly. More to convince himself, I suspected, than me. His gaze slipped past me. "Azriel, glad you made it back."

"So am I," Azriel replied.

Tao handed me one of the bags. Inside were a couple of Angus burgers with bacon and cheese, as well as a large fries. I parked my butt on the table and happily munched them down. Tao didn't join me, but walked around as he ate. It was almost as if he was afraid to stand still. Afraid the monster inside would seize control again if he did.

My phone rang just as I was working my way

through the fries, and the tone—a somber funeral march—told me instantly who it was.

"Fuck, it's Hunter. I forgot to ring her earlier." Mainly because it had totally slipped my mind after coming home to find this place a half-smoldering ruin.

"And she's only just calling you now?" Tao said. "She must be in a good mood or something, because she was in a proper snit last time she contacted me."

"And Hunter in a snit is something I really *don't* want to face—even if only on a phone."

"If you don't answer it," Azriel said, "it will only antagonize her further. That would not be wise."

No, it wouldn't. I made to jump off the table, but Azriel motioned me to stay, then disappeared. A heartbeat later, he returned and handed me my vid-phone. I hit the Answer button and Hunter's image appeared on the screen. Her face held no expression, but her green eyes promised death.

"I'm sorry I didn't get back to you sooner," I said, before she could say anything. "But things have been kind of crazy—"

"I do not care about your current problems," she cut in, her voice so devoid of life it sent chills down my spine. "And you certainly *will* be sorry. I have warned you, Risa, about the consequences of inaction."

Fear chased the chills down my spine. I swallowed heavily, trying to ease the sudden dryness in my throat, and croaked, "What do you mean?"

"You know full well what I mean," she replied, still in that same emotionless tone. "I'm sick not only of your manner and attitude, but of the delays when it comes to the keys. I had hoped my actions with the Jorōgumo would convince you of the need to take me seriously, but it appears that is not the case."

The Jorōgumo had been a spider spirit stupid enough to kill Hunter's lover. She'd tasked us with tracking it down and, when we had, she'd proceeded to kill it—by consuming it. Flesh, blood, and soul.

It had been a horrifying demonstration of just what Hunter was capable of—and how far she would go to get what she wanted.

"For *fuck's* sake," I all but exploded, despite the fact I knew anger wasn't the best option right now, "you're not the only one after the keys, and the others are not only *not* of this world, but they can do a hell of a lot more damage—"

"Perhaps," she cut in coldly, "but I am the one who lives in *this* world, and I am the one in close proximity to all that you love. Only there is now one less to love."

And with that, she was gone.

Leaving me to suddenly wonder who the hell she'd killed.

Chapter 5

"What's wrong?" Tao said. "You're as white as a ghost."

"Hunter has killed someone," I said. "Do you want to ring Ilianna, and make sure both she and Mirri are okay?"

He swore vehemently. "I was just talking to her five minutes ago. Surely she couldn't—"

"This is Hunter, so anything is possible." My voice was harsher than necessary. God, what else could go wrong? "If Ilianna is still at the Brindle with Mirri, tell her to stay there until further notice."

Surely even Hunter wasn't crazy enough commit murder inside the ancestral home of the witches.

"I would not be too sure of that," Azriel murmured.

"I'm not." I glanced at my phone, said, "Aunt Riley," and watched the psychedelic patterns swirl prettily across the screen. It seemed to take forever, but finally, Riley's image popped onto the screen. I released the breath I hadn't even realized I'd been holding. She was safe. Alive. Although even if Hunter *was* crazy enough to attack someone in the sanctity of Brindle's halls, surely even *she* wouldn't touch anyone in the Jenson pack. She might not fear Riley or her twin brother Rhoan, but surely even she wouldn't want to draw the ire of Riley's mate, Quinn. Not only was he a very old vampire, but he was also a former Cazador, and part Aedh.

"Risa," she said, her warm, mellow tones echoing the relief I could see in her expression. "You've obviously resurfaced from your drinking binge."

My smile felt tight. False. "Is everyone there okay?"

She frowned. "Yes, of course. Why?"

I hesitated. She had no idea I was working for Hunter, and that's exactly how I wanted to keep it.

"I had a premonition that someone close to me was in danger," I said, glad we were talking on the phone rather than in person. I might have the benefit of super-strong nano microcells—which were the successor of nanowires, and, like them, designed to shield the wearer from psychic intrusion— inserted into my earlobe and heel, but Aunt Riley was one of the strongest telepaths out there, and the microcells were never designed to fend off someone like her. Hell, even Hunter could catch the occasional thought—and usually at the wrong time, like when I was mentally cursing the bitch. "I just wanted to make sure you were all okay."

"Well, it's no one in my pack. You know I'd sense it if it were."

I did know, but it was still a relief to hear it said. Riley wasn't clairvoyant or anything like that, but besides being a very strong telepath, she was also a twin. She and Uncle Rhoan had a connection deeper and stronger than any psychic talent, and the two of them always knew when the other was in trouble. That bond, over the years, had extended to Liander, Rhoan's mate. And Riley and Quinn were in constant telepathic contact. If any of them were in trouble, she'd certainly know.

She added, "Are you okay? You don't look that great."

"Drinking yourself under the table will do that." I forced a smile. "It's nothing a few decent-sized steaks won't fix."

"And the key hunt? How goes that?"

"It doesn't." Which wasn't really a lie, because right now, it *was* going nowhere. "We're finding nothing but dead ends."

"Which is another reason for bringing Quinn and me in on the search. Maybe you need a fresh set of eyes on the evidence."

Not a hope in hell. It was bad enough that I'd pulled Ilianna, Tao, and even Jak into the line of fire. There was no way I would endanger the two people I considered pseudo parents.

"Thanks," I said. "But there's actually no point

because, as I said, we have no fucking clue where anything or anyone is."

"But perhaps if we—"

"Aunt Riley," I interrupted softly, "I love you to death, you know that, but right now—"

"I need to butt out," she finished for me. Her voice was amused, but there was steel in her gray eyes. "You know that's impossible for me to do."

Tension ran through me. I *couldn't* let her help me any more than she already had. I had lost my mom. I didn't want to lose my other mom as well. "Look, I promise I'll holler for help when I need it, but there's really nothing you can do at the moment. Hell, there's nothing for *me* to do."

She considered me for a second, then said, "Is Azriel still helping you?"

"Yes."

"Then I'll back off for the moment. But if you don't holler, and go get yourself dead again, I will be madder than hell at you."

I smiled, relief and amusement running through me in equal amounts. "I promise, on Mom's soul, I will call in your help the moment I need it."

She harrumphed. Meaning she undoubtedly caught the catch-22 in that statement—that I was never going to be desperate enough to call in her help on the key search—but all she said was, "Keep in contact regardless, Risa, or I *will* get involved, whether you like it or not."

"Noted," I said, and hung up. The phone rang almost immediately, and the tone told me it was Jak. I hit the vid-phone's Answer button, and Jak's image popped up on the screen. "Jak," I said, voice a mix of relief and confusion. If everyone I cared about was safe, who the hell had Hunter gone after? "Are you okay?"

He frowned. "Of course I'm okay. I'm ringing you, aren't I?"

"Well, yeah." I hesitated. "Where are you?"

"At the office, like I said I would be." His frown increased. "Are *you* okay? I mean, you look a little pale—"

That's because death is reaching her sharp little claws toward one of my friends. I swallowed back bile and said, "Look, I'm fine, but I want you to go home right now. And don't open the door to anyone but me."

"Why, if I didn't know better," he said, amused, "I'd say you were worried about my safety."

"I am, asshole. I mean, if anyone is going to kill you, I want it to be me. Now, cut the crap and just get moving."

He chuckled, and airily waved a hand—a movement I only half saw on the small screen. "No one can get into the office, Ris. Not only is there security downstairs, but the entry into this area is thumb-coded. I'm actually safer here than at home."

"Security doesn't worry vampires," I told him.

"All they have to do is take over the mind of the guard and they're in."

Or, in the case of thumb-print security, cut off said thumb.

His grin faded. "And that's what you think is after me? A vampire? Why?"

I took a deep breath, and released it slowly. "I'm not sure you're the actual target," I said, honestly enough. "But a vampire has threatened to kill someone I know, and I'm just warning everyone."

"Warning heeded." His voice was somber. "And I'll be careful, I promise. Now, do you want to hear what I found?"

I did, but I wanted him safe, too, and I couldn't escape the notion that he wasn't, no matter what he thought. Hunter *hadn't* made that threat idly. But maybe part of the torture was the waiting, the ever-tightening fist of fear, and the knowledge that sooner or later, one of my friends would be dead. The bitch would no doubt enjoy toying with me like that.

"I'll listen, as long as you promise me you'll go home, lock the door, and stay there until further notice."

"Sounds a bit extreme," he said, with a frown.

"Trust me, the bitch who made the threat *is* extreme."

He studied me for a moment longer, then nodded. "I've seen too much lately to ignore such a warning. The minute I hang up, I'll leave. That okay?"

"Okay." I'd rather he hung up and left straight-away, but I was realistic enough to know that was never going to happen when he had news to share. Why he couldn't leave and talk I had no idea—other than the fact it wasn't legal to drive while on the phone.

Not that legalities had ever stopped him from doing something before.

"Right then," he continued. "I went through public records, and discovered the company that owns that particular warehouse is a mob called Pénombre Manufacturing."

I frowned. The name rang a distant bell—I'd seen or heard that name somewhere before. Where, though? "What do they manufacture?"

"I have no idea, because I can't uncover much information about them or what they actually do. I suspect they might be a shelf company, except for the fact that they own that warehouse."

"Can't shelf companies own assets?"

"I wouldn't have thought so, given they were initially designed for people wanting to start a new company without the hassle of all the paper-work required to create one."

"When did they buy the warehouse? There has to be some records of that."

"There is." He glanced down, and I heard the clicking of a keyboard. Jak was the old-fashioned type—none of these fancy light screens and key-boards for him. Hell, he still jotted down most of his notes in an actual notebook, rather than using his smartphone. "It was purchased twenty-eight years ago."

I frowned. I'd been born twenty-eight years ago. Which didn't actually mean anything, be-yond the suspicion that it wasn't actually coinci-dental. "Who by?"

"A bloke by the name of Michael Greenfield is the registered owner of the company. Problem is, the only Michael Greenfield I can find is in the matches and dispatches database—he apparently died forty-odd years ago."

I wondered if he was any relation to Adeline Greenfield, the witch who'd taught me to astral travel. "Meaning someone is either using his name, or the Michael Greenfield registered as the owner of that building was born overseas, not here."

"Yep. I've just sent a request to an English mate to search the databases there, but I don't know anyone in the U.S. or in Europe who could help us."

"You could always join ancestry.com," I said, only half joking.

He snorted. "That wouldn't help us if he's changed his name."

True. And knowing our luck, there'd be thou-sands of Michael Greenfields out there in the wider world. "I'll get Stane on it, too."

That's if Stane hadn't had enough of my near constant requests for help.

"Between us, we might be able to find something," he said. "I'll send you through what I've found, and I've asked Jason—the English mate—to copy you on any replies he makes. If you could do the same with Stane, I'd appreciate it."

"Will do." I hesitated, then added, "Now go home and be safe."

"I really think you're overreacting but—" He paused, frowning as he glanced at something offscreen. "That's strange."

"What?" I said, my heart leaping as fear surged through me.

"The lights in the foyer just went out."

"Jak, get out of there. Use the stairs or something—" I stopped as the lights over his head went out, plunging him into darkness. "Jak? Move!"

"Moving as ordered," he said, confusion and perhaps a touch of fear in his voice.

"Hide if you can. I'll be there in a minute." But if it was a vampire—if it was Hunter—then he didn't even have a minute.

Which meant I had to get there *now*. And the quickest way to do that was to have Azriel take me. Changing into Aedh form might be fast for me nowadays, but travel wasn't instantaneous. It was with Azriel.

"Problem?" Tao said.

I grabbed a jacket from the back of one of the

chairs as I jumped off the table. It was sodden, but right then I didn't care. My handbag was in my bedroom, and I needed a pocket to shove my phone into . . . the thought barely crossed my mind when Azriel appeared in front of me, holding out my handbag.

Thank you. I glanced at Tao as I swung the bag over my shoulder. "Jak's in trouble. Can you ring the cops and the ambulance, and get them to his building ASAP?"

As Tao nodded and reached for his phone, Azriel caught my free hand and pulled me close. I had a brief moment to enjoy the press of his body against mine, to feel the warmth and strength of him, before his energy ripped through us both. He transported us through the gray fields so fast that the reapers' ethereal, unworldly homes were little more than a bright blur. We re-formed into darkness. A darkness ripe with the metallic scent of blood.

Oh *god* . . .

Azriel? Can you see anything? I swung around, my nostrils flaring, trying to catch the source and location of the blood. Trying to discover if Jak was here.

Whether his attacker still was.

The vampire is to your left. He runs for the foyer doors. Azriel hesitated. *Remember, reaper rules mean I cannot interfere unless he attacks you.*

I didn't care about his rules. Or being attacked.

All I cared about was Jak—and he'd obviously never made it to the stairs.

No, Azriel said, mind voice soft. *He dies, Risa.*

If we get him to a hospital straightaway—

It will not make a difference. He would not survive being transported, anyway. He has not the strength left.

Grief swept through me, but it was twisted with fury. At Hunter, for doing this, and at myself, for involving Jak in our goddamn quest.

I drew Amaya. The flames that flickered down her side were fierce and angry. *What did they do to him?*

He has been gutted. And no reaper waits, as it is not his time.

Gutted him, *not* drained him. A deliberate choice on Hunter's part, meant to kill with as much pain as possible. And if he died when there was no reaper here to guide his soul onward, then he would become one of the lost ones—a ghost forever trapped on the astral planes, never to move on and be reborn. Tears stung my eyes even as fury rolled through me. Damn it, no! Jak shouldn't have to pay such a price for helping me. *None* of my friends should. It wasn't fucking fair when I was doing the best that I could to find the damn keys.

I drew in a shuddery breath. Anger and grief could wait. There was a killer to hunt first.

Help Jak, I said. *Don't let him die without a soul guide, Azriel.*

You know I cannot interfere . . .

I don't care who you have to contact or what favors you have to pull in, I cut in fiercely. *Please don't let him become one of the lost ones.*

I ran for the foyer. The light burning down Amaya's sides made it easier to see the various cubicles, desks, and chairs, but it did little to rip the shadows away from the vampire. Nor could I detect his scent.

Burn brighter, I told Amaya. *I need to see the bastard.*

Fire erupted from her sides, filling the large room with her fierce light. On the opposite side of the room, far closer to the foyer doors than I was, a shadow found form. The vampire was long and lean, with dark hair and pale skin. Not someone I knew, I thought with relief. Not Markel Sanchez, who was one of the Cazadors assigned to follow me astrally. I'd only met him a couple of times, but I had a suspicion that—as far as Cazadors went— he was probably one of the more ethical ones. Not that being ethical would have prevented him from killing Jak had Hunter ordered it. From the little he'd said, even the Cazadors feared incurring Hunter's wrath.

"Stop," I shouted, "or you're fucking dead."

He made a short, sharp noise that sounded a hell of a lot like a laugh—even if a derisive one— and did the exact opposite, crashing through the doors and out into the foyer. I swore and sprinted after him. I hit the half-closed doors a second later, thrusting them back with such force that the top hinges tore free. Glass shattered, glittering with lilac fire as it fell all around me.

The vamp hadn't stopped to call the elevators, but was instead racing for the fire exit. I had a bad feeling that if he made it there, he'd escape. And that meant I had one option, and very little time.

Don't kill him, Amaya. I drew her back and threw her, as hard as I could. She flew like an arrow—albeit a flaming one—and thudded into the vampire's back, her dark blade disappearing into his body, until only her hilt protruded from his flesh. The vampire made a gargled sound, then his legs went out from underneath him and he fell face-first onto the carpet.

I slowed and approached him cautiously. Lilac fire burned where shadowed steel met flesh, but blood crept out from underneath the flames, an ever-growing pool that stained his pristine white shirt. His face, which had borne the brunt of his fall, was also bloody, although I couldn't see just how badly he'd been smashed up given he was still lying facedown. And I wasn't about to go closer or move him, even if he did look dead. Looking dead was something vampires could do extremely well.

Dead not, Amaya said. *Arrange can.*

We need to question him first. I hesitated. *Can he move, or do you have him pinned?*

Move not.

Good. Keep it that way. I paused. *Azriel, how is Jak?*

He only has a few minutes left, Risa. Hurry if you wish to say good-bye.

I scrubbed a hand across stinging eyes, then spun and raced back into the main room. Blue flame flickered in the darkness, Azriel's sword providing enough light to guide me through the office maze, just as Amaya had.

It wasn't until I was near that I realized Azriel wasn't alone. Standing several feet away from Jak's prone body was a white-haired, white-winged female figure. A reaper waiting for Jak's soul to rise. But her form surprised me. Reapers tended to wear the image of someone the soul was most likely to trust, as it made the transition easier. That this reaper had taken on the appearance of an angel meant either Jak was more of a traditionalist than I'd ever figured or that he simply didn't have anyone in his life he ultimately trusted. And that was, in very many ways, sad.

I dropped to my knees beside him. Jak's dark features were pale and etched with pain, his body shuddering and bleeding and . . . bile rose as my gaze stopped at his stomach. Blood, intestines, and god-knows what else spilled from his stomach, despite his best efforts to stop them.

I briefly closed my eyes, fighting for the strength to remain calm. To not storm back to that vampire and rip his fucking heart out.

I placed one hand over Jak's, and tried to ignore the warm blood that oozed over my fingertips. "Jak? Can you hear me?"

His eyes fluttered open. In the dark depths of his gaze, the awareness of death gleamed.

"Risa," he said, voice so soft and hoarse I had to lean close to hear him. "I think you were right about that vampire."

I brushed the sweaty hair from his forehead. "In what way?"

"Security didn't stop the bastard."

"No." I swallowed heavily as tears tracked unchecked down my cheeks. "I'm so sorry, Jak. This is my fault—"

"No, it's not. I wanted to be here, I wanted the story. My decision, not yours. I could have walked away."

Yes, he could have. But I'd known that he wouldn't, not once he had the scent of a good story in his nostrils.

He reached up and caught one of the tears on his fingertips. "You've cried enough tears over me, Risa. I don't deserve these any more than I deserved your love—" He hesitated, his face twisting, his breath becoming little more than short, shuddering gasps for air.

A sob tore up my throat. I bit my lip, and somehow held it back. "The ambulance is coming, Jak. Just hold on."

It would be too late. I knew it, he knew it, but I

didn't know what else to say. So I squeezed his hand lightly, watching as his breath became more and more labored, and his life poured over our twined fingers to soak into the carpet underneath him.

"God," he somehow croaked, "this is a bitch. The story of a lifetime in my grasp and I'll never—"

The rest of his words were cut off by a gasp. Then his eyes rolled back in his head and his breathing stopped.

The sob tore free. "Good-bye, Jak." I kissed his warm lips gently. "I hope both love and the story of the century find you in your next life."

My tears splashed across his face as I sat back and, just for a moment, it looked like he was also crying. Gossamer tendrils began to rise from his body. His soul, ascending. The winged reaper reached out one hand. Jak's soul moved toward her, and together they moved on.

I briefly closed my eyes and swiped at the tears with my nonbloody hand. While I wanted to do nothing more than bawl like a baby, now was not the time. I took a deep, shuddery breath, and said, "Who was the reaper?"

"My sister." Azriel's voice was without emotion, but his surprise echoed through me. Surprise, and something else. Something that was close to regret. "I did not think anyone would answer—especially not someone from my family."

"Why not?" My gaze met his. "It is you who caused the estrangement, not them."

"It was mutual, Risa. My decision to seek revenge for my friend's death brought shame on them." He shrugged, as if it didn't matter, even though—from the little he'd told me—families were a big part of a reaper's life. And yet I knew he didn't regret either his decision or his subsequent actions. But it was those actions that had made him Mijai—it was his punishment for breaking reaper rules and taking a life before its time.

And now, because he'd shared his life force with me, he would remain a Mijai for all eternity, until death overtook him.

"My relationship with my family is not something we should be discussing now," he continued softly. "The police are near. We should go."

Even as he said that, the distant wail of sirens began to cut across the steady murmur of traffic moving past the building. I sighed and pushed to my feet. "No. I want to question the vampire first."

He frowned. "I can pull whatever information you need from his mind."

"But that won't give us a record of confession, and I want to start protecting my ass against Hunter."

That's if he *could* incriminate her. She was a powerful telepath, and could easily have placed a block around the vampire's thoughts, preventing him from ever mentioning her part in Jak's death.

I glanced one more time at Jak's motionless body, whispered a final good-bye, then dug out my phone and hit the Record button as I walked back to the foyer.

She has not placed a block on his thoughts, Azriel said, appearing by my side again. *I can feel none of her taint in his mind.*

I glanced at him. *Which is odd. I know Hunter is head of the Directorate and therefore able to squash any investigation, but surely even she wouldn't want the questions her involvement in Jak's death would raise.*

You accord her human thought processes, and that is something she long ago abandoned. Azriel's mind voice was thick with contempt. *Besides, she would not think us capable of catching her killer. He is not a Cazador, but he is very skilled in killing. Do not step too close or give him the opportunity to attack.*

I wasn't planning to. I took several photos of the vampire—noticing in the process that Amaya didn't show up in any of them—then tucked my phone into the purse's front pocket, out of sight, but still close enough to record everything said.

"Okay, mystery man," I said, "unless you want some *serious* damage done to your back, you'd better stop faking unconsciousness and start talking."

There was no response, which wasn't really surprising. Hunter wouldn't have sent a fool to do her dirty work.

Amaya, twist a little closer to his spine.

Her chuckle—which could be described only as both gleeful *and* bloodthirsty—ran across the back of my thoughts as her blade did a slow circle in his flesh. Blood spurted, and the vampire hissed—a venomous sound if I'd ever heard one. He looked at me, face bloody and eyes narrowed. There was no pain in those black depths, no fear. Just fury. And the promise of death should I make one careless move.

"One last chance to start answering my questions, then I'll sever your damn spine." My voice was cold and flat. One look at his expression—or lack thereof—was enough to tell me I could not show any sort of emotion to this man. He was the sort to take it as weakness.

"What do you want?" His voice was controlled, even. One tough vampire, obviously.

"Everything." I crossed my arms. "Your name, and the name of the person who sent you here to kill Jak."

"I wasn't sent here to kill—"

He cut the rest of the sentence off as Amaya did a half turn. Sweat dotted his face, but his expression remained unchanged. Uncaring. Deadly.

"You're lying and we both know it." To Azriel, I said, *What's his name?*

He hesitated, then said, *Trent Fagan. He is a killer for hire. The Directorate had a death order on him, but Hunter had it removed on the proviso he work for her.*

Why would she do that, when she has the Cazadors at her beck and call?

They do not work for her, but the council as a whole. Kill orders must be cleared through the council before they can be enforced. He studied me. *She is gathering her own personal hit squad; you are one of them, Risa.*

But I don't—

Not yet, he agreed. *But it is what she wants, nevertheless. You—and the remaining keys—would give her the ultimate command over not just the council, but the world.*

I blinked. *Even she's not* that *crazy—*

Oh, but she is. His mind tone was grim. *She wants power. Hungers for it. And she will never be satisfied until all who live bow at her feet.*

Wow. Just . . . wow. And yet it certainly made more sense than the council wanting the keys so they could use hell as their own private jail. Not that I'd ever really believed *that* particular statement—or, at the very least, I'd always suspected there was something more. I had no doubt that if Hunter *did* get the keys, then she *would* use hell. It would amuse her greatly to cast those who annoyed her into that place.

I returned my attention to the vampire. "Look, I know your name is Trent Fagan, and I know you're a contract killer for hire. Tell me the truth about what happened here today, and I might just let you live."

Surprise flickered briefly through his eyes, but he remained mute.

I sighed. "Fine. But consider this, the Directorate are on their way, and we both know they had a kill order out on you. It might have been rescinded, but do you honestly think you'll be given such a chance a second time?"

He contemplated me for a moment, very obviously weighing options. "Living probably isn't in my future, given capture was never part of the plan."

"And what was the plan?"

Something flickered in his eyes. Annoyance or acceptance, I couldn't tell which. But after a brief hesitation, he said, "To kill Jak Talbott."

"Why gut him? Why not just drain him?"

"Because gutting is the more painful death."

I clenched my fists. God, what I wouldn't give for Amaya to be buried in Hunter's flesh right now. "And who sent you here?"

Again he contemplated me. "What makes you think someone sent me here? That reporter has stepped on more than a few toes in his time."

"He certainly has, but you're not one of them. Besides, you don't work for free, even on kills you desire."

That last part was a guess, but I was betting it was a correct one.

A slight smile touched his lips. "If you know so much about me, then likely you'll also know who sent me."

"I suspect I do, but I nevertheless want it confirmed."

"And if I tell you that, you'll let me run?"

"If you can still run, then yes." Even if he escaped the arriving police, he'd still have to face Hunter. She'd know in an instant I'd questioned her killer, but what she *wouldn't* expect was me recording it. "But only if you're honest with me. And I will know, trust me on that."

He smiled, but it held little amusement. "The truth will do you no good, because my employer is beyond anyone's reach. Even the Directorate's."

"She may be beyond the Directorate's reach, but no one is beyond the reach of death."

"Madeline Hunter is."

He'd finally named her, but I felt no elation. I'd need a whole lot more than this confession alone to protect me from her. But it might go a ways toward convincing both her brother *and* the Directorate that there were extenuating circumstances if—god forbid—she and I ever came to blows and I managed to survive the encounter and she did not.

If you and Hunter came to blows, Azriel said, voice grim, *she would* not *survive. And no one—not the Directorate, and certainly not her brother—would ever know of her death. Valdis would consume body and soul. There would be nothing left to find, and nothing left to move on.*

Good. Even hell was too nice a place for the

bitch. I once again returned my attention to the vampire. "Madeline Hunter? The woman in charge of the Directorate?"

"The same one." He coughed. Bloody spittle lined his lips.

"Did she say why?"

"No. And I didn't ask. I'm paid to do a job, end of story."

It was the end, all right, for Jak and for him. Hunter wouldn't let him live, and we both knew it. *Amaya*, I said, and reached out a hand.

She didn't want to leave without a kill, and she hissed noisily, the sound rebounding through my brain. But she nevertheless withdrew, her hilt hitting my palm with a heavy thump. Letting me know she was unhappy by action as well as voice, I thought, amused.

I sheathed her, then said, "As much as I'd love to avenge Jak's death with yours, I think the fate that awaits you is far worse, vampire. Enjoy what is left of your life."

With that, Azriel took me in his arms and swept us out of there. It was only when I was home that I finally allowed myself to grieve for the man I'd once loved.

Hunter's phone call came as no surprise, but it took all my willpower *not* to hit the Answer button and call her every name under the sun.

That would not only be a stupid move, but dangerous to those I loved.

"What?" is all I said. My voice was tight, and my hands clenched. It was a wonder I didn't crack the phone, so tight was my grip.

"Did you get my message?" she all but purred. A cat enjoying playing with her mouse.

And the mouse had no option but to take it. At least for the moment.

"Yes."

Her eyes gleamed with maliciousness. "And did the message get through?"

"Yes." It came out as little more than a spit of angry air. I took a deep breath, trying to calm down, and added, "But why Jak? He wasn't doing anyone any harm—"

"Which made him the perfect specimen for my little demonstration," she cut in. "I would have chosen Rhoan, even though his death would have annoyed my brother greatly, but that would also take out Riley. I have no wish to come to blows with Quinn just yet."

Meaning a confrontation with Quinn was in her cards sometime in the future?

More than likely, Azriel commented. *Your uncle is not the type to sit back and let Hunter's plans proceed unheeded. She would need him gone to openly make her move for domination of all.*

The bitch wasn't only certifiable, she was a

glimpse of our future if we didn't stop hell's gates from being opened.

Because she sure as *fuck* had to be one of hell's finest.

"But do not doubt," she continued, in that same soft but deadly tone, "I *will* take out Rhoan, Riley, and even Quinn if you do not find me those keys."

"I'm doing my best."

Her expression was amused, but the specter of death shimmered in the depths of her eyes. "Your best is not enough, dear Risa. Try harder."

And with that, she hung up. I swore and raised the phone to throw it at the nearest wall, only to have it plucked from my hands by Azriel.

"Taking your anger out on defenseless electronics is a waste of money and electronics," he commented. "May I suggest this instead?"

He offered me a melted glob of metal—all that remained of one of the dining room chairs—and I couldn't help laughing. As he'd no doubt intended. "Thanks, but it won't shatter and therefore won't ease the frustration in quite the same way."

"Ah. Shame." He placed both the phone and the globule on the glass table.

"Yeah." I sighed. "How the hell am I ever going to get free of her, Azriel?"

"I do not know," he said. "But we can always hope she personally threatens you. At that point, she is dead."

"And you don't think she'll have found some

way to counteract your presence?" After all, he had become a Mijai after coming to Earth to track down—and kill—the person responsible for the murder of several reapers, one of whom had been his friend.

"Possibly—"

"Then we don't attack her," I cut in. "Not unless we have an army behind us."

"Harry Stanford has opened that possibility."

Harry Stanford was the manager of a nightclub known as Hallowed Ground, and an archrival of Hunter's. He was plotting to bring her down—for the good of the council, or so he claimed—and he'd already tried to enlist my help. I'd refused. It wasn't as if I needed to get any more involved in vampire politics than I already was.

"No, he hasn't, because he wants me to confront Hunter without his intervention. There was never any mention of a goddamn army." I sighed. "I'm going for a shower."

Though I doubted it would do much to wash the stain that was Hunter's ever-tightening grip from my skin.

A half hour later—freshly showered and wearing a dress that *didn't* remind me of Jak—I sat on the end of the bed and said, "So where the hell do we go from here?"

Azriel shrugged. He'd resumed what had become a normal position for him in my bedroom— when he wasn't actually in my bed, that is—by my window, and the pale moonlight gave his warm skin a cool, silver sheen. "The one clear lead we have is Lauren Macintyre. Perhaps it is time we talked to her."

"She's not likely to give us anything—"

"She doesn't have to," he cut in. "It is key related, so I can force her to talk."

"That's presuming we can find her." I pushed to my feet, walked over to the wardrobe, and slipped on a pair of red leather flats. Not my shoe of choice normally, but I had no idea how long I was going to be on my feet, so heels weren't really practical. "Lauren seemed to have most of her possessions at her place on the Gold Coast, so why don't we head there first?"

He nodded and held out a hand. I placed mine in his, and let him tug me close, smiling as I stared into the mismatched blue of his eyes. "Do you really have to hold me this close when you transport me? Or does it stem more from desire?"

Amusement touched his lips—lips I really wanted to be kissing right now. Only a huge amount of self-control, and the knowledge that time was ticking away for Mirri, stopped me from doing so. That, and the fact that one kiss was never going to be enough.

"I had to be with you, follow you, twenty-four hours a day, and yet every rule said I could not touch you. Not in the way I wanted." His energy began to surge around us. "Holding you like this stopped me going crazy, without breaking the rules."

Which he ended up breaking anyway. Not that I was complaining. "No wonder you were so against me becoming Aedh. It wasn't concern for my strength at all."

"It certainly was," he refuted, voice offended but his smile growing. "It just wasn't the *entire* reason."

I laughed just as he swept us into energy. But the sound quickly died as we reappeared in Lauren Macintyre's pristine white living room.

Because I found myself staring directly into a pair of bloodshot blue eyes.

And they *didn't* belong to anything human.

Chapter 6

Demon, I thought, then found myself thrown out of the way. I hit the polished floorboards with a grunt, but rolled back to my feet and drew Amaya.

And none too soon.

A second creature came out of nowhere, oddly reminding me of a thick, hairy carpet with limbs, and barreled straight at me, its tusklike teeth bared. I swore, jumped sideways, and swung Amaya hard. The creature was big—both in height and in width—but it was surprisingly nimble, and the blade hit nothing but air.

The creature swung a paw the size of a shovel, its long fur streaming out behind it like banners. I ducked under the blow, twisted around, and sliced the back of its tendons. Blood spurted— thick, green, and stinking to high heaven—but it didn't go down. Instead it jumped high, did a midair tumble, and came down behind me—a maneuver that took barely an instant. I stabbed backward with Amaya, then leapt away. But the creature's thick fingers caught the hem of my dress and dragged me back toward it. I swore again and lashed at it over my head. Shadowed steel met hairy face, and split its skin from eye to chin. Flames leapt from Amaya's sides and danced across the creature's face, attacking its eyes and filling the air with the thick scent of burning flesh and hair. The creature howled and flicked me sideways, as if I were nothing more than a feather. I hit a kitchen cabinet with another grunt, but scrambled upright fast as the creature charged me again. Amaya's flames had engulfed its entire head, so I had no idea whether it could see me or not, but I wasn't about to take a chance. I called to the Aedh and swiftly changed, then moved around behind the creature. Taking a deep breath, I concentrated on the arm that held Amaya and brought it back into being. Then I swung my sword, as hard as I could, at the creature's neck.

Amaya hissed as she slid easily through flesh and bone alike, her sparks and the creature's blood flying all around me. As her steel came free, the creature's head rolled sideways from its neck and dropped to the floor with a wet splat. A second later its body followed. I re-formed, somehow keeping to my feet even as my head swam and bile rose up my throat, and swung around.

There were two dead creatures at Azriel's feet, and a heartbeat later a third joined them. He spun, Valdis blazing in his hand, his gaze sweeping the room. There were bloody rents across his right shoulder and thigh, but neither wound looked particularly deep.

His gaze met mine, and the tension in his shoulders eased. "Are you all right?"

"Yes." I hesitated, eyes widening a little as my stomach rose. "Make that a no."

I bolted for the sink. Azriel was beside me in an instant, and though he offered no comfort, his closeness was enough.

"To repeat my earlier question," he said, once I'd finished throwing up. "Are you all right?"

"Yes." I turned on the tap, scooped up some water, and rinsed out my mouth. "But if I'm going to spend the next nine months throwing up my dinner every time a bad guy carks it, I'm going to be royally pissed."

"So this is a result of the pregnancy?" He tucked a stray strand of hair behind my ears, his touch warm against my skin.

"Probably." I gave him a twisted half smile. "I can remember Mom saying she did nothing but throw up in the first trimester. And given that I've generally managed to hold on to my stomach when a bad guy has gone splat, it's a good bet that being pregnant is the problem."

"And is this"—he motioned toward the sink, his expression bemused—"a common problem with nonhuman females? Because it does not seem very efficient to me."

I grinned. "Is that how reapers go through pregnancy? *Efficiently?*"

"Of course. It benefits the mother and the child to do so."

"Well, *this* mother has always had problems with efficiency."

"I know." He raised my chin with one gentle finger and dropped a kiss on my nose. "It is one of the reasons I find you fascinating."

I raised my eyebrows. "I'm not entirely sure I'm happy to be called 'fascinating.' Especially when there are lots of other adjectives I'd much rather hear."

His warm smile crinkled the corners of his eyes, and made my heart do happy little tumbles. "Would 'enthralling' be better? Or 'captivating'?"

"They're a start," I said primly. Then I waved a hand at the creatures. "What were they?"

"Some form of lower demon, though not one I've come across before." His smile faded, and the room seemed cooler for its loss. "The fact they were here and waiting suggests our sorceress has fled. It is doubtful we will find anything of use."

"Probably, but we should still look."

"I wasn't suggesting otherwise." He paused and sheathed Valdis. "Perhaps we should start upstairs, in her bedroom. That is where she kept her tools of trade."

I pushed away from the bench and led the way

to the stairs. "Which she'll undoubtedly have taken if she has fled."

"Undoubtedly. But she might have left in a rush, so it is always possible she has forgotten something."

"She had a three-day head start, thanks to the fact I was drowning my sorrows rather than doing what I should have been." My voice was heavy with annoyance—at myself, at my stupidity for acting without thinking. It's what had allowed Hunter to get her claws in me, and it's the reason Azriel had been scarred—

"Risa, enough." He caught my hand and tugged me toward him. "Neither of us can change what has already happened. We can only affect the future. As for acting without thinking—" He paused, and his sudden smile just about melted my heart. "It is one of the things I adore about you. Please never lose it, because there has been far too little spontaneity in my life until you came along."

Tears stung my eyes. I blinked them away and hugged him fiercely. "Thank you," I whispered, my breath stirring his dark hair.

He gently kissed the nape of my neck. "For what?"

"For just being you. And for coming back."

"It is not logical to thank me for being me. I can hardly be anyone else."

Laughter rolled through me. I pulled back, dropped a quick kiss on his lips, and said, "That's not exactly true given you can look like anyone you wish."

"Ah, but you only ever see my true form, and I'm extremely thankful you happen to desire it. I'd hate to spend eternity attempting to look like someone else."

"But it could certainly put a new spin on sexual dress-ups." I turned and headed up the stairs. "And don't ask why anyone would want to dress up for sex, because this is neither the time nor the place to explain."

"I agree, but the concept is intriguing."

"And much fun."

The master bedroom was twice the size of mine and, like the rest of the place, pin-neat—almost sterile. The first time I'd been in here there'd been little evidence that anyone actually used this room, despite the clothes in the vast walk-in wardrobe and the pair of intricately carved Chinese sideboards that had sat in the middle of the wardrobe and radiated magic. A magic I had *not* wanted to go near.

My gaze swept the bedroom but little had changed other than the faint layer of dust now coating most of the shiny surfaces. It was obviously the maid's week off.

I walked across to the wardrobe, pushed open the double doors, and discovered emptiness. All the designer shoes and dresses, all the expensive but old-fashioned men's suits and shirts, everything was gone. As were the sideboards. Only the magic they'd held lingered, skittering across my skin like mites, stinging lightly.

"Well, shit." I stopped several feet inside the room and thrust my hands on my hips. "Looks like we're late to the party again."

And while Azriel might have told me to stop with the self-recrimination, this was *definitely* my fault. If I'd pulled my finger out instead of wallowing in self-pity, Lauren might not have escaped us so easily.

"She may have fled this place, but she will not have gone too far. She is too involved in whatever the other dark sorcerer has planned to run."

I glanced at him. "You read her mind?"

"No. But she obviously held Lucian's full confidence, and the standing stone we found in that storage locker ultimately led *here*. That suggests deep involvement."

"I guess it's unfortunate the locker is destroyed." As was the woman who'd rented it. She'd been caught in the blast that had razed the entire building and killed at least a half dozen other people.

Of course, while I had no doubt that the body found in the smoking ruins of that storage locker *did* belong to Genevieve Sands, the question that had to be answered was, was it the same Genevieve Sands we'd seen exiting the place, or had we interviewed someone who'd assumed her identity?

"The stone at the storage place might have been destroyed, but it is possible the one at the Razan's place remains," Azriel commented.

I frowned. "Would the Razan still be alive given Lucian is dead?"

"If they were Lucian's Razan, then no, they would not."

"We should check."

"Yes." His gaze met mine, his expression holding an echo of the frustration that ran through me. "It is also possible Stane was able to get surveillance in here."

"Possibly. I want to see him anyway, because I want to check the surveillance tapes for the storage unit."

Azriel frowned. "Why?"

"Something the receptionist said before she died strikes me as odd."

"She didn't say much before she died."

"She might not have said much, but she did say, 'You changed again.'" I met his gaze. "Why would she say that? The only other time she saw me was when we went in there to check out the storage locker that first time, and I'd face-shifted, so it wasn't even me she was seeing."

"That is true," Azriel said. "But you are not the only face shifter in Melbourne. And remember, the sorcerer is more than likely a face shifter."

"Yeah, but he's male. He shouldn't be able to take on the form of a female."

" 'Shouldn't' doesn't mean he can't."

Unfortunately, that was all too true. I scanned the room a final time, and caught sight of something glinting at the base of the wardrobe that had held all the men's clothing.

Frown deepening, I walked over and bent to pick it up. It was an elongated, hexagon-shaped cuff link, the setting thick gold that bore intricate scrollwork with a huge sapphire dominating its center. I didn't know much about cuff links, but I knew my stones, and this one was worth a fortune. It wasn't new, either, because the fixed back showed signs of wear. I turned it around. Two initials—RJ—and underneath the letters sat what looked like a half-moon. I held it up so Azriel could see it.

He raised an eyebrow. "And this will help us how?"

"It's handmade, and there's a maker's mark on the back." I tucked it into my purse. "If we can track the maker down, then maybe they could give us the details of the person they sold them to."

It was a long shot, but long shots were all we really had.

"Shall we head to the Razans' place next?"

"I guess." I walked back across the room. "What will we do if the Razan are alive, though?"

"We question them." Azriel wrapped his arms around me again. "If they are alive, then someone else made them. And that might imply there is another Aedh involved, one we have not yet sighted."

I glanced up and met his gaze. "Do you really think that's possible?"

"No. But I am not about to discount the possibility given—as you have often noted—the lack of help coming from the fates' hands."

His energy whirled through us, snapping us through the fields so fast I almost felt out of breath when we re-formed.

I didn't immediately move, remaining locked in Azriel's embrace as I breathed deep, tasting the various scents in the air, searching for any sign or smell of the Razan. Or anyone else, for that matter.

All I smelled was death.

"That is because the Razan lie dead in this place."

I stepped back, my gaze sweeping the room. We'd reappeared in the small but tidy kitchen. There were dishes piled up on the drainer and ants crawling all over the small bag of rubbish that was sitting on the counter. It'd been neatly tied, as if ready for someone to pick it up and take it to the bin. Outside, in the small paved courtyard, water sprayed high into the air, splattering both the pond and its surrounds and making the water lilies dance about. The two cuneiform-etched stones that had stood in the middle of the pond were gone.

"That is not surprising," Azriel said. "Our sorceress would not want them found."

"I'm not sure why she'd bother. I mean, they only led to her place on the Gold Coast, and it wasn't like anyone other than an Aedh could use them."

"The Razan could use them—the one who set the hellhounds on you in that tunnel wore a device on his wrist, remember. And Lauren would not have wasted energy on such devices without being able to use them herself." He pressed a hand against my spine and ushered me forward. "The bodies lie in the bedrooms."

Fabulous *not*, as my sword would say. I blew out a breath and hoped like hell my stomach would behave itself if their deaths were mucky. As it turned out, they weren't.

We found one body in the first of three bedrooms off the hall. Just as he had been the last time I'd come here, the Razan was sprawled stomach down on the bed. The blankets were twisted around his legs, leaving part of his butt and his back uncovered. He was muscular and thickset— the body of a wrestler rather than a sprinter—and his skin lightly tanned. He had two tattoos on the upper part of his shoulders—one of a dragon with two swords crossed above it and the other a ring of barbed wire. Lucian's mark, and probably my father's.

He looked for all the world like he was asleep,

but he wasn't. He wasn't moving, he wasn't breathing. And he was beginning to smell.

My stomach stirred and I stopped. Azriel walked over to the Razan and lightly pressed his fingertips to either side of the man's temples. Energy whisked around me, fierce and bright, but no images rose from the Razan's mind.

"He died when Lucian died," Azriel said grimly. "There is nothing left in his mind to help. The resonance of his memories has faded."

"He probably wouldn't have been able to help us much anyway. Lucian would have ensured his Razan would never betray him."

"Him, yes, but it is questionable whether he would have offered the same sort of protection to Lauren. Or anyone else who might have used the cuneiform stones."

"True." I turned and headed down the hall to check the other bedrooms. One contained the second body and the other was empty. The cuneiform stones that had stood in the third bedroom had disappeared as completely as their kin in the courtyard. "I wonder where the other Razan are?"

"Undoubtedly lying dead somewhere," Azriel said. "And if we're very lucky, perhaps those misbegotten shifters that have attacked us both times we attempted to get the keys have suffered the same fate."

I shot him a glance. "Why would they? It was dark magic that created them, not Aedh."

Amusement briefly touched his lips. "I did say *if* we were lucky." He held out a hand. "There is nothing more we can do here. Shall we move on to Stane's?"

"I think we should search the place first. Maybe we'll find something helpful."

"I very much doubt it."

But he helped me search regardless, and we found exactly what he'd expected—nothing.

This time, when he held out a hand, I allowed him to tug me into his embrace. I suppose I should have called the Directorate—or at least Uncle Rhoan—to report these deaths, but I really wasn't up to facing all the questions that would undoubtedly follow. Besides, it would take far too much time, and we didn't have enough of that left as it was.

We appeared inside Stane's electronics shop in Clifton Hill. The camera above us immediately buzzed into action, swinging around to track our movements. Not that we could go far—the shimmer of light surrounding the small entrance was warning enough that a containment shield was in action. Azriel could—and had, in the past—delivered us upstairs, where Stane's computer "bridge" and living quarters were, but Stane had just about had a heart attack at our sudden appearance.

"Hey, Stane, it's Risa and Azriel." I smiled up at the camera. "Turn off the shield so we can come up."

"Your wish is my command." His warm tones had a tinny sound as it echoed from the small speaker near the camera. The shimmer surrounding us flared briefly, then died. "And thank you for the case of champagne you sent. It makes late night gaming all that much more enjoyable."

I snorted softly and headed for the stairs at the rear of his overcrowded, dusty shop. "I would have thought alcohol and serious gaming didn't mix."

"Depends on who you're playing with." He appeared at the top of the stairs, his grin wide. "And if there's a bet involving sexual games on the line. Letting her win wouldn't be a bad thing in this particular case."

I laughed, bounded up the steps, and kissed his cheek. Stane looked a lot like his building—a slender, unholy mess. I'm actually surprised he didn't carry a layer of dust over his clothes like the building itself—although it was only the street level portion of the building that had *that* particular problem, and it didn't really matter, because the computer shop itself was little more than a front for his black marketeering. And *that* equipment, like his computer bridge, was kept upstairs in pristine condition.

"Don't tell me the lovely Holly was brave enough to challenge you to a *game*?"

Holly was a werewolf Stane had reluctantly met at the insistence of his mother—and hers.

And, to everyone's surprise but their respective mothers, fireworks had apparently happened.

"Not only that, but she's been here, and she *didn't* try to dust the place." He stepped back and ushered us through to his living area. "I think I'm in love."

"Certainly sounds like you're smitten," I said. "But is she aware that you don't wash or iron?"

"I wash *most* days," he said, expression offended but amusement dancing across his lips. "It's only when I'm deep in a game that I don't— something she'd understand because she's a gamer herself. I tell you, she's perfect."

I grinned. "So your mom was right, after all."

He grunted as he sat down in front of the curving sweep of light screens. "Something I am *not* going to tell her until I absolutely have to. The gloating will be horrendous. What can I do for you?"

"Did you and your friend in Brisbane happen to get the surveillance up and running on Lauren Macintyre's Gold Coast place?"

"Certainly did." He grinned, swung around in his chair, and lightly swiped several icons on the screen directly in front of him. Boxed images tiled onto the screen to his left. "Nothing much actually happens until this one."

He leant sideways and flicked one of the small boxes over to another screen. Lauren Macintyre jumped into view, impeccably dressed in what had to be a designer dress and shoes. She stood in the middle of the bedroom, and barked out orders to the half-dozen men moving a steady stream of boxes piled high with her designer dresses and shoes out of the wardrobe, taking them god knows where.

"When was this recorded?" I narrowed my eyes and leaned closer to the screen. There was something not quite right with those men . . .

"Four days ago now," Stane replied.

So she'd packed up and left *before* Lucian had died.

Suggesting, Azriel commented, *that she somehow discovered your intrusion into her house. Perhaps that is why the storage place was also destroyed.*

Yes. The bitch had been covering her tracks and finding a new hole to hide in—although undoubtedly it was a luxurious hole. She didn't seem the three-star type, that was for sure.

"Have you tried to identify any of the men?" I asked Stane.

"I've done a run through VicRoads's databases," he said, "but couldn't come up with a license match for any of them. I'm currently hacking into police files to see if I can find a match there somewhere."

One of the men on the screen turned to face the camera and shock coursed through me. It was one of the half-human, half-animal beings that had attacked us at the Military Fair when the second key had been stolen from under our noses.

And if Lauren was using them, then she was more tied up with the dark sorcerer than we'd figured.

"Fuck it all to hell," I muttered.

"To put it politely." Azriel's voice was grim. "Perhaps *she* is the reason the beings of those men are so twisted and unnatural. It would take a great deal of dark magic to so alter flesh *and* soul. More, perhaps, than one person—however strong a sorcerer—has."

I shot him a glance. "Could not the same be said for the ley-line gate? Perhaps it took all three of them to create it." I hesitated. "If that *is* the case, would Lucian's death have altered their ability to use it?"

"I am no expert on magic," Azriel said. "But I suspect it would not. The ley-line gate might have been created by a coalition, but I have no doubt they would have ensured it drew its power from the ley intersection itself. No human could create—even through black magic—enough magic to keep a portal onto the fields active for long."

"Damn." So much for the hope that Lucian's death might have some benefit other than just permanently getting the bastard out of my life.

I glanced at Stane, who had a somewhat bemused expression on his face. But then, while he was familiar with our key search, he had no idea what we were talking about when it came to the magic-twisted half shifters. And I didn't bother enlightening him. "Do you still have access to the security cam records of that storage place in Clifton Hill?"

"Yes, but didn't that place blow up?"

I nodded. "I want to have a look at the hours between you first contacting me about Genevieve Sands entering the building and the building blowing up."

"Sure thing." He grinned. "But you can make me a coffee and something to eat while I hunt them down again."

"Deal." I pushed to my feet and made us both a toasted Vegemite and cheese sandwich—he didn't have much else in his fridge—and by the time I'd deposited both that and a mug of coffee in front of Stane, he'd found the records and had relayed them to another screen.

I pulled up a chair and watched as I munched on my meal.

"What are we looking for?" Stane said, as he scooted his chair next to mine.

"Me."

He blinked and looked confused. "Why are we looking for you? Don't you remember going there?"

I grinned. "Yes. But something the receptionist said to me before she died—"

"You were *in* there when the place exploded?" Stane interrupted, his voice incredulous. "Are you insane?"

"*That* is a much debated point," Azriel commented dryly.

The peanut gallery can keep those sort of remarks to themselves, I said, amused.

I will restrain the urge to say that comment makes no sense.

Grin growing, I said to Stane, "I was. Someone had to check whether the explosion had destroyed that locker we were interested in."

"Which it did." He took a sip of coffee. "So what did the receptionist say that tweaked your radar?"

"Not much, just 'You changed again.'"

"As you said, not much."

"No. But when she saw me the first time, I'd face-changed. So why would she say something like that when it was actually the first time she'd seen the real me?"

"It could have been shock," Stane mused. "Or maybe the person who blew up the place was a vampire. They've been known to play hard and fast with other people's memories when it suits their purposes."

"True, but what interest would a vampire have in blowing up that place? And why make the receptionist think it was me going in there?"

"It could have been someone from the council," Azriel said. "Perhaps Hunter wanted to know firsthand what we were doing in there."

"She has the Cazadors following me around

twenty-four seven. Any one of them could have checked astrally rather than physically, and no one would have been the wiser."

"But Hunter also has enemies on the council," Azriel noted. "Perhaps Stanford has a desire to discover what lay in that storage unit for himself."

"Why would he have someone use my image, though?"

"That I cannot tell you."

"Whoever this person impersonating you is," Stane commented, "they don't necessarily have to be a face shifter. Actors have been changing the shape of their faces and bodies for years with makeup, padding, and stuff."

"True, but in this case, unlikely."

"But two sorcerers *and* two face shifters?" Stane said. "That's pushing the coincidences, don't you think?"

Probably. I took a sip of coffee as I watched the images scroll across the screen. Hoddle Street was awash with cars, but there wasn't a lot of foot traffic. Which was good, I guess—it would make spotting the fake me easier. If there *was* a fake me, and I wasn't just grabbing at straws.

"If it *is* a coincidence, then yes," Azriel commented. "But Lucian's plans were centuries in the making. It is entirely possible he brought both sorcerers into this quest not only because they were powerful, but because their abilities would make it difficult for anyone to track them down."

"There *is* one other possibility," Stane said, as he bent to put his now empty plate on the floor under his desk.

I raised an eyebrow. "And that is?"

"That you're dealing with shifters capable of *full*-body shifts," he said. "Hell, there might only be one shifter, not two, and he or she is able to take on both male and female form."

I wrinkled my nose. "We did think of that, but full-body shifters are extremely rare. And I've never heard of any shifter being able to change their sex."

"Hermaphrodites are rare, but they can and do exist. What if we were dealing with one of those?"

If we were dealing with a hermaphrodite capable of full shifting, then heaven help us, because they'd be next to impossible to find.

"It could explain why Nadler listed Harry Bulter, Jim O'Reilly, *and* Genevieve Sands in his will," Stane continued. "He was hedging his bets and relying on the fact that most people think shifters are human-to-animal capable, not human-to-human."

Nadler was the man behind the company who'd purchased most of the properties surrounding the ley-line intersection. In fact, only Stane's shop and the pub down the road remained independent. He was also, more than likely, one of the sorcerers.

I glanced at Stane briefly. "So have you found either Bulter or O'Reilly?"

Stane shook his head. "No. And I've been keeping an eye on the solicitors handling his estate—they haven't tracked them down, either."

"Well, they have to have existed at some point, because Nadler couldn't just appear out of nowhere as one of them and expect to be handed everything on a platter."

"Totally," Stane said. "Which is why I've been searching overseas databases. Not having much luck, though."

That seemed to be the story of this whole damn quest. I sighed and continued watching the images scroll across the screen as the time in the left-hand corner of the screen counted down toward the explosion at the storage place. At the twenty-minutes-before mark, my double strolled into view.

"Well," Stane said. "You were right."

Yes. And it was somewhat disturbing to look at the woman on the screen, knowing the face and body were the image of mine but someone else was inside the shell. Hell, she was even dressed like I was most of the time these days, in blue jeans and a tank top. My gaze skimmed down to her feet.

"Holy shit, the *shoes*."

I leaned forward so abruptly that coffee splashed over the rim of my mug and splattered onto my legs. I swore and jumped up, spilling yet more coffee. Azriel plucked the mug from my hand—thereby preventing more damage to either me or Stane's floor—while I quickly pulled the soaked dress away from my skin to prevent further burning.

"You okay?" Stane asked. "Do you want a cloth or something?"

"I'm fine," I said, flapping the dress a little to cool it down. "Just freeze the screen and enlarge her feet."

He did so. "I don't see anything special about the shoes, aside from the fact they're kinda ugly."

"What's special about them," I said, "is the fact I not only saw those same shoes on Genevieve Sands when we were talking to her outside the storage place earlier in the day, but in one of the boxes those shifters were moving out of Lauren Macintyre's wardrobe."

"Thereby confirming she is indeed our face shifter," Azriel murmured.

"I wouldn't call a pair of shoes a defining piece of evidence," Stane said. "It's not like a thousand other women couldn't have had the same bad taste."

"Agreed, but I just can't buy the coincidence factor in this particular case."

"But you'd think someone canny enough to be involved in the planning of this gate-creation and key-stealing venture would be smart enough to remember to change a pair of shoes when she was changing identity."

"Not if the decision to impersonate Risa and

blow up the storage unit was a decision made in haste after we'd confronted her outside that building," Azriel commented.

"I still wouldn't bank my fortune on the evidence of one pair of shoes," Stane said.

"Perhaps she just didn't think anyone would notice them." After all, from what Aunt Riley had said over the years, witnesses often had trouble agreeing on what suspects looked like, let alone the smaller details of what they were wearing, like shoes.

Stane studied the image frozen onto the screen for a moment. "Suspecting this shifter is both Sands *and* Macintyre doesn't actually leave us any closer to finding any of them."

"No." I stood up and began to pace. "How the hell are we going to find someone who can change their features at will?"

"Your only real hope is to chase the paper trail," Stane said. "Both Macintyre and Sands own properties. Perhaps our best bet is to track both purchases, and see if there's a common link. Maybe a company they both went through or something."

I nodded. It was probably a long shot, but it was better than doing nothing. "While you're doing that, check for a bloke named Michael Greenfield or a company called Pénombre Manufacturing. They own an empty warehouse in Maribyrnong that just happens to be sitting on another ley line. Jak"—I hesitated as tears stung my eyes again; I blinked them away and cleared my throat before continuing—"wasn't able to find much about them."

"Will do."

I glanced at Azriel. "In the meantime, we should go search Genevieve Sands's place. Maybe she hasn't had the chance to clear it out yet."

"Unlikely," Azriel said, his expression grim. "She blew up the storage unit hours after we talked to her, remember. It is doubtful she'd risk remaining in Prahan, given she undoubtedly knows about Stane and his computer skills, thanks to her association with the Aedh."

"God," I muttered, "the bastard is dead and he's *still* causing us problems."

"And will no doubt continue to do so until both sorcerers are dealt with."

Dealt with—the polite way of saying dead. Not that I was, in any way, doubting the necessity of it.

I sighed and walked back to Azriel. "You'll let us know if you find anything useful," I said to Stane.

He nodded. "I'll also check if the autopsy results are ready on the body parts found in the locker. If it *was* Genevieve Sands, then at least it basically confirms the shifter theory."

Because it wasn't Genevieve who'd walked back into that building just before the blast, but a shifter wearing my face. And it was a wonder the police hadn't contacted me about the events—

unless, of course, Uncle Rhoan was running interference with them.

"Draw your sword," Azriel said, as he caught
my hand and tugged me toward him. Valdis was
already in his free hand.

"Why?"

"Because she might have more guards waiting
in this place."

I drew Amaya. A high-pitched humming began
to flow across the outer reaches of my thoughts as
she happily anticipated devouring more shag-pile
demons. She really *was* a bloodthirsty little person.

Not person. Demon. Better.

I grinned as Azriel whisked us across the fields.
He released my hand as we re-formed in the middle of a bright and airy hallway, his gaze watchful
and blue fire running down Valdis's steel sides.

The place was silent. The air held an oddly
smoky, somehow electrical scent that reminded
me of the smell in air just before a thunderstorm,
but there was nothing to suggest there was anything or anyone else in this place but the two of us.

"There's not." Azriel sheathed Valdis. "Not
even her resonance lingers."

"Something does." I held on to Amaya and
swung around. "It smells like magic."

"It is, though it does not feel recent or primed
to attack."

"Why would she set a trap in one home, and

not the other?" I cautiously walked into the first room off the hallway, my footsteps echoing on the polished floorboards. The double bed had been stripped of linen, and the drawers from the bedside tables had been thrown on top of the mattress, suggesting someone had emptied them in haste. I walked across to the wardrobe and used Amaya's tip to open the door. It too was empty.

The rest of the house provided a similar story—beds and wardrobes stripped, rooms empty of everything other than large pieces of furniture. Genevieve Sands had taken everything that might have provided us with some sort of clue as to who she really was or where she might now be found.

The sudden urge to scream rolled up my throat, and I had to bite down on my lip to stop it. I sheathed Amaya and walked through the kitchen-diner, heading for the windows that lined the rear of the house. The small garden was immaculately tended and very pretty, filled with roses and other flowering plants. There was no sign of a cuneiform stone, however. Not even a bare spot in the garden to mark where one had once stood. I sighed and rubbed my forehead wearily.

"Another dead end. Just what we needed right now."

"*That* is not entirely true," Azriel said.

I swung around. He was squatting in front of one of the kitchen cabinets, and held up what looked like a torn edge of paper. "It was caught at the back of this cabinet. Obviously, whoever emptied the drawers did so in haste, and did not notice it."

I walked across. "Does it say anything useful?"

He smiled, though it failed to reach his eyes. "There is some sort of symbol resembling a stylized whirlpool and, underneath, a word that is incomplete because of the tear—Pénom."

"That *has* to be Pénombre Manufacturing. It can't be anything else." Not in this instance, surely. And that meant we'd finally caught a break, even if only a small one.

"I wouldn't think so." Azriel pushed upright. "It also gives us our next target—that warehouse you and Jak discovered."

I frowned. "But there's nothing there."

"There *will* be something there, but it is possible it can only be accessed via magical means."

"Which doesn't do us much fucking good, given neither of us is capable of magic."

"No, but it is still worth checking. Magic lingers here, which suggests its use was recent. If she did not use it to set a trap, what, then, did she do?"

"I have no idea." I flared my nostrils and drew in the electric scent again. There was an odd sense of energy and movement in its undertones and I frowned. "Maybe it was some sort of transport spell."

"Which is why we should check that warehouse. Perhaps the only way to reach whatever secrets that place holds is via the use of such a spell."

"Which still isn't going to help us."

"No, but if the scent lingers there as it does here, then perhaps we could uncover her den via more practical means."

He held out a hand, and in a matter of seconds we were inside the empty warehouse. It was pitch black and the air still and cold. Moonlight filtered in through the grimy windows, but its cool light did little more than puddle around the area immediately underneath them. I stepped away from Azriel and drew in the scents. Magic lingered, as he'd predicted.

He drew Valdis. Flames burned down her sides, casting a bright light around us but throwing deeper shadows beyond it. "Where?"

I glanced at him. "You can't sense it?"

"I can, but its feel is too faint to pinpoint." He half shrugged. "In this case, the nose of a werewolf is infinitely more capable of tracking than a Mijai untrained in magic."

"Half wolf," I corrected, and slowly turned, trying to define from which direction the scent was the strongest.

"But full wolf where it counts."

I raised my eyebrows and shot him a glance. "Oh yeah? And just where would that be, reaper?"

"Your senses," he replied, voice bland but

amusement dancing in his eyes. "What else would I have meant?"

"What else indeed." Smiling, I returned my attention to the scent. It seemed to be the strongest from the area near the stairs that led up to the next floor.

I walked across, and cast around to see if I could pinpoint a particular area the scent seemed to be coming from. After a moment, I ducked under the metal steps and bent down. The concrete here was smooth and unmarked. There was absolutely nothing that would indicate anything lay underneath it.

"There wouldn't be, given magic is used to enter and exit." Azriel squatted beside me and rested Valdis on the concrete.

"Becoming Aedh would be pointless, because I can't move through solid objects. What about you?"

He shook his head. "I need a point of reference to transfer anywhere here, be it a soul or an image. Up until now, I've basically been accessing your memories or knowledge, but you have not been into whatever lies below so I do not have the required information."

I swore softly. "If we break in, she's going to know we're onto her."

"She's well aware of *that* already. She would not have retreated otherwise."

"Yeah, but neither she nor the other sorcerer is aware that we know about *this* place."

"True." Sparks flew from Valdis's tip, hitting the concrete with sharp little hisses. An echo of her master's frustration, perhaps. "We have two choices—breach the concrete, or turn around and walk away."

"We haven't got time to walk away." Or rather, Mirri didn't. I drew Amaya, then added, "Go for it."

At my words, flames flared from Valdis's tip, then split and raced left and right, until they'd formed a two-foot-wide circle. Gray smoke began to billow, the concrete dust teasing my nose and catching in my throat, making me cough. Deeper and deeper the flames bored into the concrete, until suddenly they were through and the concrete ring dropped into a deeper darkness. The flames clung to its side, providing us shadowed glimpses of what lay below.

And what lay below were more fucking hellhounds.

Chapter 7

"You know," I said as the hounds stared up at us, their red eyes glowing with malevolence and their thick bodies little more than shadowed outlines in the fading glow of Valdis's flames, "I'm getting a little sick of being attacked by hell's creatures every time we take a step forward on this damn quest."

"It is the price we pay for tracking a dark sorceress. Stay here—"

I snorted. "Like fuck—"

"Risa," he said, cutting me off with a fierceness that surprised me. "There is *no* need for you to place yourself in danger. Not in this case. For once let me do what I was sent here to do *without* argument."

Let me take care of you. Please. He didn't say the words out loud, but they echoed through me nonetheless. I met his gaze, saw the annoyance and the caring there, and reached out, cupping his cheek lightly as I leaned forward and kissed him. "Just this once," I murmured.

"Thank you." His voice was dry but amusement tugged at his warm lips. "So generous of you."

And with that, he jumped into the hole, Valdis aflame and spitting in fury. I watched, heart in my mouth, as the hellhounds attacked and he briefly disappeared under the force of their onslaught. He emerged seconds later, Valdis a blur as he hacked right and left, dispatching the hounds with quick efficiency. When the last of them was dead, he looked up, his blue eyes glowing as fiercely as the sword in his hand.

"*Now* you may come down."

I sheathed Amaya, then gripped the edges of the hole and carefully lowered myself into the darkness. It seemed an awful long way down to the bottom, even at full arm's length.

"I'll catch you." He sheathed his sword, though her brightness still provided enough light to see by.

"You'd better, or I'll be pissed."

"Which scares me not. It's not like I haven't been subjected to your ire before."

I snorted softly, then released my grip on the edge and plummeted down. Two heartbeats later Azriel caught me, as promised.

"You," he said, voice severe as he stood me upright, "have lost far too much weight since this quest began."

And the opposite should be happening given I

was now pregnant. "Yeah, well, tell that to the bad guys who are either interrupting my meals or making me lose my lunch." I swung around. "Is there anything here besides a black hole and hell-hound bits?"

"There are no cuneiform stones, if that is what you are looking for."

Meaning our sorcerer and sorceress *weren't* using it as a jumping off point to get to their ley-line intersection chamber. I swore softly. "Is there anything else here?"

"Nothing living."

Flames flared down Valdis's sides again, lifting the shadows and lending the rough-hewn walls a blue glow. The cavern was on the small side, though there were two tunnels leading off it. A few small tables had been hacked out of the soil and stone, but there was little on them other than clean spots in the grime—indications that things *had* sat there not so long ago.

I drew Amaya and marched toward the first of the two tunnels. It was small and narrow, and cut so roughly that the sharp edges tore at my dress and skin. Thankfully, it wasn't all that long, and I soon found myself standing in another chamber. This also held empty shelves and tables hewn out of the earth, but there was one major difference here. A very elaborate protection circle had been etched into the stone floor, and the melted remains of black candles sat on each of the four cardinal points.

The twin scents of frankincense and cedar still lingered in the air, which was odd. I knew from Ilianna that frankincense was used as protection *against* evil, and I had no doubt that Lauren used this circle to *summon* evil. But maybe she used it for personal protection—it wouldn't be surprising given what she was summoning. It was what ran under those scents, however—a sharper, almost caustic aroma—that made my skin crawl.

"*That* is the scent of hell," Azriel said grimly. "This is certainly where she summoned her demons."

"Then we'd better destroy it."

"It will not be the only place from which she could summon."

"No, but one less place has got to be a good thing for us, right?"

Not waiting for his answer, I stepped forward, swung Amaya, and slashed her across the nearest part of the circle. The sharp point of her steel scored the stone, cutting the etched lines in two, thereby destroying whatever magic lingered within the circle. To use it again she'd have to redo the entire thing, and that would take time in stone this hard. I smiled grimly. It wasn't much but, if nothing else, it would annoy the bitch.

"Now all we have to do is find whatever other circles she is using." Azriel touched my back, his fingers warm against my spine. "Shall we inspect the other tunnel?"

"Might as well since we're here."

I squeezed back through the rough-hewn tunnel, gaining yet more scratches—though, thankfully, none were deep enough to bleed. The second tunnel was wide enough to walk normally down, and led into a chamber as large as the main one. I scanned the floor, but there was little more than dirt here. But there were more tables and shelves hacked out of the stone and earth, and this time, not all of them were empty. I walked across to a row of six shelves, inspecting the items stacked neatly along them, but not touching. I didn't know enough about the accoutrements of a witch to do so; what I *did* know was the fact they could be damn dangerous if you didn't know what you were doing.

There were old jars of varying sizes, and they seemed to hold little more than herbs, though there were a few that had dried up bits of animals and one that held what looked suspiciously like strands of hair. Hair that was the color of silver.

My hair, I very much suspected.

Maybe this is where Lucian had brewed the *geas* he'd placed on me that had made me unable to resist him sexually. Meaning, this place might not be Lauren's bolt-hole, but rather Lucian's.

"It's possible they both use it," Azriel commented. He stood on the opposite side of the cavern, inspecting several bags. "Lucian was certainly on Earth long enough to have become proficient in magic."

"Why would he need the help of dark sorcerers, if that is the case?" I peered closer at the jar containing the hair to see if there was any sort of visible trap or alarm, then cautiously lifted it. There was no way in hell I was leaving this stuff here for the sorceress to use and abuse. The last thing I needed was another spell or *geas* placed on me.

I unscrewed the lid, inserted Amaya's tip, and watched as she crisped the silken strands until nothing—not even ash—remained. That done, I placed the jar back on the shelf and walked across to a table that held a mix of candles, bells, a chalice, and several incense sticks. There was absolutely nothing that even remotely resembled any of the weapons that had been stolen from the Military Fair.

Frustrated, I walked over to Azriel, my shoulder brushing his as I stopped beside him. "Anything interesting?"

"In the first one, no. This one, however—" He upended the sack, and half a dozen old weapons tumbled out. There were daggers, short swords, several old-fashioned guns, and even a polished silver bayonet. I had no doubt they were part of the haul the dark sorcerer had taken from the Military Fair, because there was little other reason for these types of weapons to be here.

I raised a hand and skimmed it across them. There was no response from the Dušan on my arm, and I couldn't feel any sort of pull toward them.

"You know," I muttered, thrusting my hands on my hips as I glared at the weapons, "I'm getting pissed not only about having hell's minions constantly thrown at us, but also continually being runner-up when it comes to these damn keys."

Azriel tossed the sack back onto the table and swung around, his gaze searching the rest of the cavern. "We might not have found the key, but finding some of the stolen items in this cavern confirms that the dark sorcerer—if indeed there *are* two sorcerers involved, and not just a hermaphrodite shifter—is in fact working with Lauren. Up until this point, it was little more than conjecture."

"Forgive me if I don't get overly joyous about *that* bit of news." I turned and leaned my butt against the stone table. "With the sort of luck we've been having, I fully expect the Raziq to make an encore appearance sometime in the near future."

"It would not matter if they did."

I blinked and stared at him for several heartbeats, wondering if I'd heard him right. "What?"

He glanced at me, eyes once again gleaming brighter than his sword. But this time its source was not the fierceness of battle, but rather the desire for vengeance. And that scared me, because as good a warrior as he was, there was still only one of him, and many more of them.

"It would not matter how many there were, because I am no longer one, but two."

"Which is just about the most confusing state-ment you've ever uttered," I said. "And you've uttered a few."

He smiled. "Our life forces have been leashed. That means it's harder for each of us to be killed, because we can draw strength from the other."

I frowned. "So I'm drawing from you now? I mean, I'm not exactly in tip-top shape at present."

"No, because it will only ever happen when whatever form we are wearing is in danger of complete failure."

"But that doesn't stop them from weakening you to the point where neither of us can fight," I commented. "And it doesn't stop them from kid-napping me again."

"Yes, but the other benefit of our energies being leashed is the fact that there is nowhere they can take you—not even deep underground—that I will not be able to find you."

"That *still* won't stop them from snatching me." Or trying to tear me apart yet again.

"That is something they can no longer do. You have the life force of a reaper within you, and while they may be able to kill you, they can no longer render you to particles." He caught my hands, and squeezed them lightly. "You have nothing to fear from them. You are not what you once were. You are stronger. *We* are stronger."

"Forgive my pessimism, but I'm thinking we

still need to fear them. They'll find a way to make us do what they want."

And it would be easy enough—all they have to do is echo my father's methods and threaten one of my friends.

"But they are impervious neither to attack nor death," he said. "And if we remove the brains of the beast, the beast itself will not function."

A shiver ran through me, despite the warmth of his touch. Though it was cold down here, and I had only a light dress on, neither of those factors played a part in the chills assailing me. Rather, it was the notion that I'd be confronting the brains of the beast—Malin—sooner rather than later. Clairvoyance, I thought, sucked big time.

"Great theory, but I'm guessing it's going to be a trifle difficult to put into practice. Malin doesn't always show up when they kidnap me."

He shrugged. "We can always hope."

I half smiled. "I think hanging around me has made you a little bloodthirsty, reaper."

"It has nothing to do with a thirst for blood," he replied, voice flat. "And everything to do with revenge. As you well know."

"It was revenge that made you a Mijai in the first place," I reminded him.

"And if I had not become Mijai, I would have not met you." He stepped to one side, and motioned toward the tunnel. "But even so, I do not regret the actions that made me Mijai, and I certainly would not regret seeking revenge now for what the Raziq have done—not just for what they did to you, but for making the keys that have the potential to cause so much destruction across two worlds. Shall we go?"

There was little I could say to that. Revenge might be a dangerous desire, but it was one I could totally understand.

The main cavern was still empty of everything but hellhound blood and gore. I stopped underneath the hole in the concrete, and looked up. *What* I was looking for I had no idea. It wasn't like Lauren would suddenly appear, thereby making our hunt a whole lot easier.

"What do we do now?" I asked, after a moment.

"You need to rest—"

"I haven't got the time, Azriel. Mirri's life—"

"May well depend on you being strong enough to complete the task ahead." His voice held an edge that was an odd mix of concern and frustration. "You run yourself into the ground, Risa, and that is not good for anyone."

Not for the hunt, not for those you seek to save, and not for our son. The words echoed through me and made me smile. And yet a vague sense of irritation stirred. He wasn't telling me what I didn't already know.

Wasn't saying what I really wanted to hear.

"I know, and I will rest, I promise, when Mirri is safe."

"Then at least let us return to your apartment so you can get something to eat."

"That I can do." I wrapped my arms around his neck, then, as his arms came around my waist and drew me even closer, added, "Home please, James."

"Another ridiculous Earth saying, given my name is hardly James," he said, as his energy snapped us home in no time flat. As we reappeared in the stinking blackened ruins of the living room, he added, "Nor do I actually think I look like a James."

I grinned. "Agreed. You need a name more befitting of your bright and sunny nature."

He lifted an eyebrow. "I believe *that* is what you would term sarcasm."

"I believe you could be right."

My phone rang, the tone telling me it was Ilianna. The noise was sharp in the dark and smoky silence. Tao, I realized suddenly, wasn't here.

Concern surged. I swung around, noting the front door was wide open as I dug the vid-phone out of my bag and hit the Answer button.

"Is everything okay?" I said, the minute Ilianna's image appeared on the screen. "Is Mirri okay?"

"For the moment, yes." Her voice was calm but worry had etched fine lines around her eyes. "Both Mom and Kiandra are currently studying all the different threads of magic woven into the energy collar, in the hope it will give them some idea how to dismantle it."

It was a long shot, but right now, I guess it was the only one we had. "Tell them to be careful, because it's Aedh magic they're dealing with."

"They know, trust me." She hesitated. "Have you got any idea where Tao is? I've been trying to contact him, as we need some fresh clothes. We're going to stay here for the next day or so."

I frowned. "He hasn't called you?"

"Not recently, no." Meaning he'd disappeared not long after Hunter's phone call to me. I scrubbed a hand across my eyes and tried to ignore the growing sense of loss. Tao wasn't lost, not yet, no matter what my inner voice might be saying.

I said, "As to where he is, I don't know. He was supposed to be home keeping an eye on the place, but the door is wide open and he's gone."

"Nor is he in the near vicinity," Azriel said.

Damn, this is all we needed. *Not* that it was Tao's fault. He was trying his best not to succumb to the elemental, but the desperation in his eyes haunted me. He was losing the battle, and he knew it. "Have you tried the café?"

"Of course. And I rang Stane, but he's not there."

"God," I muttered. "I hope the fucking elemental hasn't gotten hold of him again."

"How was he when you last saw him?" Ilianna said.

"Jittery." Scared.

But wherever Tao was, whatever he was doing, I just had to pray *he* was in control rather than the thing inside of him. Because as much as it tore at me, he couldn't be my priority. That honor belonged to finding the keys and saving Mirri. "I'm sure Stane will keep an eye out for him."

"He is," she said. "He's aware of the elemental problem, Ris. Tao must have mentioned it."

He might be aware, but he was as helpless as the rest of us.

"Then there's nothing else we can do. I've got keys to find and the clock is ticking."

"I know." She hesitated, her expression suddenly holding a touch of fear. "How is the search going? As badly as I fear?"

"Yes and no. We've uncovered a few clues, but they've led to dead ends."

"Well, you *are* dealing with a dark sorceress. They don't make things easy for anyone, including themselves."

I frowned. "Meaning what?"

"Meaning dark magic is usually based on the strength and the blood of the practitioner. To summon as she does would take a toll on her physically *and* mentally."

"Meaning if she summoned enough demons to protect two different places, she'd have to lie low for a few days and recover?"

"Definitely."

Which was more than likely *why* the second key hadn't yet been used. It wasn't just that they hadn't found the correct one yet, but one or both of them hadn't the strength to actually get *onto* the fields. And that meant how much time *we* had left very much depended on *when* they'd summoned the demons. Lucian had died three days ago, and Lauren had been packing before then. The days I'd spent trying to drown my sorrows might have given her all the time she needed to recover.

"Does that sort of rule apply when you're creating something like a protection circle?"

"Not really. It's a different type of magic to summon."

"But what if you're trying to protect and hide something large? Something like a gateway onto the gray fields powered by the ley-line intersection?"

"It's still the same magic, just a larger scale." Her expression was a little bemused. "As I've already told you, the amount of magic needed should produce a magical 'hot spot' that would enable us to pinpoint its location."

And the sorcerer would *know* that, I suddenly realized. "And have you?"

"Well, no. But I did ask Kiandra about it—"

"And she said they haven't noticed any such hot spots," I cut in.

She frowned. "Yes. How did you guess?"

"Because it suddenly occurred to me that any sorcerer worth his salt is going to know just how

trackable his magic is. So either the magic conceal-
ing and protecting the ley-line gateway is Aedh
based and therefore untraceable via human means
or—"

"Or," she cut in, "he's *not* using magic. Not to
protect the intersection, anyway."

"Exactly." I began to pace. "There was a small
protection circle around the cuneiform-etched
stones Jak and I found in the tunnels under that
warehouse near Stane's. Maybe we should be
looking for something along those lines on or near
the intersection."

There was also the other tunnel, Azriel commented. *You did not examine that.*

No, I hadn't, mainly because I'd sensed something evil down there. I'd been right, too, because
that was where the hellhounds had come from.

But why have the hounds down a completely
different tunnel from the one that held the cuneiform transport stones? Had they been protecting
something else entirely—like a gateway onto the
gray fields? Had the hellhounds only been unleashed when we'd sprung the trap by falling
through the floor?

And was that trap—as well as the cuneiform
stones—the only way into those tunnels? Given
how tight the tunnels were, I couldn't imagine
someone Lucian's size actually using them with
any sort of regularity. Not without doing himself
major harm, anyway. And while it was easy

enough to get into the warehouse via the broken loading-bay door, the building was surrounded by a barrier that prevented energy forms from entering—and he had been energy, even if he'd been forced to remain in flesh. Still, how hard would it have been for someone—be it Lucian himself or Lauren—to have woven exceptions into the spell? Not very, I'd imagine.

And that meant that maybe there was another entrance into that other tunnel somewhere inside that building.

All that is more than true, Azriel commented. *But if that barrier is still active, neither of us may get back in.*

I frowned. *Why would the barrier prevent me from entering again?*

Because we now share a life force and it altered your genetic makeup, Azriel commented. *You may technically be flesh-based, but my life force now runs within you. That fact may make the shield react.*

There's only way we can test that theory.

Yes. But not before you eat.

Don't nag me, Azriel.

Someone has to. His mental tones were grim.

"I'm gathering," Ilianna said, her voice dry, "that given the silence and your sudden, somewhat annoyed expression, you and Azriel are having a telepathic spat."

"Sorry, Ilianna," I said immediately. "And yeah, we were."

She smiled. "Tell him I'm on his side."

"Hey," I said, feigning hurt, "you're *my* friend, not his."

"Yeah, but if he's telling you off, it probably has something to do with you not eating or looking after yourself. And that's good, because you don't."

"Thanks, friend," I muttered.

"No problem at all." Her smile faded. "You'll keep me updated on any progress?"

"As much as I can, Ilianna."

She nodded and hung up. I rang the local pizza place, ordered a large with everything, then shoved my phone away and said, "Happy?"

"When you actually eat it, yes I will be."

I got out some cash and handed it to him. "I'm going for a shower. If the delivery guy gets here before I'm done, give him this."

He accepted the cash with a nod, then walked over to one of the broken windows and assumed his "soldier on guard" position—hands behind his back and feet slightly apart. The occasional ripple of blue running down Valdis's length showed she was as alert as her master.

I headed for my bathroom, stripping off my dress and kicking off my shoes along the way. The light came on as I entered, and the black slate was warm under my feet, meaning neither the fire nor the water had damaged any of the electrical or heating circuits in this part of the house. Tao's insistence on having separate circuits for the various sections of the warehouse had finally paid off. I dumped the dress into the laundry chute, then stepped into the shower. The water came on automatically at just the right temperature, the sharp spray like needles against my skin. For several moments I did nothing more than stand there, lifting my face to the spray and allowing the water to run down my body. And wished it could wash away the grief and tiredness as easily as it washed away the grime.

After several minutes, I sighed and got down to the business of washing. I didn't have time to waste, and as much as I would have liked to stay there, letting the jets of hot water massage and soothe, there was too much to be done.

Once dry and dressed—this time in more sensible jeans, a sweater, socks, and boots—I headed for the living room, only to stop when I saw an envelope sitting near the end of my bed.

Trepidation raced through me. In the past, an envelope or parcel arriving on my bed had generally heralded a change of events or circumstances, and not always for the better.

But standing here staring at it wasn't going to make it go away. Nor would it uncover what delights it had in store for me this time.

Azriel appeared as I somewhat tentatively picked it up, his shoulder lightly touching mine. Warmth flowed between us, but it failed to ease the rising sense of dread. Obviously, my psychic senses had already decided this note held nothing good.

But this time it wasn't from my father. Not only was the paper quality more everyday than upmarket, but the writing on the front was very different. It simply said *Urgent* in what I'd term bold and masculine handwriting.

Mouth dry, not knowing what to expect or who it was from, I slid a fingernail under the flap and opened it up. Inside was a single white sheet of paper. The message was short—*It is imperative we meet, but we can only do so on the astral plane. I will be where we first met at one. Markel. 12:05 a.m.*

I glanced at my watch. One o'clock was only twelve minutes away. I folded the note and glanced at Azriel. "What do you think?"

"My immediate thought is that Tao must have been here at the time this was delivered. Markel is a vampire, and he could not have left this note on your bed due to the fact he has not been invited into your home."

I blinked. I hadn't even thought of that. "I'm not sure it's much of a comfort." Especially given an awful lot could happen in a forty-minute time frame. I waved the note. "Could this be a trap?"

"It is always a possibility." Azriel's expression gave little away—as usual—but his tension flowed through me, a river of energy that tingled across my skin, making it twitch. "And I can neither follow nor protect you on the fields. He may well be aware of that."

"Yes." I glanced down at the note again, and wished I had the capability to read between the lines. But other than the tension flowing through me—both mine and Azriel's—my psychic senses were giving me squat.

"The mere fact he wishes to meet on the astral plane suggests he has no desire for anyone to witness it." Azriel's voice was grim. "And that could mean this meeting would displease Hunter greatly."

And Markel was canny enough not to displease Hunter—which only made this request all the more ominous.

"I should go. Just in case."

Azriel raised an eyebrow. "In case of what? You have enough to deal with as it is, Risa. There is no need to be seeking more trouble."

"What if it's not trouble? What if it's something vital about the keys or our sorcerers?"

"If it was something vital to our quest, it would have come to us via Hunter." He crossed his arms. "But I can see there is no dissuading you."

"No. Although I don't know if I've got enough time left to get onto the plane." I was still very much a novice when it came to astral traveling, after all, and it took me longer to find the right frame of mind to astrally step out of my flesh.

"Then you had best start now." His words rang

with disapproval, but it wasn't like I hadn't felt that before.

I crawled onto the bed and got myself comfortable, then closed my eyes and concentrated on my breathing, slowing it down, drawing it deep. As my heartbeat became more measured, a sense of peace enveloped me and the tension in my limbs began to slip away. Then, as Adeline had taught me, I pictured a rope hanging above my head and reached up with imaginary hands to grasp it. It felt thick and real against those fingers, and as strong as steel . . . I pulled myself upward along it. Dizziness briefly swept over me, seeming to come from the center of my chest, but I ignored it and kept climbing that rope. The pressure grew and every inch of me began to vibrate. Then, suddenly, I was free and floating above my prone form.

I didn't hang about, simply imagined the gigantic shed that was the Central Pier function center on Melbourne's docklands district—the place where I'd not only first met Markel, but had interviewed the ghost of Frank Logan. In an instant I was there.

And so was Markel. He was tall, with regal features and a body that was as lean as a whip. He bowed as my gaze met his, his expression giving little away but his brown eyes showing a touch of relief.

It is good of you to come. His mind voice was cool,

without inflection, but not unpleasant. *I wasn't sure that you would.*

I did think about not coming. My reply, like his, was thought rather than spoken. You couldn't actually talk here on the astral plane, just as you couldn't physically move. Everything had to be done on a subconscious rather than conscious level—although that didn't restrict you from fighting or even dying on the fields. And if you died on the astral plane, then you died in real time, too. *But curiosity got the better of me. Of course, curiosity has also gotten the better of many a dead cat.*

He smiled, although it held little humor or warmth. *I did not arrange this meeting in order to harm you.*

Then why did you arrange it?

He hesitated, and that in itself was enough to send trepidation skittering through me. Markel was a *Cazador*. They never hesitated. They just did whatever needed to be done, in the most efficient way possible.

Because someone wishes to speak to you. Someone neither of us should be seen with.

And with that, he moved to one side and a second man stepped forward out of the ghostly surrounds.

It was Harry Stanford, the manager of Hallowed Ground and the vampire who wanted me to kill Hunter.

Chapter 8

Fury swept through me and the plane responded instantly; shadows crowded close and the very air began to vibrate ominously.

I flexed imaginary fingers and tried to calm down. Getting angry in a place that reacted to your every thought and emotion was damnably dangerous.

What the fuck are you playing at, Markel? I glared at him. So much for attempting to calm down. *If you were following me the day I went to Hallowed Ground, you know full well I want nothing to do with this man's schemes.*

I said as much to Harry, Markel replied, voice even and expression unperturbed. *But he insisted.*

"Harry," not "Stanford." Suggesting he and Stanford were, at the very least, well known to each other.

I snorted. *And a Cazador has no other choice but to give in to a nightclub manager?*

When that manager is not only a trusted friend, but a former Cazador himself, then yes, I do.

My gaze shot to Stanford, who was regarding me neutrally. He was a dark-haired, dark-skinned man of indefinable age, with incandescent green eyes that glowed with an unearthly fire here on the astral plane. That he was a former Cazador certainly explained the sense of danger I'd gotten the last time I'd been in his presence.

If you're a damn Cazador, I hardly think you'd need my help to take the bitch out.

A smiled teased the corners of his lips, but barely reached his bright eyes. *You've now seen what Hunter is capable of. Do you really think one lone Cazador is capable of beating her?*

The only way he could know I'd witnessed Hunter's full capabilities was if Markel had told him. And that meant Markel was more than just a messenger.

But you're not one lone Cazador, are you? I waved a hand in Markel's direction. *That he's here very much suggests he's on your side.*

Harry definitely isn't alone in his desire to rid the council of the stain that is Hunter. Markel's mind voice held a touch of grimness. *But she is also by no means alone. Too many vampires fear her, and will never risk going up against her.*

So, I commented, *the majority of council members—many of whom are hundreds of years old and very dangerous in their own right—fear to cross Hunter. And yet you're expecting me to?*

Brought down to basics, that's precisely what we're

expecting, Stanford said. *She's now killed a former lover of yours. How many more of your loved ones will have to die before you realize she will never get her hooks out of you? She owns you, Risa, for as long as you have people you care about.*

She won't kill any more of my friends. She's not that stupid.

If you honestly believe that, Markel commented, *then you are the one who is stupid.*

I wasn't stupid. I knew it was more than a possibility, but it was one I wasn't about to admit to in front of these two men. If I acknowledged their point, it would somehow feel like I was giving ground. *And are the Cazadors behind this coup attempt?*

Again he hesitated. *No. Not all of them.*

What about the other two who follow me about? Do they side with you, or with Hunter? Or are they the reason we're meeting here?

We meet here because it is safer for us all. Hunter cannot astral travel.

Meaning there was something the bitch *couldn't* do? Amazing. *That still doesn't answer the question about my other followers.*

They are not among Hunter's supporters, he said, *but neither do they side with us. They do not, in fact, know I support Harry. If they did, they would report it to Hunter, just as they would if they knew of this meeting.*

Then I guess I had to be glad they didn't know

about it. It also meant I had to be damn careful about what I said out loud from now on. I returned my gaze to Stanford. *None of this changes the fact that I have no intention of helping you.*

And if Hunter attacks more of your friends?

I'll deal with it when it happens. But would I? *Could* I? As much as I hated Hunter, as much as I'd love to see her dead for what she'd done to Jak, I very much doubted I could ever win a fight against her. And even though I knew Azriel would take the witch out if given half the chance, he could do so only if she attacked me. She wasn't stupid enough to do that, either. Besides, he'd made no secret of his desire to kill her—not even from her. She no doubt had plans—and protections—put in place for such an eventuality.

Stanford continued to regard me steadily, and there was something in his eyes that made me think he was neither surprised by my answers nor in any way put off by them.

Which made him very much like Hunter in some respects. The question was, just how far would *he* go to get what he wanted?

When she kills again—and she will *kill again, trust me on that—we will be here, ready to discuss our plans further.* His tone was still even, still unperturbed. Trepidation skittered down my spine. Its cause wasn't so much fear of him or his plans, but rather his certainty that Hunter hadn't finished her bloodshed just yet. *But you should know now that we do not expect you to go up against her alone and unprepared.*

Well that's mighty big of you. I frowned. *What do you mean by unprepared?*

He half shrugged. *There are means of—nullifying, shall we say—the more terrifying aspects of what Hunter has become.*

And what, exactly, has she become? You never did explain that.

She is a Maenad, he said, *and a follower of the Greek wine god Dionysus, who can on one hand bring joy and divine ecstasy to those who come in contact with him, and on the other brutal, unthinking rage.*

While I was absolutely positive Hunter didn't even *know* the meaning of joy, the brutal, unthinking rage certainly fit.

Stanford continued. *In ancient times, Maenads roamed the mountains and forests during what was known as the orgiastic rites of Dionysus, and often tore apart and devoured any animal or human who came in contact with them. Hunter still performs those rites today, although there are none alive who could confirm it.*

Does that mean she became a Maenad before she became a vampire?

Yes. The followers of Dionysus have no gain when it comes to life span.

But when you became a vampire, you certainly did. I studied him for a second, then said, *If there's no witnesses left alive, how do you know she's still a practicing Maenad?*

Because when you are touched by the magic of a god, as the Maenads are, it is not something you can cast aside.

So Hunter was imbued by the spirit of a god and warped because of it. I guess that made about as much sense as anything else right now.

How do you plan to stop her doing to me what she did to that spider spirit?

By trapping her in a place that breaks the connection to her god, thereby restraining what she is able to do in his name.

Which really didn't tell me a lot. *If you're able to do that, why not do it now and take her out yourselves? Why do you need me involved?*

Because, Markel said gravely, *such a death goes against the council's rules of hierarchy and challenges, and they would be honor bound to kill us.*

Meaning what? That to kill Hunter you have to formally challenge her?

Yes, Stanford said. *Such challenges must be performed in front of chosen witnesses, so that they can confirm the legitimacy of both the fight and the kill. As a fully functioning Maenad with the power of a god behind her, Hunter would wipe the floor with either myself or Markel. It is the reason she has retained her position as long as she has.*

Then make sure the fight happens someplace she can't use her powers.

It is not that simple, Markel commented. *The place has to be council sanctioned, and will be guarded against any form of interference. Restricting Hunter's Maenad nature would be seen as such.*

Trust fucking vampires to make the whole stepping-up-the-ladder scenario so damn complicated.

If she's so damn powerful, why hasn't she tried a takeover of the high council before now?

Because as much as the majority fear her, she is aware that fear alone is not enough. She may be powerful, but the weight of numbers can overwhelm even the strongest. Stanford paused, and half shrugged. The movement spun small eddies through the astral plane near him. *She has never been a fool, no matter what else she might be. But with these keys in her hand, she has hell itself behind her.*

I snorted. *Not even Hunter could control hell.*

I never said she could control it. The threat of unleashing it—of making a hell here on Earth—would be enough. There are few who would risk such a thing.

There were at least two people I knew of who could and *would* risk it. Unfortunately for everyone, they were the ones who currently had both gate keys.

Look, as much as I sympathize with your desire to kill her, there's no way in hell I'm about to be the bait in any trap to snare Hunter.

Both men studied me for a moment, then Stanford nodded. *As you wish. However, if you change your mind—and I fear that you will be forced to—then you know where to find me. Or Markel.*

I wouldn't bet the blood bank on it, I replied grimly.

I only ever bet when I'm sure of a win. Stanford didn't seem too perturbed by my refusal to fall in line with his plans, and that made me more than a little nervous. I doubted he was the type to give up easily. He added, *In this case, I certainly would bet the bank—blood or otherwise.*

He bowed—an old-fashioned but elegant movement—then disappeared. Swirls of gray were the only indication that anyone had ever stood there. I glanced at Markel. *You should have known this would be a waste of time. You've been following me around long enough to get some sense of how I'd respond.*

He shrugged. *Reminding you of your options—and the fact we can and would do our best to make it a more even fight—can never be considered a waste of time.*

Give me an army at my back and I might consider it. But one-on-one? No fucking way.

You would hardly be alone given the reaper rarely leaves your side.

And you think Hunter wouldn't be canny enough to have a means to nullify his presence? Magic can restrain him, Markel, and I'm betting Hunter has been around long enough to know such a spell.

More than likely. He hesitated. *However, if you have no intention of ever going up against her, then do nothing more to antagonize her. She walks a knife edge of sanity at the moment.*

If you know this, the fucking council must. Why won't they do something about her? Surely if they ganged up on the bitch they could defeat her.

As Harry said, we are bound by rules and conventions. It is not that simple.

I snorted. *And do you think Hunter plays by the rules? Or even cares about them?*

Perhaps not, but if we play her game, then we are no better than her. And she is not without her supporters. He hesitated. *Be wary of what you say. We hear every word here on the plane. You would not want her other followers to realize anything untoward has happened.*

I know. I studied him grimly for a moment. *What happens if they do suspect anything?*

Then I will have to take care of them.

Kill them, you mean.

He shrugged. *There is little other choice. Besides, it is what I do.*

But won't it alert Hunter that something has happened?

If an astral traveler is killed on the plane, then they die here on Earth. It would not be the first time such a death happened, and I daresay it will not be the last. It is a risk we all take when traveling.

That didn't actually answer the question.

Yes, she will suspect and more than likely question me. But she has no reason to question the loyalty of the Cazadors, and she will not suspect my involvement.

No, she'd suspect me.

Perhaps, but we work twelve-hour rotating shifts. If

the kill is timed right, it would be at least ten hours before the body was discovered. The plane is an ever-shifting environment. There would be no evidence left to find.

There'd be a ghost. Ghosts can be questioned.

It would be a fragmented ghost, and insane. They would get no information from it.

I frowned. *What the hell is a fragmented ghost?*

It happens when the part of the soul that walks the field is killed. The traveler not only dies in flesh as well as spirit, but it sends the remainder of their soul mad. It is the source of the ghosts who wail. They can do little else. He bowed slightly. *Until next we meet.*

And with that, he disappeared. I shook my head and imagined myself back in my body. I whooshed back quickly—a little too quickly, as it turned out. My eyes sprung open as I gasped in shock.

"Whoa," I said, swallowing heavily as my stomach leapt up into my throat. "Forgot all about the side effects of doing that."

The bed dipped as Azriel sat beside me and held out a can of Coke. "Would this help?"

"If I was a normal person, no it wouldn't." I pushed upright, and ignored my rebellious stomach as I accepted the Coke. "I, however, happen to have this stuff running through my veins."

He smiled. "And here I was thinking it was junk food that fueled you."

"Speaking of which, where's the pizza? If I don't eat it, you'll nag me."

He nodded toward the bedside table, then added, "What did Markel want?"

"He was basically warning me to get a move on with the keys." I leaned sideways and snagged a thick slice of pizza, then, just in case one of my astral watchers was near, silently added, *And playing middleman for Stanford. It doesn't take a genius to guess what he wanted.*

You said no?

Of course. Just because I sometimes choose to ignore consequences doesn't mean I'm not aware of them. I munched on the pizza and added, *And I think the consequence of me going up against Hunter would be me getting dead.*

Death in this form, maybe, but you would live on in energy form.

Sorry Azriel, but that's not something I want right now. Especially given it meant me becoming a Mijai. I frowned. *If I did happen to die, what happens to our child? Would he die, or would he also become energy?*

He would also become Mijai—although obviously not a serving one. Not until he reached maturity.

So by saving me, you condemned our son to a life you hate?

Yes. His gaze met mine, blue eyes hard. *Better the life of a Mijai than no life, Risa.*

It would have been better to have left things as they were meant to be—both of us dead. But then, if the Raziq had the power to call my soul back into this world, what was to stop them doing the same to my son? I might not agree with what Azriel had done, but I could certainly understand his reasons. Now that he'd actually explained them, that is.

I snagged another piece of pizza. "So, I guess the next thing we have to do is go see if we can get into that warehouse near Stane's."

"And if we can't?"

"Then unless dear old Dad comes through with a key to get into his quarters in the temples, I'm fresh out of ideas."

He studied me for a moment, then said, "What of your uncle?"

I frowned. "What of him?"

"Did he not study to become a priest?"

My confusion grew. "Yes, but that's not going to help us get into my father's quarters."

"Maybe, maybe not," Azriel replied. "But it is very rare for a half Aedh to undergo priest training, and that alone suggests he's more than likely extremely powerful."

Which was something I'd never really thought about before. I mean, sure, I knew he'd undergone training, but it had never struck me to ask *why* a half-breed had even been allowed near the temples. Unless, of course, the priests were in short supply even back then.

"Powerful or not, from what my father said, we won't be getting into his and Lucian's quarters without some sort of access code." I finished the slice of pizza and licked a few cheese remnants off my fingers. "Besides, we don't need Uncle Quinn to get into the temples. You can do that, can't you?"

"I can, yes, but it is unlikely I would be able to access the inner sanctums, and that is no doubt where your father's quarters are. Only the initiates are quartered in the outer rings, and we Mijai rarely have need to go any farther."

So once again my father hadn't been completely honest. What a surprise. "I really don't want to involve Uncle Quinn, if only because it'll drag Riley into the equation."

"Your uncle is more than capable of keeping information from your aunt," Azriel commented. "He is Aedh as much as vampire, remember."

"Yeah, but she's one hell of a telepath." And she could spot someone keeping a secret a mile away. How the hell I'd managed to keep the fact I was working for Hunter to myself for so long, I'll never know.

Of course, it *did* help that I'd recently missed our weekly cake and Coke catch-up sessions. If I hadn't, I'd probably be locked up somewhere right now while she gathered the troops and took off after Hunter.

"I still think you should talk to him," Azriel said. "He might also be able to offer suggestions when it comes to Hunter and Stanford."

"Maybe." I drained the can of Coke, smothered

a loud burp, then added, "Let's go check out that warehouse first. If we have no luck there, I'll consider talking to Uncle Quinn."

Azriel nodded, then rose and held out a hand. I placed my fingers in his and he tugged me upward. I grabbed my coat, then locked the front door and once again melted into the warmth of his arms. A heartbeat later we were outside the old West Street warehouse that contained the first of the cuneiform stones we'd found.

It was one of those old two-story, redbrick places inner-city renovators seemed to love. The wind rattled the rusted iron roof and whistled through the small, regularly spaced windows, many of which were broken, but overall it was in pretty good shape. Like many of the other buildings in the area, its walls were littered with graffiti and tags, and rubbish lay in drifting piles along its length.

But while it looked abandoned, there was an odd, almost watchful stillness about the place. It was a stillness that seemed to affect the immediate surrounds, which were unnervingly quiet. Even the roar of the traffic traveling along nearby Smith Street seemed muted.

I shivered, despite the heat rolling off the man standing so close. "Can you sense anything or anyone in or near the warehouse?"

He shook his head and pressed his fingers against my spine, ushering me forward. "Nothing but rats."

"Just like last time," I murmured. And I had to hope it was a case of second time lucky when it came to this place. I really didn't fancy falling into a pit and I certainly didn't want to confront more damn hellhounds.

There were two entrances here on West Street. The first one was heavily padlocked and seemed to lead into an old office area. The other was a roller door over what had once been a loading bay, and this was where we'd gotten in previously. I glanced down at the bottom-right-hand edge. Someone had obviously tried to fix the hole, because it was far smaller than it used to be. But there was still a section that provided just enough of a gap for a skinny person—which I certainly was these days—to get in.

"The real question here," Azriel said, "is whether you'll be able to get in this time."

"And if I can, do I really want to?" I rubbed my arms, but it didn't do much to chase away the gathering chill. "I haven't even got Jak to shore up my courage this time."

"No," he said softly. "But you could destroy the wards. That would allow me entry."

"And no doubt notify the sorcerer that we've found this place."

"True. But I suspect that—sooner rather than later—we're going to have to do that if we wish to find their gateway onto the field."

I stopped in front of the door and scanned it for

any additional signs of security, electronic or otherwise. "That's if it *is* here. There's no guarantee of that."

"It has to be here somewhere, if only because of its proximity to the intersection." He paused, then added, "I can sense no magic other than the shield."

And I couldn't sense *anything*. I took a deep, somewhat quivering breath, but it didn't do a lot to ease the growing tide of tension. "Wish me luck."

"I wish you safety," he replied. "As you have noted on numerous occasions, luck is a bitch who seems to have abandoned us."

Laughter bubbled through me as my gaze shot to his. "Azriel! Did you just swear?"

He raised his eyebrows, his expression bemused, though amusement danced in his bright eyes. "Is not a bitch a female dog? How is that swearing?"

I grinned, knowing he was teasing and trying to lighten my mood. I leaned forward and kissed him. "Thank you," I murmured, my lips so close to his I could taste every breath.

"You are most welcome." He gently tucked a stray strand of hair behind my ear. "Just be careful in there."

"I will." I stepped away from the warmth of his touch, then took another of those deep breaths that did little to calm the butterflies, and stepped toward the roller door.

Energy skittered across my skin, the sensation

sharp and unpleasant. I ignored it and got down on my hands and knees to squeeze through the small hole. The sensation increased, until it felt as if I was being swarmed by sand flies. My skin twitched and crawled, and I had to bite my lip against the desire to back out. However unpleasant the sensation was, it *wasn't* actually stopping me. I guess that was something I had to be thankful for, even if I really didn't want to enter this place alone.

Once inside, I stood up, dusting off my hands as I stepped away from the door. The stinging sensation eased immediately.

"I'm in," I said, rather unnecessarily.

"Can you see or sense anything?"

I looked around. The light that filtered in through the grimy windows highlighted the dust and rubbish lying in drifting piles along the loading bay's ramp. Three doors led off the platform that ran around the sides of the dock, and there were stairs down at the far end that led up to them. I could neither see nor smell anything or anyone out of the ordinary, but I hadn't last time, either. But there *was* something here—something that crawled along the edges of my psychic senses.

Magic.

"They haven't abandoned this place, that's one certainty." I drew Amaya. Flames rippled down her sides, casting a lilac glow across the nearby concrete.

"If this is where they hide the gateway onto the fields, it would be highly illogical for them to do so," he said. "But they will more than likely have added additional security. Tread warily."

"I did that last time, and still fell through the goddamn floor."

"So this time don't ignore intuition when it suggests something is wrong."

"That would be totally logical, and you know I don't always work that way."

"Unfortunately, that is very true." His voice was wry, and I smiled as I cautiously moved up the ramp. The last time we'd been here, Jak and I had chosen the middle door of the three that were situated on this upper level, and had subsequently triggered a trap. Maybe a change of entry point would change my luck.

I stopped at the first door and scanned it for anything out of place. It was one of those half-glass doors, but enough paint had peeled off the lower section that the grime had stained the wood almost black. There didn't appear to be any sort of security—magic or otherwise—so I reached for the door handle. The damn thing was locked. Which wasn't surprising if they wanted to direct all traffic to the middle door. But having sprung that trap once, I wasn't about to go there again.

I bent and peered at the lock. It looked solid enough, but the same could not be said about the frame. It very much looked as if sometime in the past, someone had kicked this door good and hard and had taken some of the frame with it. And though it had been patched, I suspected it wouldn't take much to force it open again. I clenched my hand and gave the door a thump. It sprung open instantly. I caught the edge before it could smash back against the wall, then closed it again, making sure it still looked locked.

The room itself had obviously been a small office, though it held nothing more than the remnants of a whiteboard, a broken office chair, and strings of dusty cobwebs. I moved on. The next door wasn't locked, and it led into a room that was long and dark. Given there was no wall to my left, it also had to be the same room that held the trapdoor into the pit. I glanced down sharply, seeing bare concrete rather than wooden flooring, but didn't immediately move. The uneasy sensation of magic crawled around me, and I wasn't about to ignore it.

"Amaya, flare brighter."

She did so. Her flames revealed the room was twice the size I'd imagined. The roof soared high above me, snaked with metal lines and some sort of conveyer system. Several small offices sat on the right-hand side of the building, and the concrete was stained with rust lines and grime, reminders of machines that had once stood here. To the left, there was that large square of wooden flooring Jak and I had fallen through the first time.

Obviously, whoever had made that trap had repaired it after we'd left.

"Why would they set the trap over only one door?" My voice echoed in the cavernous room and something seemed to stir in the shadows down the far end. Or maybe that was simply imagination and fear.

The stairs are closest to the middle door, so most of those who use them would logically choose that door. Azriel's voice held a hint of amusement. *Why do you ask the question out loud rather than in your thoughts?*

"Because I don't feel so alone." Which was stupid, because I was.

Not, Amaya grumbled. *Am here.*

Yeah, but it's not quite the same hanging on to you as it is Azriel.

Her static filled the far reaches of my mind. I might not understand it, but I was pretty sure she was swearing at me. I ignored her and stepped forward, every muscle tense, ready to jump should the concrete show the slightest inclination to drop out from underneath me. When it didn't, I took another step. The crawling sensation of magic grew no worse or better. I bit my lip and walked on, moving past the wooden flooring that concealed a trap and into the warehouse proper. Though I scanned high and low, I couldn't see anything that suggested this place had been recently used in *any* way.

I checked out the offices to the right, but didn't find anything more than rubbish—although in the last one there was a large rat's nest. It had been made with shredded paper, odd strips of material and wiring, and what creepily looked like human hair. Hair that was dark and long.

I wondered if it had come from someone who'd stumbled into the pit and, unlike us, hadn't been able to escape.

I shivered, but let the rats be and continued on. I was about halfway down when I felt it.

Not magic, but something else. Air stirred the hairs on the back of my neck, cool and almost otherworldly, sending goose bumps skittering across my skin. I stopped, my grip tightening on Amaya.

There was nothing here. Nothing but shadows in the far reaches of the building where Amaya's flames did not reach.

I glanced toward the street. Several windows had been broken along this section, so it was logical that the air would stir. The wind might be light outside, but it was nevertheless there, and it wasn't about to hurt me. I scanned those shadows again.

Still nothing.

"Azriel, has anything changed? Can you sense anything other than me and the rats in this place?"

No. But if you fear something, retreat. It is not worth the risk.

"I can't retreat every time I feel threatened," I muttered. "I'd never get anything fucking done."

The trouble with that *statement,* he said, mental tone exasperated, *is the fact you* haven't *retreated. Not once.*

"That's an exaggeration. I *have* retreated, and you know it. I'm not that much of a fool."

What sounded like a mental snort rolled down the line between us. I ignored him and continued on.

The air stirred again, this time whisking behind me, making the small hairs at the nape of my neck stand on end.

Something definitely *was* here.

I stopped again. *Amaya, can you sense anything?*

No foe, she said. *No fair.*

I half smiled, despite the tension running through me. She was obviously feeling a little put out. I mean, it had been *hours* since she'd killed anything.

Funny not, she muttered.

My smile grew. I walked on, my gaze constantly scanning the walls and the floor, looking for some clue as to what might be here, and whether it was dangerous. I couldn't see or sense anything untoward. Even the dark caress of magic began to fade as I moved farther from the pit trap, until it was little more than a faint buzz of wrongness that scratched at the far edges of my senses.

As I moved into the end third of the building, the filth and grime began to build. The sludge was thickest where machines had once stood, and it smelled to high heaven. I kept to the center, between the outline of the machines, but even so it was hard not to slip and slide.

Air whisked past me again, and for a moment it felt like someone was trying to grab at my fingers. The fleeting sensation left them tingling. I flexed them and frowned. What the hell was going on? Was it my imagination, or something more?

I stopped again. There really *was* nothing to see. Nothing but the dirt and the grime and a few rusted remnants of the machines that had once dominated this space. If there was an entrance into the caverns below, then it didn't appear to be here. The floor looked solid—although given the thickness of the grime, it was certainly possible that there *was* something here and I just couldn't see it.

Although I couldn't see evidence of anyone having walked through this place recently, either, and with the thickness of the muck, surely I would have. My footprints were pretty easy to spot.

Again, air stirred, but this time, ethereal fingers briefly entwined through mine. I yelped and jumped backward instinctively, my heart leaping into my throat even as my fingers burned with the icy touch of the dead.

Shit, I thought, suddenly realizing what was going on. It was a fucking *ghost*.

Maybe even the ghost of the person whose hair had become a bed for a nest of rats.

I swallowed heavily and tried to calm down. A ghost couldn't hurt me. Well, maybe it could on the astral plane, but certainly not here on Earth. Besides, it was grabbing at my hand, which suggested it wanted to show me something.

"Okay," I said softly. "I hear you. What do you want?"

An odd sense of excitement stirred around me, then that cool touch slid across my fingers again and tugged me to the right. Amaya flared brighter as we approached the deeper shadows crowding the corner of the building, but for once, her flames had little impact.

Because there was magic here.

It was faint, little more than a sliver of energy that barely stirred the hairs along my arm, but it was similar in feel to the shield that protected this building and kept Azriel out. And surely *that* meant there was something here they wanted to protect.

A door into the caverns below, perhaps?

If we were right in our guess that our sorcerers weren't using any sort of high-level magic to protect their gateway, then perhaps this *was* the entrance they were using to get to it. As Azriel had noted earlier, it made sense that the gateway was here somewhere, simply because it was so close to the ley-line intersection.

I directed Amaya's flames toward the floor, but the shadows refused to lift. But just for a moment, the vague outline of something small and round appeared—a stone. And it wasn't alone, because there was an even fainter shadow sitting next to it. Stones weren't something you'd expect to find in an old factory warehouse—bricks and roofing tiles maybe, but not stones the color of ink. And that could mean only one thing—there was a stone circle here—one that hid its contents as much as it protected them.

I raised a hand and pressed it closer to the screen of darkness. Energy rippled across my fingertips, its feel sharp and somehow dirty. I bit my lip and pressed harder. It felt like I was fighting glue, and the unclean sensation grew, until it felt like acid gnawed at my skin.

Eventually, I couldn't stand it, and yanked my hand back. My fingers were red and tiny blisters were beginning to appear along their tips. The magic might not be outwardly evident, but it still was powerful. There was no way in hell I was going to risk stepping into it.

"Well, fuck," I muttered. "Can nothing go our goddamn way for a change?"

Would it be worth bringing Ilianna here? Azriel said. *She's unraveled the threads of this sorcerer's magic before. Perhaps she can do the same with this barrier.*

"As much as I hate the thought of doing it, it might be our only chance of discovering both the sorcerers *and* the key before Mirri's deadline."

The ghost's touch trailed across my fingers again. This time, there was a sense of urgency in the sensation.

I frowned and said, "Azriel—" at the exact same time as he said, *Risa, hide. Someone just magicked into the building.*

I swore. *Where?*

The office on the other side of the pit trap.

And there was no cover near, and nothing else but those rat-infested offices. I dove into the first one, sending rats scattering just as the far doorway opened. I twisted around, and saw a shadowed figure step out.

Amaya snarled, the sound soft but nevertheless echoing. *Shut it*, I told her fiercely, *and flame out*.

She grumbled, but obeyed. The shadow paused and seemed to be looking our way, although it was a little hard to tell given the ink around us. After a moment, he moved on, his stride long and lithe. Shifter, I thought, for no logical reason. He certainly didn't smell like one—although that didn't really mean that much in an age of scent-erasing soap. But he obviously didn't smell me, either, and most shifters would have.

He strode past the pit trap, seemingly headed toward the shadowed corner. He wasn't the sorcerer—his build was far too short and stocky—but if he was going to use whatever lay hidden by those stones, then he was someone we needed to talk to.

Do it fast, Azriel commented. *He may be shorter than you, but he'll be stronger.*

Like I didn't realize *that*. The shifter drew closer and tension wound through my limbs, until my legs were quivering with the need to move, to attack. I waited until he'd passed the office in which I'd hidden, then rose and ran after him, as quickly and as silently as I could.

He sensed me and pivoted, lashing out with a booted foot. The blow was so fast it was little more than a blur. I twisted away, and his heel scraped across my hip rather than burying itself in my stomach. I flipped Amaya so that I was holding blade rather than hilt, and swung her hard. The blow caught him high in the forearm and knocked him sideways. He swore, the sound guttural, almost incoherent, but caught his balance all too swiftly and launched at me. I caught a brief glimpse of his features as I spun away, and realized with a sinking sensation exactly what I was dealing with. He wasn't a shifter, or even a Razan, but rather another of those beings who'd been twisted by magic. He just didn't feel as wrong as his brethren. Maybe our sorcerer was getting the hang of perverting the souls of others.

I ducked under another leap but this time he anticipated the move, somehow twisting in mid-air to crash body-first into me. I landed on my back with a grunt, briefly winded, my arms and legs tangled in his. I swore, pulled an arm free, and chopped down with Amaya. Her hilt smashed into his shoulder and something cracked. He howled, the sound one of fury and pain combined, and lashed out with an elbow. The blow struck my chin hard enough to rattle teeth, and for a moment I saw stars.

Amaya hissed in fury, a sound I could only echo. I bucked, trying to get him off me, but I might as well have tried moving a ton of bricks. He laughed and grabbed at my arms, managing to pin one to the grimy concrete, his breath thick and fetid as it washed across my face. He may not have smelled bad on the outside, but he was definitely rotting inside.

I bucked again, this time lifting him high enough to get my knees under him. I thrust him up and over my head, then scrambled to my feet and lunged toward him. Though still on the ground, he spun, one leg sweeping out, trying to hook mine. I leapt over it and landed, knees first, in the middle of his gut. As air exploded from his lungs, I smashed my fist into his chin with as much force as I could muster. His head snapped sideways and his body went limp. He was out cold.

I blew out a relieved breath, but didn't immediately climb to my feet. *Azriel, can you read him from a distance?*

Normally yes, but this creature's soul and mind have been twisted by magic. I need contact.

Meaning I have to carry him out? Bummer.

It's not far.

Says the man who doesn't have to carry him, I grumbled.

You could drag him.

Not if we want any hope of our presence here to remain unknown. The fucking floor is full of grease and muck. And while my footprints would undoubtedly show, at least there was a chance of them not catching anyone's eye, given that the twisted shifter and who knows what else came through here.

I rose, grabbed the shifter's hands, then hauled him to his feet with a grunt of effort. After draping his arms around my neck, I knelt in front of him and let his body fall over my shoulder and back. Then I lifted him, holding on to one arm and leg to keep him in place. That done, I turned and headed for the exit.

It felt like I'd run a fucking marathon by the time I reached the loading bay. The shifter might not have been overly tall, but he was thick and muscular, and weighed a goddamn ton. I eased him from my shoulder, then propped him against the roller door and sucked in great gulps of air. When the trembling in my muscles finally eased, I shifted my grip to his arm and let him drop sideways. And, in the process, just about ripped his arm out of its socket. Not that *that* particularly worried me.

I shoved his upper body through the hole in the roller door, and Azriel dragged the rest of him out. I followed, relieved to be in fresh air again.

I studied the street, making sure no one was paying any particular attention to what we were doing, then knelt on the other side of the prone form. "So, can you read him?"

"Wait." Azriel closed his eyes and placed two fingers lightly against the shifter's high forehead. After several moments of silence, he shook his head and glanced at me. "The shifter's mind is a maze of magic and blocks, and it feels like the work of the Aedh. It has not the feel of dark magic."

I frowned. "But Lucian's dead—"

"Yes," he cut in. "But these creatures were more than likely created by our sorceress while he lived, and the Aedh was more than a little aware of my abilities. He ensured I could not get information from this mind."

"So I carried this bastard out here for nothing?"

He smiled. "The Aedh was not as clever as he liked to think. There is more than one way to get information from a mind."

With that, he placed his hands on either side of the shifter's head and closed his eyes. Almost instantly Valdis's sides began to glow, showering the immediate darkness with blue sparks. Energy surged, its feel sharp and fierce, and in the space between Azriel's hands pictures began to flow— flickering images that moved so fast they were little more than blurs of color. The last time I'd seen him do this was when he'd tried to capture the lingering memories from a dead man's mind. This man was very much alive, and perhaps that was why the images were sharper, faster.

I watched in silence, catching an occasional glimpse of Lauren but little else. After a few minutes, Azriel lowered his hands and leaned back on his heels.

"Well, that was interesting."

I raised my eyebrows. "In what way?"

"He has only ever dealt with Lauren and Lucien. I could find no indication that there was another party involved in their schemes."

"Which doesn't mean there isn't," I commented. "Just that he's been extraordinarily canny about revealing himself."

"Perhaps." Azriel's gaze briefly swept the shifter, and distaste briefly touched his expression. "He was created just over a week ago. His flesh belongs to a drifter but his soul was wrenched from the fires of hell."

I frowned. "What do you mean?"

His gaze came to mine. Anger burned deep in those blue depths. "When Lauren creates these creatures, she replaces the original soul with one who is bound by her magic to obey. Her source is hell itself."

She was dragging souls back from hell? Not just demons, but *souls*? Holy fucking *crap*. "So what happens to the original soul? Do they share flesh space?"

"No. It was forced out, so it would have become one of the lost ones."

A ghost, in other words. Anger surged through me, and Amaya burned to life, her flames shooting fierce lilac streaks through the darkness. Echoing my emotions, as Valdis sometimes echoed Azriel's.

"How the *hell* could she do something like that, Azriel? I would have thought only the powers in charge of both heaven and hell were capable of such a feat."

"It is doubtful she would have attempted drawing souls from the light path, if only because they would not have the level of corruption she seems to require. But the dark path has always allowed access to those with enough power and strength of will."

"But why? I mean, the gates were created to *prevent* souls and demons escaping, weren't they?"

"Yes, but any barrier can be breached. The portals have never been totally impervious. They cannot be, when souls must constantly traverse them."

"We really *do* have to catch this bitch," I muttered, and glanced back at our shifter. "He seemed a whole lot more rational than some of the others we've come across."

"Perhaps Lauren has finally refined her technique."

I snorted softly. Nothing like refining the way

you destroyed someone's present and future lives. "What about those stones I came across inside? Could you find anything about those?"

He nodded. "It is a minor protection circle, as you have already guessed. It hides stairs that lead down into the basement."

"I wonder if the basement leads into the tunnels the pit falls into?"

"I don't know. His memories seemed to imply the magic merely protects storage areas, but that does not mean that is all there is to be found down there."

It would be typical of the sort of luck we'd been getting, though. "If it's only minor magic, Ilianna will be able to unpick it for us."

"Shall I go retrieve her?"

I hesitated. "I don't think the witches would react too favorably to your presence in the Brindle."

He frowned. "Perhaps not, but it would drain too much of your strength to transport her here in Aedh form."

And it would take longer than we probably had to drive here. The shifter had been sent here for a reason, after all, and sooner or later someone was going to miss him. I blew out a breath. "Okay, you fetch her. I'll wait here and knock our friend out again if he shows signs of waking."

"No need." Azriel briefly pressed two fingers against the shifter's forehead, and energy caressed the air. "He will not waken until I will it."

I frowned. "How come you could do that, and yet not access his mind telepathically?"

"Different sections of the brain. I have also adjusted his memories. He now believes he came out here to investigate a sound, and was knocked unconscious and subsequently robbed. I suggest you claim his wallet." He touched my hand, his fingers warm against my skin. "Stay alert. I won't be long."

"Even I can't get into trouble in the two minutes you'll be gone," I said, voice wry. But I was talking to air.

And tempting fate.

Because the words were barely out of my mouth when an odd glimmer caught my eye. It was little more than a wisp of silvery smoke that was quickly shredded as it passed under the glow of the streetlight, but my stomach nevertheless dropped.

Because it wasn't smoke.

The Ania were back.

Chapter 9

Ania were minor demons and were generally summoned to perform tasks such as harassment, assault, and murder. The last two times they'd come after me they'd done so under orders from the Raziq, and I had no doubt that was who had sent them this time.

The attack itself wasn't really surprising. If my father was aware that the sorcerer had the second key, then surely the Raziq would be. The only surprising thing was the fact they'd taken so long to get around to doing anything about it.

Another wisp of silver stirred to my left. There was more than one Ania here. But there had been the other times, too.

I rose, drew Amaya, then reached out for Azriel. *Houston, we have a problem.*

What? His reply was instant, concerned.

Ania.

I cannot transport from inside the Brindle. It will take me a few seconds—

No, I cut in, as a third flicker appeared. This one

was closer than the others. I swung Amaya lightly from side to side, a warning of what would happen if they got close, and one I knew they would ignore.

What do you mean, no? Has insanity caught hold of you in the brief time I've been away?

More than likely. Despite the situation, amusement bubbled through me. *But that's beside the point. You said it yourself—the Raziq can't hurt me.*

That doesn't mean you should let them snatch you.

But if I don't, they'll go after Ilianna or Tao instead. I won't put them in any more danger than I already have, Azriel.

You value the life of your friends more than you value your own. His frustration and anger rolled through me, singeing my soul.

I'm no happier about this than you are. I somehow managed to keep my tone even. Reacting in anger wasn't going to help the situation—I'd learned *that* from past mistakes, if nothing else. *And I certainly have no desire to be pulled apart again.*

Especially now that I was pregnant.

Then why go?

Because I do *value the lives of my friends.* The back of my neck tingled. The Ania's numbers were growing, and it was all I could do to remain still. *Look, what's the worst they can do? They can't kill me, because they still need me.*

The Raziq are capable of more horrors than you could ever imagine.

Yeah, like making me think my flesh was melting from my hands. A shudder went through me and my stomach turned. *That* was another experience I had no desire to relive. *They'll snatch me, they'll do their whole threatening spiel again, and then they'll let me go. And we gain some time and space to find the damn key.*

It is not worth—

It is, and you know it. I hesitated, fighting the urge to spin around and stab Amaya into the wispy hearts of the creatures who drew ever nearer. Amaya's grumblings grew louder in my thoughts when I didn't. *You said you can find me anywhere now—will you also be able to hear me, even if the Raziq use their shield again?*

Energy surged across my skin—Azriel, not more Ania. Though he didn't physically appear, he was nevertheless standing beside me, the warmth of his presence rolling through me. God, I felt so much safer for it.

I do not know. His mental tones were annoyed. *Perhaps.*

Not what I wanted to hear. I licked dry lips, my gaze jumping to the left as another wisp darted forward. I swung Amaya and it hesitated. Obviously they were waiting for more of their kind before they attacked. *Is there any way you can be transported with me?*

Perhaps. He hesitated. *But it would mean infusing my energy into yours, and that might cause an inappropriate reaction given the situation.*

My eyebrows raised. *Meaning what?*

Reapers infuse energy when they have sex. The result will be similar.

As in, orgasmic?

Possibly.

I couldn't help grinning. *Well, if I've got to face the Raziq, I sure as hell can't think of a better way to do it.*

It could be distracting, and that *could get dangerous.*

So un-infuse once we're in the Raziq's presence. Problem solved.

That, he said, mental tones wry, *is like asking a human male to pull out at the point of ejaculation. It's easy enough to say, but it requires a great deal of control and presence of mind to actually do.*

Are you telling me you have as little control as a human male?

When it comes to you, I think that's *a well-established fact.* He paused, and all sense of amusement fled. *Their numbers are near attacking point. If we're going to do this, we need to do it fast.*

Then do it.

Reach out your right hand.

I switched Amaya to my left hand and did so. Ethereal fingers enclosed around mine, a touch that was both electric and heated. My heart began to race, though it was a combination of fear *and* expectation.

Imagine, he said, *that your hand is on my chest. Feel the rhythm of my breath. Breathe in as I breathe out.*

It was hard to imagine *anything* when all I could see was the shimmering of the Ania.

Close your eyes. Concentrate. We have little more than a minute, at best.

I obeyed. Blocked out the awareness of the Ania and Amaya's distant rumblings of unhappiness, and remembered the last time we'd done this. Remembered the feel of warm skin under my fingertips, the strong drumming of his heart.

Feel my breath on your lips, he continued softly. *Imagine it running across your tongue and into your body. Let it fill you, become you.*

Warm air teased my mouth. My lips parted and I drew it in, filling my throat with his taste and my lungs with the scent of him, until all I could feel and all I could sense was the energy of his presence. In me, around me.

Imagine that energy inhabiting every part of you. His voice was soft, hypnotic. *Draw it within, deep within, until it infuses every atom, until we are connected not by skin, but by the essence of all that we are.*

Energy swirled through me, around me. His and mine, burning bright, within and without, making me tremble. Ache. He was right. This *was* dangerous. But there was no other way. Not if we wanted to be absolutely sure he was there by my side to confront the Raziq.

Draw it in, accept it, he said quietly. *Let flesh and energy truly become one.*

I drew a deep breath and his energy became a

river that flooded every part of me, until the music of his being played through my body and mine through his. It was a dance, a caress, a tease. Heat and movement and desire, and I slipped into the firestorm we'd created so very easily.

Power of a different kind spun around me. Ania. Fear surged and it was all I could do to ignore the dark and uneasy particles twisting around my flesh. Then the music of Azriel's being surged anew, and awareness slipped away again, until there was nothing but him and me and the pleasure of the moment.

And god, it was *glorious.* It carried me away, made me soar ever higher, until I felt lighter than air, brighter than the sun . . .

Then it was gone, ripped away as I crashed back to earth—literally. I hit hard enough to knock the air from my lungs and, for too many seconds, breathing became impossible. I couldn't even groan. The energy that was Azriel re-formed beside me, on his back. Though I felt the shudder of surprise that ran through him, he nevertheless scrambled to his feet, Valdis ablaze in his hand.

He scanned the area, then bent, grabbed my arm, and hauled me upright. *Are you all right?*

Yeah. A little shell-shocked after your abrupt departure from that rather pleasurable experience, but otherwise okay. I paused and glanced around. *Where are we?*

Underground.

Deep underground, if the stale air was anything to go by. I swung Amaya around. Her purple light parted the night, revealing the rock that surrounded us. Like the previous times the Raziq had kidnapped me, they'd dropped us into a cavern that didn't seem to have either an entry or an exit point. Our tomb—for that's what they always felt like—was about ten feet wide, and about the same height. At least we could stand, which was a definite improvement over previous occasions.

I glanced up at the ceiling. Once again, there was a faint, multicolored shimmer that reminded me of oil on water. I swore softly. *That* shimmer was a field of magic designed to prevent me from reaching for the Aedh—something I'd discovered the hard way the first time. At least *this* time, unlike the others, I wasn't alone.

Wasn't alone before, Amaya muttered. *There was I. One time, not the other.*

Fault yours.

True. And it was the reason I rarely removed her these days. I glanced at Azriel. *Can you sense them?*

They are near.

But not near enough, I gathered from the edge in his voice.

Will they be able to read my thoughts? Hear me talking to you?

No. That applies to flesh beings and Aedh. You are more than either now.

Which explained why my father didn't catch

my thoughts when he'd confronted me earlier. It should have been a relief, but it only ratcheted up the tension. After all, if they couldn't read my thoughts, they might be tempted to do something about it.

Not while I draw breath, they won't, Azriel commented.

Does an energy being actually need to draw breath?
He half smiled. *You know what I mean.*
I do. And thank you.
He glanced at me, eyebrow raised. *For what?*
For always being here.
It is both my duty and *my desire.*

His words warmed me more than I could ever say. He was finally admitting to emotions, even if it was desire rather than love. But once upon a time he would have denied even that, even if his behavior suggested otherwise.

I scanned our surroundings again, knowing the Raziq were drawing closer but still unable to spot them. After a few seconds, an oddly dark surge of electricity ran across my skin. It made the little hairs at the back of my neck stand on end and my soul shiver away in fear.

They'd come within sensory distance. Whether that meant they were also within range of the swords I had no idea.

Unfortunately, no. The edge in Azriel's mind voice was deeper, the frustration stronger.

It's really not surprising given they'd sense your pres-

ence. The Raziq might be greater in numbers, but they weren't fools. And they certainly had no desire to risk their lives—as evidenced by their continuing use of the Ania to do their dirty work. Not that either *that* fact or Azriel's presence in any way lessened my fear of them. I licked my lips and gripped Amaya a little tighter. "Show yourself, Malin."

My voice sounded oddly small in the damp, stale confines of the cavern.

"Malin is not here." The disembodied voice was male, and while it held no threat, it nevertheless sent a chill down my spine. This was the Raziq I'd spoken to the first time I'd been captured—the Raziq who'd invaded my brain and made it seem like every part of me was being torn apart. A Raziq I thought I'd killed. Obviously, I was wrong.

Not. Sound same, Amaya said. *Tasted sweet. Want more*.

And I'd love to give you more. Trouble was, I doubted the Raziq would so foolishly expose themselves like that again.

"And even if she *were*," the disembodied voice continued, "she would not be foolish enough to show herself with the Mijai present. His desire for revenge is so fierce it stains the fields."

I snorted. "The only thing staining the fields is you lot. You're the ones who made the goddamn keys and created this mess we all find ourselves in."

"We do not need to justify our action to the likes of you—"

"No," I cut in fiercely, "but you sure as hell have to depend on *my* help. And you know what? It's about time you started remembering that. Because without me, there is no way on earth you're going to get your greedy little mitts on those keys again."

Risa, Azriel warned. *As much as I agree with what you're saying, antagonizing them might not be wise.*

Well, I've fucking tried everything else, with little success. Maybe a little anger is precisely *what's needed.* I hesitated. *Are they close enough to attack yet?*

No. They remain outside the barrier.

You can't breach it?

Given time, Valdis could, but I see little point in weakening either of us that way.

Especially when the Raziq might be waiting for that very thing to happen. A weakened Mijai would be a far easier target.

"Do not think either yourself or your reaper are beyond the reach of our wrath," the Raziq replied. "What I did to you, I could so easily do to him."

"I suggest you look a little closer, Yeska." Azriel's voice was edged with contempt. "You would not find either of us such an easy target now."

I gave Azriel a sharp glance. *You know him?*

We have crossed paths previously. He glanced at me, eyes glowing brightly in the blue and lilac light of the swords. *He is Malin's second. Valdis has tasted his blood in the past.*

If the fierce flare of fire along Valdis's sides was

anything to go by, she longed to do so again. *Why would a Mijai be sent after a Raziq?*

When it became evident they were behind the systematic killing of Aedh priests. Yeska was caught and questioned.

Why wasn't he killed? Reaper rules?

Yes. If we had known their ultimate plan, however, then perhaps intervention would have been ordered. Instead, it was simply left to the fates.

I snorted. The powers that be obviously had a *hell* of a lot more faith in fate than I did.

"Interesting," the disembodied voice that was Yeska replied. "Two have become one. That would explain the lack of response in the device we placed in your heart."

He could have been discussing the weather, for all the emotion in his voice. And yet, that device had been the only way they'd had of knowing when I was in my father's presence, so it was a good bet there was a lot of background anger and frustration happening right now.

"Yes," Azriel replied evenly. "And if you think to rectify the situation in *any* way, be prepared for the consequences. She is Mijai now. Attack one, and you attack all."

That certainly explained the attitude of the reaper bearing the two swords. It wasn't just that I'd made Azriel fail, it's that I'd put them *all* in a bad light.

"We have no need to attack either of you," Yeska replied, a hint of amusement in his tones. "She will comply when the lives of her friends are at stake."

"No, she won't," I spat back. "Because if you harm one hair on the head of anyone I care about, I promise you, the remaining keys will be broken into little pieces and placed where absolutely *no one*—"

"Do *not* threaten us." His fury whipped around us, snatching my breath and stinging my skin.

Amaya reacted instantly, her fire almost sunbright. Just for a second, I caught a shimmer of energy behind the shield. The Raziq, and more than one of them.

Kill can, Amaya said.

I glanced at her sharply. *How? Valdis can't break the shield, and she's stronger.*

Am smarter, Amaya replied. *Use floor.*

I glanced down. Fuck, she was right. The floor *wasn't* shielded. None of the cavern floors had been shielded, when I thought about it.

They'd see you coming. And see me throw her.

Flame out can.

Yeah, but there was still the whole throwing problem. Amaya could move under her own steam, but I suspected it would be easier for her to cut through the stone if she had some momentum behind her.

Under different circumstances, it would be a good

plan, Azriel said. *But it will achieve little in this in-stance, and only amplify the danger to your friends.*

Then we need to nullify that first.

There is no reasoning with the Raziq. As with all Aedh, it is only their plans—their desires—that matter.

Then maybe that's *the tack we need to take.* To the Raziq, I said, "Look, I don't give a frig who actu-ally gets the keys. I just want to get back to normal life again."

That statement has a scarily fierce ring of truth about it, Azriel said.

I ignored him and continued on, "So, really, it behooves you to actually do what you can to *help* me rather than offering a long and tedious line of threats to both my near and dear."

"We cannot help find the keys, because we have no idea where they are hidden."

"No, but you can help me find the bastard who keeps stealing them from me."

"That is not possible. We do not interact with the human world."

Unless it was to fuck or torture us, of course, but I bit *that* remark back. "No, but you interact with the fields, and the sorcerer has to use magic to access the fields and the gates. Therefore, he must have a particular entry point somewhere on the fields." After all, a door always opened into the same room. I didn't know much about magic, but it seemed logical a transport portal would do the same. "If you shut that point down, it confines him to Earth, and gives me more time to find him and the key."

"Why shut it down, when all we have to do is find it, and then wait for him to step through?"

Well, there was *that*. I hesitated, thinking fast. "Except he has to know that's a possibility now that he no longer has Lucian to guard and guide him. He may wait until he has both the remaining keys to make his next move. The fact that he hasn't used the second key even though he's had it for several days certainly suggests this is a possibility."

And I mentally crossed my fingers that Azriel was right, that the Raziq and my father *couldn't* read my thoughts. That they'd believe this was a very real possibility, and *not* realize that the only reason our dark sorcerer hadn't used the key was the fact that he still didn't know which of the artifacts he'd stolen it was.

"Even so, all we would have to do—"

"No," I cut in. "You're not getting it. Our sorcerer was working with an Aedh—someone *you* not only tortured, but abandoned on Earth. Let me tell you, he wanted revenge, and he wanted it *badly*. And he was canny enough to ensure that, even if he *was* killed, you'd never get your mitts on the one thing you truly wanted."

Dark energy flowed around me, thick and threatening. Amaya's mental hissing ratcheted up another degree, and my heart began to pound a whole lot faster.

Azriel's fingers entwined through mine and he squeezed them gently. *It is not a threat. It is merely anger.*

At whom?

The Aedh. He continues to taunt them, even when dead.

That's presuming Lucian did actually do what I'm suggesting.

It is a logical line of thought, Azriel said. *After all, the Aedh seeded Ilianna and Lauren so his genes would live on if he died. It is logical he would also ensure his plans for the keys lived on.*

Ha. Me thinking logically. Who'd have thought that was possible?

Wisely, he refrained from saying anything about *that*. He squeezed my fingers again, then released them—leaving me mourning the loss of heat and strength that had flowed through the brief contact.

"How will finding the sorcerer's entry point on the fields help you find this sorcerer?" Yeska eventually asked.

Great question. I hesitated again, then mentally shrugged. The Raziq probably knew as much about dark magic as I did, so a little bit of improvisation wasn't going to hurt. And hey, there just *might* be a chance I was on the right track. "Portals use direct lines to go from one point to another; therefore, wherever his opening on the field is, it should be mirrored here. And if we can find his place of power here, we can use it to track him down."

"And get us the key," he added.

"And get the key," I agreed. Who I gave it to was another matter entirely.

No, it's not, Azriel said, tone sharp. *For the safety of all, the Mijai must hold the keys.*

And do you really think the Raziq will refrain from attacking the Mijai to get them back?

We are greater in number—

And they can use magic. My gaze met the steel of his. *You said it yourself, Azriel—only their desires matter. They could very well decide to erase the reapers just as they have the Aedh.*

They would not dare—

Why not? I cut in. *Why would they care about reapers or souls being unguided? They don't—their desire to permanently close the gates is evidence enough of that.*

It would not be allowed.

I snorted softly. *Who wouldn't allow it? The powers that be? They could have stopped this whole mess in its tracks by stopping the Raziq before they got started, but they preferred to let fate have her way. Do you really think their decision would be any different when it came to reapers?*

He didn't answer. Maybe he couldn't, simply because there *was* no real answer.

"If you do *not* hand us the keys," Yeska said, voice flat, yet somehow filled with venom, "then all those you care about will not only lose their lives in *this* time, but in all their future times. They will be forever locked in this world, never to know life or love again."

His words chilled me to the core. Yet fury rose, and it was all I could do not to throw Amaya. Threatening my life was one thing. Hell, I could understand them threatening the lives of my friends—even if I didn't like it—but stripping them of all their futures and making them ghosts? That was totally unacceptable.

And it had to stop. Somehow, somewhere, I had to find a way to end all this and make my friends—and the world—safe.

"Fine," I muttered. "Just let me know where the sorcerer's entrance onto the fields is, and we'll take it from there."

"Do not double-cross us," Yeska warned.

"I get it already," I said, voice tight. "Now just get us out of here so we can get on with the business of tracking the key."

"The reaper can get you out," he replied. "Once we retreat, the shield will go down."

"What, don't you trust us?"

But there was no reply. The dark energy that was the Raziq had gone. I sheathed Amaya and let out a slow breath. "Well, that certainly went better than I expected."

"Yes." Azriel pulled me into his embrace and wrapped his arms around me. "I fear, however, you have only delayed the inevitable."

"I know." I closed my eyes and listened to the

steady beat of his heart, feeling so safe it had tears stinging my eyes. But it was an illusion. None of us were safe. Not even a Mijai warrior with centuries of fighting behind him. *But I'm hoping that by the time they realize I have no intention of giving them the key, we'll have figured out a way of stopping them from hurting anyone.*

It is possible. Though more than likely impossible. He didn't add that last bit, but the words hovered between us nevertheless. *Shall we go get Ilianna, and see if she can create a doorway through those stones in the warehouse?*

Yes. There wasn't much else we could do right now.

A second later we were standing outside the Brindle. It was a white four-story building that had been built in the Victorian era—a grand old lady from a bygone time that was a whole lot more than she seemed. It was the home of all witch knowledge, and was protected by a veil of power so strong that there were very few in this world—or the next—who would dare test its boundaries. Though I'd never considered myself overly sensitive to magic, I'd always been aware of its presence here. But the sensation I got from the place now was weirdly different. It wasn't just awareness—it felt like the power was alive. Energy crawled across my skin, its touch sharp, electric. Probing. The Brindle didn't suffer evil to enter, but it had never reacted to me like this before Azriel's presence in my life.

"It happens because you are now Mijai in waiting." Azriel pressed his fingers against my spine, lightly guiding me toward the steps.

"But this was happening before you pulled me back from death."

"Possibly because I was linked to your chi."

It was more than that, and we both knew it. He'd been linked to my chi—or life energy, as Ilianna called it—from the beginning of this mess, and it was only very recently that the Brindle had begun reacting to me.

But I let the matter drop—at least for now—and took the steps two at a time. The huge, medieval-looking, wood and wrought-iron doors were open, and a slender, brown-haired, tunic-clad figure waited to the left of them—for us, I suspected.

"Risa, Azriel," she said softly, as I approached. "Please follow me."

We obeyed, our footsteps echoing softly on the marble tiles. The energy of this place was so strong that every step was accompanied by a spray of golden sparks. The Brindle's interior tended to be somewhat austere, though the foyer's brickwork had been painted a rich gold that added a warmth that the entrance otherwise lacked. We were led to the end of the hall and down some stairs, then into a wide hall that was lined with darkly stained timber and filled with shadows, despite the morning light. Sconces flickered on as we approached, then went dark once we'd passed, fueled by magic rather than electricity.

We turned right at the end of this hall, and went down a second set of stairs. After traversing another hallway, we reached the end and two large, intricately carved wooden doors. The slender witch opened one of these, ushered us through, then closed it. The room beyond reminded me somewhat of a medieval hall, with its gabled wooden roof and walls lined with tapestries. But it was the large protection circle that caught my eye—that, and the four women standing within it. Ilianna, Mirri, Kiandra, and Ilianna's mom, Zaira.

I stopped immediately. Magic eddied around us—tides of power that itched at my skin—and I didn't want to risk getting any closer in case my presence disturbed it in some way. For several minutes, no one moved; then Ilianna sighed and glanced my way.

"Are you having any luck unravelling the cord?" I said.

"Not yet." Ilianna stepped carefully from the circle, then walked toward me. Her face was pale, strained. "Neither Mom nor Kiandra have come across anything like this before now, but I guess that's natural, given the source. They're relying on my limited knowledge in their attempts to unpick the various layers."

"Well, you did reroute the magic in the warding stones my father left at Mom's."

And I had to wonder if *that* had been deliberate. After it, those stones were all that was stopping the Raziq from entering our home—the thought stalled, and I blinked as excitement surged. Maybe the damn answer to the Raziq problem had been sitting right in front of my nose all the time!

"Rerouting the magic of the stones was easy compared to this," Ilianna said. "This collar is interlaced and complicated. I just don't know if we're going to have the time to dismantle it."

Tears briefly shone in her eyes, but were rapidly blinked away. No time for tears. Not yet.

I looked at Mirri. Her expression was stoic, but fear lurked in the depth of her eyes. "You will. Have faith."

"Faith is something I'm rapidly losing." Ilianna paused, and glanced at Azriel. "Sorry, but it's hard to keep believing when your bosses are doing squat to help the situation as far as I can see."

"They tend not to interfere unless absolutely necessary."

"Seems to me the opening of hell and the possible destruction of both Earth and the gray fields would make interference a *necessity*."

"Hence the reason I am here," he replied. "More Mijai are not practical in this situation."

"Meaning if it was warranted, more would come?"

"If necessary, then yes."

"I guess that's something." She returned her gaze to me. "I'm gathering you're not just here for a progress report."

"No." I hesitated. "But I have a question about the warding stones before I get into that. Are you able to replicate the spell on the stones? And if so, would it be possible to make some sort of personal protection circle using it?"

She frowned. "I could repeat the spell, no problem, but I don't know—"

"It's possible," Kiandra cut in.

I glanced past Ilianna. Kiandra's attention was still on the cord wrapped around Mirri's neck, but she'd obviously been keeping tabs on our conversation, despite the fact we'd been speaking softly.

"But," she continued, "the spell would need to be fed into the energy of the wearer to have any long-lasting benefit."

"That sounds like we'd be stepping into blood magic territory."

"No, we would not," Kiandra said. "Tapping into the wearer's aura or life force is no different from drawing strength from the elements or from the earth."

"But," I said, "drawing power from the elements or the earth has its cost—it saps the witch's strength and leaves her vulnerable to attack from darker forces if the drawing isn't done within a protection circle. You can hardly employ a protection circle in the case of a portable warding device."

"Who'd have thought you knew so much about magic," Ilianna murmured, a smile touching her lips.

"I have been hanging around a witch for most of my life," I said dryly. "Some stuff rubs off, even on someone as thickheaded as me."

Azriel's amusement rolled through the back of my thoughts, soft and enticing. *If I had said that, you would be very annoyed.*

You may not have said it, reaper, but you certainly thought it.

That, he replied, amusement stronger, *is undoubtedly true.*

"The difference in this case," Kiandra said, "is that the wearer would be performing no magic, so there is no need for a protection spell of any sort."

Which didn't mean it wouldn't still drain the energy of the wearer. "How would it work?"

"It would be similar to the micro cells you wear. Four stones would need to be worn on four points of the body, which would then create a self-sustaining continuous circuit of energy and provide protection against any force they were set to."

"In other words, if they were set to protect against the Raziq, the Raziq would not be able to either physically or mentally harm them?"

"In theory, yes."

Right now, theory was all we had. "How soon could you start making half a dozen sets of these stones?"

Kiandra blew out a breath. "Mirri is our priority—"

"I know," I cut in. "I meant once Mirri is safe."

"A few days, at the very least. And only if Ilianna is willing to be involved in their creation."

I frowned at the odd note in Kiandra's voice. Ilianna didn't immediately reply, but her expression had clouded over. She looked . . . wary. Scared.

"Ilianna," I immediately said, "you don't have to do this. We can find another way."

I might not know what was wrong, but I didn't want—in any way—to put her in a position that would give the Brindle some sort of hold over her. Because I suspected that was what was involved. That her staying there, creating magic, would be a step onto a road and life that Ilianna had fled when she was a teenager. A path that Zaira had said, not so long ago, would find her daughter again.

"Are these stones really necessary?" she asked eventually. Her voice was even, but her expression was still troubled.

"The Raziq snatched me again tonight." I hesitated, but she had the right to know exactly what we were all facing. "They threatened to not only kill everyone I care about, but make them ghosts. If these stones don't work—"

"Heaven help us," she finished, then nodded. "Fine. Once we unravel the energy imprisoning Mirri, I'll help the Brindle make the aural wards."

I couldn't help but give a silent sigh of relief. Ilianna might well be stepping onto that path, but better that than her being dead. Or worse, a ghost. "Thanks, Ilianna."

She nodded. "Anything else?"

I hesitated. "Yes, but it doesn't matter now given you can't really leave Mirri—"

"Just tell me what you need," she cut in, voice flat. "If I can help, I will."

"We need someone to create some sort of doorway into a warding circle."

She frowned. "I do not think I could spare—"

"You do not need to," Kiandra cut in. "I'll send one of the fifth-year trainees. They will be more than capable of handling such a task."

Being a trainee at the Brindle didn't mean you were new to magic. It was quite the opposite, in fact. Witches came here to hone their skills and to become both a master and a teacher. I knew it took at least ten years to reach the master rank, so she was sending someone pretty damn proficient.

"Thank you, Kiandra."

She nodded without looking at us. "Ilianna, I believe Rozelle is available. But look after her, reaper, or I will be displeased."

Azriel bowed, the movement regal. "You have my word no harm will befall her."

Ilianna caught my arm and guided me back out the door. "Has there been any word from Tao yet?"

"No."

She grimaced. "I fear for him, Risa. I can't see anything but fire in his future."

"He'll pull through this. He's stronger than you think."

"I hope you're right." But her expression said that I wasn't.

And maybe she *was* right. Maybe there wasn't any future for him. But that didn't mean I could give up. I wouldn't, not until every single option had been explored and abandoned.

We went back up to the next level and into a section that I knew from past visits held the sleeping quarters for the witches stationed here. Rozelle was tall, pretty, and looked all of twenty. Which meant she had either become magic proficient at a very early age, or she was much older than she looked. Most witches didn't usually begin the master's training until they were at least thirty.

Ilianna explained who we were and what we wanted, and Rozelle bounced up from her seat, gathering magical bits and pieces and carefully placing them into a carryall.

"Right," she said, "Let's go."

Her warm tones held an edge of excitement that made me smile. Obviously, things had been a little slow here at the Brindle lately. I gave Ilianna a hug, then said, "Keep strong. We'll all get through this, I promise."

She smiled, but didn't say anything. Because she knew, like I knew, my promise was empty. No one knew how all this was going to pan out.

Not even, I was beginning to suspect, fate.

Azriel transported us, one at a time, back to the warehouse.

"Wow," Rozelle said, blinking rapidly and wavering a little as she reappeared. "That's certainly a novel way to get about. Not something I'd like to do too often, though."

"Yeah, sorry," I said. "But we're on a tight deadline and it's the quickest way to travel."

"Then let's get on with—" she stopped, and her gaze widened a little. "That man's not dead, is he?"

I glanced down at the shifter. "No. He's merely in an enforced sleep."

"Oh, good." She cleared her throat, then added, "Let's get to these stones. Although I'm hoping they're not the ones creating the barrier around this building, because that is *way* beyond my capabilities."

My eyebrows rose. "You can sense that?"

She nodded. "Although it has an energy that feels rather weird."

"That's because it was created by a dark sorcerer, and designed to keep me out," Azriel commented. "It will not, however, prevent you from entering, nor will it harm you."

"Oh, good," she repeated, then paused, her eyes narrowing a little. "In case you're interested, the source of the energy seems to be coming from under the building, which is rather odd. Shielding stones usually have to be placed at each corner for them to work efficiently."

I glanced at Azriel. *If the source is underground, maybe that's what the smaller circle is protecting.*

Possibly. What we need to discover, however, is what this building might be protecting beyond the shielding stones and the transport gate you found. There has *to be something else here.* He paused, then added out loud, "Be careful."

"You keep saying that," I said, amused. "Anyone would think you don't trust me to look after myself."

"Well, you do have the unfortunate habit of stepping into trouble." His voice was dry. "And remember, I cannot help you if you find it here."

"I have Amaya. We'll cope." I dropped a kiss on his lips, resisted the urge to do a whole lot more, then said to Rozelle, "Follow me."

I led the way into the building, retracing my steps to prevent creating too many obviously new footprints in the muck coating the floor.

"Well," Rozelle said, her gaze narrowing as she stopped several feet away from the inky wall that masked the stone circle. "That's particularly nasty, isn't it?"

"Yeah." I lifted my hand and showed her the red marks where the blisters had been. "I wouldn't get too close, either."

"I wasn't intending to." She handed me her carryall, then walked the length of the wall, examining it warily. She stopped close to the back wall and said, "Okay, here's the sorcerer's point of entry."

"How can you tell?"

She glanced at me, her expression amused. "Because I'm a witch and that's what I'm trained to do." She walked back around until she was standing on the opposite side of the circle to the doorway. "We shall make our entrance here. Our sorcerer is less likely to sense it. My bag, if you would be so kind."

I handed over the bag. "Won't he sense the break in his magic?"

"Perhaps, if he is looking for it." Her gaze met mine. "There is no other way to enter this circle, though."

"Then do it."

She drew out her athame and made a protection circle, then sat cross-legged on the ground and began the incantation to create the doorway.

After several minutes, the shadows began to retreat, until a gap that was about two feet square had formed. It revealed not only several black stones but the concrete and metal steps beyond them.

Rozelle sighed and opened her eyes. "That is the best I can do. The spell around these stones is more intricate than I first thought, so if I create anything larger, it may be visible to our sorcerer."

I frowned. "Surely he'd notice the fact that there's now no shadows around one section of his circle?"

"No, because it was designed to be visible to only you and me. But as I said, if he's looking for intrusion, he *will* notice the threads I have woven into his magic."

"A chance we'll have to take. Thanks for your help, Rozelle."

She nodded, but didn't move. "I'll wait here, just on the off chance you need me down there."

I frowned. "I'm not sure that's wise. Azriel can't get into the building if something goes wrong, and we promised Kiandra—"

"No one and nothing is getting into my circle," she replied, amusement in her tones. "I made sure of that. Go. I'll be safe, I promise."

I hesitated, but really, short of dragging her free of her circle—not something I was convinced I could do given the strength of the barrier she'd raised—I had no other option but to proceed.

I dropped to my hands and knees, took a deep breath that didn't do a whole lot to bolster my courage, and went in.

Nothing jumped out at me.

I rose and drew Amaya. Light flared down her sides, shifting the shadows and gleaming off the metal stair rails. I walked over and peered down. All I could see was deeper shadows.

Something, Amaya said.

I frowned. *Meaning what? That there's something or someone waiting down there for us?*

Magic, she said. *Some kind.*

Great. Not.

I briefly thought about retreating, but that really wasn't an option. Not if I wanted to find the keys and save Mirri. Ilianna might yet be able to unravel the cord, but I wasn't about to bet Mirri's life on it. I gripped Amaya a little tighter and cautiously headed down. My footsteps echoed on the metal, and the sound reverberated across the thick silence. I bit my lip, my nerves crawling, as each step took me farther into the bowels of the earth and whatever it was Amaya had sensed.

My foot had barely touched the bottom step when I heard it. A low rumbly sound that had the hair on the back of my neck rising.

I paused, listening. The sound was not repeated, but something definitely was down here.

Amaya?

Magic ahead.

Maybe it was, but magic didn't make low rumbly noises. Not any sort of magic I knew, anyway. I raised Amaya and let her light fan out across the shadows. The room was long and cavernous but it wasn't a cavern, rather an actual, concrete-lined storeroom that was filled to the brim with dusty, somewhat rusty metal shelving. Meaning it, like the stairs, was part of the building rather than something our sorcerers had created. I guess that made sense; why build something when it was easier to protect what was already here?

But did the fact the shelves all appeared empty mean there was nothing here to find?

Something, Amaya repeated. *Magic. Life.*

What sort of life. Demon?

No. Living.

Which really didn't clarify things. I bit my lip, then stepped onto the concrete.

And found more of that trouble Azriel had mentioned cannoning straight at me.

Chapter 10

The creature came out of nowhere, a skinny mass of filthy matted hair and gleaming canines. I raised Amaya instinctively, realized what was actually attacking us, and flipped my sword around midswing. The hilt smashed across the dog's head and sent him flying. He hit the left wall and slithered down to the floor. He didn't move.

I took a deep, somewhat quivery breath and cautiously walked over. The dog's eyes were closed, and there was a slight trickle of blood coming from a wound just above its right eye. Thankfully he was still breathing. Beside the fact I didn't want any more blood on my hands than necessary, the last thing I wanted was to kill a dog that was only doing what it had been trained to do. Although given the condition the poor mutt was in, maybe killing him would have been a kindness. He was literally skin, bone, and matted brown hair. Obviously, he wasn't fed all that often. Maybe that was what the shifter had come here to do. Or maybe they didn't bother, and simply got a new guard dog whenever the old one died. Lauren seemed the type to do something like that—although maybe that was just my hatred of her showing.

I turned, my gaze skimming the room. There didn't seem to be anything in this room beyond shadows and the shelving.

Where's the magic, Amaya?

Back.

Which I couldn't see. I walked on carefully, gaze constantly moving and my sword held at the ready. Nothing else jumped out at us. Eventually, we neared the rear wall. It looked solid and I had no sense of magic of any kind.

Is, Amaya said. *Left.*

I raised a hand and skimmed it along the wall. After several seconds, energy skittered across my fingertips. Its feel was dark, and oddly dirty. I resisted the urge to jerk my hand away from its touch and kept on walking, trying to discover the full extent. The patch of magic was about six feet high and four feet wide. If it wasn't a door, I'd eat my hat. If I'd been wearing a hat, that is.

The last time we'd discovered a concealed door had been in the pit Jak and I had fallen into when we'd first raided this warehouse. Maybe this entrance led into the same tunnels as that one had, or maybe it led to somewhere else entirely. The only way I was going to find the answer was to discover another way to open it.

Can't press through, Amaya said. *Magic not same.*

Meaning that, unlike the hidden doorway in the pit, this wall was *actually* solid rather than merely looking it.

I tried anyway, but succeeded in doing little more than breaking my nails. I swore softly, and turned around. "Rozelle, are you able to come down here?"

"Sure. Just give me a moment."

I raised Amaya, letting her flames chase back the shadows again and, after a few seconds, Rozelle appeared.

She stopped beside me and frowned. "Another nasty piece of work," she muttered after a moment. "I'm afraid this one is coded. Unless you have the proper key, it'll kill you."

"No way you can get past it?"

"Not without a lot of time and effort." Her gaze skimmed the wall. "And I couldn't create a doorway myself without knowing what was on the other side."

"That I can't say, because I don't know." I paused. "The shifter who was outside—he was coming here. Is it possible he could have a key of some kind?"

"I could check."

"Then let's check." There was nothing else we could do. And if the shifter didn't have a key, then we'd hit another wall. Literally, in this case.

Once we were back outside, Rozelle knelt beside the shifter and ran a hand above his body, her expression intent. After a moment, she sighed and sat back on her heels. "There is some form of magic within him, but it does not feel the same as the magic that guards that door."

Meaning we *had* hit another wall. Fabulous.

I sighed. "Thanks for the help, Rozelle."

She nodded. "I could stay here and work on that door. As I said, it'll just take time—"

"No," I said softly. "Thanks, but it's far too dangerous for you to remain here unprotected."

"I am able to protect myself—"

"I have no doubt of that under normal circumstances, but the person we chase is far from normal." I hesitated, seeing her doubt, and added, "She can take any form she wishes; tell me, if you saw Kiandra walking toward you, would you not be inclined to trust her?"

"I would sense a glamour—"

"This wouldn't be a glamour. It's not that type of magic. We're chasing a shifter capable of full body transformation. You wouldn't know it wasn't the real Kiandra until it was far too late."

"Oh." She swallowed. "Then perhaps it *is* wise not to be alone. However, that lock *can* be broken. If you need it done, we can arrange protection—"

"It's not worth the risk right now, Rozelle."

Her expression was doubtful. "Are you sure?"

I lightly squeezed her arm. "For the moment, yeah."

"What about the shield around the building?"

I frowned. "I thought you said it was beyond your capabilities?"

"It is, but that does not mean it cannot be broken."

"We don't need it broken. We just need it altered enough to enable Azriel to get inside."

"That is certainly an easier option than breaking it. All we would need to do is unpick the spell enough to enable us to weave a variation through it."

"And would the shield's creator be aware of your handiwork?"

She hesitated. "If we broke it, yes. But, as with the doorway I wove into the stone circle within this building, the creator would only sense it if he or she happened to be looking for it."

I glanced at Azriel. "It's worth a shot. If the gate we're searching for is down there, at least you could get in."

He nodded, and looked at Rozelle. "If I take you back to the Brindle, would you be able to make the necessary arrangements for this?"

She nodded. "We could be back here in an hour."

"That would be brilliant," I said.

She smiled. "Trust me, it is my pleasure. It is a rare opportunity to practice what I have been taught."

Azriel glanced at me. "Will you stay here, or return home?"

I hesitated, then said, "Home."

"I shall meet you back there, then."

With that, he took Rozelle's hand, then the two of them disappeared. I grabbed the shifter's wallet, then became Aedh and returned home. The apartment was dark and silent. Tao still wasn't here. I bit back the instinctive urge to ring and check if he was safe, knowing there was little I could do if he wasn't, and walked into my bedroom. I'd left the door open and the acrid smell of smoke was stronger this time. My nose twitched and I briefly wondered if we'd ever be able to rid the place of it. Or if, indeed, we'd even bother rebuilding it. Especially if the worst happened with Tao . . .

I slumped wearily onto my bed and rubbed my forehead, half wishing for coffee but not having the energy to actually walk down to McDonald's to grab one.

"Which is why I did," Azriel said, as he reappeared. He handed me not only a coffee, but a double Quarter Pounder.

I raised my eyebrows. "And just where did you get the money for these?"

"One does not need money when one can simply arrange for them to be given."

"You *stole* them?"

"If they are gifted, they are hardly stolen."

I grinned. "So if I feel the sudden need for diamonds, you could arrange for them to be 'gifted'?"

He raised an eyebrow. "Diamonds are hardly necessary for your health."

"You obviously have no understanding of women and diamonds."

Amusement creased the corners of his bright eyes. "I think we can take that as a given. Eat."

I did. Once I'd finished the burger, I took a sip of the coffee and said, "So what do we do now?"

"Until the Raziq or your father comes through with some way of finding either of our sorcerers, I do not know." He paused. "I would suggest sleeping, but I already know the answer to that."

"Yeah." I grimaced. "It just feels wrong to sleep when the clock is ticking for Mirri. But I could go see Uncle Quinn."

Surprise flitted across Azriel's expression. "Why?"

"Because, as you noted earlier, if there's one person in this world of mine who might know how to stop these bastards in their tracks, it would be Uncle Quinn."

And not just the Raziq, but my father and, hell, maybe even Hunter. They had to be stopped, all of them. And while I knew I was going to have hell's chance of stopping Quinn from subsequently joining any battle, it was a risk I might have to take.

Because I was beginning to think it could be the only way *anyone* was going to get out of this . . . the thought froze as my phone rang. The tone told me it was Uncle Rhoan, and I fought back an odd mix of trepidation and grief. Because I knew he'd be ringing about Jak. And that he'd be madder than hell.

Only trouble was, the pain of Jak's death was still so raw I might end up saying something I'd ultimately regret.

"Then ignore it," Azriel said, ever practical.

"If I do, he's more than likely to order me arrested."

He frowned. "Why would he do that?"

"Because I'm betting he wants answers about Jak's murder and why Hunter would want him dead."

And how could I explain any of that without stepping into territory that could ultimately lead him into danger? Because Hunter *would* kill him if she thought it necessary to both keep her secrets and me on the leash.

I took a deep, somewhat quivery breath, then reached for the phone and hit the vid-screen's Answer button. Rhoan appeared. To say his expression was thunderous was something of an understatement.

"What the *fuck* is going on, Risa?" he all but exploded. "Why the hell would Madeline Hunter want Jak Talbott dead?"

I was tempted to tell him that was a question he should ask the lady herself, but I didn't actually want him anywhere near the bitch. Not when she was so intent on teaching me a lesson. I licked my lips and said, "I don't know—"

"Don't give me that shit." A dangerous light glittered in his gray eyes. "You know *exactly* why she ordered the hit, and I'm guessing you knew it even *before* you put a sword through the back of the assassin. Tell me what the fuck is going on, or I'm going to haul your ass into the Directorate and make the investigation official."

Part of me wanted to snarl some smart remark right back at him; the other, more sensible part just wanted to run. The last thing I wanted was a confrontation with Uncle Rhoan, but I guess it was always bound to happen. As I kept fucking noting, it wasn't like fate had shown any propensity to give me a break.

Which meant I had only one choice.

Honesty.

I swore internally and scrubbed my free hand across my eyes. "Do that," I said, my voice holding an edge I couldn't quite prevent, "and you might well kill everyone we both care about."

His expression didn't change. If anything, it got more dangerous. "What the hell are you talking about?"

"Look, we can't do this over the phone. Meet me at the café." I hesitated, then added, "Come alone, and don't tell anyone else you're doing it. Not even Aunt Riley."

"I'll be there in ten minutes. Don't fuck me around on this, Risa. I'm warning you."

"I won't."

He hung up and I threw the phone back into my bag for a second time.

What of your astral watchers? Azriel said. *If Markel is on duty, you will—most likely—be safe against the possibility of the meeting being reported to Hunter. It is doubtful that the others would be so recalcitrant, given what Markel has said about them. And Hunter's reaction will be swift and deadly.*

I know. Just as I knew that if I wanted to stop my astral watcher from reporting back, there was only one way I was going to do it.

But could I take that step?

Could I take the life of someone who was doing nothing more than their duty?

Soldiers throughout history have lost their lives doing nothing more than their duty, Azriel commented. *It is the way of war, be it waged on the fields or here on Earth.*

Yeah, but this isn't a war.

That's where you're very *wrong. This* is *a war, and perhaps the only one that has ever mattered. You're not only fighting for the lives of your friends, but for the souls of mankind and the existence of two—very different—worlds.*

I knew all that. But I'd been hoping—perhaps naively—to survive this whole mess with as little blood on my hands as possible. I sighed. *Let's just hope it's Markel following me, then.*

You would need to be sure before you meet your uncle.

Yes. But we have ten minutes. More than enough time to step onto the astral plane.

More than enough time to take a life.

Ignoring the horror that spun through me at the thought, I lay down on the bed and closed my eyes. Several seconds later, I stepped onto the astral plane.

It wasn't Markel who watched me.

This vampire was short and thickset, with steel gray hair, swarthy features, and dead black eyes. His gaze, when it met mine, showed neither interest nor surprise, but rather the natural wariness of a warrior who has seen many battles.

My stomach began to churn. I didn't want to do this. I didn't want to take this vampire's life and make him a ghost, with no future to look forward to. But I had no choice. I had to protect my friends and family—and Rhoan and Riley were the only family I had left. Hunter *wasn't* going to take them from me. I wouldn't let her.

Amaya, I said, imagining her shadowed in my hand. *Get ready. And for god's sake keep quiet.*

Her weight appeared in my hand, but her blade was hidden, at one with the shadows that surrounded us.

If the vampire sensed the surge of energy that had briefly accompanied her shift in position, he showed no sign of it.

He raised his eyebrows. *Why do you travel the fields?*

I need to question a ghost.

What ghost? Jak? Is that what Rhoan Jenson asked you to do?

So he'd been close enough to hear at least *some* of our conversation—and it was enough to place Rhoan's life on the line if it was passed on to Hunter. The churning in my gut got stronger, and I briefly wondered if it were possible to be physically ill on the astral plane.

What other ghost would he be interested in? I said, striding forward. Not directly toward him, but off to one side.

Even so, his stance shifted and his eyes narrowed. He sensed something was off, even if he wasn't sure what. *And does this sudden desire to question a ghost have anything to do with Jenson suspecting Madeline Hunter's involvement in the death?*

Fuck, fuck, *fuck*! He'd heard entirely too much and I really had no choice now. I didn't know when Markel was back on watch duty, and I simply couldn't risk this vampire reporting what he'd heard to Hunter.

My grip tightened on Amaya. Her excitement burned through my mind, thick and hungry. I was almost within killing distance. A few more steps, and his life would be mine. His soul Amaya's. I wanted to run. Wanted to hide. Wanted to throw up so badly the bitter taste of bile stung the back of my throat.

I did none of those things. Just kept one foot

moving in front of the other. *I need to find out what Jak might have done to annoy Hunter.*

He did nothing, and you know it. His gaze swept me. *What is this truly about?*

This is about saving lives. Nothing more, nothing less.

And with that, I stabbed Amaya into the heart of him. Her flames exploded in and around him, capturing him, consuming him. It was murder, nothing less, and it sickened me to the core.

I'm sorry, I whispered mentally. *So, so sorry. But I have to protect the people I love.*

He opened his mouth; no sound came out. But his eyes burned, damning me, and my cheeks were wet, though I had no idea if tears were even possible here. The plane around me grew dark and heavy, bearing down on me, as if the weight of this death was something I would carry for the rest of eternity.

And I would. I knew I would.

Amaya continued to devour the vampire, until there was nothing left of him. Not even ash.

I closed my eyes and imagined myself back in my body. The minute I was, I rolled onto my side and was violently, completely ill.

The bed dipped. Azriel didn't say anything, didn't do anything, just sat behind me and placed a hand on my shoulder. He didn't need to do anything else. His presence and his touch was enough.

"I am sorry you were forced to do this." His

voice was filled with compassion and understanding. "I would have, if I could have."

"I know." I pushed upright and leaned back against him.

He wrapped his arms around my waist and brushed a kiss across the top of my head. "We'd better get moving. It would not be wise to be late."

"I know," I repeated. "Just let me clean up."

"Ris, it can wait."

"You've obviously never had the taste of vomit in your mouth." I forced myself away from him, climbed off the bed, and headed for the bathroom. For several minutes I did nothing more than scrub my hands, trying to remove blood that didn't actually exist. Blood that had drained into my soul and become a weight I'd never be free of. I swallowed heavily, then grabbed my toothbrush. After brushing my teeth and rinsing my mouth, I cleaned up the vomit, then tossed the towels down the rubbish chute rather than the laundry one. The last thing anyone would want was my vomit rolling around with their clothes. Although given the state of the living room and kitchen, washing clothes would be the last thing on anyone's mind, even if they *didn't* have bigger problems right now.

"Right," I said, returning to Azriel's side. He'd resumed his regular position near the window. "We'd better go meet Uncle Rhoan."

He turned to face me. His expression was back

to its usual noncommittal self but the compassion lingered in his eyes. "How do you wish to handle this?"

I frowned. "What do you mean?"

"I mean, I could touch his memories, make him forget. Would that not make things easier?"

"In some ways yes, in other ways no." I grimaced. "Uncle Rhoan is basically a psychic dead zone. He can't be touched telepathically. It's what has made him such a fantastic guardian."

"While there are some minds I cannot read, Rhoan Jenson is not one of them. I could—"

"No," I cut in. "It wouldn't be fair, and it wouldn't be right. Rhoan deserves more out of me than that."

"He does. But it nevertheless is a dangerous path to tread given Hunter's murderous bent."

"I know." I stepped into Azriel's arms. "Let's get this over with."

We reappeared in the upstairs office area of the café. The room was dark and smelled faintly of tobacco. I frowned, then vaguely remembered Ilianna's mentioning that she'd asked our accountant, Mike, to find someone to come in and do the business activity statement and salaries. I'd had no time lately and Margie, our new manager, had enough on her plate just keeping the café running smoothly.

That scent, however, suggested Mike himself had come in. It certainly wasn't a scent I'd come across anywhere else but in his office. And while I would have thought doing accounts a little beneath him, he did seem to think that—because of his past relationship with Mom—he owed it to her to keep a "fatherly" eye on me. Maybe this was his way of doing so.

I switched on the lights and walked across to my desk. The accounts had been neatly stacked, the "done" pile much larger than the "to be processed," and Mike's bold scrawl noting receipt numbers was on several of them. I half smiled. In some ways he reminded me of Jak—he'd never entirely trusted computers, and tended to have paper backups of all legal documents.

I once again pushed down the grief that threatened to overwhelm me—grief that came from Jak's death and the deeper, older loss of my mom—and pressed the vid-phone's button for downstairs. Margie answered on the second ring.

"Hey, boss," she said, a smile crinkling the corners of her dark eyes, "when did you sneak in?"

"Only a few minutes ago," I replied. "I'll be down later, but right now, I'm expecting a visit from my uncle—"

"If he's the red-haired gentleman with the thunderous expression, I just sent him up." She hesitated. "That's not a problem, is it? He said he was expected."

"No, it's fine. Thanks." I hung up.

Footsteps echoed—Rhoan, taking the stairs two

at a time. I swallowed nervously, then squared my shoulders. I could do this. I had to, for everyone's sake.

"Uncle Rhoan," I said, the minute he appeared. There was no way in hell I was giving him the opportunity to vent all over me. Not without making him hear me out first. "Sit down, shut up, and *listen*."

He blinked. Whatever welcome he'd been expecting, it hadn't been *that*. "I'll listen if it's the damn truth, but there's been too little of it coming out of your mouth of late."

"Rhoan," I said, more forcefully this time. "Not another word. Just sit. Please."

He studied me for a moment, then spun a chair around so he could sit with his arms resting on the back. He waved a hand, motioning me to continue.

I briefly met Azriel's gaze. *Am I doing the right thing?*

Yes. He has every intention of confronting Hunter if you do not answer his questions satisfactorily.

Something I *had* to prevent. I'd killed a Cazador to stop Hunter knowing of this meeting. I'd be damned if I'd let that death be wasted by Rhoan marching up to Hunter and demanding answers.

And that, I realized suddenly, was *precisely* what she wanted. What other explanation could there be for her failing to block the mind of her assassin?

"I'm waiting." Rhoan's voice was soft, but held

an element of ice that chilled me to the core. This wasn't the uncle I knew and loved. This was the guardian. Coiled and ready for action.

"Jak Talbott was killed to teach me a lesson," I said bluntly. "But he's just the first part. You're intended to be the second."

That last bit might be a guess, but the more I thought about it, the more likely it seemed. Hunter wasn't a fool, and there was no way she'd have allowed that vampire to give us her name. And she'd have known Rhoan would have demanded to be placed on the investigation because of Jak's links to me. This *had* to be part of her game plan. She wanted to bring me to heel, and if she had to kill one of the Directorate's most valuable assets to do it, then she would. As Azriel had noted, Madeline Hunter had abandoned any pretense of humanity. At least when it came to me.

"Why would Madeline Hunter want to teach you a lesson?" Rhoan said, voice still far too cold.

"Because she wants the keys to hell, and she wants me to get them for her. Only I'm not doing it fast enough."

And if I could get him to believe that was the extent of my relationship with her, then at least I could avoid the fallout that would inevitably follow if I had to tell him I actually worked for her.

He regarded me for a minute, his gray eyes glittering and expression flat. Still the guardian, not the uncle. "Why would she want the keys to hell?"

I snorted. "Because the woman is fucking insane, that's why."

"Risa—"

I sighed. "Look, she told me she—and the council—want to use hell as their own private jail."

"And you believe that?"

"I believe it's insane. I also believe the council has nothing to do with Hunter's desire for the keys, and everything to do with Hunter's desire for power and ultimate control."

"A comment that suggests you've had a whole lot more to do with her than you've admitted so far."

"Given the bitch wants the keys to hell, and I'm the only one who can find them," I replied, "it would be fair enough to say she's been in my face recently."

"So why not come to me or Riley? We could have—"

"You could have gotten dead," I cut in, voice flat. I met his gaze, and I had no doubt the anger and frustration so evident in his was just as fierce in mine. "Didn't you hear what I said? Jak was just the *start*. You, and then Riley, and then maybe even Quinn would have all followed—"

Rhoan snorted. "Do you honestly think she would be fool enough to hurt Riley? In any way? She knows Quinn's vengeance would be swift and deadly."

"But she doesn't have to physically touch Riley. Killing you would effectively do that for her."

Rhoan accepted that with a grunt. "Even so—"

"Even so, you're talking about a woman who has *every* intention of challenging a Mijai *warrior*, and who fully believes she will best him."

Rhoan blinked and glanced at Azriel. "Seriously?"

"She is delusional, but not stupid," he replied. "She would employ fair means *and* foul to assure victory."

"Foul meaning what? She's a vampire—a very old vampire, granted—but what fear would any vampire hold for the likes of you?"

"Mijai can be killed, and not just when in flesh form. Hunter knows that."

"Besides," I added, "she's *never* been just a vampire. She's far more. And she knows magic."

Rhoan met my gaze again. "And Jack?"

Jack Parnell was senior vice president of the Directorate and the man in charge of the entire guardian division. He also happened to be Hunter's brother. "I'm not involved with either the Directorate or Jack. How much he knows about Hunter and her plans, I have no idea."

"He's her half brother, so one would imagine—"

"Not necessarily," Azriel commented. "While Jack has some tolerance for Hunter's more excessive nature, he would not condone what she is currently attempting if he knew about it."

Both Rhoan and I glanced at him. "When did you read him?" I asked.

Azriel's gaze met mine. "When you were brought in on that Directorate case. I read the minds of all you meet. It is always better to know who and who isn't a potential threat."

"So how much does he know?"

"He knows what she is, and tolerates her excesses in that regard—"

"And what, exactly, is she?" Rhoan cut in.

"A Maenad," I replied. "Or so we've been told. They're supposedly the female followers of the Greek wine god Dionysus, and have the whole orgasmic-rites and tearing-people-apart deal going."

"Huh." His gaze came to me again. Though some of the anger had fled, it still glimmered in the background, ready to erupt at a moment's notice. "So perhaps our next step would be to talk to Jack—"

"You can't," I said, alarmed. "She *will* kill you if she thinks you've discussed this with me in any way. I don't want—"

"Give me a little more credit than that," he cut in. "No one at the Directorate knows I contacted you. I made the call in a secure dead zone."

Meaning secure from both electronic *and* psychic intrusion. "Even so—"

"No," he said bluntly. "I'm paid to do my job, and do it I will. However, no one needs to know I've already talked to you. I will take this to Jack, and see what he says. What happens from there very much depends on his reaction."

In more ways than one. "Be careful, that's all I ask. And watch your damn back. Jack may hold to the middle ground when it comes to his sister, but she has plenty of support in the Directorate—"

He snorted. "I've been traversing Directorate politics for a while now. I know who to trust."

"Yeah, but there's a whole lot more on the line with this. You mustn't tell anyone about my involvement with Hunter or mention the key hunt to Jack. Promise me you won't."

"You can't deal with Hunter alone—"

"She isn't alone," Azriel cut in. "Hunter won't ever touch her. I promise you that."

She didn't need to; all she had to do was hurt the people I loved. But both men were aware of that fact, and that wasn't the point Azriel was making anyway.

Rhoan met Azriel's gaze for several moments, then nodded once. An agreement reached, I suspected. Rhoan returned his gaze to me. "We'll know soon enough where Jack stands. As for Hunter—" he hesitated. "I'll hold my tongue for the moment. But if anything else goes wrong, if anyone else dies, then she *has* to be confronted. And, one way or another, stopped."

"If you *do* have to confront her, don't do so alone. Promise me that much."

Just for a moment, the need to fight, to act, flared in his eyes. Rhoan, like Riley, had never been one to give up or back down, and it very obviously grated to do so now. And yet, he'd become second in command of the guardian division precisely because he *didn't* often act without first thinking through the consequences.

"Only if you promise me the same."

"I'm not alone. I have Azriel."

"Yeah, but you've also said Hunter desires his death. So, just humor an old man, and promise you'll contact me if you decide to confront the bitch. Otherwise, you and me *will* have a *serious* argument."

I half smiled. "Promise."

Whether I kept it was another matter entirely.

He studied me long enough that I began to suspect he'd caught that last thought, even though he wasn't telepathic. Eventually, though, he rose and pushed the chair back toward the desk.

"I probably wouldn't be able to confront Hunter alone anyway. Riley has a way of sensing things like that, and she'd insist on accompanying me."

And if she went with Rhoan, then Quinn undoubtedly would, too. But even then I doubted it would be enough to take down the likes of Hunter.

But it was at least a concession, and I was lucky to get that much. I stepped forward and dropped a kiss on his cheek. "Thank you," I said. "And I promise, I'll be careful."

"You'd better," he all but growled, then left.

The tension that had been riding me since his phone call didn't really ease much though. He was about to talk to Jack, and it was anyone's guess where Jack fell in the scheme of things. Azriel might insist Jack wouldn't condone what Hunter was doing, but she *was* his sister. In the end, blood might be stronger than loyalty to the Directorate.

"What now?" Azriel said.

I thrust a hand through my hair and sighed. "I'd better make an appearance downstairs, just to see how things have been going in our absence."

He nodded. "Get yourself something to eat while you're at it."

I half smiled. "You're nagging again."

"Someone has to nag, otherwise you'd be skin and bone." He caught my hand and tugged me into his embrace. "Besides, you carry my son. It is important you keep your strength up."

Hurt flicked through me, but I forced a smile. "I'm not about to do anything that would endanger his life."

"But you all too readily endanger your own, and one cannot be without the other."

Tears prickled my eyes. Which was stupid, because his concern was perfectly natural. My health *could* adversely affect the health of our child, and there was no denying I really *hadn't* been taking the best care of myself lately, what with the drinking and the lack of eating. And I *did* know that he cared for me. Trouble was, caring wasn't enough. Not anymore.

I pulled out of his embrace and headed for the door, adding over my shoulder, "I won't be long."

"Risa—"

I didn't stop, just said over my shoulder, "I'm fine, Azriel. Don't worry about it."

"If you were fine, you would not be close to tears. We need—"

"I'm pregnant, and pregnant women tend to get irrational," I cut in. "You'll probably have seen a whole flood of tears by the time this child is born."

And with that, I retreated down the stairs. Not that running would do much good when the man I was running from could pop into existence anywhere he chose to. He didn't, though. Maybe he knew that there was nothing he could say to ease the irrationality. Nothing but one simple four-letter word; a word that probably wasn't even in reaper language.

I paused on the bottom step, searching the room for Margie. She was easy enough to find—she was built like an Amazon and towered over most of the patrons by a good six inches. She was clearing a table near the front door, so I made my way through the crowd toward her.

"Good to see we're so busy," I said, as I neared.

She glanced up, and her bright smile flashed. "Yeah. Been meaning to ask if I could get another waiter or two. It's been insane these last couple of days."

"Go ahead. I'm not sure when Ilianna or I are going to be back—things are hectic elsewhere at the moment."

She nodded, obviously unfazed by our absence. Which was one of the reasons we'd singled her out to become our manager. That and the fact she'd passed her business course with honors. "Excellent. I'll get the ad in the paper tomorrow. Oh, and the accountant left a note for you. It's sitting under the till."

"Thanks. Any other problems I need to know about?"

"Jacques wants to change the menu again, because he's bored cooking the same things, but other than that, no."

I smiled. Jacques was our sous-chef, although with what Tao was currently going through, Jacques had all but become our head chef. He was damn good, too—which is why we paid him so well and, subsequently, why he remained, even though he hated cooking burgers. Fancy burgers, but burgers all the same. "Tell him he can change one item to anything he desires, but don't expect a rush of orders. Ninety percent of our clientele are werewolves, and they like their burgers."

She smiled. "I told him that. He doesn't care."

I chuckled softly, and headed over to the till to grab the note. *Need to talk to you ASAP about a couple of problems*, Mike's bold scrawl read. *How about we do so over dinner?*

I frowned at the note, trying to decipher the intent behind the invitation. Mike and I had always had an easygoing relationship—mainly because he'd been dating my mom, even if their relationship had never been confirmed or even acknowledged until after her death. I'd never been entirely sure *why* she'd wanted it kept secret, but had always figured it had something to do with the fact it would probably be considered unethical for Mike to be in a relationship with one of his clients.

What I didn't understand was why in the hell he'd want to meet me for dinner, when up until now we'd only ever talked at his office or mine.

Or was this merely an extension of his need to keep an eye on me for my mother's sake? It probably was, but it nevertheless made me uneasy.

Of course, just about everything was making me uneasy these days.

I glanced at my watch. I couldn't ring him now—Mike had said in the past he was an early riser and liked getting into the office closer to eight rather than nine, but given that it was barely five a.m., I doubted even he'd be up. I folded the note and shoved it in my pocket as I headed into the kitchen. I'd deal with Mike later. Right now, I needed to grab something to eat, before my reaper started hassling me again. Besides, who knew when I'd get another chance—especially given Mirri had fewer than twenty-four hours left before the rope around her neck began to tighten.

*   *   *

Tao still hadn't arrived home by the time we got back there, and the worry that sat like a weight in the back of my mind ratcheted up another notch. As much as I kept telling myself he'd be okay, that we'd get him through this, the longer he remained unfound—the longer the fire elemental remained in control of his body—the harder it would be for us to pull Tao's spirit back. That's presuming the fire spirit *was* in control, and Tao hadn't just decided to follow in my recent footsteps, and drink himself into oblivion.

"If he was drunk," Azriel said softly, "he could be found. But his essence has disappeared, which can only mean the elemental has overtaken him again."

"I know that," I snapped, then sighed and scrubbed a hand across my eyes. "Sorry. I shouldn't be taking my frustration and anger out on you."

He shrugged. "Is it not better to release such emotion than to restrain it?"

"Depends who's at the end of the release." If it was Hunter, maybe. She deserved my anger, and a whole lot more. Azriel didn't.

"I have broad enough shoulders. I can take it."

"And it's just as well, given the grief I've been dumping on you lately." I looked around the room, not really seeing the mess, until my gaze fell on an odd-shaped plastic globule sitting near the remains of the dining table. The computer. And while we'd had everything backed up, spotting that globule oddly reminded me of the cuff link I'd found at Lauren's place on the Gold Coast. I'd shoved it in my purse and had promptly forgotten about it, which was stupid, given that finding out who'd made the thing might just provide our next step forward.

I got my phone and Googled "maker's marks using the letters RJ." Over a dozen different links immediately popped up, so I headed into the bedroom, plopped down on the bed, and started going through them. After trawling through nine different sites and coming up empty, I hit a U.S.-based site that listed trademarks and contact details for artists and metalsmiths, both in the U.S. and overseas. And that's where I hit gold—or silver, given most of the smiths listed on the site appeared to deal more in that than gold. The maker was one Rubin Johnson, originally from Santa Fe, but now living and working in Sydney, Australia. It listed a shop address rather than a home one, so I checked the yellow pages and confirmed the address was still current. A search for his home address didn't reveal anything. Maybe his listing was private.

"Do you wish to talk to him?" Azriel asked.

I glanced at my watch. "Yes, but not right now. It's barely six. He's not likely to be there until nine."

"Which leaves us with three hours to fill. Unless, of course, you have something else you plan to do."

I half smiled. "I know what I'd love to do, but I'm thinking you might veto the suggestion."

"You'd be thinking right." His expression was severe but amusement crinkled the corners of his blue eyes. "I would love nothing more than to be with you physically, but we cannot afford the distraction given the Raziq, your father, and Hunter all want to assure your allegiance is to them alone."

"Yeah, but none of them can get into our home. Not with my father's wards in place."

"The wards will not stop Ania, and your father is as capable of enforcing his will on them as the Raziq. And Hunter will have many contract killers who are not vampires she could call on."

I poked his chest with a stiffened finger. "You, reaper, are such a spoilsport."

He caught my hand, raised it to his lips, and kissed it. "Trust me, if we survive all this, I intend to make love to you so often and so well that you will beg me to stop."

I laughed and stepped close enough that my breasts were pressed against his chest. "I'm part werewolf, remember. You could be waiting a long time for me to beg off."

"I should hope so." He kissed me, long and slow, before finally adding, "In the meantime, you should rest."

I sighed again. "I guess if you're going to insist—"

"And I am."

"Then you'd better escort me to bed, James."

He did. And, frustratingly, did nothing more than that.

The first thing I did when I woke was ring Mike at his office. It was eight thirty, so I had no doubt he'd be there by now.

"Good morning, Risa." The voice was plummy and feminine, and belonged to his secretary, Beatrice. "You're calling early—hope there's not a problem."

"There's not." The vid-phone was turned off on her end, so I couldn't see what color her hair was this month. But the last time I'd been at the office it had been pale purple, and the month before that a vibrant red. Despite her age, she loved hair color variety as much as I loved Coke and cake. "Mike left me a message to give him a call ASAP. Is he around?"

"Just a moment, and I'll put you through."

There was a click, a brief moment of silence, then Mike's aristocratic features came on-screen. I didn't actually know how old Mike was—he didn't look old, and yet he didn't seem young, either. His hair was black but cut short, the dark curls clinging close to his head like a helmet. His eyes—a clear, striking gray—seemed to hold eons of knowledge behind them. Given Mom had once commented that he had a genius-level IQ, I guess that was to be expected.

"Risa," he said, his voice low and pleasant, "thank you for ringing back so promptly."

"I thought I'd better. It sounded urgent."

"Not so much urgent, more a warning."

I raised my eyebrows. "About what?"

"About the tax department's crackdown on small businesses. I just wanted to make sure you have all receipts in order, just in case RYT's is in line to be audited."

"Aside from the last couple of weeks, yes." And he knew that, so why ring me? It wasn't like the possibility of being audited was new, but as far as I knew, businesses like our café were generally only targeted when certain flags were thrown up. "Have they contacted us?"

"No, I just wanted to ensure everything was in order on the off chance we were."

I frowned. I wasn't sure why, but something just didn't feel right. "Mike, is everything okay?"

One dark eyebrow rose. It made his nose look overly large. "Yes, of course it is. Why?"

"You just seem . . . out of sorts." I cleared my throat. "And then there's the dinner invitation, which basically came out of nowhere."

"Not really. Your mother and I—"

"I'm not Mom," I reminded him gently. "I can't give you what she gave you."

Something close to horror flitted across his face. "Good god, you don't think I want to—"

"No," I cut in hastily. "I don't. But I do think that perhaps you're missing her, and I'm the next best thing to being with her."

But even as I spoke, I couldn't help noticing that for all his outrage, his gaze remained steely. Calculating.

Something was *definitely* going on, and maybe I needed to find out what. And hey, what was one more problem on an already overloaded plate?

"I do miss her," he said. "Enormously. But to imply I might wish to capture what I had with her with you is beyond—"

"I didn't mean to offend you, Mike," I cut in again. "The invitation surprised me, that's all. And I'm more than happy to have dinner one night."

"I have no desire to make you uncomfortable," he replied, voice cool.

"Mike, it's fine. I'm busy for the next day or so, but I'm free anytime after that." If the Raziq, my father, or the wanna-be queen of the world didn't have other plans for me, that is.

He sniffed. It was an oddly regal sound that stirred the edges of memory, though I wasn't entirely sure why. "Friday then?"

"That would be lovely. Thank you."

"I shall let you know when and where. Until then, good-bye."

And with that, he hung up. Great. I'd managed to offend the man my mother had not only trusted financially, but apparently depended on emotionally and physically for a good part of her life. It seemed to be my lot of late to make all the wrong moves.

"You have trusted your instincts up until now," Azriel commented. "It would be foolish to ignore them, even if the person involved was a friend of your mother's."

I twisted around. He was back in his usual spot, his arms crossed as he stared out the window rather than at me. The morning sunshine caressed his skin, lending it a warm golden glow.

"Which is why I agreed to meet him for dinner. It's easier to sense when someone is lying face-to-face." I eyed him for a moment, sensing tension even if there was no evidence of it in the way he stood. "Are you annoyed that I'm meeting him?"

"No. And you do not have to explain your motives to me."

He might be saying he wasn't annoyed, but the emotion swirling through the link between us suggested otherwise.

"I agree—I don't. I just wanted to." I flipped the bedcovers off my legs and walked over to him. He didn't move, so I wrapped my hands around his waist and rested a cheek on his shoulder. "Misunderstanding, an unwillingness to trust, and sheer pigheadedness—all mostly on my part, granted—is no way to start a relationship. I'm trying to make up for all that, but you have to do the same, Azriel."

"I do not understand what you mean."

But he did. The tightening of his shoulder and arm muscles was evidence enough of that. If his hands had been visible, I very much suspected they'd be clenched.

"Why are you so annoyed that I agreed to have dinner with Mike?"

He was silent for a moment, then said, "I do not actually know. It is irrational given I know full well your reasons for doing so."

I couldn't help grinning. "It may be irrational, but it makes my little heart sing."

He turned and wrapped his arms around my waist. "And why would that be?"

"Because that particular irrationality is called jealousy, and it means you really do care for me."

He studied me for several heartbeats, a smile tugging at his lips and his expression somewhat bemused.

Then he sighed, shook his head, and said, "For a very smart woman, Risa Jones, you are sometimes extraordinarily dumb."

Chapter 11

I blinked. To say I *hadn't* been expecting a comment like that would be the understatement of the year—in a year that had been full of them.

"I'm gathering you *have* got a reason for insulting me like that. Or are insults some weird reaper way of showing affection?"

He smiled. "It is hardly an insult when it is the truth. And you have had the answer to the question you fear to ask for some time now."

"You know, you're not making anything any clearer."

His amusement grew. "Why do you think you are pregnant?"

My eyebrows rose even as I wondered what the hell *that* had to do with anything. "I got pregnant because we had unprotected sex."

"Yes. And as I told you once before, a reaper can only ever have a child with his Caomh."

Caomh. The reaper term for life-mate. I could only stare as the word echoed around my brain, unimaginable and impossible.

"But nevertheless fact," he said softly. "You carry the truth of what has lain unspoken between us since the very beginning."

I swallowed heavily, not daring to believe that fate had, against all the odds and two very different worlds, made this man mine.

"Believe," he said. "You are my body, my soul, the energy by which I live, and the song in my heart. It was not for our son, or the keys, or the fate of our two worlds that I pulled you back to life. I did it because I cannot live without you."

And with that, he kissed me. It was a fierce thing, his kiss; fierce, and passionate, and joyous. It was everything I'd spent half my life searching for, everything I'd ever wanted, all wrapped up in one glorious action.

But it didn't end there.

He touched me, caressed me, even as I ran my hands over his beautiful body, teasing him as thoroughly as he teased me, until sweat stung our skins and the smell of desire was thick in the air.

I wanted him; dear god, how I wanted him, but I didn't immediately give in to the need. Instead, I wrapped my arms around his neck and kissed him again, pressing my body hard against his, until it was difficult to tell where his skin ended and mine began. Desire and heat burned through and around us, until even the very air we breathed seemed to be boiling.

He slid his hands down my back, then cupped

my butt and lifted me with little effort. A heartbeat later, he was in me. It felt like heaven and, for several seconds, neither of us moved, simply enjoying the sensations and the heat that rose with this basic joining of flesh. Then the heat became too great to ignore and he thrust deeper—harder—his cock sliding in and out of me with growing urgency. Energy flickered across our skin, dancing between us, tearing through us, until the music of his being played through me, and mine through him. It was a dance, a caress, a tease. It was movement, and heat, and desire. It was crazy and electric, a firestorm that ripped through us even as we remained in flesh. It fueled the urgency and heightened the pleasure, and the desire coursing through my body built, until it was all I could do to keep hold of the pleasure that threatened to tear us both apart.

His movements became more and more urgent, until my whole body shook with the intensity of them. I burned, tightened, until I couldn't breathe and it felt like I would shatter.

"Please," I somehow whispered, "please."

He responded instantly, his movements fierce. I shuddered, my control crumbling as my orgasm began to sweep through me, intense and violent. A heartbeat later, he cried out, his body stiffening against mine as he came.

For several minutes neither of us moved. He leaned his forehead against mine, his breathing harsh against my lips.

I smiled, and touched his cheek gently. "If you continue to love me like that for eternity, I will be one contented woman."

"I do not believe I would have any complaints, either." He lowered me gently. "As much as I would like to linger here, with you, we should continue with the key search."

I sighed. "Yes. I'll just grab a quick shower first."

He nodded and stepped aside. I padded across to my wardrobe, grabbing underclothing, jeans and a T-shirt, then headed into the bathroom.

Twenty minutes later we were standing in front of Rubin Johnson's little store, situated in McMahon's Point, just across the bay from the opera house. The shop itself was one of those quaint, single-front two-story Victorians that were everywhere in Sydney, although this one was in the process of being renovated, if the splashes of paint across the windows were anything to go by.

"*That* is not paint," Azriel said, voice grim.

I glanced at him sharply, then stepped closer. Unlike the shops on either side, the window here was only half frame rather than full. A wide shelf stretched the length of it, and was lined with necklaces, bracelets. No cuff links, but then, they'd certainly be easier to pocket than the intricate and heavy stone and silver work currently displayed.

The brown splatters I'd presumed were paint had a crusty, cracked look close up, which dried paint didn't usually get. It was blood—old blood.

My gaze skimmed the jewelry, but none of it appeared to have been splattered. Not that I could see from this angle, anyway. But there were several globs of rusty red near the right end of the shelf and a spray of the stuff up the nearby wall. It was the sort of spray that could happen only when a major artery had been cut.

My gaze jumped to the interior of the shop. It had an open plan, with glass display cabinets lining the long wall to the left and a glass display table situated in the middle of the room. A counter stretched the length of the rear wall and, behind it to the left, a set of wooden stairs led upward. Nothing seemed out of place or disturbed, and there was no sign of anyone—dead or alive.

"That is because the body lies underneath this window. You cannot see it because of the thickness of the shelf."

"We need to get in there." I stepped back and scanned the walls. The place was alarmed, but there was no camera, at least out here. I hadn't noticed one when I was peering in the window, either. I pulled my sleeve over my hand and tried opening the door. "It's locked. We'll probably set off the alarm when we go inside, but we should have enough time to examine the body before either the cops or the security firm get here."

"Then let's go."

He caught my hand, and we reappeared just inside the door. The first thing I saw was the alarm

panel. Neither the door's nor the windows' indicator lights were lit, meaning the system had been
switched off. Suggesting, perhaps, that Rubin
Johnson had not only known his killer, but had
invited him in.

I turned and saw the body. He was barefoot,
and wearing an old-fashioned woolen dressing
gown that was so well worn the blue check was
faded and patchy. He'd been shoved under the
shelf like so much rubbish, his limbs at impossible
angles to his body.

Azriel walked over and squatted next to him.
"He has no head."

"What?"

He glanced at me, expression neutral but his
anger burning through my mind. "His head has
been removed."

"Why the hell would someone remove his
head?" I scanned the rest of the room. He'd obviously been killed here—the arterial sprays across
the wall and floor were evidence enough of that.
"Surely no one would want a trophy *that* size."

Or that macabre.

"I do not think it has anything to do with a trophy, but a means of stopping us. Or rather, me."

"So you can't read his thoughts."

"Yes."

"Which would imply whoever did this is fully
aware a reaper can access the memories of the
freshly dead."

"Yes."

Meaning Lauren had either realized she was missing the cuff link, or she was simply taking out anyone or anything that could pin down her location. And if the latter, that undoubtedly meant there had been something here that could give away her current whereabouts. Maybe she was a longtime customer.

That's presuming our dark sorceress was the one responsible for this murder.

"If it was not Lauren, then it confirms there is another sorcerer involved. The taint of dark magic lingers in the air."

"Meaning the bastards are still one step ahead of us."

He pushed to his feet. "Unfortunately, yes."

I stared down at the broken body. From this angle, I couldn't actually see the stump of his neck, thanks to the shadows and the depth of the shelf, and of that I was glad. I'd lost the contents of my stomach far too often in the last twenty-four hours, and I had no desire to test its stability again.

"He's wearing a dressing gown, so he obviously lived upstairs. It might be worth doing a quick search through the whole premises, just in case he keeps a record of buyers somewhere."

"Is that likely?"

I shrugged. "Right now, we can't afford to overlook any option. I'll take upstairs."

He nodded, and I headed for the stairs. The upper level consisted of a small living area, a separate bathroom and bedroom, and what could only be described as a kitchen nook. There was also a balcony off the kitchen that provided nice views over the bay.

I grabbed some gloves from under the sink and went searching. There were no filing cabinets, so I went through his drawers. I found all sorts of bills, tax records, notes, as well as various bits of design artwork, but no clientele records.

Which was pretty typical of our luck, really. I clomped down the stairs. "Anything?"

Azriel shook his head. "There is an index of names and addresses, but none of them are our sorcerers or the Gold Coast address."

"Lauren's sharing that place with a man, so maybe he's one of the names listed."

"Perhaps, but as I said, the Gold Coast address was not listed."

"Which doesn't mean he can't be in there. It just means he might have a secondary address. It might be worth taking the index cards with us and getting Stane to do a check."

"Why not your uncle? Would it not be easier for the Directorate to conduct such a search?"

"Yeah, but that would mean involving Rhoan again, and I'm not about to do that unless it's absolutely necessary."

"And yet you're willing to involve Stane?"

I grimaced at the unspoken implication, even

though it was perfectly true. I *was* more prepared to risk Stane's life than Rhoan's, even though, of the two, Rhoan was more capable of defending himself. "The one thing my uncle has that Stane doesn't is Hunter as his ultimate boss."

"You can be certain that Hunter is well aware of Stane's participation in this quest."

"Oh, there's no doubt about that." Hell, thanks to the Cazadors, she knew everything I did and everyone I talked to. Except for the last couple of hours, that was. I shivered and tried not to itch at hands that still felt bloody, even if no blood had actually been spilled. "It's just that if I lose Rhoan, I'll more than likely lose Riley, thanks to their twin bond. And it may be brutal, but I'd rather risk Stane's life than two people I consider pseudo parents."

Although I was hoping like hell it *didn't* come down to that. Jak had already lost his life to this quest. I really, *really*, didn't want that to happen to anyone else.

And yet the notion that others *would* be lost before this quest was over was one that wouldn't go away and wouldn't be ignored.

Azriel picked up the index cards, his expression unreadable and little emotion evident in the link. I really had no idea what he thought of my reasoning, but surely he understood. After all, reapers did what was necessary to get the job done.

"We head to Stane's, then?" was all he said.

I hesitated, then nodded. "After that, we might go to Adeline Greenfield's place, and ask whether our Michael Greenfield could possibly be her brother."

Azriel frowned. "I thought you intended to see your uncle next?"

I grimaced. *"I did, but after that confrontation with Rhoan, I've rethought the wisdom of that."*

In other words, cowardice had come to the fore. But one angry confrontation a day was really all I could handle at the moment.

"It is not cowardice to wish to avoid a confrontation that might set those you care about on a crash course with death," Azriel said softly. *"And that is what all of us involved in this quest face."*

My gaze flashed to his. "You stay alive, reaper, no matter what. I have no intention of raising our child alone."

He smiled. "Trust me, I have no intention of going anywhere. Whether the fates give me that choice is another matter entirely."

"Well, they fucking better," I said, as I stepped into his arms. "Because if I survive all the chaos they've created, I think I deserve some sort of reward."

He raised an eyebrow, amusement evident. "And I'm to be that reward?"

"You'll do for starters."

He laughed, and delight skated through me. I cupped his cheek and lightly brushed my thumb across the small laugh lines near his mouth. Lines that hadn't been there when he'd first made an appearance in my life. "You should do that more often."

"Once we are through this, perhaps I will."

And with that, he swept us to Stane's.

Only Stane wasn't alone. Tao was with him.

I stared at him for a moment, taking in the haunted eyes, hollowed cheeks, and dusty, partially burned clothing, then all but threw myself into his arms. He caught me with a grunt and his arms wrapped around me, his grip so fierce my ribs were in danger of cracking. I didn't care. He was here, he was whole, and that was all that mattered.

"God," I muttered, wrapping my arms around his neck and holding him as fiercely as he held me. "I'm so glad you're safe."

"So am I," he said softly. "So am I."

I pulled back, my gaze searching his. The flames had totally retreated and there was little more than ash and desperation in his eyes.

"What happened?"

He shrugged and scraped one hand across his chin. "I don't really know. One minute I was home, and the next I was flat on my face in a field the other side of Sunbury, near the landfill center there."

"The elemental was heading back to where it was created again."

"Yes." He shook his head. "And it was close to getting there by the time I regained control. Up until that point I was—" He paused and a shudder went through him. He briefly closed his eyes, his voice breaking as he added, "I was nowhere. I was nothing. No matter what I did, no matter how hard I fought, all there was were flames and heat and endless agony. I think I'd rather be dead than go through that again."

"Tao—"

His gaze hit mine. Fierce. Angry. "Don't say it, Ris. Don't you *dare* say it. You have no idea what it's like to lose your entire being to another force, and until you do, don't lecture me or feed me platitudes."

I didn't say anything. Couldn't really, simply because anything I did say probably *would* come off sounding like one or the other.

Tao knew how I felt and what I believed. I'd told him often enough already. He knew we were there for him, no matter what. Just as I knew that, right now, he was angry and scared; who wouldn't be, placed in the same position?

So I simply dropped a kiss on his ash-stained cheek, then stepped back, took the index cards from Azriel, and handed them to Stane. His gaze, when it met mine, was sympathetic. Maybe he'd tried comforting Tao as well, only to receive a similar response.

"Where did you get these?" He flicked through

the cards with a slight frown. "It's very old-fashioned to store information in this form these days."

"They were stolen from the premises of a dead man. Maybe he didn't trust computers."

Stane snorted. "It's far easier to steal information from these things than it is from computers."

"Says the man who hacks for fun and profit."

He grinned. "Well, yeah, but I'm an extraordinary individual. The common man generally isn't as clever as me and my kind."

His kind meaning hackers and black marketeers, not werewolves, obviously. "If we haven't already overwhelmed you and your computers with requests, could you do a search through these and see if there's any link—however tenuous—to Lauren Macintyre?"

"Sure. Could take a while, though. There's a fair few names in here, by the look of it."

"I know, and I'm sorry, but it could be the only way we're going to track down our sorceress." And maybe the only way to save Mirri. But there was no point adding that. Stane would do his best, as usual. "We need to know the minute you find anything."

"Speaking of findings, I managed to get the autopsy results for the body parts and teeth the cops found at the storage place that blew up." Stane reached over to the second of his desks and flicked a screen. Several documents flashed onto it. "Long story short, the bits *did* belong to Genevieve Sands. Problem is, she was dead long before this blast tore her apart. The coroner picked up evidence that the body had been frozen."

"Just like the real John Nadler." My voice was grim. "It's beginning to look more and more likely that we're dealing with not only a full-body face shifter, but one capable of taking multiple male *and* female forms."

"If that *is* the case," Azriel said, "then it is possible the clothes we saw in Lauren's wardrobe might well have belonged to her alternate *male* identity."

I glanced at him. "Yes. Which means that cuff link might yet lead us to her, even if a search through the index cards doesn't."

He raised an eyebrow. "How? It is an inanimate object, and in and of itself can provide no clues."

"To you and me, yes. But to someone who has psychometry skills, maybe it can. We have to go see Adeline Greenfield about her apparently resurrected brother; maybe she can point us to someone who can help."

"Why not ask the Brindle?" Tao said, voice a little strained, but overall sounding a whole lot less tense than a few moments ago. "Surely they have witches capable of that there?"

"Yes, but their first priority has to be Mirri—"

"Fuck," he said, cutting me off. "I'd forgotten. How is she? How is Ilianna?"

"Okay for the moment. Ilianna's mom and Ki-andra are both helping to try to get the threads unraveled before the deadline."

He hesitated. "And have they any hope?"

"Who knows?" I half shrugged. "But Ilianna *did* manage to unravel the magic in my father's warding stones, so she has at least a basic level of understanding of what's involved."

"Fuck." He thrust a hand through his tangled, matted hair. "We've made a right old cock-up of everything, haven't we?"

"Not we," I refuted softly. "Me."

"Ris—"

"Don't," I cut in. "And for exactly the same reasons you gave me only minutes ago."

He stared at me for several seconds; then the faintest trace of a smile touched his lips. "Fair enough. Although I will remind you that you can hardly be held to account for your father's stupidity in losing the keys in the first place."

"True, but that doesn't absolve me of responsibility for everything else that has happened." My voice broke, and I swallowed heavily. Damn it, I *wouldn't* cry. Not again. There'd been enough tears shed for Jak for the time being, and I refused to cry for Tao or Mirri. It wasn't over yet. They *weren't* dead. And until it was all done and dusted and we knew . . . I paused, not wanting to think about the rest of that sentence, but it ran through my mind nevertheless.

. . . we knew who survived and who didn't, there was no point in grieving. Hell, there was a fair chance I wouldn't survive, let alone anyone else. And that would be the pits given the possibility of a happy ever after had been dangled in front of my nose.

I returned my gaze to Stane. "Any luck finding more information on Pénombre Manufacturing?"

He shook his head. "For all intents and purposes, it's a shelf company, as I said. I have no idea how they can own that Maribyrnong premises given it shouldn't be possible."

"So there's no connection to either Genevieve Sands or Lauren Macintyre?"

"None that I can find. Doesn't mean there isn't one, of course." He leaned across to another screen. "There is, however, a link between Sands and Macintyre. It's tenuous, and I'm trying to uncover more details, but it would seem that twenty-eight years ago, Sands invested in a property that Macintyre subsequently purchased."

My eyebrows rose. "The Maribyrnong warehouse was purchased by the shelf company some twenty-eight years ago, too."

"Yeah. Odd coincidence, don't you think?" He half smiled. "Macintyre no longer owns the property. According to records, she sold it five years ago."

"And the new owners?"

"It went through several, and ended up being one of the properties purchased by the consortium owned by John Nadler."

"And round and round the circle goes," Tao commented. "Only it seems to stop at exactly the same spot."

Stane glanced at him. "Yeah. I'm currently doing a search on all the owners between Macintyre and Nadler, just to see what I come up with."

"It's worth a shot." If nothing else, it might give us some home addresses to search. I mean, sooner or later, we *had* to hit gold. Or, in this case, a legitimate address that actually had the person registered as the former owner actually living there.

"Anything else?" Stane said.

I smiled. "That's enough, don't you think?"

"Well, I am becoming accustomed to my crates of top-shelf champagne. Not sure how I'll manage once all this over."

My smiled grew. "You could actually purchase them yourself."

Shock claimed his expression, although his brown eyes twinkled. "Buy them myself? Good god, I don't buy *anything*, dear woman. I'm a trader. Unfortunately, crates of Dom Pérignon aren't something I often come across in the electronics market."

"Then you need to get better contacts." I glanced at Tao. "Are you heading home?"

He shook his head. "I have a feeling if I do, the elemental might wrest control from me again. I seem to do better when I have company."

I hesitated, wondering if his being here was actually safe for Stane, then mentally slapped myself. Stane was probably in more danger from *my* actions than from any possibility that Tao would hurt him. So I simply said, "Do you need anything brought here from home?"

He shook his head. "Whatever I need, I'll borrow from Stane. I just don't—" he paused, and half shrugged. "Keep in contact."

"I will." I squeezed his arm gently, and tried to ignore the heat so evident in his flesh, even through the barrier of his clothes. The elemental was far from finished with this battle.

Fear washed through me yet again, but there was nothing I could do but ignore it. And hope that fate had a better plan for him than an eternity locked in nothing but fire. I turned to Azriel. "Let's head to Adeline's, and see if she can help us."

He nodded, caught my hand, and a heartbeat later we were standing outside Adeline's front gate. I raised an eyebrow. "Why not inside?"

"Because she would not appreciate such an unannounced intrusion, and given we wish her help, I thought this wiser."

"Good thinking," I said, and opened the wrought iron front gate.

"Someone in this team has to do it," he replied evenly.

It took a moment for me to realize I'd just been insulted. By Azriel, of all people. My gaze shot to his, and I saw the amusement lurking underneath the serious expression. "I can't believe you just said that!"

"Is not such a comment almost expected in this world?"

I grinned. "Yeah, but it's not something I expected from *you*."

The amusement grew. "Alas, the more time I spend in flesh, the more human my tendencies become."

"So I've got a lifetime of insults to look forward to?"

"Only if you do something that would warrant such a comment."

"I've hardly done something now."

"No." His smile broke free. "But it seemed an opportune moment to practice."

He touched a hand to my spine, gently ushering me forward. I snorted softly and headed along the tiled pathway that wove its way to Adeline's front door. Her house was one of those beautiful old Victorians filled with character and age. Two graceful old elms dominated her front lawn, but underneath them lay a riot of colorful flowers that filled the air with perfume. It should have overwhelmed my olfactory senses, but it didn't.

I made my way up the steps and walked to the front door. A little gold bell sat on the right edge of the door frame, its rope cord swaying gently in the breeze. I rang it a couple of times, and the joyous sound it made had me smiling.

Footsteps echoed inside; then the wooden door opened. Adeline Greenfield was a short woman with close-cut gray hair, weathered features, and round figure. She reminded me of the grandmotherly types so often seen on TV sitcoms, and it wasn't until you looked into her bright blue eyes that you began to suspect she was anything other than that. Her eyes glowed with a power that was almost unworldly.

"Risa," she said, opening the security door with a welcoming smile. "Perfect timing."

I raised my eyebrows. "You were expecting me?"

"Of course." She stepped aside and waved us in. "I'm glad your reaper chose to be polite, however. I do so detest visitors popping into my home unannounced."

"Which suggests you get more than your fair share of visitors popping in unannounced." I stepped past her.

"Just head for the sitting room, dear," she said. "And yes, I do. Ghosts have no sense of privacy these days, I'm afraid. It's the new generation. No manners."

I smiled and walked down the hall, my footsteps echoing on the old wooden floorboards. The air inside Adeline's house generally smelled of ginger and various spices, but underneath them this time ran the warm, rich smell of coffee. She really *had* been expecting me, because Adeline didn't drink it—she preferred tea to coffee. Her sitting room was cozy and dominated by a log fire. Embers glowed within the ashes and lent the room extra warmth. Two well-padded armchairs sat in front of the fireplace and, in between them, there was a small coffee table on which sat a teapot, a bone china cup and saucer, and the source of the coffee smell—a large mug of it, in fact.

"Please, sit," Adeline said. When I did so, she handed me the mug, then glanced at Azriel. "Would you like anything, young man?"

"No, thank you," Azriel said, amusement in his voice. I guess there were a few people who actually called him young *man*.

"Right, then," she said, sitting down on the chair opposite and pouring tea for herself. "What can I do for you?"

"I'm afraid we're here to ask your brother, Michael—"

"Michael?" she cut in, with a light frown. "He's been dead for forty-odd years now."

"Yes, I know, but we came across his name in our search"—I hesitated, then remembered I'd told her at least some of the story the last time we'd been here—"for the keys to heaven and hell's gates, and were just wondering—"

"I assure you," Adeline interrupted again. "Michael would never be involved in such a theft. Alive *or* dead."

"I didn't mean to imply that he was. It's just

that we think someone might have assumed his identity. In which case, we need to know more about Michael in order to track down the fraud."

She studied me for a moment, then rose and walked over to the mantelpiece. She picked up a small, framed photograph and offered it to me. "That's Michael. It was taken just before he died."

The man in the photograph was silver haired, with blue eyes and round, kind features and a build not dissimilar to Adeline's—although he was far thinner than she now was. "How old was he here?"

"Nearly thirty. Gray hair runs in the family, I'm afraid."

"And do you have any contact with his friends? Was he close to anyone in particular, or did he make a new acquaintance just before he died?"

"Not that I'm aware of. Why?"

I ignored her question, asking instead, "And how did he die?"

"Accident. He was heavily into the motor cross scene, and slid off during a race and hit several trees. Unfortunately, one of the smaller ones speared him. He never recovered."

So, an accident rather than murder, Azriel commented. *Perhaps in this case, the shifter merely appropriated the name of someone with few relatives.*

Sounds like it. Still, it couldn't hurt to be sure. "And he was buried appropriately?"

Her frown grew. "Of course. I ensured he could

not be raised, if that is your next question. And it isn't as if a zombie would be much use to anyone anyway. They are very obviously dead."

But they could still be damn dangerous if raised by the wrong person.

"True, but that wasn't the point of the question. You see, Michael is not the only person whose identity our shifter has stolen, but up until your brother, he's murdered all those whose lives he's stepped into. I just wanted to make sure Michael wasn't another of his victims."

"Ah," she said softly. "Then no, he isn't. It was very much an accident—there were plenty of witnesses to the event."

At least that was something. I handed the photograph back. "If someone *is* using his identity, is there any way you could trace them?"

"Magically, you mean?"

When I nodded, she grimaced. "I'm afraid not. I'd have to have something of theirs to even attempt a reading."

I dug into my purse and retrieved the cuff link. "We found this, although we have no real idea if it belongs to our fake Michael Greenwood or someone else."

She plucked it from my fingertips and studied it for several minutes. "I think it might be possible to trace whoever owned this item. It is not, however, something I wish to do without some form of protection."

"Why?"

Her gaze rose to mine. "Because whoever owned this cuff link has a particularly nasty resonance."

"We think the owner might be a dark sorceress."

"That would certainly explain the resonance." She paused, her expression curious. "How is the sorceress connected to whoever might be using Michael's identity?"

"We suspect our sorceress is a face shifter who is able to not only make a full body shift, but can become male or female, too."

"Which is an extremely rare occurrence."

"I know."

She glanced down at the cuff link, then rose abruptly. "Come along then."

She bustled out of the room and didn't look back. I hastily placed my coffee mug back on the table, the movement so sudden liquid splashed over the rim, scalding my fingers and spilling across the table. I grabbed a napkin, dropped it over the mess, then ran after Adeline. She led us into a room farther down the hall—one opposite the room in which she'd taught me to astral travel. Energy caressed my skin as I went through the doorway, a warning that wards were very active here. The décor was simple—a small round table, a half dozen thickly cushioned chairs, and warmly colored tapestries on the wall. Candles burned in the four corners of the room, their aroma filling the air with lavender and sage. They were also the only source of light. This, I suspected, was the place she did most of her business and, in very many ways, it reminded me of the room Mom had used when she had clients wanting to talk to relatives who'd moved on.

"Please, sit." Adeline waved a hand to one of the chairs, then sat down opposite. "I'll attempt lithomancy, which is a form of divination using stones. I think there is enough of a resonance within the sapphire to at least give me some idea as to who might have owned it. Whether I can pull current location information from it might well depend on how long they have owned it. I will need your help, however."

I nodded. "Just tell us what to do."

"Reaper, please sit between myself and your charge."

Azriel obeyed without comment. She placed the cuff link on a small velvet cushion sitting in the middle of the table, then sprinkled it with sage, which I knew from Ilianna was used for cleansing or purifying. Adeline slid her chair back slightly, opened a drawer, and produced a small crystal ball. This one, unlike most, had a small indent in its base, and it was this section she placed over the cuff link.

"Now," she said, her voice brisk and business-like. "This will work along similar lines as a séance, only instead of spirits we will be seeking to connect to the essence of whoever owns this piece. As I said, what we see in the crystal will very much depend on how long the stone has been in the possession of its owner."

"So we join hands and chant?"

"Join hands, yes. Chant, no. I just need you two to focus on the cuff link. I will channel our energy into drawing whatever the sapphire holds into the crystal so that you might see it." She hesitated. "I cannot guarantee we will see anything, however. Lithomancy is generally used to 'see' the past, clarify the present, or predict the future. It is rarely used for what we are about to attempt."

I nodded. She held out her hands, palms up. I placed one hand in hers, the other in Azriel's. Her skin was warm against mine, and far softer than Azriel's more calloused grip—naturally enough, given one was an earthbound witch and the other a gray-fields warrior. Adeline closed her eyes. After a few moments, energy began to rise, a heartbeat that seemed to fill the silence. As it grew stronger, the small crystal began to cloud over. It cleared again after a few moments, revealing a small, book-filled room. A study of some kind. The view shifted, and revealed the back of a woman. She was thickset, with almost manly shoulders and short colorless hair. It wasn't white, wasn't gray, wasn't anything, really. It reminded me somewhat of an unwashed canvas, waiting for the arrival of paint.

A sorceress in her true form, perhaps? Azriel commented softly.

Perhaps.

The image shifted again. This time we got a side view of her; she had a large, almost regal-looking nose and thin lips framed by deep lines. Not someone who smiled very often. It wasn't, however, Lauren. Or not as we knew her, anyway.

She rose and walked across the room. Our viewpoint followed her. She gathered several armloads of papers and returned, dropping them all in a suitcase and closing it. She left the room, but moments later returned, carrying another case.

She was packing up.

Which meant if we didn't get there soon, we'd lose her. And yet there wasn't enough information coming through the crystal to give an indication of *where* this was all happening.

The woman moved across the room again, her stout fingers brushing the edges of a framed painting. After a moment, the painting slid aside and revealed a wall safe. She opened this and took out four small items—three daggers and a broken bayonet.

Excitement surged through me, but it was tempered by panic. I had no doubt one of those things was the key to the second gate, and if she had it narrowed down to the four of them, then it wouldn't take her very long to find the correct one.

Damn it, we were so close! All we needed was the where and the who . . .

. We didn't get it. The clouds closed over the image, then faded away. It was all I could do not to scream in frustration.

Adeline sighed and pulled her hands from ours. "I'm sorry, but that's all I could get. As I said, this is not the usual way I use lithomancy."

"Thanks for trying, Adeline. At least we know she's out there." To Azriel, I added, *Could you transport us to that study?*

No. There wasn't enough information. All we saw were bookcases and a safe. It could be anywhere.

I slumped back in my chair and wearily rubbed my eyes. Damn it, why couldn't things just go our way for a change? "How are we going to find the location of that place?"

"You could always try astrally."

I frowned. "How could that help?"

"Well, for astral travel, you simply imagine where you want to be. It's not the actual address that matters."

I abruptly sat up. "Of *course*." I could transport myself to that study, and from there, gather enough information for Azriel to take us there.

"It would be best, however," Adeline continued, "if you did it here, where I can keep an eye on events and intervene if need be."

Which Azriel could not, if something happened. It certainly made sense, but I still asked, "Why? I mean, it's not like she could sense my astral presence, is it?"

"Many witches can, and you've already mentioned the possibility that this woman is a dark sorceress. And while you should be safe enough from any form of magical attack originating from this plane, if she *is* a dark sorceress, it would not be beyond her skill to mount an attack astrally."

"Which I have no doubt she would do if she in any way suspected my presence."

She'd certainly shown a propensity to cover her bases and attack so far. And while I might be doing little more than scooting out of that room to see where she was located, there was no way in hell I was going to risk getting attacked, astrally or otherwise. Been there, done that, and had no desire to do it again.

I added, "Are you available to try this right now?"

"I left the day free," she said with a smile. "I expected you might be needing additional help."

"I don't know how I can ever thank you, Adeline."

She waved the comment away and rose. "Stop these idiots, and that will be thanks enough."

"That we can do."

She nodded. "Let's go, then. I suspect we don't have much time, given she appeared to be packing up."

I took off my shoes and padded after her. The room on the opposite side of the hall smelled faintly of lavender and chamomile, and my feet sank into a thick layer of mats and silk that covered the entire floor area.

"Lie down and make yourself comfortable," Adeline said. "Do you need guidance?"

"No, I've stepped onto the plane a few times since I was last here."

"Then I shall simply monitor." She sat cross-legged near the door, her hands folded neatly in her lap.

I glanced at Azriel, who stood guard near the closed door—more for reassurance than anything else—then released a long, slow breath and imagined the tension within flowing out with it. Then I followed the routine Adeline had taught me. Within minutes I was not only on the astral plane but in the place we'd seen in the crystal. The woman was still in the study, although all four items from the safe were now neatly bubble wrapped and packed in the second case. Part of me wanted to move closer to the items, just to see if I was able to pick up any sort of vibration that would tell me which one was the actual key, but I resisted the temptation. I had no idea whether this woman would sense my astral presence or, if the key *did* react, whether she'd be able to sense *that*.

The last thing I needed right now was to give her any more of a head start than she already had.

Instead, I imagined myself standing outside the building that housed this room, but just as I did, the woman abruptly straightened. I hoped like

hell she hadn't sensed me—that she'd just finished her packing—but I couldn't be certain, because the astral plane whisked me outside. The
study was housed in a two-story brown brick warehouse that had been converted to a living accom-
modation. Unlike ours, however, this one—if the
buzzers near the entrance were anything to go
by—had more than one apartment within its four
walls. Which wasn't a whole lot of help given we
could hardly go knocking on every door to find
the right one.

I tried again, this time imagining myself standing outside the front door of the apartment that
housed that study and, with very little sense of
movement, I was suddenly in front of a very upmarket wooden and glass door. HARRIET MONTER-
REY, APARTMENT 1B, the little sign under the buzzer
read.

Which was all I needed.

I imagined myself back in my body, and scrambled to my feet the minute I was. The room spun
abruptly around me, and if not for the fact that
Azriel grabbed my arm to steady me, I would
have fallen.

"Whoa," I muttered. "Did that way too fast, obviously."

"Obviously," Adeline said, voice dry. "But were
you successful?"

"Yes, and I'm sorry, but we have to run. Thanks
for the help and the coffee."

She smiled. "You're welcome to both, but perhaps when this is all over, you can actually stay and chat."

"When this is all over, consider it a date." It was the least I could do, after all. I glanced at Azriel. "You know where we're going?"

"I have picked the necessary information from your memories, yes."

I smiled. At least mind sharing sometimes saved the necessity of words. "She's on the move, and she may have sensed me."

"Then we go in ready to fight. Draw your sword."

I did so, then stepped into his embrace. A second later we were in the study we'd seen in the crystal.

The woman and the cases were gone.

She had, however, left something behind for us—demons.

There were half a dozen in all, insubstantial wisps that were all teeth and claws. The bigger brothers and sisters of the Ania, I suspected.

Two of them came straight at me. I backpedaled fast and raised Amaya, sweeping her from left to right. She hissed, her flames splattering across the floorboards as her sharp point tore through one of the approaching creatures. The demon moaned—a sound abruptly cut off as its remaining fragments were swept up in Amaya's trailing fire and burned to a crisp.

The second creature swept around to my right, attempting to attack from behind. I spun, and was confronted by the sight of a fistful of wickedly barbed teeth coming straight at my face. I swore and dropped. The demon whooshed over my head, the breeze of its passing strong enough that my hair was tugged after it. I twisted around, saw the creature's wispy form spreading like a sail as it tried to break and turn, and I thrust upward with Amaya, twisting her steel into the creature's tail. It screamed, the sound one of fury, then swung and bit her blade. There was enough force in the attack that her steel vibrated, and I'm not sure who was more surprised—me or Amaya. Then she made a sound suspiciously like a chuckle and her flames flared, wrapping around the creature, capturing it tight as she slowly—almost lovingly—consumed it.

I shuddered—although you'd think I'd be used to my sword's bloodthirsty bent by now—and looked past her. Azriel stabbed Valdis through the heart of a creature, literally exploding it, then swung around. His fierce expression became one of relief as his gaze met mine. Then he turned and ran, leaving me flatfooted with surprise. I swore and galloped after him, catching a brief glimpse of his disappearing butt as he dived through a doorway farther down the hall.

I was three steps away from repeating the procedure when the goddamn room exploded.

Chapter 12

Air hit with the force of a hammer and sent me tumbling backward. Wood, plaster, and dust rained all around me, and I threw my hands over my head in an effort to protect myself.

Amaya screamed in fury as her flames erupted to form a protective cocoon around my body. And none too soon, because it wasn't just wood and plaster coming down, but concrete tiles. The fucking roof had collapsed.

Not that it mattered. Nothing mattered right now, except the reaper who had gone into that room a heartbeat before it exploded.

Azriel! Desperation filled my mental scream. *Are you okay?*

For several seconds there was no reply, and my fear skyrocketed. Then he said, his mind voice somewhat groggy, *Yes. Valdis shielded me from the worst of it.*

What the hell were you trying to do? I pushed into a sitting position. Several large sections of wood rolled off Amaya's shield and dropped onto the top of the mess that surrounded us. There wasn't much left of the hallway—just several skeletal wooden frames bereft of plaster. Wires dangled from the ceiling, and I fervently hoped they were not going to attack me the minute I moved. Water was spraying from broken fire sprinklers, dampening down the worst of the dust, and somewhere in the distance alarms were ringing. The fire brigade and police would undoubtedly be here soon.

I was attempting to catch that sorcerer before she escaped. His voice was clipped. Angry at himself for not succeeding, I suspected.

So why didn't you zap yourself to that room instead of running?

Because, as I have said, I cannot zap myself into unknown places without having at least some point of reference. When I was a reaper, it was the resonance of the soul, but in this case, I could not get a fix on her.

I frowned and rose. Amaya's shield pulsated around me, moving as I did. *Why couldn't you get a grip on her resonance?*

Because it was shifting.

Meaning she was?

I suspect so.

At the far end of the hall, a pile of timber and tiles began to move, sliding away as flames began to pulsate through the pile. A second later, Azriel appeared, surround by a halo of blue fire. It faded as he turned, his gaze searching the ruins and stopping when it met mine. Blood oozed from a wound near his temple, but other than that, he appeared unhurt.

"I guess from all this"—I waved a hand at the mess around us—"that she sensed me."

"She might be powerful enough to summon demons at a moment's notice, but the explosion would have taken longer to set up." He stepped over a pile of broken plaster and tiles and walked toward me. "There was a transport gate in that room. I saw her step through, and had a brief glimpse of shadows and stone before the explosion."

"She's heading for hell's gate." My voice was grim.

"Undoubtedly—though the gate she just escaped through would not get her onto the gray fields. It was nowhere near powerful enough." His voice held little emotion, but his fury and frustration echoed through me, as sharp as my own. "But she knows we're close now, so I have no doubt she is headed to the gate that *will*. She would not want to risk us reclaiming the key before she has a chance to use it."

"And if she does use it and the Raziq are waiting, the key is theirs." I thrust a hand through my hair. "Fuck!"

"Yes," Azriel said. "Our best chance now lies in finding her access onto the fields."

"And how the fuck are we supposed to do that? There was nothing useful in either of the goddamn warehouses!" Nothing we could access without a lot of time and effort—the first of which we were running dangerously low on.

"We cannot be sure of that because we have not explored the entirety of the larger warehouse. Remember, there was a second pathway you did not explore."

"Then I guess we have no choice but to go there now and do just that." Only my skin crawled at the thought of doing it alone. That section of the tunnel had felt *nasty*. Besides, it was more than likely where the hellhounds had come from, and I certainly didn't feel like facing more of them alone.

"Perhaps it is time to call in your uncle—" He stopped abruptly and spun, Valdis blazing brightly in his hand. "I sense your presence, Yeska."

"Only because I intended it, Mijai." Amusement, and perhaps more than a little contempt, was evident in the Raziq's voice. "You would otherwise be dead."

"You overestimate your skill yet again." Azriel's voice was even despite the tension so evident in his stance and in the flow of his energy through my mind.

"I overestimate nothing, Mijai. But I am not here to harm you." He hesitated, and though he had no physical form, it was not hard to imagine a particularly nasty smile as he added, "Not at this present time."

Azriel didn't reply. He didn't need to when Valdis burned black and her desire to kill was so fierce the air was thick with it.

"Look," I said quickly, sensing it wouldn't take much for either being to attack the other right now. "As charming as this little catch-up moment is, the bitch with the keys might now be readying to open the second gate."

Yeska's attention turned to me—something I felt rather than saw. It hit like a punch in the gut, leaving me feeling a little breathless. "If the sorcerer steps onto the fields, then he or she will be stopped."

"You have found the location of her gate?" Azriel asked, before I could.

"On the fields side, yes. We have the location under surveillance."

Meaning she hadn't *yet* tried to access the fields. We still had time to stop her. "And are you going to share the coordinates or are you intending to keep the information all to yourselves?"

"I am here, am I not?"

"Then give us the grid reference, or face the consequences," Azriel all but growled.

Yeska snorted. "You would not overstep your precious rules, Mijai, and we both know it."

"I would not be so sure of that—"

"Guys," I cut in again. "How about we drop the machismo and just concentrate on the keys? You can rattle each other's chains all you want once we catch this bitch, but let's just first catch her."

"Indeed, let's." There was amusement in his tone. For supposedly unemotional beings, the Raziq—and Aedh in general—seemed to be full of emotion.

"The location of the gate is at -37.7925000, 144.98635. And remember, if you find this sorcerer first—"

"I've got to give you the keys or you'll kill my friends' present and future lives," I cut in wearily. "I know, and trust me, I *am* trying to get the key."

"Then try harder," he replied equably, and disappeared.

"That conversation would have been so much more pleasant had he made the slightest threat toward you," Azriel mused, sheaving a still blazing Valdis.

"Only because it would have enabled you to kill the bastard."

"Yes. Yeska's time is long overdue."

"Well, you can blame your people for his presence here. You could have done something when you first held him for questioning."

"With the advantage of hindsight, that is obvious." He turned. "I suspect those coordinates will take us to the warehouse near Stane's. Let us hope Rozelle and her friends have been able to break through that shield."

Otherwise I'd be entering that damn place alone. Again. "It's probably better to check the location on a computer first, just so we have some idea what to expect. And while we're home, I can fix that cut on your head."

He smiled. "It will heal soon enough."

"Yeah, but humor me anyway."

His smile grew. "I have heard it said it is unwise to argue with a pregnant woman."

"I'm betting that'll happen only when it suits you."

"A statement I am about to prove. We have not the time to delay. Even now the sorceress could be at the gate, invoking the magic that will lead her into the grasp of the Raziq."

He was right, damn it. I got out my phone, typed the coordinates into Google maps, and a second later we had our result. It was the location of the warehouse near Stane's.

Two seconds after that, we were once again standing in front of the building. Rozelle spun as we appeared, one hand going to her chest. "You could give some warning before you pop in like that," she muttered. "It's enough to scare ten years' growth out of a person."

"We did not mean to scare you," Azriel said.

"Under normal circumstances you wouldn't, but in a place like this, when we're dealing with a spell like this, then, yeah, arrival announcements are definitely appreciated."

I glanced past her, and studied the three women sitting cross-legged within a protection circle drawn in chalk in the loading bay's concrete driveway.

Sweat beaded their skins and their expressions were intent.

"How is it going?"

"We're close." She glanced at Azriel. "Actually, you couldn't have timed it better. We need to weave an echo of your energy into our threading spell so that you can cross through it unimpeded."

"What do you wish me to do?" he asked.

"Take my hand."

He did so. One of the women in the circle raised a hand; Rozelle clasped it, her fingers glowing slightly as she breached the barrier of the protective circle. For several seconds nothing appeared to happen; then the air began to hum with energy and electricity began to dance from Rozelle to Azriel and back again, forming a circle that looped around and around for several minutes. Then it faded.

Rozelle sighed and released Azriel's hand. "Just a few more seconds, and we should be finished."

I nodded but couldn't keep still, and began to pace instead. Azriel merely crossed his arms and watched the witches impassively. I wished I had half of his calm. Right now, my stomach was so full of knots it was getting painful.

Then the witches in the circle sighed and rose. The oldest of the three stepped from the circle and stopped beside Rozelle.

"It has been completed," she said, her voice etched with weariness. "The reaper's energy has been woven into the spell surrounding this building. He may move about within freely, but must keep to flesh."

"Thank you," I said. "We appreciate—"

"Stop this person," she cut in. "And that will be thanks enough."

"We plan to."

"Good." She waved a hand toward the broken roller door. "You should enter and exit from that point. It was the weakest section of the spell, and therefore the easiest place to create our doorway."

Azriel pressed two fingers against my spine, ushering me forward. I crawled into the loading bay yet again, then rose, dusting the dirt off my jeans as I scanned the area. Nothing had changed, and I couldn't smell the shifter's presence.

I glanced around as Azriel climbed to his feet. "The only way we can get into the tunnels is via that pit Jak and I fell into."

"Given I must retain human form while in this building, our only option is to fall into it once again."

"Or we could grab something heavy, and spring the trap first."

"That would also work." He paused. "There were chair remnants in the room next door, were there not?"

"Yes."

"Then I will retrieve them."

We headed up the stairs. Magic crawled across

my fingertips as I opened the door to the pit room, its touch stronger and dirtier than before. Either I was becoming more sensitive to magic, or it had changed somehow.

Azriel appeared with the chair remains. I stepped aside, giving him room, and watched as he tossed them into the middle of the dark room. For a second, nothing happened. Then, with a crack, the entire floor dropped. As it hit the cavern floor far below, dust bloomed, making me sneeze.

Azriel drew his sword and squatted near the edge of the hole. Valdis's flames fanned out, lifting the darkness and revealing the all too familiar pit. It was about ten feet square and smelled of earth and age. But there was something there this time that hadn't been there the last—wooden stakes.

An over-the-top response to our previous intrusion into the place, no doubt.

"The bitch is getting nasty," I muttered.

"She has always been nasty," Azriel commented. "But I believe she is becoming desperate."

"And desperate people make mistakes." Or so the saying went. There didn't seem to be much evidence of it so far. My gaze swept the floor. The stakes had been set in a semicircle that covered the area immediately below the doorway—the place where most people would fall. The other half of the small pit was unencumbered by any additional security measures. Nothing that was so blatantly obvious, anyway.

"Can you jump that far?" Azriel asked.

I nodded. "Just be there to stop me falling back onto the stakes."

He nodded and rose. After sheaving Valdis, he took several steps back, then ran at the pit and leapt. I watch, heart in mouth, as he dropped down, hit the dirt, and rolled well clear of the stakes.

He rose, dusted off his hands, then glanced up. "Your turn."

I pushed upright, and tried to ignore the twisting in my stomach as I backed away from the pit. I took a deep, steadying breath, then ran and leapt. I cleared the stakes by several feet, hit the dirt hard, and rolled a little too fast and far. It was only thanks to the fact that Azriel grabbed my arm and yanked me to an abrupt halt that I didn't smack headfirst into the pit's wall.

"Thanks." I climbed to my feet and rotated my shoulder to ease the ache. "The concealed entrance to the tunnels is over here."

I drew Amaya and walked across to the wall where she'd found the exit for us last time. Flames flickered down her dark steel, sparking brightly off the quartz that lay embedded in the pit's walls. I ran the tip of her blade along the wall until she hit the exit and disappeared.

"Let me enter first," Azriel said.

"For once, I am not about to argue." I stepped back. "The hellhounds, if there are any, are all yours."

"That is very sensible of you."

I smiled. "I can be, when I want to be."

"So it would seem."

He pushed through the barrier and disappeared. I followed, sword first. As before, it felt like I was walking through molasses—the magic creating the illusion of a solid wall was thick, syrupy, and unclean. I shuddered, my skin crawling with horror as it clung like tendrils to my body, resisting my movements for several seconds before abruptly releasing me into the tunnel. It was a tight fit—there was little more than an inch between my shoulders and the tunnel's walls. Azriel, several inches taller than I am, not only had to stoop but stand slightly sideways.

"Which way?" Valdis was ablaze in his hand, and her fire lent the dark stones around us a bluish glow.

"The transport stones Jak and I found were to the right, so we need to head left." I eyed that end of the tunnel warily. The last time I'd been here, I'd had a sense of something waiting down that end, something that was inherently evil. Given the hellhounds had more than likely come from that direction, my senses had been right. While I wasn't getting a similar sensation right now, something still didn't feel right.

"No," Azriel agreed. "There is magic down there. Dark magic."

My gaze shot to his. "As in demons lying in wait to munch us up, or something else?"

He half smiled. "Something else. And demons hardly munch. They rend and tear, or swallow whole."

"Oh, that's *so* comforting," I muttered, and lightly pushed him forward. "After you."

With the twin blazes of the two swords lighting the way, we crept forward. The tunnel continued to narrow, forcing me to go sideways. Azriel, already sideways, was in worse shape, the rocks and debris in the soil tearing across his shoulders and back. The scent of blood stung the air, an aroma that would call to any demons who might wait ahead.

"They don't," he commented. "Whatever magic lies ahead, it has not the feel of either hell's creatures or something living."

"Meaning the sorceress isn't here."

"Or that she's already gone through the gate, if that is the magic we sense."

"If she's gone through, the Raziq would have her."

"If they did, I daresay we would know."

I frowned. "How? It's not like we're in constant contact with them."

"No." He paused, squeezed through a particularly nasty narrow section, scraping both his back and his chest in the process. "But Yeska would inform us. He has a predilection for flaunting his victories."

I snorted. "The more I learn about the Aedh, the

more their reputation for being unemotional beings bites the dust."

"They *are* unemotional, at least in the sense that
humans view emotions. Love, desire, caring—
they are unnecessary states in the minds of the
Aedh. Hence the reason they do not live in family
units."

"So how come they developed a completely different mind-set to the reapers? I mean, you're both
energy beings, so I would think you'd both have a
similar evolution."

"Just because one comes from the same source
does not mean evolution will follow a similar path."

"True enough."

It was my turn to squeeze past the tight spot.
The stones that had torn into Azriel's back now
tore into mine. I winced and tried sucking in my
gut in the vague hope it would also suck in my
breasts, with little success. Thankfully, my sweater
bore the brunt of the damage, the stones snagging
the fleece and tearing several large holes into it. I
guess I should be thankful I wasn't overly en-
dowed in that area, because the damage would
have no doubt involved a lot more skin.

The tunnel continued to narrow, making me
wonder if anyone else but hellhounds actually
used this. The Razan Jak and I had seen in the
other tunnel certainly hadn't been thin, and yet
he'd had none of the scrapes on his body that we
seemed to be collecting. Maybe he'd been using a

special oil or something that allowed him to slip through.

"The end is nigh," Azriel said, after a few more minutes.

"I hope you're talking about the tunnel and not anything else," I muttered, and yelped as a particularly nasty stone caught my left breast. I rose on my tiptoes, squeezing past it without damaging my other breast, then sighed in relief as the tunnel immediately widened.

We finally came out into a cavern that had been hacked out of the stone and earth by something *other* than nature itself. The floor was mainly stone, and in the middle of it stood two massive stones. They were more than eight feet tall and a good four feet in diameter at their base, but rising to an almost needlelike point at the top. Unlike the stones we'd discovered in the other tunnel, which were mostly gray, these two glowed as brightly as a harvest moon. The flames of the two swords sparked the quartz within the stones to life, and sent rainbow-colored flurries across the earthen walls. These stones, like the others, were etched with symbols and markings. It was a form of cuneiform, and an ancient and powerful language that people from a long dead civilization had once used to call the Aedh to Earth.

My gaze swept the cavern's floor. Surprisingly, these stones weren't guarded. Not by a protection circle, at any rate.

"Perhaps not," Azriel said, "but there is some form of magic active here."

He took a cautious step forward. Energy trembled across my skin, its touch light and yet oddly distasteful. "Azriel—"

"I know." He raised a hand. Sullen orange sparks danced across his outstretched fingertips as he moved to the left, feeling out the barrier's dimensions. Predictably, it ringed the two stones completely. "I cannot feel any sort of break in it."

I crossed my arms. "Unsurprising given neither of us knows much about magic. Do you think she's already been here?"

He stopped beside me. "No. There is no lingering resonance in the air, and there surely would have been had these stones—positioned as they are on a major ley-line intersection—been used."

I frowned. "So where the hell is she? I mean, she has to know we're onto her now. You'd think her first port of call would be these stones and the gray fields. Surely she'd want that gate opened before we could stop her."

"That is presuming, of course, she has created only one gate."

I glanced at him sharply. "What makes you think she'd have more than one gateway?"

"Because, in many respects, it would make sense to do so." He cupped my elbow and tugged me over to the far wall, away from the tunnel's entrance and out of the immediate sight of anyone who might enter. Not that, I suspected, he actually expected anyone to enter.

"Why? I mean, creating gates that size"—I waved a hand toward the two stones—"has to take a lot of power, even if it is standing in the middle of a ley-line intersection."

"Yes, but does it not seem odd to you that we found this building very easily? It's not as if a great deal was done to conceal its presence."

I frowned. "Well, it wasn't exactly *easy*. I mean, the paper trail alone was hell—"

"Yes, but if she *really* wanted to hide it, she could have done so magically. Also, neither Ilianna nor the witches could find any great energy output coming from this area."

I sat on my haunches and leaned back against the wall, even though my feet itched with the need to move, to do something *other* than just sit here. "Which was explained by some sort of spell restraining any visible output."

"Perhaps." He half shrugged, but his expression suggested he wasn't buying it. "It also occurs to me that the Aedh"—he paused, his expression suggesting even the mere *thought* of Lucian was distasteful—"was never one to leave anything to chance. His actions in trying to impregnate you, Ilianna, and indeed the sorceress herself were indication enough of that. He would not be foolish enough to rely on only one entrance to the fields."

Especially when he'd had centuries to plot every little detail of his revenge on both the Raziq and my father. "Yeah, but I thought gateways were straight-line things. You know, point A to point B with no offshoots or detours. And there's only one gate here."

"Yes, but a ley-line intersection holds enough power to create more than one gateway into the gray fields, so why would they not do so? The Aedh undoubtedly knew enough about magic to siphon the intersection's energy down lesser lines. I cannot believe he would not have done so, especially given he knew—at least from the moment he became involved with you—that both your father and the Raziq were well aware of his presence."

"And doing fucking nothing about it," I muttered.

"They did not see him as a threat. In their eyes, he was lesser than he was, and therefore unimportant."

And that lack of foresight had cost them—and us—the first key and might yet cost us the second.

Although to be fair, Azriel, at least, had seen Lucian's true colors from the very beginning.

"If there's more than one gateway, surely the Raziq would be watching both," I said. "They want to stop this bitch—or bastard, depending on which form she's wearing—as much as we do."

"But what if the sorceress's gray fields gateway is in the one place no one would ever think to look?"

"But there's nowhere—" I paused, suddenly realizing what he was implying. "Surely even Lucian wouldn't be *that* devious."

"Why not? Are not the quarters he shared with your father as his chrání the perfect position for such a gateway? Your father cannot enter the temples without alerting the Raziq to his presence, and the Raziq cannot enter your father's rooms. Nor would they even *think* to look there, given they do not think the Aedh a threat."

"I wonder if *that's* the reason he left the coordinates of that warehouse. It wasn't so much the coordinates here on Earth that mattered, but the positioning on the fields."

"It is possible, although that would mean there is a gateway somewhere in that warehouse."

I jumped up. "We'd better go investigate—"

He caught my hand. "It would be useless to do so because we have not the means to get in or out of your father's rooms."

I frowned. "But if we find the gateway, it will take us into them."

"Yes, but the private residences of the Aedh within the temple areas are all shielded. You cannot get in *or* out without the correct means of doing so."

"Fuck it, why can't something be *simple* in this damn quest?"

"Because that is not the way of your world or mine." His voice held a slightly bitter edge. "However, your father said he was creating a means by which you could freely access his rooms. Perhaps you should check if anything has been left at your home while we were away."

"*That* means going back through the damn tunnel. And risking the sorcerer coming here when we're gone."

"That is a risk, yes."

Great. Damned if we did, and damned if we didn't. I bit my lip, then half shrugged. "I guess we just have to take the chance."

"We are right in this, Risa. I'm sure of it."

I wasn't, especially given lady luck hadn't been all that generous to us to date. Still, what else could we do? It was either stay here—and risk losing her—or chase down our theory and hope like hell we were right. And at least with the latter, we were actually *doing* something.

Even if it ultimately proved to be the *wrong* something.

We made our way back through the tunnel. Progress was slow, and the delay ate at my nerves. The longer we were stuck here, the more chance there was of the bitch escaping us.

Although if Azriel's theory was right, there was a good chance she already *had*. Our only hope lay in the fact that she hadn't yet figured out which of the four items she'd stashed in her case was the key in disguise.

We finally reached the pit. I stood near the outer

ring of stakes and glared up at the floor high above us.

"I may be part werewolf, but even I can't leap that far."

"I'll boost you."

I raised an eyebrow as I glanced at him. "And how are you going to get up?"

"I'll jump. You'll catch me."

"You're putting a hell of a lot of faith in my catching skills."

"Because I figure you would not want the father of your child staked." He cupped his hands. "Up you go."

I stepped into his hands and, with a grunt of effort, he flung me high. I grabbed at the ragged ends of the pit and hauled myself onto solid ground, then hooked my feet on either side of the doorframe and leaned back over the hole.

"Okay, go for it."

He leapt up. A heartbeat later his outstretched hands were in mine. I gripped them fiercely, but his weight hit like a ton of bricks and just about ripped my arms from their sockets. I hissed in pain but slowly inched backward, drawing him with me. After a few seconds, he released one hand, caught the edge of the pit, and drew himself up beside me.

I rolled onto my back, breathed a sigh of relief, then scrambled upright. With the shield still in place, neither of us could shift to energy form within the building, so the sooner we got out, the better. I jumped over the loading bay railing, landed neatly, then ran for the gap in the door. Azriel followed me out, and a heartbeat later, we were standing in the burned-out remnants of my living room. I spun around, scanning the room, but couldn't see anything different. And the front door still appeared locked. Which meant either my father hadn't yet delivered on his promise, or it was sitting outside. I strode across the room, unlatched the door, then stepped out onto the metal landing to check. And there, tucked into the corner shadows of the top step, was a small brown box.

"Found something!"

Azriel appeared beside me as I opened the box. Inside were two black cords twined with a silverish thread that had an almost ghostly glow about it, and a note. I quickly unfolded it.

The cord will allow both entry into the temple's inner sanctum and the rooms I shared with the chráni, it said. *There is a second for the reaper, as you should not access the temples without his guidance. It is a dangerous place.*

I glanced at Azriel. "Why would the temples be dangerous?"

"Because while the priests no longer physically guard the gates, there are . . . remnants . . . left behind."

My eyebrows rose. "Remnants?"

He nodded. "They are not ghosts, as such. More echoes of the beings they once were."

"So when Aedh die, their energy doesn't return to the stars like the reapers?"

"They do, but the Aedh priests have sworn an oath to protect the gates, so remnants of their beings remain."

"I wouldn't have thought echoes of beings would be all that dangerous."

"You have not yet encountered the echoes of the priests." His voice was grim. "Trust me, if they decide you are an intruder, they can cause great harm."

"Then let's hope we don't encounter them." And that the sorceress *did*. I glanced down and read the rest of the note. "The third key lies in the southeast, on a palace whose coat of arms lies the wrong way around."

"Which," Azriel said, "apparently means as little to you as the previous clues, if your current expression is anything to go by."

"Yeah." I folded the note and shoved it in the back pocket of my jeans. "But Google helped us find the last one, so maybe it'll help with this. Besides, finding the third key isn't our priority right now. But there *is* another problem."

Azriel raised an eyebrow. "The Raziq?"

I nodded. "The minute I appear on the gray fields, they're going to know. We need a distraction."

"I could—"

"Not you," I cut in. "My father. He keeps telling me how mighty and powerful he is, so how about we give him a chance to prove it?"

"Neither he nor the Raziq will be fooled for long. As you have noted, they will feel your presence on the field."

"Perhaps, but we can always hope they're too busy fighting each other to immediately do anything about our presence. Besides, what other option have we got?"

"None." His voice was grim. "You had better contact your father quickly, as the sorceress might already be on the fields with the four items."

I spun around and headed for my bedroom to retrieve the communication ward my father had given me. Azriel appeared, a knife he'd found who knows where held in one hand, as I sat cross-legged on the floor and placed the ward in front of me. The rainbow colors within it seemed to run faster, as if it knew what was coming.

"Thanks," I said, accepting the knife. With little ceremony, I jabbed the point into my finger, then, as blood began to well, turned my finger upside down and let the blood drip onto the communication ward. As the droplet hit, the rainbow stopped moving, and everything was still. Silent.

Then light erupted from the center of the stone and briefly blinded me. When I was able to see again, I was encased in a cylinder of white.

"Father, are you out there?"

There was a pause, and then he said, "You have found the second key?"

"Yes, but I need your help to retrieve it."

"I cannot interact with your world—it is the reason you were bred."

I snorted softly. Nice to know the only reason I existed was because my father had a feeling he'd need an extra pair of hands here on Earth. "The problem isn't here on Earth. It's on the gray fields."

"Explain."

"We suspect the sorceress has two gateways onto the fields. The Raziq currently guard one. The other, however, is in your rooms—"

"Impossible. No one can get into my temple residences without the proper—"

"Lucian could," I cut in. "And he was working with the sorcerers."

"He would not—"

"You keep saying that," I interrupted again. "Trouble is, time and again he was doing *exactly* what you said he shouldn't or wouldn't be."

Annoyance swirled around me, thick and heavy. But all he said was, "What is it that you want?"

"The location of the gate the Raziq guard is -37.7925000, 144.98635. We need you to provide some sort of distraction."

"Such as?"

"I don't know, and I don't particularly care.

Hell, you can take the bastards out for all I care. You keep saying you're far more powerful than either Malin or her people will ever be, so how about proving it?"

"That is a truth not even she would deny."

There was no conceit in my father's voice, no hint of boasting in his words. He merely stated a fact as he saw it. I dare say Malin held the exact same opinion about *her* prowess. Aedh, from what I'd seen, certainly weren't backward about admitting their strengths. Their weaknesses were a different matter entirely—in fact, most seemed to think they didn't actually *have* any.

"Whatever you decide to do, I just need them kept occupied while we go to the second gate and try to capture the sorceress."

"And the key."

"That goes without saying." Whether *he* got it was another matter entirely. I'd sure as hell be making sure Mirri was safe before I handed the key over to *anyone*.

"When do you wish this to happen?"

"Now."

"I shall see what I can do."

It was on my tongue to snap, "You'd better do your best," but I restrained the urge. There was no point in antagonizing him when Mirri's life still lay in his hands.

"I'd appreciate you hurrying. The Raziq are going to know the minute I step onto the fields."

"They will be too busy saving their puny lives to worry about your presence."

And with that, the white light died and I found myself blinking furiously against tears as I stared at Azriel.

"You were successful?" he said.

"I think so." I pushed upright. "Do we head over to that other warehouse now, and try to find the other gate?"

"There is no need. I can transport us to the co-ordinates the Aedh left us once you are on the fields."

I frowned. "I thought you said you could only transport to a place you have some physical point of reference to, likc a soul?"

"Here on Earth, not on the fields."

"Ah. Good." I hesitated, then added, "I take it you can't transport me onto the fields themselves?"

"No. If I were a reaper, I could guide your soul upon death, but that is not what we desire to happen anytime soon."

I half smiled. "Been there once, and I'm in no hurry for a repeat." I climbed onto the bed, made myself comfortable, then added, "What about the other Mijai? Will they be able to help us at all?"

He hesitated. "In the inner reaches of the temples, no."

"What about if the sorceress reaches the gates? There are Mijai stationed there, aren't there?"

"There is currently only one, as breaches have fallen over the last few hours. But if our sorceress gets that far, more will be called. They will aid us to stop her."

So at least we weren't going to be entirely alone. Which was a damn good thing if the Raziq happened to appear. They certainly weren't going to be pleased the moment they realized I'd deceived them.

I hesitated, then asked, curious, "How will they react to my presence on the field?"

He shrugged. "You may or may not see them, depending on whether they decide to acknowledge your presence."

Charming. "I'll see you on the field in a few minutes."

He nodded and disappeared. I closed my eyes and took a deep breath. As I slowly released it, I released awareness of everything around me, concentrating on nothing more than the slowing beat of my heart and freeing my psyche, my soul, or whatever else people like to call it from the constraints of my flesh. It was similar, yet very different, to stepping onto the astral plane, mainly because the plane was of *this* world and the gray fields were not. On the fields, the real world was little more than a shadow, a place where those things that could not be seen on the living plane became visible. It was also the land between life and death, a place through which souls journeyed to whatever gateway was their next destination, be it heaven or hell.

As the awareness of my world began to fade, warmth throbbed at my neck—Ilianna's magic at work, protecting me as my psyche pulled free from my flesh and stepped onto the gray fields.

The Dušan immediately exploded from my arm, her energy flowing through me, around me, as her lilac form gained flesh and shape, until she looked so solid and real that I wanted to reach out and touch her. She swirled around me, the wind of her body buffeting mine as her sharp ebony gaze scanned the fields around us. Looking for trouble. I wondered if she actually sensed it, or if she merely reacted to the growing knot of tension in the pit of my stomach.

I looked around for Azriel, and spotted him easily enough. He was a blaze of sunlight in this ghostly otherworld, a force whose very presence throbbed through my body. As if he, like the Dušan and Amaya, were a part of me. And I guess, given what he'd done, he now was.

He stopped in front of me and held out a hand. Though in this place we were both energy rather than flesh, when I placed my hand in his, it felt real and warm.

Just because we wear no flesh doesn't make us any less real. His mental tone was gently chiding. *Let's go to your father's chambers and see if our sorceress is there.*

I'd barely nodded when the fields blurred, and suddenly we were standing in a place that was ghostly and surreal. A place filled with impossible shapes, high soaring arches, and honeycombed domes sitting atop floating towers.

I frowned. *This doesn't look like living quarters.*

As you know them, no. But there are divisional walls here; you just can't see them.

He was right, I couldn't. All I could see was the wide expanse of ghostly, glowing buildings. Oddly, the temples appeared far more structurally heavy than the ethereal beauty of the reaper buildings I'd seen, even if their shapes seemed just as far beyond the realms of possibility.

I turned around, my frown deepening. *I can't see any form of transport gate here, nor does it appear as if the sorceress has arrived.* I paused. *And where the hell are the Dušan?*

They are not able to enter this place. They wait in the temple grounds. He paused. *There is energy coming from the right. I suspect our gate might lie there.*

I followed him through the ether, and tried not to get distracted by the otherworldly beauty of everything around us. Azriel swung right, and the buildings disappeared, replaced by a honeycombed tunnel, along which ran various oddly shaped doors. Some glowed, some did not. And from one of them came a strange humming sound.

What's that noise? I reached back for Amaya. She might not be needed, given I had Azriel to protect me, but I certainly felt easier with her in my hand—*not* something I'd ever thought would happen when she and I were first introduced.

It is not of this place, he replied.

Flames flickered down Valdis's sides, and an answering hum came from Amaya. Whatever that noise was, the two swords were anticipating meeting it.

Have you any idea where it's coming from?

From the star-shaped door. He glanced over his shoulder. *There is movement inside. Be ready to fight.*

My grip tightened against Amaya's hilt, and her humming ratcheted up several notches. *Is it our sorceress?*

It is not a reaper or Aedh, so I would think it must be.

So you can't tell from the energy itself?

No. He hesitated. *It has not the feel of anything I've come across before.*

If our theory was right, and both the sorceress and Lucian had been using dark magic to transform their beings into energy so that they could get onto the fields, then it was logical that he wouldn't be able to recognize whoever or whatever waited inside that door. Azriel placed a hand on the odd-shaped door. It reacted to his touch, emitting a warm, nonthreatening light. I briefly wondered how it would have reacted had we not been wearing my father's bracelets. He glanced at me. *Are you ready?*

I nodded and tightened my grip on Amaya. Her humming became a hiss of expectant fury, the noise jarring against the silence that surrounded us.

He pushed the door open and stepped through. I quickly followed, Amaya raised and my gaze scanning the surrounds. The room was large and circular in shape, with ghostly honeycombed walls defining its area. There was no furniture or adornments—or nothing that I recognized as such—nor did there appear to be anyone here.

But there was some*thing* here.

I may not have been able to see it, but I could damn well feel it. It was an uneasiness, a shadow, in a place that was bright and light.

Then that shadow moved, became two, and then three, and I realized what they were.

Dušan.

But these weren't like our Dušan. These were dark and twisted, their beings radiating a wrongness that sickened me to the core.

And they weren't alone.

Chapter 13

The Dušan attacked as one, all teeth, claws, and fury. And behind them rolled a writhing mass of sinuous, sluglike forms that had stalks for eyes and that seemed to bleed a white substance from all over their bodies.

I'd battled *them* on the fields once before. That time, the Raziq had set them on me. This time the source had be our sorceress, but where the hell was she?

Running. Azriel raised Valdis, his voice grim. *There's a door to our right. Go after her. I will deal with these abominations.*

And with that, he dived into the midst of the Dušan, Valdis ablaze and spinning fire through the ether. I did as he ordered and ran to the right of the room. The door was easy enough to find—it was a larger honeycomb shape in a sea of them. I paused long enough to punch it open, and found myself in another long corridor. Ahead, disappearing into the grayness, was a long, thin shadow. Our sorceress. It had to be.

I bolted after her. I had no idea if I was running in the sense that I knew, and I guess it didn't matter as long as I caught the bitch ahead. But it was a weird sensation, being surrounded by honeycombed walls through which other structures were visible, but everywhere was silence. There was no sense of life in this place and no sounds, not even from the battle raging behind me. I hoped like hell that Azriel was okay, that he could cope with three Dušan as well as the slug ball . . .

The thought froze as air hit from behind. I staggered a little, caught my balance, and swung around. The slug mass *hadn't* remained in that room. It was here, chasing me. Fuck!

I sidestepped at the last moment and swung Amaya with all my might. Her blade hit the slugs and stuck hard, just about yanking me off my feet as the mass rolled on, forcing me to run beside it or lose Amaya. She screamed in fury, spitting fire that sizzled and flamed out the minute it struck the oozing sides of the writhing mass. Then I remembered the white muck was glue. I swore again and dug my heels in, pulling back with all my might. She came free with an abruptness that sent me tumbling ass over backward. This world might *seem* ethereal, but it had the same power to wind if you hit it hard enough. Air stirred around me again, a warning I didn't dare ignore. I scrambled to my feet just as a second, smaller mass of slugs swept into the corridor. I swung to face it, but it arced away, avoiding the sweep of the blade. As it rolled past, white mucus exploded from its sides, forming a weblike structure as it spun toward me. I twisted away from it, and it splattered against a section of honeycomb wall, immediately sizzling and smoking. Within seconds, there was little left of either the net *or* the wall.

Obviously, the sorceress had added her own special touches to these slug balls, because the ones the Raziq had sent after me certainly *hadn't* had that effect on the gray fields themselves. And if it could affect the fields like that, what the hell was it going to do to me?

There was no fighting these things; not before, and certainly not now that the sorceress had apparently upped their firepower. Not with just Amaya, anyway. But, unlike last time, I simply couldn't retreat. There was a sorceress to catch and a key to retrieve.

Which left me with running.

And that's exactly what I did. The slug balls were after me with alarming alacrity. Amaya was a fierce storm battering my thoughts, wanting to stand and fight, and frustrated that we weren't.

Later, I promised her. *We need to catch the sorceress first.*

Kill, she muttered. *Feed.*

If we catch her, you can do both.

Faster run, she muttered.

I snorted softly. Like I wasn't *already* running as

fast as I could. The trouble was, even though this world was destined to become mine on my death, it wasn't yet, and the constraints of flesh were affecting me here. I wasn't a particularly fast runner in the real world, despite being part werewolf, and that—unfortunately—translated over to the field.

But at least the promise calmed Amaya's storm. She still wanted to fight, but the promise of blood had quieted her for the moment.

The wind of the approaching slug masses grew stronger. I bit my lip, reaching for greater speed. The slender shadow I chased was no longer in view, so either this corridor turned or she'd already left it.

Door, Amaya said. *Left*.

I flung out my free hand, saw an answering flare of warm light, and threw myself through it. As I hit the ground and rolled, the slug balls went past. I jumped up, pressed a hand against the door to close it, then ran after the shadow.

We were in a wide expanse of what looked like a courtyard. Buildings soared above us, casting no shadows even though they dominated the skyline. Something swooped, and I ducked instinctively. Two forms appeared out of the gray, one that was black and winged, the other lilac and serpentine. The Dušan—mine and Azriel's. Relief slithered through me. The Dušan might have as little luck against the slug mass as me, but at least they'd be able to delay the progress of the things.

Maybe enough for me to catch the bitch ahead, anyway.

From behind us came an odd cracking. I glanced over my shoulder. One section of the honeycombed tunnel was smoking, collapsing. A heartbeat later, the two massed balls rolled through. They didn't even slow, just made a beeline for us.

The Dušan screamed and dove into their midst, sending gray forms scattering as they bit and slashed. Several rolling lumps re-formed out of the main two masses, the smaller ones immediately skirting around the larger two to come after me.

Amaya, flame and encase!

I jumped out of their path and swung Amaya. Purple fire trailed from her blade, hit the two masses, and rolled around them, sizzling and spitting as it encased the sinuous forms in a flaming lilac cage but *didn't* actually touch them. The mass writhed with greater agitation and white muck splattered against the fiery cage. Amaya hissed and the trailing edge of her flames snuffed out, leaving the mass encased together but free. It did a long looping turn and came at me again. I jumped aside, then ran like hell.

The shadow had disappeared around the corner of a building that had an impossibly small base against a wider top, reminding me somewhat of a pyramid turned on its end. As I rounded the corner, the Dušans screamed. I glanced back, saw the Dušans rise from the midst of the two larger masses, their skins dripping with white matter and god knows what else. They twisted in midair, then dove again, teeth wide as they chopped down on gray forms and flung them left and right. They might be stopping the main two masses, but every time they tore them apart, they were creating new, smaller masses. And those smaller masses were coming after me.

I swore, but kept running. There was little else I could do. The sorceress had to be stopped, and it seemed I was the only one who could do it.

God help our worlds, I thought bitterly.

I wasn't gaining on that shadow, but I wasn't losing ground, either. We ran across a vast empty space, but in the distance the vague outline of a structure gradually became visible. It seemed to glow with an odd light—it was neither bright nor warm, and yet it wasn't cold or unwelcoming. But it seemed to draw me forward, as if it were something I *had* to see.

It is the gates that lie ahead.

The voice was male, and it came from everywhere and yet nowhere. It hung on the ethereal air and yet reverberated through my mind. It held no threat, but I sensed it could kill without a moment's hesitation or thought.

My grip tightened on Amaya, and yet—oddly—she didn't react. Whatever—whoever—this being was, my sword had no sense of immediate threat.

Which didn't mean there *wasn't*.

Meaning that light is the gates? If a mind voice could come out croaky with fear, then mine undoubtedly did just that.

Yes. It is what you would call the gates to heaven and hell.

Surprise rippled through me but it was quickly pushed aside by frustration as a small sphere came out of nowhere and charged toward me. I leapt over the top of it, but it flung white goo at me, forcing me to twist in midair to miss it. I landed awkwardly, and felt pain ripple up my leg. But was that even possible when I was energy rather than flesh?

The mass began a long looping turn. I kept an eye on it, and said, *Wait, what do you mean gates? Are they both here? Together?*

Why should they not be? There was an odd sense of amusement in the reply, and it filtered across the gray world in much the same manner as his words did.

Because . . . My reply faded. In all honesty, I couldn't actually think of a reason *why* the gates to heaven and hell wouldn't be together. I guess I'd just imagined the two would always be separate. Instead I asked, *Who are you?*

Who am I? He seemed to ponder the question for a second, then said, *I am of this place. I am all that remains of what we once were.*

You're a priest? The small slug mass had completed its circle and was coming at me again. They were persistent bastards, that was for sure. A Dušan appeared—Azriel's, not mine—and grabbed it with a snap of its teeth, then flung it away. Then it whirled around me, buffeting me forward with the force of its wings. It was almost as if it were telling me to hurry, that they couldn't contain the slug masses for much longer.

But given what Azriel had said, why wasn't the priest doing something about them? If anything was an intruder, it was these fucking things.

Once, yes, the voice replied. *I remain to protect.*

The structure up ahead drew closer, clearer. It consisted of two high, soaring but simple arches that stood side by side, neither one particularly ornate. At least they didn't appear so from this far away.

Well, you're not doing a particularly good job of it, are you?

Up until that point, I'd felt no real malevolence from the remnant that was the priest, but the moment the words were out of my mouth, that changed. The air grew dark and thunderous, and it suddenly seemed like I was teetering on the precipice of an endless pit. And that the priest stood behind me, ready to push.

Amaya's hissing ran through the far reaches of my thoughts, but her noise was muted, wary. It was as if she sensed the being who confronted us was not something she should ever attack or have any hope of beating.

You have no justification—

I haven't? I cut in. Perhaps stupidly, given Azriel's earlier warning about the remnants being able to cause great harm if they decide you're an intruder. *Then why is hell's first portal open? And why the hell have you allowed a sorcerer bearing the second portal key to get so close to opening it?*

There is no one in this place but you and me and the reaper who battles the twisted Dušan within private temple quarters.

No one here? Incredulity filled my mental tones. *What the fuck do you call the shadow who runs ahead of us? And what do you call the things that chase me?*

The heavy sensation of danger briefly lifted, and an odd sense of bafflement ran across the ether surrounding us. *The Dušan battle something, but I cannot sense what.*

I frowned. How was that even possible? He might be a remnant, but he was still of this place, these temples. The sorcerer was not, so how could she disguise not only her presence, but that of her creatures?

And if this priest couldn't sense her presence, what chance would the reapers who guard hell's gate have of seeing her?

The answer, I suspected, was a big fat zero.

There is magic at work, he continued. *Magic that is powerful and dark. It has the taste of hell, and yet this place runs through it.*

This place? What the hell did he mean by that?

And then it twigged. *Lucian.* Maybe he'd not only been teaching the sorceress Aedh magic, but dark magic as well. He'd been trapped on Earth for centuries after all—certainly more than long enough to become proficient at *all* types of magic, be it light or dark.

And maybe *she* was his very last throw of the dice. Maybe, if all else failed, the destruction of the place that had become his prison was part of his ultimate end game. That, and the destruction of the Raziq's grand plans for freedom.

The shadow that was the sorceress ran through the left arch and disappeared. I swore. Time had run out. We had seconds left, if that, to stop her.

Can you stop the intruders hidden within that magic? Or, at the very least, contain them?

Here, yes. At the gates? No.

Naturally. I mean, it wouldn't be that fucking easy now, would it?

Why not? I thought Aedh priests are the guardians of the gates?

I am not what I once was, he said, his voice so heavy it seemed to press down on me. *I can contain the things that chase you, but I am no longer able to enter the portal's sacred space.*

Why not?

Because I will be forced to move on, and this place would be left unprotected.

Are you all that is left?

No, but we are still few.

*Then gather the few and stop the things that chase
me. I'll take care of the sorceress.*

He seemed to contemplate this suggestion, then
said, *Stray not from hell's path, reaperess, or you will
find yourself compelled into a realm that is not your
destiny.*

And with that, the heavy sense of impending
doom abruptly disappeared. A second later, the
two Dušan were circling around me, eyes afire
and skin dripping with the muck and flesh of the
slugs. Thankfully, there was no sign of the slug
masses themselves.

I ran on, pushing for every scrap of speed I was
capable of. The gates soared high above me, otherworldly, but very plain. Which was something
of a disappointment. The gates to hell, at least,
should have been dramatic. Or at least reflected
the hell that awaited the souls who journeyed
through this gateway. Had either of these arches
been on Earth, I wouldn't have given them a second glance. The only decoration was the stone
vines that crept around the soaring pillars. Then I
noted that the arch on the left, which at first glance
looked identical to the other, had tiny thorns
twisting through the leaves. Hell's gate, I presumed.

If there was a Mijai warrior here anywhere, I
couldn't see him.

I ran through the arch and into a different space
entirely. It was light, restful, and filled with a

warmth that was extremely comforting. Not what I'd expected from the antechamber of hell at *all*.

I slowed. For some odd reason, haste didn't seem to be appropriate—or indeed welcome—here. I was several steps in before I realized I was alone. I paused and looked behind me. The Dušan flew in agitated circles, trying to get in but unable to do so. Obviously, whatever force prevented them from getting into the inner sections of the temples also forbid entry here.

Meaning it was just me and Amaya against whatever the sorceress could fling at us.

Cope can, Amaya said. *Kill will*.

I wish I had *half* her confidence. I gripped her tighter, but felt no easier as I moved through the warm light. Sound began to leach through the air as I moved farther into the antechamber. It was a heartbeat, soft and deep. Goose bumps ran across nonexistent flesh. Hell's heart wasn't all that far away.

Which meant the sorceress couldn't be, either.

The golden glow around me darkened slightly, and air tugged at my form, as if trying to hasten my progress. I glanced down. A pathway had appeared beneath me—it was brighter than the fading warmth of the antechamber, yet it seemed to have a darker essence. On either side, what looked like skeletal wisps of hands reached for—but didn't quite touch—me. But it was the wind of their movements that I could feel urging me on.

But given the priest's warning, hurrying was the last thing I could do right now. There was no way in hell—or out of it—I was going to risk falling off the path and into those wispy hands.

I had no doubt that they would guide me straight into the bowels of hell if I did.

The path ran ahead of me, a new section appearing with every step forward. It did a slow looping turn and then, without warning, stopped.

As did I.

Because before me lay gates, and they didn't even *remotely* resemble anything I'd ever imagined the gates to hell would look like. In fact, these delicate creations, enhanced with exquisite depictions of glowing beings, trees, and animals, were so similar to what I'd thought the entrance to heaven might look like that, for a moment, I wondered if I'd somehow taken a wrong path.

Then I saw the snake. It was small, and in one corner, a tiny blot of darkness in an otherwise glowing image. But its eyes seemed to burn with an inhuman awareness, and fear crawled through me. *That* thing was watching. Waiting. Judging.

Gatekeeper, Amaya said. Her thoughts were wary. Respectful. *Fate his.*

As in, he decides which section of hell is to be your particular pleasure?

Not alone. All portals.

I scanned the gate and the immediate surrounds, looking for our sorceress but unable to spot her. But she couldn't have disappeared. She had to be here somewhere. *What happened to the first gatekeeper now that the first portal is open?*

Remains.

I frowned. *But the gate no longer exists.* Or at least, we didn't appear to pass it.

Still there. Not see open.

Huh. I moved forward cautiously. I still couldn't see the sorceress, but maybe I wouldn't. She knew I chased her, after all, and I had no doubt she also knew how to conceal her presence in this place. What I should be searching for was the key. I'd feel it if I was close enough.

Only trouble was, I had no desire to step off the path, nor get any closer to that damn snake.

Something moved.

Something that was long and sinuous and had a mouth full of teeth.

A snake. Not *the* snake, but just as nasty.

It formed out of the wispy ether surrounding us and lunged straight at me. Amaya screamed, her flames fierce and bright in this place, a sharp, clean contrast against the shadows that suddenly seemed to be gathering.

Hell's gate, I realized, was about to be opened.

I swore and swung Amaya as hard as I could. Her blade swept through the snake's form and sent it scattering. I had no idea whether she killed it and I didn't care. I ran forward, not worrying about whether I stayed on the path, as my gaze swept the gates. There was no evidence of the sorceress's presence anywhere near the gates themselves, which is where, logically, one would expect a lock to be. But this was the gray fields, and logic didn't exactly apply here. I veered to the left, off the path. Wispy hands began to tear and drag at me, as if desperate to force me into their bitter, painful darkness. I swung Amaya left and right, sending the shreds whirling away. Energy slithered across my being—a caress so light it felt like little more than sparks that hit, then disappeared.

The key was near.

I ran on, my gaze on the warm light to the side of the gates. I still couldn't see the sorceress, but she was there, somewhere.

The shadows grew thicker, the sense of impending doom stronger. Then I saw it—a flicker that grew into a flame. A flame that became a dagger, then became something else entirely—something that shone with an intensity I've never seen before.

The key.

The sorceress had found it.

I wasn't going to get there. I couldn't stop her. I swore and did the only thing I *could* do—I flung Amaya, with as much force as I could muster.

She arrowed through the air, her flames trailing behind her like a comet and her scream rolling across the rapidly darkening antechamber like a call to arms. The hands tearing at me seemed to pause; then as one they turned and raced after Amaya, quickly overtaking her and rushing on.

Too late.

We were all too late.

There was a blinding flash of light, followed by an explosion. Air hit, the force smashing into Amaya and sending her spinning away. A second later it did the same to me.

As I tumbled over and over, the air around me began to shudder, gently at first but gathering strength, until it seemed as if the entire field was about to shatter. Then it shifted. *Dropped.* The warm brightness of the antechamber flickered and, in the brief darkness, the gossamer fingers rushing forward found shape and form, became beings who were twisted and misshapen, and whose very countenance spoke of pain. Eons of pain. Then the warmth reinstated itself and the wisps became nothing more than reaching hands.

The gates were gone.

There was nothing but space in their place. Nothing but a deep and threatening sense of uneasiness.

I'd failed again.

But there was still the chance to stop this bitch going after the third key. Still a chance for some good to come from this goddamn mess. I swooped, picked up Amaya, and ran toward the fading light of the second key.

But the hands got there before me.

They pulled the shadows from the sorceress, then grabbed her, tore at her, as they ushered her forward, ushered her *down*. If she screamed I didn't hear it. In fact, she didn't even appear to struggle as she disappeared into the ether. Maybe she couldn't. Maybe the magic that had taken her safely to this point had faded away, leaving her defenseless.

I stopped. I had a bad feeling I didn't want to go anywhere near those hands right now. That if I did, they'd take me with them.

Where are they going, Amaya? Into hell?

No. Pens.

Pens? Even as I watched, the last part of her was swept away. The hands stopped moving, but the calm warmth of this place didn't reinstate itself. There was only one gate left. Only one gate to protect the Earth and the fields from all of hell's demons.

Because of me. Because I'd failed to do what I'd been sent here to do.

I closed my eyes and flung myself back into my body. The force of it sent me toppling off the bed and onto the floor. Where I screamed and ranted and cried at the unfairness of it all. And at my own stupid uselessness.

Hands eventually touched me, cocooned me. I wrapped my arms around Azriel's neck and pressed my cheek against his chest, drawing in the sweaty, bloody, and very *real* scent of him as I listened to the steady beat of his heart and wished mine was anywhere near as calm.

"I'm sorry," I whispered eventually. "I tried."

"I know." He brushed a stray strand of hair away from my cheek, his touch so warm against my skin. "The blame for this lies not just with you, but all of us who seek the key."

I sniffed. "The rest of you weren't at hell's gate. I *was*."

"Yes, but the path that led to that place is where the blame can be placed." His voice was grim. "That road is scattered not just with *our* failure, but the failure of the Raziq to guard the place they desecrated with their conceited slaughter of the priests, and by the failure of your father to fully tell us what his chrání was capable of. And it also lies with those of us forced to take over guard duties and yet who still do not understand all the magic of that place."

"Was it magic that prevented the Mijai at the gate from interfering?"

"Yes. He was not aware that anything was amiss until the gate opened."

"But he sensed my presence?"

"Yes, and thought nothing of it because you wore the marks of my tribe and my energy resonated within you. But he had no sense that anything was wrong. Not until I was able to slaughter the sorceress's Dušan and get into the temple grounds. By then, it was all too late."

Because I'd failed to do what I'd gone there to
do. He could dance around it all he liked, but that
was one fact we were never going to escape.

"Will the pits hold her?"

"It would depend on how much knowledge the
Aedh passed on to her."

I shifted so I could look into his eyes. "Meaning
what?"

"Meaning the priests have always been able to
enter either gate at will. As the Aedh was your
father's chrání, he will have gained some—if not
all—of that knowledge."

"You should have ignored my wishes and killed
that bastard when you had the chance," I muttered. I scrubbed a hand across my eyes, smearing
the remaining tears. "So what the *hell* do we do
now?"

"Now," an ominous, all too familiar voice said,
"your friend dies."

I scrambled to my feet, Amaya suddenly in my
hands and screaming her fury. Valdis joined in the
noise as Azriel rose beside me.

My father's energy filled the room. How he'd
gotten so close without us noticing I had no idea,
because technically, he shouldn't have been able
to get *into* this place. Ilianna's wards were still active, and they should have prevented *any* Aedh
other than the now dead Lucian from getting in.

Of course, my father had created those wards,
even if Ilianna had rerouted the magic within

them. And it would be just like my parent to have created a back door within the original magic for such an eventuality as this.

"One move, Hieu," Azriel said, voice soft and yet filled with death, "and it will be the last move you ever make."

Amusement spun around us, thick and sharp. "Save your meaningless threats, Mijai. I have no intention of harming anyone here. Elsewhere, however, it is a different matter entirely."

My eyes widened. "Don't you dare touch Mirri—"

"Touch? I assure you I have no intention of *ever* touching another human, even if I *had* the capacity and the form to do so."

"Then why threaten—"

"Oh, I do not *just* threaten," he murmured. "I do. And your friend is not human as the word is defined in this world. And she is, unfortunately, no longer a part of this world."

Someone screamed a denial. I wasn't sure if it was me or Amaya or both of us. Suddenly she was no longer in my hand, but aiming toward the wash of heat and power that was my father's presence in this room. Only she did so silently, and in full shadow. She was an unseen and unheard arrow of revenge.

Azriel gripped my arm, as if to hold me in place. He was speaking, I knew he was speaking, but I couldn't hear the words, neither aloud nor in my mind. All I could see, all I could hear, all I wanted, was death.

And that's exactly what I got.

Amaya sliced deep into the heart of the energy that was my father. For a moment, nothing happened. There was no immediate response from my father, and no reaction from Amaya.

Then her chuckle filled the silence.

There was nothing nice about that chuckle. Nothing nice at all.

Azriel swore, but the words were distant, meaningless. My mind was still with Amaya, with the destruction she was about to wreak.

He spun, wrapped his arms around me, and transported us out of there. We'd barely reappeared in the street when the entire warehouse—and everything Ilianna, Tao, and I owned—exploded into a million different pieces.

And deep within the heart of that explosion, my sword consumed the energy that was my father, sucking him dry until there was nothing but dust and memory left.

And those remnants she burned.

My father was dead. Gone.

I had my revenge, but I felt no better for it. I just felt . . . empty.

As empty as Ilianna's life would be without Mirri . . .

Oh god, *Mirri*.

I didn't think, I just reacted. In an instant I was

in Aedh form and streaking across the city. The fierce energy that was the Brindle's protective field reared up in front of me but just as abruptly gave way. I raced unimpeded through the shadowed halls, not changing shape until I neared the chamber where Ilianna, Kiandra, and Zaira had been attempting to free Mirri from my father's noose. I hit the doors at a run, and with enough force to slam them back against the walls. The crash reverberated through the silent halls and, in the room, three figures spun.

Three, not four.

A sob tore at my throat. I stumbled, tried to catch my balance, and failed. I hit the stone floor hard enough to shred my jeans and skin my knees, but I didn't care.

My gaze met Ilianna's. There was nothing there. No anger, no grief. No pain. Nothing other than surprise.

I swallowed hard, and somehow managed to say, "Mirri? Is she—?"

Zaira said, "What the hell—" about the same time as Azriel appeared behind me and said, "Risa, there is no need—"

"Ilianna!" I cut them both off, my voice rising to a near shout as I added, "Is Mirri *okay*?"

She didn't answer, just stepped to one side. And there, sitting on the floor, looking shocked and a little worse for wear, was Mirri.

She waved a hand as my gaze met hers, but

didn't actually speak. Though there was no sign of the energy collar around her neck, her throat was red-raw and decidedly painful-looking.

But she was alive, even if hurt, and the relief that swept through me was so great that if I hadn't already been on my knees, I soon would have been. I closed my eyes and took a deep, shuddering breath. At least one thing had gone right. It might not have been the most important thing—at least in terms of what was at stake for both this world and the other—but on a personal level, this was the *only* thing that really mattered. I'd done a lot of things wrong, but at least I hadn't killed Ilianna's heart.

Ilianna walked over, knelt in front of me, and wrapped her arms around me. She didn't say anything, and neither did I. Not for the longest time.

"Tell me," she said eventually.

I drew in a deep, shuddering breath and pulled away from her embrace. "My father said he'd killed her. I had no reason to believe he lied but—"

"You came here to check anyway." Ilianna smiled, but there was a fierce light in her eyes. "We didn't break the collar, but we did beat the bastard at his own game."

I frowned. "Meaning what?"

"It was you who gave us the idea, actually." She rose, dusted off her knees, then offered me a hand.

I accepted it, and climbed wearily to my feet. Azriel touched my elbow, not holding me up, but there in case I needed him.

"Or rather," Ilianna continued, "our discussion about creating personal wards and using the wearer's life force or aura to power the devices."

"I'm not seeing the connection."

Ilianna smiled. "Neither did we, not at first. But once we realized the cord hadn't tapped into Mirri's aural shield, it was then a matter of where else could it be getting its energy from."

"The source was its creator," Azriel commented.

Ilianna glanced past me and nodded. "Yes. And as Risa had pointed out, I'd learned enough of the magic to subvert her father's wards to our own use, so it was simply a matter of unpicking the appropriate threads in the collar and rerouting those."

She made it all sound so easy when it was obvious from the haggard appearance and tired stance of all three women that it had been anything but.

"So when my father tried to kill her—"

"The energy rebounded back to him."

"Which would explain the fierceness of the explosion," Azriel commented. "It wasn't just Amaya."

"Explosion? What explosion?" Ilianna said.

"The explosion that killed my father and destroyed our home."

"If losing our home is the price we have to pay to rid the world of that bastard, then good riddance, warehouse." Her voice was grim. "And the key?"

My gaze went to Kiandra. Even though her expression gave little away, I had no doubt she knew what had happened.

"The key is lost," she said, immediately confirming my thoughts. "The second gate is open."

"Yes."

"Oh, *fuck*," Ilianna said.

"Yeah," I said. "That, and a whole lot more."

"The sorceress?" Kiandra asked.

"Gone." I hesitated. "Maybe."

She nodded, her expression stoic. But I had a strange feeling that nothing I'd said had surprised her. That the loss of the second key and the opening of its gate were events she'd long known would happen.

"There is still hope left," she said softly. "At least there is as long as you and the last key remain in play."

"If the safety of the world depends on my actions," I said bitterly, "then heaven help the fucking world."

She blinked; then her gaze refocused. I suddenly realized she'd been seeing into the future.

"To use a worn-out cliché, the fate of the world hangs in the balance. You must not give up, Risa, no matter what it costs or however much you might want to."

I wouldn't.

I couldn't.

Hell on Earth might be one step closer, but there

was no way I was about to bring *my* child into a world overrun by hell's spawn.

Somehow, I'd find a way to stop the Raziq and secure the third key.

We'll find, not you'll *find*, Azriel corrected, voice stern. *Whatever we do from now on, we do it together.*

I twined my fingers through his but felt no safer for the comfort of his touch.

Because I knew, just as he knew, just as Kiandra undoubtedly knew, that even together we might not be strong enough to win the last, and perhaps the most important, battle of all.

The battle for life.

Don't miss our special preview
of *Darkness Falls*, the thrilling
conclusion to Keri Arthur's
fantastic Dark Angels series . . .

The Raziq were coming.

The energy of their approach was very distant, but it blasted heat and thunder across my senses and sent them reeling. But even worse was the sheer and utter depth of the rage that accompanied that distant wave. I'd known they'd be angry that we'd deceived them, but this . . . this was murderous.

Up until now, the Raziq had used minor demons to kidnap me whenever they'd wanted to talk to me—although *their* version of talk generally involved some kind of torture. This time, however, there would be no talking. There would be only death and destruction.

And they would take out everyone—and everything—around us in the process.

It was a horrendous prospect given we were still at the Brindle, a place that not only held aeons of witch knowledge, but was also home to at least two dozen witches.

"We cannot stay here." The familiar masculine tones broke through the fear holding me captive.

My gaze met Azriel's. In addition to being my guardian, he was my lover, the father of my child, and the being I was now linked to forever, in both life *and* afterlife. When I died, I would become what he was—a Mijai, a reaper warrior tasked with protecting the gates to heaven and hell, and hunting down those demons who broke through hell's gate to cause havoc here on Earth.

Of course, reapers weren't actually flesh beings—although they could certainly attain that form whenever they wished—but rather beings made of energy who lived on the gray fields, the area that divided Earth from heaven and hell. While I *was* part werewolf and therefore flesh, I was also part Aedh, who were the energy beings who'd once lived on the fields like the reapers and who were the traditional guardians of the gates. My father had been one of the Raziq—a group of rebel Aedh who were responsible for not only the destruction of the Aedh, but for the creation of the three keys to the gates—and he was also the reason they were currently lost.

Or rather, only one key was still lost. I'd found the first two, but both had been stolen from under my nose by the dark sorceress who'd subsequently opened two of hell's gates.

Things hadn't quite gone according to plan for her when she'd opened the second one, however, because she'd been captured by demons and dragged into the pits of hell. I was keeping everything crossed that that's *exactly* where she'd remain, but given the way luck had been treating us of late, it was an even-money bet she wouldn't.

"Risa," Azriel said when I didn't immediately answer him. "We *must* not stay here."

"I know."

But where were we going to go that was safe from the wrath of the Raziq?

I closed my eyes briefly and tried to control the panic surging through me. And yet that approaching wave of anger filled every recess of my mind, making thought, let alone calm, near impossible. If they got hold of me . . . My skin crawled.

It took a moment to register that my skin was *actually* crawling. Or at least part of it was. I glanced down. The wingless, serpentlike dragon tattoo on my left forearm was on the move, twisting around like a wild thing trapped. Anger gleamed in its dark eyes, and its scales glowed a rich, vibrant lilac in the half-light of the room.

Of course, it wasn't an ordinary tattoo. It was a Dušan, a creature of magic that had been designed to protect us when we walked the fields. It was a gift from my father, and one of the few decent things he'd actually done for me since this whole key saga had begun.

Unfortunately, the Dušan was of little use here on Earth.

It shouldn't even have been able to move on this plane, let alone partially disengage from my skin, as it had in the past.

"What's wrong now?"

I glanced at Ilianna—my best friend, flatmate, and a powerful witch in her own right. Her warm tones were rich with concern, and not without reason. After all, she'd only *just* managed to save the life of her mate, Mirri, from my father's foul magic, and here I was again, threatening not just Mirri's life, but Ilianna's, her mom's, and everyone else's who currently stood within the walls of this place. Because not even the magic of the Brindle, as powerful as it was, would stop the Raziq. It had been designed to protect the witches from the evil of *this* world. It was never meant to be a defense against the evils from the gray fields.

"The Raziq hunt us." Azriel's reply was flat. Matter-of-fact. Yet his anger reverberated through every inch of my being, as fierce as anything I could feel from the Raziq. But it wasn't just anger; it was anticipation, and *that* was possibly scarier. He drew his sword and met my gaze. If the ominous blue-black fire that flickered down the sides of Valdis—which was the name of the demon locked within the metal of his sword, who imbued it with a life and power of its own—was anything to go by, she was as ready to fight as her master. "We need to leave. *Now.*"

Ilianna frowned. "Then go home—"

"We can't," I cut in. "Home's gone."

It had been blown to smithereens when I'd thrust the black steel of my own demon sword into my father's flesh and had allowed her to consume him. And it was an action I didn't regret, not after everything the bastard had done.

"Yes," Ilianna replied. "But the wards your father gave us should still be active. I placed a spell on them that prevents anything or anyone other than us from moving them."

Azriel's gaze met mine again. "If they *aren't* active, then we stand and fight. They still need you, no matter how furious they might currently be."

Yes, but they didn't need *him.* And they would destroy him, if they could. Still, what other choice did we have? No matter where we went, either here or on the gray fields, others would pay the price. I swallowed, then stepped toward Azriel.

"Good luck," Ilianna said.

I didn't reply. I couldn't. Azriel's energy had already ripped through us, swiftly transporting us across the fields. We reappeared in the blackened ruins of the home I'd once shared with Ilianna and Tao—although to call them "ruins" was something of a misnomer. "Ruins" implied there was some form of basic structure left. There was nothing here. No walls, no ceiling, not even a basement. Just a big black hole that had once held a building we'd all loved.

I stepped away from Azriel and glanced up. The faintest touch of pink was beginning to invade the black of the sky; dawn wasn't that far off.

Time appeared. The familiar, somewhat harsh tone that ran through my thoughts was heavy with displeasure. *Alone should not be.*

Sorry. I felt vaguely absurd for even issuing an apology. I mean, when it was all said and done, Amaya was a *sword.* But somewhere in the past few days, she had become more of a friend, more than merely a means of protection.

And in this case, she certainly deserved an apology. In my desperation to see whether Mirri had lived, I hadn't given Amaya a second thought. Obviously, neither had Azriel; otherwise, I'm sure he would have collected her. I picked my way through the rubble and found her half-wedged in the blackened soil. I pulled her free, and felt a whole lot safer with her weight in my hand.

"The Raziq have split," Azriel commented.

Confusion—and a deepening sense of dread—ran through me. "Meaning what?"

The ferocity that roiled through the connection between us gave his blue eyes a hard, icy edge. "Half of them chase us here. The rest continue toward the Brindle."

"Oh, fuck!"

"They plan to demonstrate the cost of misdirection, and there is nothing we can do to prevent it." His expression hardened further, and I hadn't thought that was possible. "And before you say it, I will *not* let you endanger yourself for them."

"And I will *not* stand here and let others pay the price for decisions I've made!"

"We have no other choice."

"There's *always* a fucking choice, Azriel. Standing here while others die in my place is *not* one of them."

"Making a stand at the Brindle will not alter the fate of the Brindle."

"Don't you think I know that?" I thrust a hand through my short hair and began to pace. There *had* to be an answer. Damn it, if only Ilianna had had the time to create more protection stones . . . The thought stuttered to a halt. "Oh my god, the *protection* stones."

Azriel frowned. "They are still active. I can feel their presence."

"Exactly!" I swung around to face him. "You need to get them to the Brindle. It's the only chance they have against the Raziq."

"I will not—"

"For god's sake, stop arguing and just do as I ask!"

He crossed his arms and glared at me. His expression was so fierce my insides quaked, even though I knew he would never, ever hurt me.

"My task here is to protect you. No one else. *You*. I cannot and *will* not leave you unprotected, especially not *now*."

Not when there is life and love yet to be explored between us. Not when you carry our child. The words spun through my thoughts, as fierce as his expression and yet filled with such passion my heart damn near melted. I walked back to him and touched his arm. His skin twitched, but the muscles beneath were like steel. My warrior was ready for battle.

"I know it goes against every instinct, Azriel, but I couldn't live with myself if anyone at the Brindle died because of me."

"And I would not want to live without you. There *is* nowhere that is safe from the wrath of the Raziq."

"Maybe not—" I hesitated, suddenly remembering what he'd said about the Aedh temples and the remnants of the priests who still haunted that place. They weren't ghosts, as such, more like echoes of the beings they'd once been, but they were nevertheless damn dangerous. I'd briefly encountered one of them when I'd chased the sorceress to hell's gate, and it had left me in no doubt that he could destroy me without a second's hesitation.

"*That* is not a true option," Azriel said, obviously following my thoughts. "And there is certainly no guarantee that the priests will even acknowledge you again, let alone provide any sort of assistance."

"That's a chance I'm willing to take." And it was certainly a better option than letting the Brindle pay the price for my deceit. "Those who haunt that place weren't aware of the Raziq's duplicity, Azriel, but I think they might be now. And you're the one who told me that if they decide you're an intruder, they can cause great harm."

"But the Raziq were once priests—"

"*And* they're also the reason the Aedh no longer exist to guard the gates," I cut in. "This might be the only way both of us are going to survive the confrontation with the Raziq, and we *have* to take it."

He stared at me for several heartbeats, then swore viciously. Not in my language, in his. I blinked at the realization I'd understood it, but let it slide. Right now it didn't matter a damn how or when *that* had happened. All that did matter was surviving the next few minutes.

Because the Raziq were getting closer. They'd breached the barrier between the fields and Earth and were closing in even as we stood here.

Azriel sheathed his sword, then caught my hand and tugged me toward him. "If we're going to do this, then we do it somewhere your body is going to be safe while you're on the fields."

"Not the Brindle—"

"No."

The word was barely out of his mouth when his energy ripped through us again. We appeared in a room that was dark but not unoccupied. The scents in the air told me exactly where we were—my aunt Riley's, who was the very last person I wanted to endanger in *any* way. I wasn't actually related by blood to Riley, but after my mom's death, she and her pack were the only family I had left.

But before I could make any objection about being there, she said, "I'm gathering there's a good reason behind your sudden appearance in our bedroom at this ungodly hour of the morning."

Her tone was wry, and she didn't sound the slightest bit sleepy. But then, she'd not only once been a guardian, but one of their best. I guess old habits—like sleeping light—die hard.

"The Raziq hunt us," Azriel said, his voice tight. He didn't like doing this any more than I did, although I suspected our reasons were very different. "I need you both to keep Risa's body safe while she's on the gray fields."

And with that, he kissed me—fiercely, but all too briefly—then disappeared. Leaving me reeling, battling for breath, and more frightened than I'd ever been. Because I was about to face the wrath of the Raziq alone, even if only for a few minutes.

Not alone, Amaya grumbled. *Here am.*

Yes, she was. But even a demon sword with a thirst for bloodshed might not be enough to counter the fury I could feel in the Raziq.

And why the hell could I even feel that? Had it something to do with whatever Malin—the woman in charge of the Raziq, and my father's pissed-off ex—had done to me that time she'd tortured me? I didn't know, because Malin had also erased the knowledge of the procedure from my mind to prevent my father from uncovering what she'd done. But with him dead, maybe it was time to find out.

"Risa?" This time it was Riley's mate, Quinn, who spoke.

And he was the reason Azriel had brought me here. While Riley might once have been a guardian, Quinn was a whole lot more. Not only was he a vampire who'd once been a Cazador, which was basically a hit man for the high vampire council, but he was also what I was—a half-breed Aedh. One who'd undergone priest training. If there was anyone on Earth who could stand against the wrath of the Raziq for more than a second, it would be him.

I swallowed heavily, but it didn't do a whole lot to ease the dryness in my throat. "There's no time to explain," I said. "I have to get onto the fields immediately. People will die if I don't."

"Then, do it." Quinn climbed out of bed and walked to the wardrobes that lined one wall of their bedroom. "No one will get past us."

I hoped he was right, but it wasn't like I was going to be around to find out. I sat cross-legged on the thick, cushiony carpet, saw Quinn open a door and reach for the weapons within, then closed my eyes and took a deep breath.

As I slowly exhaled, I released awareness of everything around me, concentrating on nothing other than slowing the frantic beat of my heart so I could free my psyche, my soul—or whatever else people liked to call it—from the constraints of my flesh. *That* was what the Raziq were following; not my flesh, but my spirit. Hopefully, they would follow me onto the fields and not wreak hell on the two people I cared most about in this world.

As the awareness of everything around me began to fade, warmth throbbed at my neck—a sign that the charm Ilianna had given me when we'd both still been teenagers was at work, protecting me as my psyche pulled free and stepped onto the gray fields. There the real world was little more than a shadow, a place where those things that could not be seen on the living plane became visible. It was also the land between life and death, a place through which souls journeyed to whatever gateway was their next destination, be it heaven or hell.

But it was far from uninhabited. The reapers lived here, and so did the Raziq who remained.

And right now it was a dangerous place for me to be. The Raziq could move far faster here than I could. My only hope was reaching the Aedh temples that surrounded and protected the gates.

I turned and ran. The Dušan immediately exploded from my arm, her energy flowing through me, around me, as her lilac form gained flesh and shape, became real and solid. She swirled around me, the wind of her body buffeting mine as her sharp ebony gaze scanned the fields around us. Looking for trouble. Looking to fight.

The Raziq were coming. The thunder of their approach shook the very air around us.

Fear surged, and it lent me the strength to go faster. But running seemed a hideously slow method of movement, even if everything around me was little more than a blur. I wished I could transport myself to the temples instantaneously, as Azriel had in the past, but I wasn't yet of this world, even if I was destined to become a Mijai upon death.

The Dušan's movements were becoming more and more frantic. I swore and reached for every ounce of energy I had left, until it felt as if I were flying through the fields of gray.

But even when I reached the temples, I felt no safer. This place was as ghostly and surreal as the rest of the fields, but it was also a place filled with impossible shapes, high, soaring arches, and honeycombed domes sitting atop floating towers. And yet it no longer felt as empty as it had the first

time I'd come here. There was an awareness—an anger—
now, and it filled the temple grounds with a watchful energy
that stung my skin and sent chills through my being.

I stopped in the expanse of emptiness that divided the
temple buildings from the simply adorned gates to heaven
and hell. The Dušan surged around me, her movements
sharp, agitated. I tightened my grip on Amaya as I turned to
face the oncoming Raziq. She began to hiss in expectation,
the noise jarring against the watchful silence. But none of the
priestly remnants appeared or spoke. I had no doubt they
were aware of my presence, but it seemed that, for now, they
were content to watch.

Leaving me hoping like *hell* that I hadn't been wrong,
that they *would* interfere if the Raziq got too violent.

Electricity surged, dark and violent. Without warning
both the Dušan and I were flung backward. I hit vaporous
ground that somehow felt as hard as anything on Earth and
tumbled into the wall of a triangular building that stood on
an impossible point.

Amaya was screaming, the Dušan was screaming, and
their joint fury echoed both through my brain and across
the fields. The Dušan surged upward, briefly disappearing
into grayness before she dove into the midst of the Raziq,
snapping and tearing at beings I couldn't see, could only
feel. A second later she was sent tumbling again.

If they could do that to a Dušan, what hope did I have?

Amaya screamed again. She wanted to rend, to tear, to
consume, but there were far too many of them. We didn't
stand a chance . . . and yet, there was no way in *hell* I was
going to give up without a fight. Not this time. I pushed to
my feet, raised Amaya, and spit, "Do your worst, Malin. But
you might want to remember you still need me to find that
last key. And if you kill me, I become Mijai and beyond
even *your* reach. Not something you'd want, I'd guess."

For a moment there was no response; then that dark energy surged again. I swore and dove out of the way, and the
energy hit the building that loomed above me. Its ghostly,
gleaming sides rippled, the waves small at first but gaining
in depth as they rolled upward, until the whole building
quivered and shook and the thick, heavy top began to
crumble and fall. I scrambled out of the way, only to feel
another bolt arrowing toward me. I swore and dove to my

left, but this time I wasn't quite fast enough. The energy sizzled past my legs, wrapping them in heat, until it felt as if my flesh were melting from my bones.

A scream tore up my throat, but I clamped down on it hard, and it came out as little more than a hiss. I wasn't flesh; I was energy. *This* was nothing more than a mind game.

A mind game that felt painfully real.

Damn it, no! If I was going to go down, then I sure as hell was going to take some of these bastards with me.

Amaya, do your worst. And with that, I flung her, as hard as I could into the seething mass of energy that was the Raziq. They scattered, as I knew they would, but Amaya arced around, her sides spitting lilac flames that splayed out like burning bullets. Whether they hit any targets I have no idea, because I wasn't about to hang around waiting for another bolt to hit me. I scrambled to my feet and ran to the right of the Raziq. Amaya surged through their midst, still spitting her bullets as she returned to me. The minute she thumped into my hand, I swung her with every ounce of strength and anger within me. Steel connected with energy and the resulting explosion was brief but fierce and would have knocked me off my feet had it not been for my grip on my sword. Amaya *wasn't* going anywhere; she had a soul to devour, and devour she did. It took barely a heartbeat, but that was time enough for the rest of the Raziq to rally. Again that dark energy cut across the silent watchfulness of the temple's fields, but this time it felt stronger—wider—than any of the others.

Amaya, shield! I dropped to one knee and held Amaya in front of me. Lilac fire instantly flared out from the tip of her blade and formed a curved circle that encased me completely.

And just in time.

The dark energy hit the barrier, and with enough force that it pushed me backward several feet. Amaya screamed in fury, her shield burning and bubbling where the Raziq's energy flayed her. She held firm, but I had to wonder for how long. Not very, I suspected.

Damn it, where were the priestly remnants? Why weren't they intervening? The Raziq were the reason we were all in this mess—they were the reason the priests were dead. Did they not realize that? Did they not want to avenge that? I know the Aedh were supposedly emotionless beings, but they were not above pride and they *certainly* weren't above anger. Surely to god the priests had to feel *something* about their demise.

But if they didn't know or care?

Maybe it was time to remind them of their duty to protect the gates.

"Killing me won't solve your current problem, Malin." I had to shout to be heard above both Amaya's screeching and the thunderous impact of the dark energy against her shield. I had no idea where the Dušan was, but she was still very much active if her bellows were anything to go by. "As long as there's one key left, you — as an Aedh priest — cannot be free from the responsibility of caring for the gates. If you so desperately want to close them permanently and therefore end your servitude to the gates, then you're better off trying to sweet-talk me."

"'Sweet-talk?'" The voice was feminine, and decidedly pleasant. There was none of the malevolence I could feel in the dark energy, yet it nevertheless sent chills down my spine. Malin could charm the pants off a spider even as she dissected it piece by tiny piece. She'd dissected me once. That time, at least, she'd put me back whole, though not entirely the same. This time I suspected she would not be so generous. "You defy us at every turn, you do not take our threats seriously, and you expect us to simply accept your games of misdirection? Since when did insanity become a thread in your being?"

"I suspect it happened the day you lot entered my life." It was probably not the wisest thing to say, but hey, what the hell? It wasn't like she could get any angrier. Although the fresh burst of energy that hit Amaya's shield very much suggested I was wrong. And the fact that *she* was no longer screaming was an ominous sign that her strength was weakening.

Is, she muttered. If there was one thing my sword hated, it was admitting she wasn't all-powerful. *Yours must draw soon.*

Her drawing my strength was the very last thing *I* wanted right now, but again, until Malin and the rest of the Raziq calmed down a tad, it wasn't like we had another choice.

Presuming, of course, they *would* calm down.

"And insanity aside," I continued, "it doesn't alter the fact you still need me to find the final key."

"Not if we have decided that pursuing the remaining key is no longer viable *or* necessary. Not when it would be easier to simply destroy the gate itself."

My body went cold. If they did *that*, then heaven help us all. Hell would be unleashed on both the fields and on Earth, and I very much suspected neither world would survive.

But would the fates and the priestly remnants allow that?

The continuing silence — at least when it came to the priests — very much suggested they might.

"You can do that?" I said, voice hoarse.

"We can now. With two gates open, the magic that prevents its destruction is muted."

"But how would destroying the last gate free you from their service? The other two are still active, even if they are open."

"Which is precisely why we have concluded destruction might be the better option." I could hear the smile in her voice, even if I couldn't see her. "The gates are all linked. If you can destroy one, you destroy them all."

"The mere fact you make such a threat shows just how far the Raziq have fallen." Azriel's voice cut across the noise and the anger that filled the temple grounds as cleanly as sunshine through rain. Relief made my arms shake, and tears stung my eyes. I blinked them away furiously. It wasn't over yet. Not by a long shot. It was still him and me against all of them.

"You no longer deserve the name of 'priests,'" he continued, voice ominously flat. "And you certainly no longer have the umbrella of its protection."

"Do *not* make idle threats, Mijai." Any pretense of civility had finally been stripped from Malin's voice. It was evil personified — nothing more, nothing less. "We both know you would not dare to violate the sanctity of this place."

"Not without the permission of the fates," he agreed. "And *that* we now have."

With those words lingering ominously in the air, he appeared.

And he wasn't alone.